FELICITY PRICE is the author of the successful novel *Dancing in the Wilderness* which met with critical acclaim in 2001. She began her writing career at *The Press* in the 1970s where she was a reporter and feature writer. Felicity has since written for the *NZ Woman's Weekly*, the *Listener* and *North & South*. She was a panellist on TVNZ's Beauty & the Beast and also a journalist at TVNZ and Radio New Zealand. In 1987 Felicity started her own award-winning public relations company which continues today. She has an MA(Hons) in English. Felicity is married with two children and is currently working on her third novel for publication in 2003.

www.felicityprice.com

Also by Felicity Price

Dancing in the Wilderness

What they said about *Dancing in the Wilderness*:

'Felicity Price's first novel offers something rare in New Zealand fiction – pace and tension. You can't bear to put it down… Price is gifted enough to write her story with a precision, eye for detail and balance that make it feel authentic… Price is a gifted storyteller who has gone to serious lengths to research her plot.'

– New Zealand Herald

'An action-packed debut novel links two periods of New Zealand history that have an ever-present relevance.'

– North and South

'Quite apart from being a good yarn, it is well informed about issues that should concern us all.'

– Wairarapa News

'Price puts a human face with strong woman characters to unique parts of New Zealand history. She has the pace of a good storyteller and the development of character that absorbs the reader into the lives of those women.'

– The Press

'Price spins a captivating tale… The book is well crafted and engaging, and impressive for a first novel. I hope it is the first of many.'

– The Nelson Mail

No Angel

Felicity Price

HP

HAZARD PRESS
publishers

www.hazardonline.com

ISBN 1-877270-31-8

Published by Hazard Press Limited
P.O. Box 2151, Christchurch, New Zealand
email: info@hazard.co.nz
www.hazardonline.com

Cover design by Graeme Hobbs, Hobbs Graphics
Printed by Griffin Press Ltd, Australia

Dedicated with love to Chris

Acknowledgements

My grateful thanks to the following people, without whom this book would not have been possible:

Caroline and Charles Reid, for sharing their inestimable knowledge about vineyards and making wine; Robyn and Evan Price and Jane and Nigel Price, Nelson; Joanna Murray; Susie Moncrieff and Donna Ching, of the Montana World of WearableArt; Mike and QiQi Li, for assistance with the maritime chapter; Bettina Wallace, for help with German identities; Suzanne Walker, for help with Italian identities; Dave Quested, for advice on cocaine and drug dealing details; Paul and Sherrill Cutler, for advice about CBS; Mike McLeod and Mike Fitzgerald; Steve Astor; Sue Tumahai; Fiona Farrell and Sue McCauley for their encouragement; Graeme Hobbs, for his clever cover; the team at Hazard Press – Quentin, Antoinette and Danielle Wilson, and editor Sam Gill; and my support team – Chris, Amelia, James, Mum, Christine Smith, Vicki Blyth, and fellow author Paddy Austin.

Historical note

The Maungatapu Murders, in which five men were killed by the Burgess gang as they crossed the Maungatapu Saddle on their way to Nelson in 1866, shocked the country at the time. The leader of the gang, Richard Burgess, who learned bushranging from the same teacher as Australia's notorious Ned Kelly, spent as much of his life behind bars as at large until his execution at Nelson Gaol in October 1866. Burgess wrote his own autobiography, *The Confessions of Richard Burgess*, while awaiting trial for the murders. He was assisted editorially by Alfred Hibble, editor of the *Nelson Colonist*, who is thought to have passed the manuscript on to the *Lyttelton Times* (the forerunner of *The Press*) which published it in a 48 page booklet later that year. The author is indebted to the information about his life and times, and also to Ken Byron's explanatory notes to the Confessions in his book *Guilty Wretch that I Am – Echoes of Australian Bushrangers from the Death Row memoirs of Richard Burgess*.

Blending fact with fiction, *No Angel* extrapolates the facts of Burgess's life, including the whirlwind romance and impregnation of his live-in mistress, Carrie, into a gripping tale of those times.

The contemporary characters of this book, however, with the exception of the political and other well-known personalities of today, are entirely fictional. Any resemblance to any person, living or dead, is entirely coincidental. In the same way, the contemporary organisations depicted are also fictional and do not represent or resemble any actual company, voluntary organisation or activist group.

Prologue
Christmas, 1866

Cradled in Carrie's arms, Christina was on the verge of slumber. Her fragile pink eyelids flickered in the last vulnerable moments before sleep, her rosebud mouth pursed, making miniature movements in and out, subconsciously still sucking at the breast.

Carrie's pale, freckled face – furrowed from lack of sleep and careworn from anxiety – relaxed for a moment over the sleeping baby. Christina was just four weeks old and was beginning to bring her mother more joy than she felt she deserved. The terrors of the past few months faded as she pressed her face against the tiny head with its soft sprinkling of downy hair. She inhaled the familiar smell of the gentle glycerine soap she'd made especially for her new baby and suddenly felt terribly alone.

'Oh, my little one,' she said softly, 'what's to become of us?'

Carrie looked out the uncurtained window on the other side of the upstairs room in her two-storey cottage which was nestled on a lower slope outside Hope, near Nelson. The flickering candlelight behind her was dim enough to allow the stars to shine brightly in the cloudless sky. There was no moon; the big hill in the distance was a vague silhouette.

'Sweet and low, sweet and low,' Carrie sang the Tennyson lullaby softly.

'Wind of the western sea,
Low, low, breathe and blow…
Blow him again to me,
While my little one,
while my pretty one, sleeps.'

She paused, staring out the window at the stars, wishing she were not so utterly alone.

'Blow him again to me,' she said wistfully.

She was still gazing out the window, the sleeping Christina in her arms, when the sound of a disturbance outside brought her back to earth. She could hear people shouting, chanting almost. And in the corner of the window she could see the flickering of torches.

Alarmed, she jumped up and ran to the window, waking the baby, who started to fuss and whimper.

'Oh, my God!' she cried. In front of her, surrounding the gate to her cottage, was a mob brandishing torches and long garden pikes, their faces hard with anger. Listening carefully, she could just make out their words:

'Whore! Whore! Murderer's whore!' they chanted.

Christina, seeming to sense danger, started to wail.

'Whore! Whore! Murderer's whore!' it continued, unbroken.

'Oh, Christina, what am I to do?'

Christina's cries became louder.

Outside, she could see some of their faces and recognised her neighbours – people who only yesterday had been perfectly civil to her, or at least to her face. One of them broke away and unlatched the gate before walking up the path. A few seconds later, there was a loud knock on the front door.

Part one

1: The Vintner's Luck

When the call came, David Rossini was gazing contentedly out the window, fidgeting absent-mindedly with his reading glasses on the cluttered desk in front of him. The big bay window took up most of the south-facing wall of his first-floor office, and from his desk David could see more than half his vineyard. He'd been surveying the neat rows of chardonnay vines, their plump yellow-green grapes just a few weeks away from harvest, the lower leaves starting to turn in the hot August sun. Line after line climbed up the steepening hillside to the thickly forested maple and redwood just visible at the top of the window. He'd put *Tosca,* his favourite opera, on the CD player behind his desk, the speakers filling the room with Kiri Te Kanawa. Lost in thought about this year's harvest, which he knew would be the best in many years, he was dreaming of gold medals, of accolades in wine columns across America, of demand outstripping supply, of prices skyrocketing and profits rising even higher. The lines in his chubby, tanned face were relaxed in a beatific smile as he pictured the coming vintage. He was so engrossed in thought and in the divine music that he didn't hear the phone on his old oak desk until the ninth ring, when he dropped his glasses on a pile of papers, reached behind to turn down the volume, and picked up the phone.

'Hello,' he said. 'David Rossini.'

'Hello,' said an unknown voice. 'This is Mike Gibbens, CBS News. I would like a few minutes with you, if that's possible. I have a couple of questions I'd like to ask about last year's vintage.'

'Oh really?' David said as calmly as he could while his mind snapped to attention. If CBS News was interested, they were hardly likely to be giving his wine a free promotion, especially last year's vintage. It had been one of the most difficult years he'd had, with too much rain before all the fruit had a chance to set. The rain had continued to plague his part of the valley when he needed lots of sun to ripen the fruit. They'd lost almost half the crop and had produced only a very average vintage. He didn't have a good feeling about this call. Mike Gibbens was well known for going for the jugular. He wouldn't be out on some patsy story. He'd be after blood. David prayed it wasn't his blood.

'What sort of questions?'

'I'd rather talk about that when I see you,' the reporter said. 'I'm in the Napa now. How are you placed in, say, ten minutes?'

David gulped. Ten minutes! The reporter must be almost at the vineyard gate!

'What's the rush?' he asked. 'I'd really rather have some idea what this is about.'

'Well,' Gibbens replied. 'We've had a tip-off about allegations of wine-blending, as well as a complaint to the Institute of American Wineries. A complaint about blending wine. That's what I want to talk to you about.'

'Whose wine is supposed to be blended?'

'Look, I'd rather talk about it when we meet,' Gibbens said. 'I'll be there in ten minutes. Okay?'

David had a sinking feeling it was his wine Gibbens was investigating. Yet he'd heard nothing from Danny Ineson at the Institute. He knew better than to refuse to talk to CBS. But at least he could play for time.

'Make it two o'clock,' David replied. It was now just after 12.30. If he had a bit of time, he could find out what was going on and deal with it properly. 'Two or nothing. I'm a bit tied up right now, but I'll make time to see you at two.'

'Okay, two it is. See you then,' Gibbens said and hung up.

Without pausing to replace the receiver, David hit line two and dialled Ineson's mobile phone. As he punched the buttons, dark sinews stood out on his big brown hand, which was shaking with tension.

'What the hell's going on, Dan?' he asked his long-time friend, for once by-passing pleasantries. 'I've just had CBS News on the phone. That rottweiler Gibbens. He's on his way to see me. He says you've had a complaint about blending. Who's the complaint against? It'd better not be Rossini's.'

There was a foreboding silence. The usually voluble Ineson was taking a long time to answer. David could feel his anger on the rise. He had a reputation for having a bit of a temper, although once expressed, his anger was quickly spent. He would have to be careful with Ineson. It wouldn't pay to shout at him, but he hated being kept in the dark, especially when it was about his family's business. It had been a long hard struggle getting Rossini's established, and he wasn't about to see some vicious smear campaign wipe out his father's years of back-breaking labour. Nervously, David rubbed at the back of his hand.

'Er, well… yes,' Ineson said at last, 'Rossini's. We got a letter this morning. An anonymous letter. Someone thinks your *Don Giovanni* label has been blended. In fact, they sent us a batch to test. I was going to phone you this afternoon, as soon as I'd checked out a few things.'

'Is that so? Well, thank you very much,' David said sarcastically, doing his best to contain his mounting fury. 'Nice of you to keep me in the picture. Perhaps you'd be so kind as to tell me the whole story.'

'There's not much more to it than that,' Ineson said. 'As I said, we got an anonymous letter alleging your *Don Giovanni* chardonnay had been heavily blended with semillon, which would mean, as you know, it wouldn't comply with your AVA. You don't grow semillon at Rossinis, so there'd be major repercussions. We'll run a few tests on the bottles they sent in with the letter of complaint, and no doubt that'll put you in the clear.'

'But it's an anonymous letter. It must be a hoax. It's a malicious libel.'

'Sure,' Ineson said placatingly. 'I'm sure there's nothing to it. But with a couple of sample bottles enclosed, we have to take it seriously. We're legally obliged to investigate. And CBS is coming to interview me too. I'm expecting him any minute.'

David couldn't believe it. He knew for certain there was nothing wrong with the wine. Only chardonnay grapes from his own vineyard had been used, pressed, and then fermented in the Limousin oak barrels Pietro had imported from France. All the usual processes had been followed. He'd been there every step of the way. Analysis of the bottles would put him in the clear, he was sure of it.

'When will you know the results?'

'A couple of days to have the preliminaries. Confirmation a week or so later.'

'A week! Our reputation could be ruined in that time. I can't wait a week,' David groaned. 'CBS is going to be knocking on my door any minute. What am I going to tell them? That they'll have to wait a week? Anyway, how did they find out? Did someone in your office leak it to them?'

'That wouldn't be possible,' Ineson said firmly. 'Only my board and I know about the allegation, and they know they can't say anything.'

'I hope you're right,' David said. He didn't share Ineson's confidence. There were one or two people on that board he wouldn't trust to keep quiet, especially when one of their competitors was in the gun.

Ineson cleared his throat, clearly embarrassed. 'Look, David, I know this is a bit of a setback, but…'

'Setback?' David growled. 'You bet it's a bloody setback. My family has worked day and night for over thirty years to build up this vineyard. We've put everything we own into it, every cent. I'm damned if some malcontent is going to ruin all that with slander and doctored wine. If there's anything out of the ordinary in those bottles, you can bet someone's added it with a syringe. I know for sure there's been no blending at Rossini's.' David banged down the receiver and thumped his other hand hard on the desk as he spoke, immediately regretting it with the pain of impact.

This couldn't be happening. It felt as if he were in someone else's movie. How could anyone believe he would add anything to his wine? He and his father had been avid guardians of Napa Valley controlled appellation when it was introduced in 1978. The Rossini vineyard's name appeared on all their labels, which was the family's guarantee that the wines contained at least 95% of their own grapes.

He didn't dare mess with the AVA. His reputation, his whole livelihood was at stake. The Californian wine industry's reputation would suffer. He'd always been sure the contents of each bottle delivered exactly what the label said. And he'd always been sure that Rossini's chardonnay – one of the best in the valley – was pure chardonnay, from his own vineyard. He glanced up at the wall of awards and medals the Rossini label had won. Every other time he'd looked at them, he'd felt proud to be a Rossini, proud of what he and his father had achieved. Now after the call to Ineson, they'd lost their sheen. The more he thought about it, the madder he got. 'What would Alex do?' he wondered out loud.

Alex! If he had any sense, he realised, he'd get her here as soon as possible. Alex, PR pro that she was, would know just what to do and would help keep the media at bay. He'd first hired her to help with the fallout over the landfill he'd put in on unproductive land. She'd been terrific. Turned the whole fuss around to make him look like God's gift to the environment by pushing the recycling side of the business and downplaying the rest of it. That land would be usable one day. And in the meantime, his nephew was making a pretty good living from it. The finings, the grape pomace, skins, seeds and stems left over from all the neighbouring wineries up the Valley were now composted and sold back to locals to nourish next year's crops. And last year, they'd bought a machine and started extracting grapeseed oil and selling it 'cold pressed' for a tidy profit. They could hardly keep up with the demand.

Alex had driven up from San Francisco at the speed of light in that sporty little BMW of hers, bringing along all her environmental case studies and she'd encouraged them to try new ideas. She'd stayed on for a while after the fuss died down and helped organise their first *Opera in the Vines*. It had been a huge success. He'd kept her on as an occasional adviser ever since, making sure she visited at least quarterly to keep in touch with what was going on. Anna insisted on Alex staying for at least one night every time. 'At least I can see that the poor girl has one good meal and a good night's sleep for a change,' Anna would say. Alex had gone back to San Francisco only a few weeks ago after organising the programme and the publicity for the latest *Opera in the Vines*. He smiled as he recollected the mercurial Alex, always rushing somewhere, surrounded by singers, stagehands, an entire orchestra – nothing phased her.

He picked up the phone and auto-dialled Alex's home number. An answerphone clicked on with a man's deep gravelly voice: 'Lucian and Alex are unable to come to the phone right now…'

Who was Lucian? he wondered. It must be serious if he'd moved in with her. And why had she not told Anna about him? Alex confided in her. Unless she'd become unusually sensitive or protective of this Lucian, whoever he might be. David wondered if he would prove to be another one of her disasters. He smiled to himself as he recalled some of the awful scrapes Alex had gotten into with men in the past. She seemed to attract real bounders, men who were self-centred, mean and totally lacking in the ability to acknowledge the achievements of anyone but themselves.

The beep of the answerphone system waiting for his message brought him back to the present with a jolt. He didn't leave a message but tried her mobile instead. She answered straight away.

'Hi. Alex Zerakowski,' The sound of her warm, reassuring voice was almost enough to make him cry out with relief.

'Alex, it's David,' he said.

'Hi David. How's it going?'

'Terrible. Something terrible's come up, Alex. I need your help.'

'Sure, David. Anytime. That's what I'm here for. What is it?'

He explained the call from CBS and the subsequent conversation with Danny Ineson.

'How soon is the reporter coming, did you say?'

'At two. I haven't got long. I wish you were here, Alex. You'd know just what to do.'

'Well, there's no way I'd be able to make it before he arrives,' she said. 'Even if I could get away right now, which I can't. I could leave in a few hours, though. The freeway will be pretty tied up by then, but I should be able to get there in time to watch you on the news.'

'Yeah, and I'll have stuffed it up for sure by then,' David said ruefully. 'But I'd really appreciate it if you could make it up here as soon as you can. I just know this'll be all over the newswires tonight and there'll be reporters everywhere.'

'Sure, David. I'll drive up as soon as I can get away. In the meantime, though, remember the procedure…'

'I know, I know, write down three key messages and stick to them,' David laughed despite himself.

'And think about what they'll ask you.'

'You'd know that better than me…'

'Well at this stage, with only CBS on the case, it's fairly straight-forward I guess. He'll push you to say something about adding semillon, he'll want to know why you'd want to add something, and if you hint that it might be tampered with, he'll want to know who would do that and why…'

'…Slow down, slow down,' David interrupted. 'I'm trying to write this down.'

'Sorry,' Alex chuckled. 'Good work.' She paused, waiting for him to catch up.

'Go on,' he said.

'He might ask a few technical questions – you know, like how you check wines before they leave the winery, what quality controls you have, what the AVA means to you, that sort of thing. But until the results are known from the lab, he can't really get stuck into you. You'll be fine!' she finished breezily.

'I wish I had your confidence,' he said.

'You know what to do. You've handled TV before, David. You'll be just fine.'

'I sure hope so,' he said. 'Look, I'd better go now, get ready for the grilling. You'll make it tonight?'

'I will. I'll look forward to seeing you again.'

'I'll tell Anna. She'll be delighted to have you back so soon. See you tonight then. And thank you, Alex. You're a gem.'

'No problem, David. See you tonight.'

He put down the receiver and looked out the window again, seeking solace in the view that never failed to uplift him. But now the sparkle had gone from the sunshine on the vines, the view no longer provided calm. The rows of vines looked more like armies marching towards him.

His phone ran again. He wasn't sure if he dared answer it. After the fifth ring he gave in. It was his father, Pietro.

'David, what are you doing? Your mother is expecting you for lunch. Surely you didn't forget?'

David struck his fist against his forehead. He'd completely forgotten about the weekly family lunch. Anna would be making excuses for his absence, twisting the long fronds of hair on the side of her face the way she did when she was annoyed, placating her in-laws yet again for her husband's preoccupation with work, and their eldest daughter Maria, home for a few days from UC Davis, where she was doing an oenology degree, would be leaving soon to return to the campus. He'd probably miss her if he didn't go over to lunch.

'Sorry Papa. Something's come up that I have to deal with. I'm going to have to raincheck lunch today. Please give my excuses to Mamma and Anna, and can you tell Maria I'll try to get over before she has to go.'

'What is it, David? Anything I can help with?'

'No, Papa. I can handle it. I'll come and see you later.'

'Well all right then. You know what you're doing.'

With a feeling of mounting dread, David put the phone down and headed for the winery to find Manfred, his German winemaker. Although the Rossini family knew everything about growing the best chardonnay and pinot noir grapes, about getting the best out of the land, they knew just enough about winemaking to hand that highly skilled and delicate craft over to a qualified and proven craftsman. Manfred, who'd been with them for nearly ten years now, had been the perfect choice, winning award after award.

The 210-acre vineyard had been his father's lifeblood since he'd bought it in the early 1960s, before the boom. The previous owner had to sell some of his land to save his vineyard from going under. That was before the rest of America had woken up to the joy of wine, before people appreciated the long-forgotten treasures hidden away in the Napa Valley. Those early years had been hard going for his father, and for his mother, bringing up seven children on next to nothing. They'd all had to pitch in, helping with the labour because they couldn't afford to hire anyone. At home in Umbria, the green heart of Italy, they had grown olives, selling up on his mother's brother's advice to come to California. Already there and settled in the Napa Valley, his uncle had told them it would be their promised land. And it had been, eventually.

At first, they'd survived by trial and error, learning how to cope with the vagaries of the weather. But no sooner were they starting to get it right and build a reputation for quality wines, they'd fallen victim to the "superlouse" – a new strain of the phylloxera that meant they had to rip out all their vines and start again. Pietro had been devastated; had wanted to throw in the towel. The sight of his precious zinfandel vines being ripped out of the ground day after heart-breaking day seemed to take something out of him that would never be replaced. But David had been reading the trade journals. He'd persuaded his father to replant with fresh chardonnay rootstock – much better suited to the western hills with their afternoon shadows and cooler evenings while the soil was still warm from the morning's hot sun. He also showed his father how to arrange the vines in a different pattern, closer together than before and increasing the size of the harvest. It had taken time for Pietro to come round, but once the vines started to produce fruit, he had to admit the changes were worthwhile. The chardonnay, plus a few hectares of pinot gris and sangiovese – in homage to Italy – had proved a good choice, providing the family with a reasonable income since their first harvest. They'd done so well they'd been able to buy more land and plant pinot noir. Even more satisfying was the knowledge that all the land had rocketed in value in the last ten to fifteen years. By the time he was ready to hand it on to his children, David reckoned it would be worth a small fortune.

Pietro had acknowledged David's role in helping to revive the vineyard and, along with it, the family's fortunes by turning over the management to him after Pietro's brush with bowel cancer some years ago. He'd had a small tumour removed and undergone a short but draining course of radiotherapy treatment which had knocked the stuffing out of him for long enough to make him realise – with a bit of a push from Mamma – that he should take things easier.

Under David's care, and with his depth of knowledge about viticulture and his ability to pick top winemakers, the vineyard prospered. Thanks to Manfred and his predecessor Henne, the Rossini brand became well respected and sought after across America. And particularly in demand were their special labels, *Don Giovanni* and *Il Trovatore*, named after the operas that were his father's passion. Pietro adored opera – Italian opera in particular. He sang himself, a fine, strong baritone. His renditions from *The Barber of Seville* would ring out from deep inside the vineyard, making it easy to find him, wherever he might be. He believed he was distantly related to the great Rossini, composer of some of the best Italian operas ever. David had always doubted the relationship himself, having never seen any hard evidence, but it made a good story to help them sell their opera-themed vintages.

David was damned if that was going to change now. To Pietro, Rossini's was everything. David couldn't let his father down.

He found Manfred in the barrel hall, where row upon row of oak barrels lined the deep cave David and his father had blasted out of the rocky hillside six years previously.

'Manfred, something's come up. We need to talk,' he said.

'Oh?' said the big German in his soft, quiet voice. 'What is it?'

'Not here,' David said. 'We need to talk privately.'

'Oh,' Manfred said again. 'One moment, then.' He replaced the bung in the barrel he'd been topping up and then allowed David to usher him into the tiny records room at the entrance of the cave. David shut the door behind them. He didn't want anyone overhearing. The winery was open throughout the day and, although there was no-one else around just at this moment, guided tour groups came through regularly and other staff could be around.

It was rare for David to ask for privacy and Manfred looked surprised and slightly apprehensive as he turned to face David in the tiny office.

'What's wrong?' he asked.

David pushed a pile of papers aside and sat on the edge of the bench. He indicated for Manfred to sit in the only chair.

As he sat, the winemaker pulled his neatly-pressed chinos up at the knees, exposing tanned feet encased in leather sandals. He leaned back in the chair and looked up at David.

'Last year's vintage. That's what's wrong,' David replied grimly. 'There's been a complaint against us for blending the *Don Giovanni*, presumably for adding grapes from another source. Is it true?' David came straight to the point.

'No!' Manfred looked shocked. 'I would never do that, you know I wouldn't. My reputation is worth more than anything. I'm always strict about the AVA. It must be a lie.'

'I hope you're right,' David said. 'They've got a couple of bottles of the *Don Giovanni* and they're testing them right now. If there's been any excessive blending, they'll find out.' He watched Manfred closely for any flicker of fear or guilt. There was none. The sturdy blond German looked him directly in the eye.

'There's still some *Don Giovanni* left in the cellar,' Manfred said. 'Let's go and get a few bottles and test it ourselves. We won't be able to do the full analysis the Institute will get from the mass spectrometer, but we should be able to detect any additives simply by tasting. If there's semillon in there, we should be able to tell.'

David looked at his watch. Just on one. He would have time to look at the wine before CBS arrived. He felt it might be worthwhile bringing the CBS crew into the big underground cellar to show them the wine and declare its purity. He was increasingly sure the wine must have been doctored. But that still wasn't going to get him off the TV news.

He followed Manfred through to the cellar, feeling the sudden coolness on his skin as they entered. He closed the door behind them. Ahead stretched a seemingly endless cave drilled into the rocky hillside, lit at regular intervals by unshaded halogen lights high above the dark oak barrels, stacked eight deep, as far as the eye could see into the dimness. David turned to the right and followed another tunnel containing neat rows of wine bottles from floor to ceiling. He picked out several bottles and suggested they return to the office. There he handed Manfred two bottles to open and pour.

Each man took a glass and held the clear yellow-green liquid up to the sunlight pouring in through the shallow windows running the width of the building just below the roof.

'That looks clear and clean to me,' David said.

They inhaled the heady aroma: melon and peach mixed with oak and grass.

'Smells good too,' Manfred said.

They swirled it around in the bowl of the glass and took a sip. David held it in his mouth for a moment, waiting for the warmth to bring out the full flavour. The familiar gutsy taste of fruity fullness, of butterscotch and melons made him sigh with pleasure until he remembered the reason for the tasting. He looked expectantly at Manfred. If anything were amiss, he would detect it. But Manfred was looking just as pleased as he was. He wondered briefly if Manfred was as trustworthy and honest as he made out, then he felt ashamed of himself. Manfred wouldn't cheat on him now. He was part of the family. He was the reason their wine was so highly regarded. He wouldn't risk throwing all that away with surreptitious blending. Who else could have done it? Who else might have had access to the vats? That would mean sabotage. And he didn't know of anyone who had it in for him or his family.

Together, they collected a sample of the wine in a test tube to send off to the lab for analysis.

'Could anyone have added anything without you knowing?' David asked.

'I don't see how,' Manfred said. His slow, measured words were even slower than usual. David could tell he was deep in thought. He looked at his watch. It was just after one-thirty and that damned TV reporter would be arriving soon. After what seemed like an eternity, Manfred said, 'There was that man you had to let go. Remember? It was just before we laid the vintage down. He could have done something.'

David sucked a lung full of air through clenched teeth, involuntarily making a whistling sound. It was indeed a possibility.

'That Wade fellow? What was his name? Wade... Spargo.'

He remembered the whole sorry episode. He'd caught him smoking dope in the cellar and had sacked him on the spot.

'But I don't see how he could have accessed the wine after I fired him,' David added. 'I asked him to leave there and then. He wasn't around to cause trouble.'

'He could have slipped back in after he'd collected his things, I suppose,' Manfred said. 'I was tied up in the processing area all afternoon and away from the bottling line. But it would have been hard to sneak in past Anna and do any damage.'

Every year, Anna regarded it as her personal responsibility to get the wine into the bottles, even though they now had a fancy machine to do all the hard work for them. But there was no way David was going to ask Anna if she'd seen anything. Not yet, anyway.

He wished Manfred hadn't remembered about Wade. He was pretty sure Wade wouldn't have done any doctoring – he'd have been too stoned to manage it. But he'd rather not have it nibbling at his conscience when he had a giant TV lens pulling in for a close-up on his face. The scrutiny of the nation would be on him. Rossini's name depended on it. Sighing, feeling the full weight of the responsibility, he stood up and clapped Manfred on the back.

'Wish me luck,' he said, resigned. 'Mike Gibbens from CBS News will be knocking on my door any minute wanting to give me the third degree. I might bring him over here and show him the *Don Giovanni* we've got left and offer him a bottle to test for himself. Okay with you?'

'Of course,' Manfred said. 'But I'd rather not go on camera if you don't mind.'

'I wouldn't put you through that, don't worry. I'd better go and prepare for them.'

Back in his office, with just on fifteen minutes spare, David wrote down a few key words on his deskpad, just as Alex had taught him to. He looked at them again, crossed some out, wrote a few more, and juggled them around until he was happy with the result. He held up the piece of paper on which he'd jotted the questions Alex said they'd ask and checked that he had them covered. She always seemed to know what reporters would want to know. He grimaced. The closer the interview, the more he wished she were there.

He heard the sound of an approaching vehicle crunching on the gravel, drawing closer. He could tell by the clattering of its diesel engine that it was a small SUV. It pulled up in the carpark in front of his office. He looked up from his desk and out the window. A zippy white four-wheel-drive with the CBS insignia gleamed menacingly in the bright sun. Get a grip, David, he told himself. You're an old hand at this.

He took one last glance at the list of things he wanted to say, clenched his fist purposefully, stood and strode to the door then hurried downstairs to catch the crew before they got into the public tasting room and wine shop beneath his office.

'Can I help you with something?' he said as he opened the door, forcing a welcoming smile as a tall, thin man stepped out of the van, and proffered a hand. Behind him, David could see two others waiting expectantly in the vehicle.

'Mike Gibbens,' the reporter said. 'Thank you for making the time to see us.'

'Come in,' David said, gesturing towards the door.

2. On the Road Again

Alex ended David's call and dropped the powder blue mobile phone in her bag beside the desk. Then, while she autodialed her friend Magda Schimanski on the office phone, she pulled a memo pad out from under the client project she was working on and started to note down what she needed to do before she left town and what she needed to take with her. Waiting for Magda to answer the phone, she picked up a pen and drummed it on the black lacquered surface of the Japanese-style desk.

She got Magda's voice mail.

'Hi there Shimmy,' she said when Magda's message finally finished, 'I've got to go up to Rossini's for a few days. You'll see why when you watch CBS news tonight. So I doubt I'll make the crisis comms seminar on Wednesday. Can you cover for me, please, pretty please with sugar on top? Sorry to drop you in it like this. I'll email you my notes and the case study I was going to present, if it's any help. But you'll be fine without me up there on the dais with you – you can do this sort of stuff standing on your ear. Give me a call when you pick up this message and I'll grovel in person.'

She hung up, flipped open her Filofax and looked through the next few days to see what else she'd need to sort out. Fortunately the two major projects she was working on for clients could be put on hold for a few days without any problems. She ticked off the appointments. Lacey, the PA she shared with fellow crisis communicator Sharon Villeneuve, would be able to change those. And since Sharon was familiar with both projects, she could step in if anything urgent arose. She put a line through the Wednesday seminar – she'd dealt with that. Then she noticed Wednesday night, August fourteenth, she was supposed to be going to her brother Max's place for her father's birthday dinner. Damn! She'd have to excuse herself to Max and that would mean eating humble pie for Patricia for the next few months, if not years. Max's wife had little else to do all day except moan about Max, who could never do enough or earn enough to keep her happy, or skite about her snooty daughter Annelise. An expert in putting on airs and graces way above the station of a city council architect's wife, Patricia had inveigled her way into a clique of similarly shallow friends and had adopted the excessively pretentious name Patrice. Alex kept on calling her Trish.

She quailed at the thought of having to confess to Max that she wouldn't be there. And not just because of the spiky response she'd get from Trish. Dad was difficult enough on his own; when confronted with his family he became even more contrary. Alex, the only sibling who was still single, was regarded by both Max and her sister Kate as being the one who should take responsibility for the old man. Not that he was that old – but now that he was retired, now that he didn't have the work routine of turning up at the Sacramento state government offices every day to run their HR department – he seemed at a bit of a loose end. He played golf, badly, and went to bowls regularly – mainly because there were plenty of widows and divorced women to be found there – but she could tell he still yearned for the frantic pace of industrial and human relations.

Putting off making the call, she emailed some notes to Lacey and Sharon about the projects she was working on. She was just finishing an explanation of a complicated industrial issue that had cropped up during the communication process when she thought of Kate, who worked part-time in industrial relations. Of course! She could phone Kate and make her excuses. She pressed the autodial for Kate's mobile – that way she would catch her whether she was at work or at home.

'Kate Sweeney,' she answered.

'Kate, you're never going to believe what's happened,' Alex said.

'Don't tell me. You're not going to be there Wednesday for Dad's birthday.'

'How'd you know?'

'How long have I known you?'

'Okay, okay,' Alex laughed. 'So I'm true to type.'

'So what's the excuse this time?'

'I've got to go up to the Rossini's for a few days. Something's happened. It's highly unlikely I'll be back before Wednesday.'

Kate snorted. 'Trish will be absolutely furious.'

'You mean Patrice.'

They both laughed.

'Doug'll be upset too. He always relies on you to keep him entertained when "Patrice" is around.' She pronounced Patrice slowly, with a slight sneer.

Kate and Alex didn't see eye to eye on everything but when it came to their brother's wife, they were in total agreement. They'd argued over almost everything after their mother had died. They'd fallen out time and again, but the animosity never lasted long. The worst row was when Kate's marriage looked as though it was about to spread-eagle itself on the rocks and Alex had a go at her for being so hard on Doug and putting the blame on him for their inability to have children while refusing to consider artificial insemination. They'd ended up not speaking to each other for almost three months. In the end, Kate had relented, though whether this was because they'd just been told there was a baby available for adoption through the church or because she was genuinely sorry, Alex never knew. But that was a long time ago. The adopted baby – Alexander, named after Alex – was now in his teens and had a younger brother and sister, backing up the myth that a supposedly infertile couple need only stop worrying about being infertile.

'She's such a silly bitch, I can't imagine what he sees in her.' Alex must have said this a hundred times. But she still couldn't believe that her sensible, staid brother could want to put up with such an empty-headed social climber for so long.

Kate exploded into laughter. 'Give it up, Alexandra. You know he adores her. Theirs has been the one stable relationship in our whole family. There's no point in analysing it. It just works. It doesn't matter why. I only wish I'd had such an easy time of it.'

'Well you're not doing too badly now, Katharina.' Alex mimicked Kate's use of her full name.

'Don't call me that, you know I hate it.'

'Kath-a-rin-a,' Alex repeated, emphasising each syllable.

'Right, that's it. I'm not going to make excuses for you on Wednesday.'

'Sorry, Kate. I just can't help myself. You've got to tell them, Kate,' she begged. 'I can't tell Max. He'll hit the roof. Please do it for me and tell them I had to go out of town on an urgent job.'

There was a brief silence then Kate exploded into laughter again. 'You're impossible Alex,' she said. 'What it is to be single and fancy free. I wish I could just dash off like that, without having to worry about whether the kids'll get to school or the dog'll get fed.'

Alex joined in the laughter. 'It's not as simple as you think,' she said. 'I've still got to sort it out with Lucian.'

'Lucian!' Kate snorted. 'Best way to sort it out with him is to tell him to push off.'

'Don't start that now,' Alex pleaded. 'He's going to be really pissed off when I tell him I'm off out of town again. He hates me leaving him to cope on his own.'

'That's only because he hates having to do his own washing and cooking.'

'Stop it, Kate. He's not that bad.'

'Hmm,' was all Kate would say.

'Dad likes him.'

'Well he would, wouldn't he? They're both vain and self-centred.'

'I don't believe you just said that!'

'Well it's true.'

Alex fought off the inclination to defend Lucian. He *was* a bit like Dad. They both spent ages in front of the mirror preening, combing their hair and adjusting their clothes.

'I'd better get out of here and go home to break the news,' she said. 'He should be home by the time I get there.'

'All right, you go and enjoy yourself. I'll bear the brunt of your absence on Wednesday.'

'You're an angel, Kate. Thank you.'

'Don't worry. I'll get you to make up for it some time.'

'I know you will,' Alex agreed and the two hung up.

She gathered up the client files and took them out to Lacey.

'I'm going to have to leave all this with you and Sharon to deal with,' she said to the PA, who was poring over the profit and loss account. She plonked the heavy folders down on Lacey's desk. 'I've got to whip up to Rossini's for a few days. There's a bit of a crisis. I haven't got time to explain, but you'll see it on CBS tonight.'

'Oh dear,' Lacey said. 'Is there anything I can do to help them? They're such nice people.'

'No thanks, hon. Kind of you to ask, but I've got to be there to deal with it. What you can do, though, is hold the fort while I'm gone and see that Sharon gets all this. Give her all the support you can. There's not much that needs to be done until next week, but I've made a few notes for her to follow.'

'No problem,' Lacey said. And Alex knew that it would be done. Lacey was the most reliable PA and office manager she'd ever had. She managed to cope with Alex's ups and downs, with her clients no matter how demanding, and with Sharon's emergencies without showing any change in her unflappable demeanour.

She handed Lacey her Filofax and a couple of notes she'd made about the appointments.

'Here, you'd better photocopy these pages. I need you to phone everyone and put the meetings off until next week, please. You'll know what to say.' She shoved a pile of folders and papers onto Lacey's desk. 'And these are the things I've got coming up I need you to deal with.'

'How long do you think you'll be gone?'

'Oh, probably until the weekend. Or maybe a few days after that. But I can't stay away too long. I've got to get back onto the airline case before the weekend after next or I'm in trouble.'

'Don't you worry about a thing, Alex. I'll sort it for you.'

'You're wonderful, Lacey. I don't know what I'd do without you.'

'Just you keep those pay checks rolling in, Alex. A little bit more every year. That'll keep me happy.'

'A woman of simple needs.'

'Don't you believe it!' Lacey said as Alex disappeared back into her office.

Alex gathered up Rossini's file with its own media lists and background info, picked up her bag, her water bottle and all the bits and pieces she thought she'd need over the next few days, collected her diary, hot off the photocopier, from Lacey and said goodbye as she headed out the door.

'You go, girl!' were Lacey's parting words.

She took the lift to the basement, got into her car and headed off home. The powder blue BMW convertible purred through the traffic, which wasn't too bad yet. She looked at her watch. It was just before three. If she could get back to the apartment in less than thirty minutes, pack in fifteen minutes, she could hit the road again before rush hour started in earnest. But the road out to the Napa would still be pretty clogged. She'd be lucky to get there in time for the news. She sighed and turned up the stereo. *Figaro* was in the CD player, with the gentle strains of 'Voi, che sapete' just beginning. She settled back to listen as she negotiated the traffic.

'You're early!' Lucian looked up from the ballgame grumpily. He was surrounded by half-eaten food and an array of beer cans.

'I've got to go away on a client job for a few days,' she said. She'd decided on the way home not to tell him where she was going. She could do with a few days' peace, and it would do him good to stew about where she might be. 'So I've come home early to pack.'

'Oh,' he said. 'Where are you going?'

'Up north. I've got to get to the airport to catch a flight in a couple of hours,' she fibbed. 'With all that check-in security stuff now, I've got to get moving.' She took off to the bedroom before he could question her further and he turned back to the ballgame on TV, apparently uninterested in further information.

The whole lounge, she noticed, was a terrible mess. Newspapers, beer cans and empty food wrappers were scattered over the cowhide couch and dotted the black pile rug like confetti. In the kitchen, the mess was even worse. The stainless steel benches and Gaggenau hobs – usually pristine and uncluttered – were littered with unwashed dishes, half-filled glasses and coffee mugs which, on closer inspection, were swimming with cigarette butts. By the time she reached the bedroom she felt like screaming. The bed she'd made this morning before leaving, the tidy clean room was now a jumble of clothes and pillows, with a collection of crumbs and magazines congregated on the cover. It looked as though Lucian had been home all day, which was unusual. If she'd had more time, she would have gone back out to the lounge, muted the television, quizzed him as to what was going on and asked him to clean it up. But as it was, she had precious little time to pack, so decided to leave it until she got back. Besides, she reasoned, Lucian would only mess it up again while she was gone, so she might as well leave him to it.

She was just zipping up her bag when he popped his head through the door.

'Sorry about the mess, doll. I was going to clean it up before you got back.'

'You shouldn't let it get that bad,' she couldn't help herself from saying. 'It's gross.'

'It's not that bad,' he said.

'It is. It's gross,' she repeated. 'You've dropped towels all over the bathroom floor, the kitchen's a tip, and look at this.' She swept her hand around the bedroom, evidence enough, she thought, of total chaos.

'You're so picky,' he said, his voice rising. 'A guy can't do anything around here without getting picked on.'

'Oh, come on, Lucian. I'm pretty tolerant really.'

'Yeah? Well not in my book.' He stumped back out to the TV, slamming the lounge door behind him.

Alex stood there, wrestling with her desire to rush after him and argue the point. She'd let him get away with so much these past few weeks. Every time she'd wanted to have it out with him, she'd pulled back. It never seemed to be the right time to talk about their relationship and where it was going. And now she was frantic to get out on the freeway and beat the rush-hour traffic, with a client in desperate straits at the other end.

Repressing her anger, she picked up her jacket and bag, crossed the hallway, opened the lounge door and called out, 'Goodbye, Lucian. I'm off now.'

Silence. His back was to her; his eyes were glued on the television set, the ballgame now so loud he probably hadn't heard her. She stepped forward until she was in his sights, said goodbye again and waved, saluted almost, with her free hand. He ignored her.

'Suit yourself, then,' she said under her breath as she turned on her heel and departed, banging the front door with a vicious jerk as she left.

Out in the carpark, she flung her case in the boot and plumped herself down on the soft cream leather seats. She drove out into the traffic, *Figaro* still running on the CD player, but now it failed to soothe her soul.

The traffic seemed interminable, although she figured she was more impatient than usual. Once over the bridge and out on the freeway, she lowered the drop-top and turned up the stereo even louder. 'Dove sono', she sang along with the poignant lyrics. Like the countess in *Figaro,* she too couldn't fathom why she was being dealt such a raw deal by her man. She sang double forte, letting the full force of her lungs cry out the pain she was feeling inside until tears welled up in her eyes at the unfairness of it all. She wiped them away with the edge of her sleeve.

'Fuck you, Lucian,' she cried out at the top of her voice, the wind whipping the words out of her mouth. 'Fuck you.'

She changed down, switched into the fast lane, and ran through the gears, putting the little BMW M3 through its paces. They'd promised her Formula 1 gear changing and every now and then she liked to see how good that felt. She could feel her back hit the leather of the seat as the G-force kicked in. The convertible gathered speed and carried her faster than she'd driven it for some time through the gathering night to Rossini's.

3. Ripe for the Picking

Collapsing in front of the TV, which was built into the corner of the large, comfortable family room of their sprawling, Tuscan-style villa, David closed his eyes and felt the weight of the family name on his shoulders. He rubbed at the bridge of his nose where a headache had been building up all afternoon then dug his fingers into his closed eyelids, trying to obliterate the sharp, stabbing pain between his eyes.

'It can't be that bad,' Pietro said as he came through the door off the porch and saw the anxiety in his son's eyes as he looked up at him.

Pietro was in his late seventies, thin and wiry; a little shorter and a lot smaller than his well-built son whose size was due in no small measure to being unable to resist his wife's cooking, as well as a preference to swallow the wines he tasted rather than spit them out as his colleagues usually did. Both father and son had thick dark wavy hair, although Pietro's was now sparse at the temples and greying. Both had clear brown eyes that looked right at you, with nothing to hide. And the old man had the heart and strength of men half his age. When he handed the management of the family vineyard over to David a few years ago it was on the condition that he could still work the vines, keep his hand in – and his heart. Without his daily walk through the vines, singing in his fine baritone when he thought no-one was listening, nicking off excess tendrils or leaves as he went, David was sure his father would lose his reason to live.

Mama, still in her apron and wearing her usual full black skirt and rose-patterned cardigan, was standing behind Pietro, who'd sat down on the sofa. Mama's small, strong hands fidgeted with the gold cross hanging on a fine gold chain around her neck, the only sign that she might be as nervous as everyone else in the room. Mamma wasn't known for displays of emotion.

'I think it will be.'

Mamma put her hand on Pietro's shoulder.

'I'm going out to the kitchen to see to the dinner,' she said. 'I can't bear to watch it.'

'I understand,' Pietro said, patting her hand.

Mamma quietly departed.

David had told his family. The last thing he wanted was for them to hear about it first on the evening news so he'd told Anna then, armed with her support, he'd crossed the yard and told his parents. Pietro had been furious, but not at his son. He'd raged against the Institute, blaming them for leaking the complaint.

'I've a good mind to take them to court,' he'd said.

David had agreed with him. Once this whole thing was proven to be groundless slander, litigation was quite on the cards. But in the meantime, he had to pull Rossini's through what was shaping up to be one of its most difficult times yet.

Anna came up quickly behind him and massaged his shoulders. He could smell the faint woody citrus of her *Paloma* perfume.

'Tsss, David. Your muscles are much too tight,' she said. 'You shouldn't get so wound up about things. I'm sure it'll be fine.' She continued to knead around the base of his neck as if her strong, small fingers could erase everything with a few well-aimed firm but tender strokes. He could feel her rings, as always, tapping gently against his spine – her wedding ring, her mother's wedding ring, and her mother's before her, in that order. Anna liked to wear them all on one finger, as if she was carrying the wisdom and understanding of three generations there. Knowing Anna, she probably was. But the square of gold and diamonds on her finger was the only jewellery she wore. She refused to wear a watch, yet she always seemed to know what time it was. On special occasions, David could remember her putting on pearls and earrings. But that was all. He loved her down-to-earth, no-nonsense approach to everything. She was the backbone of the business, yet she was warm and earthy, and a queen in the kitchen. And for the last couple of years, the whole region had been able to benefit from her tasty recipes by listening to her cooking programme on local radio. It was just a small station, but nevertheless she'd become a minor celebrity in the Napa, where celebrities were two a penny. Her occasional cooking classes and demonstrations were usually sold out days in advance, and her weekly winter-time radio series was popular with people who appreciated her self-deprecating, quick wit, her unassuming nature, her knowledge of ingredients and her obvious love of food – Italian and Californian.

Even Mamma had to admit that Anna's sundried tomato pesto and handmade pasta were better than hers. There wasn't a drop of Italian blood in Anna's body, yet her culinary skills, business acumen and ability to live life to the full were equal to any David had encountered among all his relatives – and there were many. The musky whiff of her *Paloma* made him want to bury his head in her ample bosom and wait for the world to disappear. If only it could.

Briefly, he acknowledged her comfort by reaching up and patting her plump bare brown forearm, stroking the taut muscles firmed from season after season working the vines.

'It'll be okay David, I'm sure. We've been through worse,' she said, taking his hand.

He gave his wife's hand a quick squeeze then picked up the remote control and turned up the volume so they could all hear the worst. For he was sure it would be bad.

The anchorman seemed to be taking an eternity getting through each item. There was nothing in the first segment, then the inevitable ads. He clasped Anna's hand. She was sitting beside him now, his rock in uncertain times. But he couldn't sit still. He rearranged the magazines on the coffee table into a neat pile, then rearranged them in date order. Would these ads never end? He fidgeted with the remote again.

Manfred knocked on the open ranchslider. The outside lights on the wide, slate-tiled verandah made his usually tanned face look very pale and white. Behind him, the square plastered, pale-ochre pillars supporting the verandah beams looked like eerie sentinels. David motioned for him to come in and sit down.

'I hope I said the right thing,' he said as Manfred joined them.

The phone rang, but he ignored it.

'Don't answer it,' he said to Anna. There'd already been a string of calls from other winemakers in the Valley. 'Have you heard the trailer on CBS?' they'd all said. 'Do you know who it is?' He'd had to tell them it was Rossini's, that he reckoned they'd been framed, that Manfred had even tested some of the bottles of *Don Giovanni* from the cellar and they'd been fine. Nothing added. After about the tenth call he'd stopped answering and let the answerphone click in. Much as he wanted to clear his name, to explain the real situation to everyone that called, he couldn't find the words any more. He'd dried up.

If only he'd dried up earlier with Gibbens. He knew he shouldn't have talked so much. He'd got carried away telling his side of the story. Alex would never have let him do that. As if his turn of thoughts had drawn her, Alex suddenly burst through the door.

'Am I in time?' she asked.

'Yes, yes. Nothing yet,' David said quickly. 'Here, take a chair.' He indicated an empty armchair. Alex collapsed on it. There was no need to say anything more at this stage. There would be plenty of time for talking afterwards.

Alex had arrived nearly an hour ago, bumping into David as she'd been tearing past the winery on the way through to the house. It had been dark and they hadn't seen each other until it was too late.

'Hey, watch it!' David had exclaimed then, seeing it was her, 'Alex! You made it! It's great to see you.' He'd stepped back to look at her. 'You always *were* in a hurry to get somewhere. You can slow down now. You're in the country.' He'd paused as he took her in. 'Look at you. You've cut your hair!'

'It was always getting in my eyes, David. It had to go.'

'Well, it looks pretty spunky now. Anna will be bowled over.'

Anna had indeed been bowled over.

'*Cara mia*,' she'd cried, running to her and enveloping her in a warm hug the minute she entered the kitchen. There was a familiar smell of olives and pesto and fresh bread. Alex could see three round flat loaves of foccaccia on the kitchen table. '*Cara mia*, welcome'. Anna moved back a few inches and studied her. 'Hey, I love the hair! It's terrific. It's just right for you,' she exclaimed.

'It's certainly a lot easier to look after,' Alex laughed.

'And you're looking good too – although still too thin, *cara*.'

Alex laughed, delighted to have someone fuss over her and call her *Cara mia* again. It had started with Pietro, who'd seemed to adopt her as a wayward but trainable daughter when she was here the first time and stayed for so long, and then Anna had taken it up, slipping easily into Italian as she did when conversing with Pietro and Mamma Madelena around the dinner table.

Anna laboured long and hard in the winery and out in the vines, but had always been a size twelve to Alex's eight. Her tanned skin, though, made her look much healthier and attractive than she did, Alex noticed. She recalled more or less the same conversation when she'd lived at Rossini's in the landfill days.

'I know, I know. I just can't help myself. There's just so much to do, I don't seem to eat until the evening. And then I don't want to go to bed.'

'Tssss,' Anna said. 'You're so pale, *cara*. That big city has been no good for you at all. You need sunshine and fresh air.'

'I'm fine, really,' Alex protested. 'But I'm certainly looking forward to your home-made pasta again.'

'You say that every time,' Anna laughed. 'I'll make sure there's plenty for you tonight. We'll have dinner late – after the news. There's no way David will be able to eat before that's over. And he has a new sticky wine that he wants you to taste. He's very proud of it and it'll provide him with a diversion from this dreadful business with the wine-blending,' Anna said. 'Let me show you back up to your old room. David's already taken your bag there and, if you're quick, you might even have time for a nice hot soak in the tub.'

'That sounds fabulous. I might be able to squeeze it in before the news. Might as well enjoy it while I can – before the proverbial hits the fan!'

'Indeed. It sounds awful.'

'Nothing we won't be able to fix, I'm sure,' Alex had said with more assurance than she felt.

'You're a life-saver,' Anna said. 'It's lovely to have you back for a few days again. I love it when you're around, with all the people you seem to attract – the parties and the talk.'

'I'm taking it more quietly these days, Anna.'

'That can mean only one thing – a serious relationship. Come on, own up. How long has this been going on?'

'Oh I met him a few months ago…'

'A few months! Why didn't you tell me?'

'Well there wasn't anything to tell for a while. It was on again, off again. It wasn't worth mentioning. But then he moved in last month…'

'Yes, David told me there was man's voice on the answerphone. It must be serious, then? So who is he?'

'Oh, just someone I met through work. His name's Lucian. He's a computer whizz.'

'Tsss. Computers eh? What's he like?' Anna turned back to Alex who was following her down the long hallway towards the guest bedrooms, located off to the side of the single-level home.

'Tall, dark and handsome, of course,' Alex said.

'Just like all the others.'

'Just like all the others,' Alex repeated, laughing.

'Well I hope he's better behaved than the others,' Anna said, turning as they reached the door to Alex's old room and admonishing her, shaking her forefinger.

'Probably not,' Alex said ruefully. 'I'm afraid he's shaping up to be a bit of a pain.'

'Tsss, *cara*,' Anna stood in front of the door, facing Alex. 'You seem to have some sort of fatal attraction for Mr Wrong. When are you going to find someone who's not tall dark and handsome, someone who'll give you love and security instead?'

'If only I knew, Anna. I seem to scare off all the nice ordinary guys.'

'You're such a lovely, intelligent, hard-working girl. I just can't understand it.'

'I think that's my problem. They're frightened of my success.'

'But the ones you go with, all these Mr Wrongs, they're not frightened of you.'

'No, they treat me like a dumb blonde. And I suppose I act like one to keep them interested.'

'Well, *cara*, we're going to have to see if we can find you a nice boy in the valley somewhere.'

Alex laughed, despite her sensitivities on the subject. Anna was one of the few people who could get away with quizzing her like this. She hated talking about her personal life – probably because it was such a mess.

Anna opened the door and stood aside for Alex to enter.

'It feels like home,' she said. 'Oh, I meant to tell you, I copied one of your recipes last week off Bay Radio.'

'I don't believe it!'

'Yes, and I've even tried it out. The braised lamb shanks with tomatoes and olives. I had a dinner party at the weekend and everyone was really impressed. They were really something.'

Anna laughed. 'You never cease to amaze me, *cara*. All those fancy Gaggenau appliances you told me about and you hardly ever get to use them – except the microwave to heat up take-out dinners. You're the last person I'd have expected to see writing down recipes off the radio.'

'Oh, I got the recipe off Bay Radio's website afterwards. You're right. I never thought to write it down at the time.'

'Well I'm glad to know I've got at least one fan.'

'You'll have a fan club before you know it.'

'You're getting a bit carried away. It's just a little community station, you know!' Anna said, laughing again. 'I'll leave you to it, now. There're fresh towels in the bathroom. You let me know if there's anything else you need.' Alex thanked her and gave her an impromptu hug. 'Thank you, Anna. It's great to be back. I love it here. Tell David I'll be along in time for the news.'

When Anna had gone, Alex shut the door and looked around. The room was just as she'd left it – plain but homely, the painting of the

Umbrian countryside on the butter yellow wall, the blue, yellow and terracotta striped bedspread and curtains, the worn, comfortable bucket-shaped easy chair by the window. She looked outside, across the lines of ripening vines to the hills beyond, hazy with the lowering sun. This was the view she'd missed, that she'd dreamed of during those hot, windless nights in the city: the cool green vines, the smoky purple haze of the surrounding hills and now it was almost fall, the dark red maples set against the deep green conifers and redwood beyond the vineyard boundary. She sighed appreciatively, and turned to unpack her bag.

Shucking off her well worn beige Lauren loafers, Alex zipped open her case, lifted out her toilet bag, padded into the ensuite and turned on the bath. Anna had left some Gucci *Rush* bath foam out for her.

'Thank you, Anna. You remembered how much I adore it,' Alex said out loud, and squeezed a few drops under the running tap. She inhaled the heady aroma. Heaven. Just what she needed after such a frantic day – and before the inevitable storm ahead.

She left the bath to fill, emptied the contents of the toilet bag on the vanity, picked out what she'd need immediately and returned to her suitcase.

Although she'd packed in a hurry, she was confident she'd have everything she'd need. After leading a fairly transient lifestyle, she'd become adept at throwing things into a case at short notice. And with a wardrobe that she deliberately kept to beiges, browns, pastels and grey, it was pretty easy to mix and match without having to think much about it.

She picked out her running gear first and laid it out on the settee at the end of the bed, ready for the morning routine. She liked early morning runs up here in the fresh clean air. The worn old Nikes were due for replacement soon, but they should last the summer.

Next she took out her clothes: the Jones New York pale grey suit, a couple of years old now, but still with plenty of wear in it; two pairs of slacks – slinky beige and dark grey; two easy-care shirts and three other casual tops. And for cold nights, the chunky brown Claiborne cardigan.

She unrolled her good Prada taupe linen-look dress from the side pocket of her bag, uncrushed, and hung it in the small built-in wardrobe, catching her reflection in the long mirror as she passed. Her clothes had seen better days, that was for sure. Her Levis were faded at the knees, the long white Hugo Boss shirt was creased after a long day. She needed to go shopping again – not her favourite pastime. For one, she never seemed to have the time, and with Lucian around, there was never enough money. Alex didn't shop for clothes often, but when she did, she tended to buy well made clothing that would last. Before her mother died, she'd managed to impress on Alex that clothes should last much longer than one fashion season and should suit your figure rather than the latest fad.

Instinctively, she sucked in her tummy then laughed at herself. There was nothing much there to suck any more. Those dark, unhappy days after Pete had left her and she'd put on thirty pounds were well behind her now.

Lucian, though, was a more recent problem. On her way down Route 29, she'd resolved to resist temptation to phone him and make up. She needed time out to think about what she should do. He was using her, she knew that much. And he was bad for her. She'd finally worked that out. Her friends had been telling her for months to get rid of him: 'He's spending all your money and borrowing from everyone else,' they said, 'dragging you down, making your life a misery,' etcetera, etcetera. But she'd never been able to ask him to leave. Whenever she'd steeled herself to do it, he'd manage to disarm her with that big, wide smile of his that made him look so sexy. It was almost as if he knew she was wanting to get rid of him. He'd bought her flowers, found the book she'd been looking for and given it to her with a love poem in the dedication. It was impossible to throw him out after that. But when she'd looked her credit card bill up online, she found he'd charged all his generous gifts to her card over the internet.

The next few weeks would show if she could be happier without him. And after that? Well, she could always run away to New Zealand. There'd been a contract offer there to help out a winery company in a place called Nelson that was putting in a landfill, a bit like David had done. They'd studied David's example and had emailed Rossini's many times. But they'd encountered trouble with protesters, many of them from neighbouring wineries, and had tracked her down and asked her to go and help out. The call had come out of the blue last week. She'd said she would have to think about it and would get back to them. It was unlikely, she thought. She couldn't see herself several thousand miles away in an unknown country. She'd promised to email them back within ten days, so she'd have to make up her mind soon.

Settled into the Rossinis' comfortable armchair two hours later, refreshed after a bath, Alex wished she could relax. But the dreaded item had yet to appear on the news. The string of stories was followed by another ad break; another gaggle of jangling commercials.

She sat up sharply as soon as she recognised the picture postcard scenes of the Napa Valley, followed by a series of quick shots of the vineyard – the main building, the vines, and stock footage from a past

Opera in the Vines concert. David turned up the volume with the remote.

'Shock allegations of wine blending have rocked the Napa Valley today. A complaint has been made to the authorities that last year's award-winning *Don Giovanni* chardonnay, from Rossini's Winery is in breach of the wine-labelling rules,' the anchorman was saying. 'Mike Gibbens was on the scene today, tracking down the story.'

Gibbens' face appeared in the middle of a vineyard – not Rossini's – saying how such serious allegations could affect the whole region.

'CBS News has been told that the Institute of American Wineries received a complaint…'

'Someone's leaked it to them,' Pietro interrupted, his voice choking with anger. 'It better not have been that Ineson. There's only half a dozen people on that committee. It must have been one of them.'

'As soon as this is over I'm going to find out,' David said. 'They'll rue the day they did this to us.'

Anna kept quiet. This was not a time to add fuel to the fire.

Gibbens was gesticulating at the vines around him, explaining the American Viticultural Areas, or AVA, rules about not being allowed to blend more that five percent of wine from outside the vineyard. An interview with Ineson followed.

'The Institute has to take such allegations seriously, of course,' Ineson was saying. 'Although so far, from what CBS has shown me, and from the reports I've seen, there is no evidence of any blending with other grapes.'

Then David's face flashed on the screen with a caption: 'David Rossini, Rossini's Winery,' it said. To David, the letters might as well have been ten feet high. The phone started to ring again.

'Leave it,' he said. Eventually the answer machine clicked on.

'It's absolutely impossible,' the David on the screen was saying. 'Rossini's always follows the AVA rules rigidly. I would never allow that sort of thing to happen.'

David couldn't help but smile at the righteous indignation on his face.

'Mr Rossini showed CBS through his winery and let us select a couple of bottles of *Don Giovanni* to test ourselves,' Gibbens was saying. The picture cut to the cool dark cellar, with the reporter holding up the *Don Giovanni* then tasting it. There was a second's silence, then a long satisfied sigh. 'Well it certainly tastes pretty good,' Gibbens said to the camera. David could remember that bit and he felt pleased with himself. Taking the camera crew into the winery and the cellar was a good move.

'Well done, David,' Alex said.

The next shot was of Gibbens in a laboratory, holding up a *Don Giovanni*.

'However, another allegation has been made that there are additives in the wine. CBS News purchased several bottles of *Don Giovanni* chardonnay at four randomly selected liquor stores around California and had them independently tested by two experts – one at UC Davis and the other at Seabrook Laboratory.'

It cut away to a lab technician, a thin, peaky, pasty-faced, mousy-haired man with thick, dark glasses – the sort that change colour in the light. It made him look shifty.

'Dr James Seabrook,' the caption said. 'Oenologist, Seabrook Laboratory.'

'Yes, well…' Seabrook said hesitantly. 'At first analysis it looks as though there's at least ninety-five percent chardonnay in this bottle. Which is exactly as it should be.'

David breathed an audible sigh of relief. Pietro said indignantly, 'So what's all the fuss about then?'

'But chemical analysis of this bottle and of several others has detected a small amount of glycol in the wine.'

A close-up shot of test reports from the two laboratories showed more than half the bottles contained a small amount of glycol.

Everyone in the room cried out in protest.

'It's a set-up. It has to be,' Pietro said. He'd jumped to his feet and was pacing up and down the side of the room like a trapped game animal.

'What on earth…' said Alex.

'That can't be true,' said Anna.

'What's glycol?' Alex asked.

'Anti-freeze,' David said quickly. 'The stuff east coasters put in their cars to stop radiators freezing in winter. It's got a slightly sweet taste.'

Alex thought it sounded bizarre.

Ineson's face came back on screen.

'I find this hard to believe,' he was saying, holding the laboratory reports that Gibbens had obviously just handed to him. 'There is no way a winery with such a top reputation as Rossini's would do this. It would be professional suicide. I just don't believe it.' Ineson was shaking his head.

The shot cut away to Gibbens again. 'David Rossini couldn't believe it either,' he said.

Then there was a close-up of David. Alex could tell from the look on his face that he was struggling to hold back his anger.

'We would never, ever add anything to our wine like that,' he said, pronouncing each word with deliberate emphasis. 'Our wines win awards for their quality and taste. We would never compromise our good name by adding *glycol*.' He almost spat the word. 'I can't understand how these tests can produce such a result. It's impossible…'

The camera lingered briefly on David's shattered expression of utter devastation and the item was over. His face was replaced by the confident, authoritative face of anchorman Dan Rather.

'We'll be looking further into these allegations so be sure to be watching CBS news tomorrow night.' The anchorman then started reading the next news item. Another lamb to the slaughter, David thought, and switched the TV and then the video recorder off with the remote.

'I just can't imagine anyone who'd want to do this to us,' Pietro continued. 'I know everybody on that committee. I wouldn't say they're all beyond reproach, but none of them would set us up like this.'

'I can't see it either,' David agreed. 'The whole reason for their existence is to protect the reputation of the Napa Valley. It's just not in their interests to leak something like that. Even our fiercest competitor would know there's nothing to gain by smearing us, because it would bring the whole valley into question. Besides, it seems as though the claims about glycol were made to CBS two or three weeks ago.'

'Glycol!' Pietro said. 'Why ever would we want to add that dreadful stuff into our precious wine?'

'You know the old horror stories, papa. A couple of wineries in Europe added it to their wine one year when the grapes hadn't been able to ripen properly. It's supposed to make it taste sweeter.'

'Pah!' Pietro spat. 'It makes wine taste absolutely disgusting. As if we would ever do a thing like that.'

David looked at his father, who was getting more and more upset. He'd have to be careful or he'd get breathless again. Pietro didn't handle stress all that well these days. It was imperative to find out what this awful stuff was in the *Don Giovanni*.

Then he remembered the suggestion that Manfred had made about that fellow Wade Spargo. Could it have been him? He turned to Manfred, who'd been watching the news item from behind the sofa and had remained silent throughout.

'That Spargo fellow… perhaps it *was* him,' he said. 'Perhaps he leaked it to the media as well.'

'He certainly had a grudge against us,' Manfred replied.

'I don't know of anyone else who has an axe to grind. Do you know where he went after he left us? Can we track him down?'

'Maybe we should call the police,' Pietro suggested.

'Good thinking, Papa,' David said, 'I wouldn't want to be held responsible what might happen to him if I got my hands on him.'

'Police?' Alex said. 'Do you have any proof that he did anything? What will you tell them?'

'No proof, no. Just a suspicion that he's doctored the wine somehow out of spite and has now told CBS news about it.' David turned to Anna. 'Do you remember him? That short fellow with the long wispy hair and the goatee. We had to let him go when I caught him smoking dope.'

'Of course I remember,' Anna said.

'Well,' David said, turning to Alex as well, 'Manfred reckons he might have come back in afterwards and done something then. Put something in the wine, maybe. Did you see him later that afternoon, Anna?'

Anna cast her mind back to that day when David had told her about Wade. She'd never really liked him anyway. He was always slow and seemed to have lost the plot. And he had little, bright, staring eyes amid blond, almost invisible eyelashes. She thought he looked a bit like a weasel. Had he come back in later? She'd been so intent on the bottling line she might not have noticed.

'Honestly David, I don't recall seeing him. But I was pretty tied up then. I could easily have missed him. That was the day that the labels wouldn't stick properly.'

'Damn, so it was,' David said shortly. 'I wonder if Wade had anything to do with the defective labels?'

'The more you say, the more it sounds like something for the police,' Pietro said.

'You're right Papa. That's exactly what I'm going to do. But I'll call from the office. I want to look up his file over there first.'

Upstairs in his office, David pulled Wade Spargo's file out of the filing cabinet and scanned through it. A brief CV, an address and phone number – probably out of date now. He sat down at his desk and went to pick up the phone. The message light was flashing frantically. No doubt there'd be dozens of messages – a few from friends and sympathisers and the rest from every reporter in California, and probably even beyond, hot for a story. He'd deal with them later. He dialled his lawyer then, on getting his approval, called the local sheriff, Dan Sheldrake, about his suspicions. Dan said he'd send someone over to take details in the morning.

Feeling much better now that he'd put some of his problems into Dan's and Alex's much more capable hands at dealing with crises, he decided to check his messages.

4. Torpedo

Timing his step to meet the pitch and fall of the big steel ship, Zhi Kingston made his way along the unsteady corridor to his room. He opened the door, stepped over the ledge and flung his papers and workbooks on the narrow bunkbed. His roommate, Curtis, was upstairs in the computer room, so he'd decided to grab this rare quiet moment to check his personal emails and catch up with what was going on in the outside world. Twelve-hour shifts staring at a computer screen and checking charts and records required such an intense focus that he often found he got quite out of touch with the real world unless he made an effort to keep in contact with friends and family, and check some of his favourite internet news sites.

He looked out the oblong window at the grey-green sea and the dark grey sky turning to black on the landward horizon. Whitecaps were whipping spray into the air. Not too promising. The forecast was for a big cold front coming through with a southerly gale behind it. By the look of it, the front was about to arrive. And here – aboard *Pacific Explorer II,* looking for oil off the coast of New Plymouth, on the westernmost part of New Zealand's North Island – he had no choice but to ride it out and hope it would be a short one. He'd seen a fair few storms in his time on the *Explorer,* travelling round the Pacific Rim – off Korea, the South China Sea, Indonesia and Australia. But the New Plymouth coast certainly knew how to dish out weather. Storms here could be fierce, especially at this time of the year. It was mid-August, almost spring in the southern hemisphere, which meant the start of the equinoxial gales. Staring wistfully out at the cold blackening sea, he realised he couldn't be further away or more cut off from his family in Saratoga. It would be midsummer there now.

Turning away from the window, Zhi pulled a chair up to the built-in desk, turned on his networked computer and connected to the internet.

'You have seven new messages,' his email told him. He scanned down them to find his sister Xanthia's name. He opened it first and smiled at Zannie's subject heading: 'How are the grandchildren?' Mum must have been at her again. Their mother had inherited the gift of the gab from her maternal Irish ancestors and fiery Hispanic pride from her Spanish father's side. And now that her five children were old enough to have progeny of their own, she never lost an opportunity to push the point. It was her consuming passion and so far, not one of her offspring had obliged. Zannie was the most gorgeous looking black-haired beauty. Men fell at her feet, but she never seemed to take any of them seriously enough to settle down with. She was having too much fun, she'd say, playing the field. Zhi's excuse was that he was never in one place long enough to form a serious relationship. But it didn't wash with Mom.

Sure enough, Zannie's email was full of Mom's latest ploy to marry her off to the son of some old family friend to produce a grandchild.

There was another email from Sarah, his old college friend. He'd known Sarah since they'd lived next door to each other in suburban Saratoga, and they'd both ended up at UCLA. They'd meet for lunch, hang around with the same crowd, go to watch the Dodgers play occasionally. But they'd never been an item. That way, they'd remained really good friends. Her email was a breath of fresh air. She made all her dates sound like part of a script for a romantic comedy and her job, in the marketing department of a big LA real estate chain, sounded like a breeze. But then Sarah always did make everything seem to be more fun than it really was. He was concerned to read she and her latest boyfriend were indulging in more than a few spliffs when they were out together. 'You'll have to join us sometime,' she wrote. Zhi and Sarah and the crowd they used to hang out with at UCLA had enjoyed smoking dope at parties and on the odd occasion in between. But Zhi couldn't touch the stuff while on the ship. It just wasn't worth the risk – it could jeopardise weeks of work on the oil survey, could even put people's lives at risk and besides, there were regular and random checks on the crew – both maritime and exploration – to make sure they didn't have a stash somewhere. There wasn't even much alcohol consumed while they were at sea. Which is probably why he made up for it in spades when he was ashore.

He chuckled to himself as he read the rest of Sarah's email. She referred to some photos she'd attached – forgetting that her network stripped out all attachments because they were too risky for spreading viruses. He sighed. He'd like to have seen them. It would be nice to go back home for a while. The oil exploration company he worked for – US Western Pacific Consortium – paid for him to return home to San Francisco twice a year if he wanted to. It was time he went home again, he decided. He'd see about making a booking next time he had extended leave.

He looked up and caught a glimpse of himself in the mirror above the desk. He pushed his thick black hair off his face where it had flopped down, covering his eyes. It was too long, he thought. Time to get it cut.

The ship suddenly lurched to starboard and he steadied himself against the desk. He could hear the wind screaming outside. The storm had obviously arrived. Oh well, he thought, batten down the hatches – again. Nothing he hadn't coped with before. He and the *Pacific Explorer II* – and the ships and rigs he'd been on before her – had weathered many a storm at sea. He glanced around the room and tidied away the loose or moveable things before turning back to his messages. Time to reply to Zannie and Sarah before dinner, he decided.

Bracing his knees on each side of the built-in desk, he planted his feet firmly on the heaving floor to steady himself against the pitching and rolling of the ship. He picked up his portable CD player – *Led Zeppelin II* was still in there – put the headphones in his ears, pressed 'play' and turned up the volume to block out the sound of the wind and the rain now rattling against the window. As always in a storm, he thanked his genetic inheritance for giving him a steady stomach that rarely suffered seasickness. His mother told him it was the blood of his Spanish seafaring ancestors. He concentrated on the screen and what he wanted to say.

He was in the middle of relating a story to Sarah about last night's card game, trying to make shipboard life sound lively, when the computer screen plunged into darkness.

He waited a moment or two. This sort of thing had happened before and usually the system came on again as the back-up kicked in. But the screen stayed blank.

'Damn!' he said aloud. He'd have lost his well-chosen words to Sarah – he never found it easy writing letters, even on email – and he'd have to go back up to the control room to help solve whatever problem it was this time.

As he stood up and turned to pick up his workbooks and papers, the lights went out.

Bloody hell. This was no time to lose power, he thought. The storm was only just starting – there'd be hours to go before it passed over, and the ship'd be in danger without power.

He knew they'd be rushing about in the engine room activating the stand-by generator. It should start up within minutes. But he couldn't fathom why the computer system had gone first. He looked out the window. The rain was pelting against the double glass and running down in thick rivulets. He could see the storm raging outside, feel the floor rising and falling, smell the ever-present diesel and salt of the ship. But there was no generator and no engine. It was spookily quiet.

Zhi grabbed his wet-weather gear from the peg on the door and exited. The eerie white emergency lighting and the fluorescent green strips stuck to the base of the wall guided him along the rolling corridor. He hurried forward, as fast as the uneven pitching would allow him. Now that they'd lost power, the ship was tossing in all directions, at the mercy of the sea.

He pulled open the door of the seismic control room.

'What's going on?' he called out to Curtis, who was at the main keyboard, looking bewildered. Behind him stood their boss, Franklin, the chief observer, who was holding the useless telephone receiver as if it were a dead fly.

'I can't work it out,' Curtis said, barely looking up. 'The system's gone down completely. There's just no response to anything I do.'

'Everything's dead,' Franklin added, slamming the unresponsive phone down on the desk and crossing over to the bank of data-storage equipment. Nothing was working. All the lights, which usually winked on and off as the data was processed, had gone out. During a storm, data gathering would cease anyway because the noise of the sea would make it impossible to pick up the seismic information. But even from the doorway Zhi could see that all their expensive gear was out of commission.

'It can't be,' Hank Durillo said. 'We must be able to get something working again. Here, let me try.' The officious accountant, who had tried everybody's patience for the five weeks he'd been on board on an 'acquaint' from one of the oil companies, elbowed Curtis aside from the main keyboard and started punching the keys himself. Client representatives like Hank ended up getting on everyone's nerves and they always got in the way when things went wrong. With a bit of luck, the storm would get to Hank's finely-tuned New York equilibrium and he'd soon be retreating to his cabin to spend the rest of the day chucking his lunch into a bucket.

'Give up, Hank. There's no point. It's…'

Franklin was interrupted by the deafening screech of the evacuation siren.

'Shit,' Curtis said loudly.

'That's *all* we need,' Franklin shouted. 'Come on guys, we gotta get out.'

'Muster stations,' said Zhi.

'But my laptop,' Hank said, turning away from the keyboard at last. 'I can't leave it behind in my cabin. It's got irreplaceable data on it.'

'Sorry, mate. It'll have to stay where it is for now. When the sirens go, that means there's an emergency. You gotta go up on deck,' Franklin ordered. Still Hank hesitated. '*Now!*'

'But…'

'Look mate, this is *my* control room, and when I say you gotta get out and get up on deck, then that's what you gotta do. Get it?'

By now, Franklin was standing over Hank and by the look of him, was about to grab Hank by the shirt collar and drag him out single-handed.

Hank got the message and stood, reaching for a pile of papers at the corner of the desk.

'For Christ's sake, what do I have to do to get you to realise this is an emergency! You can't stop for papers or your bloody handbag. You've got to get out.'

Zhi was standing by the open door, knowing that he should run for it, but not wanting to miss the entertainment of seeing Hank getting his come-uppance at last for behaving like an absolute jerk.

When Zhi reached their muster station, Buzz, the second mate, was organising who was to do what. Hank was asked to join the detail sent to close all the ventilation hatches in case of fire.

'Right, that's got him sorted,' Buzz said as Hank departed forard. 'You three are wanted up in the bridge. Captain Williams wants to talk to you.'

With the sirens still wailing in their ears, Zhi and his mates donned their bright yellow wet-weather gear then took the nearest companionway up to the bridge. The wind drove the salty spray into his eyes and mouth and pelted against his hardy plastic jacket. Stepping over the ledge, Zhi entered the spacious operations centre.

Rex Williams, the captain was standing in front of his chair, staring out the enormous windows, which were blurred with rain and sea-spray. Beside him stood the first mate and the navigator.

'You wanted to see us, Captain Williams,' Franklin said loudly over the sound of the siren. The captain turned to face them.

'Ah, yes, Mr Delaney,' the captain replied in his big, deep voice. 'My chief engineer tells me that this situation – the failure of the seismic system and the loss of power – would've started with a malfunction in your computer system. What can you tell me about it?'

Franklin looked extremely uncomfortable. Zhi was glad it wasn't him having to do the explaining. He didn't like the way the captain was addressing Franklin by his surname. He usually called everyone by their first name.

'I, er… I can't say, at this stage, sir,' Franklin said approaching the control panel next to the captain and looking him in the eye. 'I won't be able to work it out until we get power back on and I can start the system up again. Then we'll…' Suddenly the sirens stopped and his raised voice echoed around the room. 'Then,' he continued with less force, 'we'll be able to look at the incoming data.'

'I see,' Captain Williams said. 'I was hoping you'd be able to give us *something* concrete to go on, so that we could fix the problem at source.'

'Afraid not, sir. We're as much in the dark as everyone else until there's power.'

'You don't think it could've been one of those computer viruses, by any chance?'

'It shouldn't be a virus, sir, no. We've got every available protection against viruses, and they're updated continuously. There's a firewall on the system so thick it would be impossible for anything like that to get through.'

'What about the processing computer?' Zhi asked. 'Could someone have picked up a virus downloading a software update from the FTP site?'

'That's a possibility,' Franklin said. But it doesn't explain why the engineering plant has shut down, or what's caused the short circuit.'

'Well, Mr Delaney, I look forward to your report as soon as the power's on again. I'm hoping to start the engines as soon as we've cleared the ship for fire and are sure it's safe.'

The captain turned to talk to the first mate who'd just come in the door, shaking the water off his coat as he hung it on a nearby peg. Zhi couldn't hear what they were saying, but could see the tension in the captain's face despite his efforts to appear calm.

'Keith tells me that the systems failure has set off a short circuit in the engine room, which is why we are without power, but it can be fixed soon,' he said loudly so they could all hear over the roar of the wind and rain.

'Jim, I want you to go below and tell Jeff to start the engines. Tell him to try everything until those damn engines are going again.' The officer donned his yellow wet-weather jacket, pulling the hood over his head, and went out the door, letting in an icy blast of wind and rain.

Suddenly, the ship started to roll wildly and Zhi was flung against the wall before he could steady himself for it. Around him, various books and papers and the few things not tied down or attached crashed to the floor. He picked himself up and braced himself against the doorframe, feet wide apart, trying to stay upright as the ship rolled through what must be forty degrees. The captain was standing steadily in front of his control panels, one hand on the captain's chair fixed into the floor, the other against the control console, talking to the first mate through gritted teeth.

'Bring her round, Keith,' he was saying, 'Can't you bring her round?'

'I'm trying, sir, but she won't respond without power.'

Zhi looked out the big, outward-sloping bridge window. Without power to hold her on course, the ship was now beam on to the waves and was getting a hammering. He could see the rails on each side dipping under the sea and for the first time felt afraid. He'd never seen that before.

The ship continued to roll dangerously. Zhi looked at his boss, veteran of hundreds of exploration voyages. Franklin was looking as if he wanted to throw up – but whether from fear or seasickness, Zhi didn't dare ask.

'Well sir, if there's anything else…' Franklin prompted the captain.

'No, that'll be all for now. But I shall expect your report soon after the power's back on.'

Zhi followed Curtis and his boss to the door, glad to be out of the hot-seat, under suspicion of blame for the dangerous situation they were all now in. However, as soon as they stepped outside, the sudden blast of icy wind-driven rain and salty spray lashed his face, forcing him to shield his eyes. He could hardly see, such was the force of the water. His face was drenched in seconds. He stumbled behind Franklin, blindly feeling his way down the companionway and back to the muster station.

He wondered how serious the situation might be. There were thirty-eight men on board – fourteen exploration crew, mostly Americans and the rest, maritime crew, mostly New Zealanders. All were well drilled in emergency procedures. Just the same, when he'd looked out the bridge window at that maelstrom crashing across the deck, it hadn't looked that great.

As he reached the muster station again, Zhi heard the deep thrum of the engines starting up.

'Thank God for that,' he said quietly.

The ship reverberated as the powerful twin screws began to bite through the water. He could feel her bow steadily coming round to confront the seas head on. At last, the terrible death-rolling stopped and he could stand on his own, without having to hold onto the doorframe any more. It was still a very heavy sea. The deck fell away before him as the ship plunged into a wave, its spray washing all around him then draining quickly over the side as she climbed steeply out of it again.

'We'd better get back to the computer room and find out what happened,' Franklin said, indicating Zhi and Curtis should follow.

The room was a shambles, with papers strewn all over the floor and around the keyboards. Franklin let out a cheer when the switches responded to his touch and the lights started flashing again. He busied himself getting everything going again, asking Curtis to start up the main computer again. Zhi stood behind him, waiting nervously to see if it would log in properly, and what it might reveal. But there was no sign of life. It would start up, but the screen remained blank.

'Damn!' Franklin said and picked up the phone, which was going again. Zhi could see he was auto-dialling head office in San Francisco. He looked at his watch. It would be early morning there now. He hoped there would be someone on duty with a few clues. He'd met a couple of guys doing night shift once and not been very impressed. He'd wondered if perhaps they'd had something to do with this mess. He heard Franklin talking to their boss and could tell from his expression and the monosyllabic answers that things were grim. After a few minutes, he put down the phone and turned to face him and Curtis.

'Bad news, I'm afraid. We're the fourth ship to phone in with the same problem. The entire fleet seems to have been wiped out. All communications are down, and they can't track anything because their system's down too.'

'Do they know why?' Zhi asked.

'They think it's a computer time bomb,' Franklin replied.

Zhi and Curtis knew perfectly well what Franklin was referring to. Everybody in their business did. A time bomb was usually devised by someone working with the computer system, someone who might have a grudge against the company or who might want an insurance policy against being fired. They planted the unexploded 'bomb' inside the system with a weekly or monthly tag. A bit like a fuse. And if they weren't around when the reminder popped up again – if they'd been fired for example – then without them there to defuse it, the time bomb would go off. He'd heard of them before. One of his friends had been called into help fix up a big retail system that had been blitzed with a bomb. It had taken weeks to get it running properly again. But he wasn't aware that they could disable an entire ship, let alone the whole fleet.

'They think someone planted it inside the mainframe some time ago, someone who's obviously not working there any longer, who knew how to affect the whole company with just one hit,' Franklin concluded after a short silence, while he seemed to be letting it all sink in.

'We won't be able to continue with the exploration work without inputting all the necessary data back into the system,' Curtis said. Franklin nodded.

'That could take ages.'

Franklin nodded again.

'At least a week, I'd estimate,' he said.

The phone rang on the desk. Franklin answered it.

'Franklin Delaney.' There was a pause. 'Yes sir.' Another pause. 'Sir,' he said and put down the receiver then turned to the others. 'That was the captain. He says we're heading south to the Port of Nelson. The owners have told him he has to go there. He says it's the closest port where there's an agent who can fix our software system while the local shipping engineers work on the engine room. If no other disaster befalls us, we'll be docking in Nelson tomorrow.' He punched away at the keyboard over Curtis' shoulder. The screen remained blank. 'And Captain Williams wants my report on his desk first thing in the morning. I'd say we're in for a night of it. We'd better get to work.'

Zhi and Curtis both groaned.

'Oh, and by the way, all shore leave's cancelled until the system's back up and running properly again.'

5. No News is Good News

Alex put down the phone and made another tick on her list – the fifth list of the day that she'd meticulously worked through. That was the last of the calls she had to make to the West Coast media. She'd spoken to the community papers along the Napa Valley and into Sonoma; she'd emailed her contacts at the *San Francisco Chronicle* and the evening paper, the *Examiner*, as well as the *LA Times*, just to be sure; she'd spoken to all the radio newsrooms; and to the assistant news director at KPIX Channel 5 – the CBS offshoot, whose *KPIX Eyewitness News* wanted to do something for their regional news programme. Rival channels didn't seem to be interested, which was a blessing. If one station got the story as a scoop, the others often shunned it or tried to discredit it. She'd work on that too.

Since she'd arrived at Rossini's two nights ago, she'd moved quickly into damage control mode, and already the story was looking a whole lot better. She loved this sort of work and excelled at it – planning in detail what had to be done then, at the speed of light, getting it all done with military precision. To look at her, you would have thought Alex would be the last person to get it all together. Her streaky blond hair was short and spiky now, but still managed to look tousled and tangled, as though she'd just got out of bed. She'd had it cut a few weeks ago. Just a bit of gel once she was out of the shower and she could leave it to dry knowing it would still look cool by lunchtime. She never had time to mess around with hairdryers or make-up in the morning, and breakfast was usually a cup of coffee and, if she'd remembered to buy it, a bagel on the way out the door. Her sole focus in the morning – once she'd been for a run and taken a shower – was to get to work and get on with the challenge in hand. David's conundrum over glycol was typical of the work she lived for.

After a short and sharp meeting with David and his lawyer on Tuesday, the morning after she'd arrived, Alex had swung into action and drafted a press release claiming the whole fiasco was a sting and that the wine had been doctored. They still hadn't managed to track down that Spargo fellow David suspected of sabotage, but Manfred had carried out a check on the remaining bottles of *Don Giovanni* and had tasted the oiliness of the glycol in four of them. He'd sent the wine from these bottles off for analysis.

Allegations of doctoring, on this basis, seemed convincing enough and gave them the opportunity to go on the offensive. She quoted David as saying that a former employee was suspected of adding a harmless substance to a small percentage of the *Don Giovanni* label, and that the matter was in the hands of the police. On the advice of the lawyer, they'd added a strong warning to the media about defamation and suggested the media contact the sheriff. The phone had hardly stopped ringing all day.

True to expectations, Tuesday night's CBS news had been a little kinder. It was mainly a rehash of the first story, with the additional information about the suspected sabotage. There'd been a small piece in the *Chronicle* which had been very conservative, she thought, possibly as a result of the legal angle to her press release. But today was eerie. Her mobile phone was unusually quiet; her laptop in front of her on the desk, temporarily still. No new emails. And most of the day, the desk phone in her office had been silent. She looked around the room at the familiar honeyed lemon walls, the still life wine glass and grapes painting she'd come to know well, the same blond wood desk, all in the same place as last time.

An hour ago she'd persuaded David to issue a product recall notice through his distributor. Alex had arranged to place a small advertisement into the *Chronicle* and the *LA Times* to this effect. She'd also added this to the press release, making it sound as if Rossini's was being highly responsible and perhaps even overly cautious. If glycol had got into the wine, it wouldn't hurt anyone; but if they were to preserve the good name of the winery, they had to get every bottle off the shelf. The task of fully restoring Rossini's winemaking reputation would be dealt with in the days ahead. For now, she was concentrating on damping down the story, turning the focus onto the police and away from the winery.

She pushed back her chair, stood up and walked across the room to the window, with its view across the winery entrance, the carpark, and the driveway beyond. A big tour bus of visitors was disgorging two or three score eager wine-tasters, falling over each other in their haste to be the first in the line-up. Another tour bus was slowly filling up with departing guests, many of them carrying a bottle or two in the winery's signature slate blue and cream carry-bags. The wine-blending story had obviously not crossed their radar.

Beyond the tour buses, down the long olive-lined driveway, a sudden glint caught her eye. She squinted against the bright sun and looked closer. A light-coloured SUV vehicle was parked on the road, with two or three people standing around. The flash of light she'd seen must have come from them. Then she could see it: a TV camera pointing right at her and the winery building. Damn!

Alex grabbed her mobile, her keys and a copy of the press release she'd sent out earlier, ran down to her car in the back yard and drove it at a deliberately casual pace down the long drive and out into the road. She pulled up at a spot just beyond the camera crew, on the opposite side of the highway. The vehicle had a CBS logo on the side. She got out and strolled over.

'Can I help you with something?' she said, trying to appear nonchalant.

The camera crew had been watching her as she crossed to them. The reporter now turned to face her. She recognised Mike Gibbens instantly.

'I'm Alex Zerakowski,' she said, smiling and looking welcoming. 'I work at Rossini's. Anything I can help you with?'

'Just getting some wallpaper shots, thanks,' Gibbens said. 'We'll be finished in no time.' He turned away to the crew and gave them some instructions, which Alex couldn't hear properly. Then he swung back to face her again.

'Actually, there is something you can help me with. This former employee of yours, what was his name?'

'You know I can't tell you that,' Alex replied carefully. 'I would have thought the police would have been able to tell you, though.'

'Not yet they haven't,' Gibbens said. 'They're waiting until they find him first. We could name him though for you, help you track him down quicker.'

'Thanks for the offer, but I'll have to leave it to the police to give out names,' she said. Not wanting to appear unhelpful, she went on, 'But there is something I can tell you. We're recalling all remaining bottles of *Don Giovanni* so that there's none left on the shelf that could have been tampered with. As you'll know, glycol is harmless in such small quantities. It's our reputation that's been harmed, rather than our customers. But our reputation is extremely important and we've decided to move quickly to minimise damage.'

She noticed Gibbens was taking notes.

'That so?' he said. 'How many bottles would you have to recall then?'

'Not many now. It was a limited edition in the first place and sold quite quickly. There are only about a thousand bottles left on the shelves and fewer than a hundred at the winery.'

'Any of it exported?'

'No, it went too quickly for that. Most of it stayed in California. The small amount that was sent to the East Coast sold long ago.' She paused. 'Look, would you like to interview Mr Rossini about this? I'm sure he'd be only too happy to tell you himself.'

Gibbens agreed, so she called David, arranged the interview and managed a few minutes with him alone to prep him for it. She thought it went well. When it was over, she went back to her office, checked her list and decided to call it a day. She'd done as much as she could now, spoken to all her contacts, ticked all the items on all her lists. The news would be on in a couple of hours, so she closed the office door and headed for the house.

Back in her office the following day, Thursday, Alex tapped her ballpoint on the desk in irritation. She'd already dealt with an irate call from Max for missing the family dinner last night. And this call told her the wine-blending project was getting nowhere fast.

'Sure, Kaz, I understand,' she said, resuming the tapping as he continued.

Nick Kazukaitis was her number one source for finding out what the big city media were up to, what stories they were planning on using, what tomorrow's front page leads might be. A stringer for several major dailies including the *San Francisco Chronicle,* Kaz seemed to know everyone who was worth knowing, as well as all the goss. In return for hot tips and first cut at her press releases, Kaz gave her the good oil on what the media were up to and who was in trouble. But today, she couldn't get a thing out of him. That meant that either the wine-blending story had died or whoever had it was keeping it close to their chest.

'Thanks for trying, Kaz. I'll call you tomorrow. But you'll let me know if you hear anything.'

'Sure, honey. Do anything for you, you know that.'

She put down the phone and wondered what she should do now. She'd been here three days now and she was finding it hard to pick which way it would go. Today was the crucial day. Today she would learn if the story was going to die quickly or linger on like a bad smell. That was what she had to prevent happening, somehow, but it was proving very difficult when the laboratory analysis was taking a long time and when the main suspect couldn't be found. She needed resolutions, and she needed them fast.

She was checking her mobile to see if she'd missed any calls when David popped his head around the door.

'Can I come in?'

'Of course, David. Everything's gone curiously quiet.'

'Well it won't be for long. The sheriff, Dan Sheldrake, has just been here. They've found Spargo and questioned him and of course he denies everything. But when they found him he had a stash of drugs in his van, and so they've charged him and can continue to check out his story. The sheriff seems to think they've already found something that will nail him.'

'I suppose that's a relief, then,' Alex said. 'It'll lead to another story on the news tonight, but then with a bit of luck, it might die down.'

'Yes,' David looked thoughtful. 'The sheriff said they'd be issuing a statement to the media in an hour or so.'

Alex looked at her watch. Three-thirty. That would give Gibbens and his ilk enough time to get it to air tonight.

'D'you think they'll release his name?'

'Don't think so. They didn't say. But I suppose it will get out as soon as he appears in court tomorrow.'

Damn, that would be another day the story would remain alive, although the court appearance probably wouldn't make national television.

'Don't look so worried, Alex. It's looking a lot better now than it did forty-eight hours ago. I'm not nearly so upset about it now. You've done a great job.' He smiled at her. 'Not that I'd expect anything less from you of course. You set yourself a prodigious record of achievement first time round with the landfill.'

'You're very kind, David,' she said, smiling back. 'It's funny isn't it? Here we are trying to stop the media from going to town on Rossini's and yet not all that long ago we were trying to get as much publicity as possible out of them for *Opera in the Vines*.'

'The fickle finger of fate…' David said.

6. A short, dark stranger

Carrie O'Neill would remember the afternoon of Wednesday, January the twelfth, 1886 as the turning point in her life. It was an unusually hot summer's day and the saloon bar of the Golden Age Hotel where she worked was unbearably close. The heat made her feel languid; she would much rather be down by the river in the cooling shade of the willow trees, trailing her fingers in the dark, clear water and watching the fish quiver in the shallows. Instead, she was dazzled by piercing shafts of sunlight. It bounced off the mirrors and rows of shiny bottles of spirits behind the bar and illuminated millions of specks of dust hanging in the air before flooding the uneven wooden floorboards with a soft yellow light. The saloon was comparatively quiet, with just one table of card-players in the corner, well away from any prying rays of sun, and a couple of regulars clinging to the bar. One of them was trying to catch her eye.

'Come on, now, Carrie lass,' Billy said, when she refused to pay any attention to his winks and raised eyebrows. 'You know you fancy me rotten.'

Carrie shuddered inwardly. Billy showed every one of his forty-eight years, most of them as a hard-living, heavy drinking digger. At least half of his teeth were missing, his lined, worn face was sporting a bristle of stubble, and he smelt of stale sweat and whisky. She made herself smile at him and kept polishing the glasses, carefully laying each one upside down on the shelf. She knew Billy well enough to let the remark go. He'd soon get tired of teasing her. He always did.

At that moment, the saloon door banged open and Carrie looked up from the glass she was polishing to the sight of a blazingly handsome, black-haired and bearded stranger, who paused to confer with his companion – a man of similar appearance, though not quite as good-looking – then swaggered towards the bar. She noticed he had an unusual gait, perhaps a slight limp or over-compensation in his left leg. He was wearing a dark, three-quarter-length coat over lighter, pin-striped trousers, a matching waistcoat, a crisp white shirt and blue silk cravat. They all looked new and were impeccably tailored, fitting neatly on his lean frame. He looked like a real toff – far too grand for a place like the Golden Age saloon bar at the far end of Revell Street, Hokitika. He couldn't be one of the gold diggers from the Kaniere, not even if he'd discovered a fortune. A digger would never dress like that. Whoever he was, she thought, she would like to get to know him. Such well-dressed, handsome men were rare in this rugged, isolated corner of the world. She guessed he was slightly older than her, perhaps in his mid-thirties. He wasn't perfect, mind you. He was short of stature and the hair was thinning on the top of his head, showing a bronzed, high forehead and making him look highly intelligent and thoughtful. And his limp, though almost imperceptible, made him seem somehow vulnerable. But his eyes made up for any slight imperfection. Light, bright blue, they were almost iridescent under his thick black eyebrows. As he approached, he caught her eye. Carrie thought she would faint from the intensity and clarity of his gaze.

'Good afternoon,' he said in a rich, deep voice. His accent was familiar: he sounded like a streetwise Londoner, and certainly not the toff he appeared to be.

'Afternoon, sir,' she replied. 'Welcome to the Golden Age. What can I offer you to drink?'

The man turned to his companion. 'What's your poison, Tom?' he asked then, after getting a reply, turned back to Carrie. 'Two whiskies, please. Straight. And two glasses of your best ale, too.'

Carrie's boss, the weaselly, money-hungry Mr Hewson, sidled up to her. He hated missing out on any fresh gossip. As was his custom, he attempted to engage the two men in conversation, trying to get them to reveal who they were. But they managed to evade him, the older man going off to find a table and the younger – the one with the eyes – giving him a bland answer before turning to Carrie to pay for the drinks.

The pair settled themselves at a table away from the hot sun where, to Carrie's annoyance, the bright light from the nearby window made it almost impossible to see their faces. They were silhouettes; the man she'd just spoken to was facing her.

Throughout the afternoon, as they sat there, ordering more whiskies and beer, joining another couple of newcomers in a game of cribbage, she often felt his eyes on her and flushed with excitement. But his conversation with her was confined to the bare minimum – what they wanted to drink, how nice a day it was, and thanks for being of service. Even when she cleared their table, he paid her no more attention than normal, not even patting her bottom like so many of the other patrons liked to do.

The sun was setting, throwing a rosy glow across the room, and their game was growing noisy, when the man pushed back his chair, stood up and approached her again, smiling invitingly.

'This calls for a celebration,' he said. 'I think it's time to get out the champagne. And I would like you to come and join us, Miss… er…'

'Miss O'Neill,' she finished for him, her heart pounding so loud she could hardly get the words out, 'Carrie O'Neill. That's very kind of you, sir, but…'

'And I am Richard Davies,' he'd said. 'You have been very kind to us this afternoon, Miss O'Neill, and I would like to invite you to help me celebrate my luck. No ifs, no buts, just pop the champagne cork and come and have a drink with me.'

'But I have to serve behind the bar,' she said. 'Mr Hewson does not like me drinking with the customers.'

He'd protested and gone off to ask Mr Hewson's permission while she'd climbed down to the cellar to fetch a bottle of French champagne – and take a quick peek in the mirror out the back to make sure she was looking her best. She primped at her long, red hair, pinched her pale, freckled cheeks to make them pinker, pursed her lips to check their red fullness, and then pushed up her breasts to the top of her corset, adjusting them slightly to show off her cleavage. She wished she'd worn her blue dress instead of this dull green one, but it was too late now to run upstairs to her room and change.

When she returned, Mr Hewson took the bottle off her.

'You go and sit down with those gentlemen,' he said, indicating Mr Davies and his friends behind him. 'And mind you look after them and keep them happy. We have plenty more bottles like that if they want to spend their money. You make sure they order up plenty more before closing time.'

And so it had begun. Her love affair with one of the most notorious outlaws in the whole of New Zealand had started over a bottle of French champagne and a false identity. It was, she realised later, portentous of what was to come. But on that warm summer's day, and the wonderful evening that followed, the future was far from Carrie's mind.

Richard Davies, as she knew him then, had paid her compliments, poured her champagne, and included her in the group of friends. By dinnertime, she was tipsy from the wine as well as the lavish attention. She was sitting close to him while he played another game of cribbage – being careful not to give anything away about his easily visible hand – and she could feel his warm breath on her bare shoulder. It made goosepimples tingle along her arm. She put her hand to her chest, finding it hard to breathe.

'Now, Carrie, what is it? Are you feeling all right?' he asked, sotte voce, between games.

'I've never felt better,' Carrie replied, blushing. She wasn't used to a real gentleman taking interest in her like this and she could feel the eyes of Mr Hewson boring into the back of her neck. She smiled at Richard over the top of her glass of champagne. 'I'm having a lovely time, thank you.'

'Well, how'd you like to join me for dinner? Would it not be pleasurable to go into the dining room and have a nice quiet meal, just you and me?'

Carrie thought she'd pass out from excitement. 'I'd be delighted to join you, of course I would,' she said, trying to sound nonchalant. 'I'll have to ask Mr Hewson if I am allowed, though. I am not sure how long he will let me off the bar.'

'I shall have a word to him for you,' Richard said, 'I am sure you will be fine.' He turned to his card-playing friends, 'Excuse me, gentlemen. I shall be back in a minute.'

Carrie watched him anxiously as he approached Mr Hewson, but her attention was diverted by Thomas, who looked like Richard's older brother. In reality, she'd found out later, he was his comrade in arms, the notorious outlaw Thomas Kelly – a man with no qualms about drawing a pistol or knife to defend himself, no difficulty in asking men and women to stand and deliver.

'Ah, I can see you are taken with young Richard there,' Thomas said, touching her elbow to get her attention. 'My brother's a fine young man, always popular with the ladies.'

Carrie wasn't sure how she was supposed to take this. Was she meant to be jealous? Or simply pleased that he'd paid some of his attentions to her instead of all these other ladies, whoever they may be.

'Oh,' she said. 'He's asked me to join him for dinner.'

'Has he now,' Thomas said. 'Well that's a step up for him.' Thomas looked at Richard and, observing him to be deep in conversation with Mr Hewson, leant closer to Carrie's ear and said in a low voice, 'I would be careful, Miss O'Neill, if I were you. Be careful with your affections.

You see, he's a busy man, my brother, always rushing hither and thither on business. He doesn't like to settle down in one place for too long.'

'Oh,' she said again, confused, not knowing where to look. At that moment, Richard came back to the table and sat down beside her again. She was sure he would notice her discomfort.

'I hope that brother of mine has not been telling you bad things about me in my absence,' he said, taking her arm gently and brushing her face with the back of his hand. But before she could think of a response, he continued, clearly unconcerned about anything that Thomas might have said. 'Mr Hewson says you are welcome to have dinner with me. Isn't that wonderful? I managed to allay any fears he might have had about losing any custom or having to work any harder,' he said, laughing and rubbing his finger and thumb together to indicate that money might have changed hands. Thomas joined in on the joke. Carrie blushed with embarrassment. Mr Hewson would accept money from anyone and would promise anything in return. She hoped he hadn't entered into a contract with Richard over her. It wouldn't be the first time. But she wanted this to be different, to be like a normal courtship.

'It's a pity your friend Fanny isn't here,' Richard said to Thomas, laughing heartily. 'We could have made a handsome foursome over dinner. You'll have to join the others down the road at the Shotover.'

The Shotover was a scabby little hotel with a dining room that didn't stretch much beyond mutton stew and mash. At mealtimes, it was crammed full of sweaty, grimy, half-drunk diggers. Carrie wouldn't be seen dead in there.

Dinner in the grand oak-panelled dining room of the Golden Age flew by in a flash. It seemed that, no sooner had she ordered than they were drinking their coffee and Richard was selecting a large, fat cigar. She could hardly recall what she'd eaten or drunk, she had no idea what she'd said even, just that Richard had completely won her over and mesmerised her with his eyes. She'd done her best to ignore Eliza, the waiting girl. Eliza was a nice enough girl, and would completely understand her predicament, that she didn't want to be seen to be friendly with the serving staff now that she was playing at being a lady. She'd managed to produce a shawl and touch up her hair and her face on the way into dinner, so that she didn't feel too under-dressed when dining across the way from the local doctor and his wife. Besides, she told herself as they'd been shown to the table, if I'm attractive enough to be courted by this dashing gentleman, I can hold my head up in any company.

The meal had settled her a little and she sipped her coffee thought-fully, aware that she'd had far too much wine to drink, and wondering what Mr Hewson had offered on her behalf.

'Penny for your thoughts,' Richard said.

'Oh, I'm sorry. I did not mean to be rude. I was miles away.'

'Thinking about me, were you?'

'Maybe.' She blushed – couldn't help herself. She didn't know what else to say. There was an uncomfortable silence.

'Let's go dancing,' he said. 'We can finish our coffee and then go down to the Corinthian Hall. There is a dance on there tonight. I saw an advertisement in the *Times*.'

'I would love that,' she said, her eyes shining. It was many months since she'd been out dancing with a man. She knew she was attractive to men. They would comment on her long red hair, which she tried to tame by piling it fetchingly on the top of her head, but it usually escaped in tendrils down her back and wisps would frame her face. And she often caught them ogling her smooth, white breasts, deliberately pushed out by her tight gown to form what she'd often been told was a spectacular cleavage. But her entertainments had largely been confined to sharing a drink with some of the nicer young men who visited the saloon, and joining in on a game of whist or cribbage. Sometimes, if she particularly liked them and there was enough money in it, she would take the young man up to her room at the back of the hotel. The first time she'd got caught, Mr Hewson said it was all right as long as he got a cut of the fee. That had put her off trying it again for many months, but the money was too much of a temptation. Mr Hewson paid her as little as he could get away with for working all afternoon and evening and usually well into the early hours of the morning, six days a week. So a little bit extra on the side, and only with the men she found attractive, seemed just reward for such an easy task as pleasuring a nice young man.

But this gentleman, he was different. She cursed herself for not going up to Mr Hewson and asking for the night off herself. With Richard doing it, she had no idea what, if anything had changed hands and whether Hewson had offered her to Richard for a small fee. But she'd a strong suspicion that he would have. If there was money to be made, Hewson would be in on it.

Declining a port, Carrie sipped at her coffee while Richard puffed on his cigar. She'd seen some of the other girls take up cigar-smoking too, but she had no inclination to try it. She thought it looked disgusting for women to behave like men, smoking and cussing and spitting on the floor.

Suddenly, Richard pushed his chair back, stood up, put his cigar down in an ashtray and crossed over to sit on the arm of her chair.

'Oh, Carrie, my little Carrie,' he said, stroking her long hair. 'You are such a pretty little bird trapped in a tiny, dull and lonely cage. I would like to show you how to fly, to help set you free.'

'You would?'

'Yes,' he said firmly. 'I can tell by the honesty in your eyes and the unspoilt appearance of your face, that you don't belong here in this place. Perhaps, if you put your trust in me, I could show you a better way.'

Carrie remembered the warning words of Thomas. 'But I have only just met you,' she said, then cursed herself for being so timid.

'Of course, my little canary,' he said. 'I'm sorry. I should not rush you so.'

'No, no, you're not rushing me,' Carrie stammered. 'It's just… the wine… I am just so overawed by it all, by this wonderful meal, the champagne…'

'You need to lie down,' he said. 'Perhaps I could take you home?'

'Not far to go, which is just as well,' Carrie said, stumbling slightly as she stood. 'I live here, in the hotel, in the staff quarters.'

Richard paid the bill, leaving a large tip for Eliza and pocketing another cigar on the way out. He escorted her gently up the stairs and along to the back rooms of the hotel. When they came to Carrie's room, she fumbled in her reticule for her key, dropping it on the floor and spilling its contents – her rouge and powder, a comb, lavender water and a few coins, hairpins, handwritten notes and a white linen handkerchief.

'Oh, bother,' she said and bent to pick it up. But Richard was already there, scooping her belongings back into the bag then holding up the handkerchief to the light, before bestowing on its lacy corner a tender kiss.

'I hope you will let me keep this, as a memento of a wonderful evening,' he said.

Then, seeing her unlock the door and pass, somewhat unsteadily into her room, he said, 'You need to rest, my little chick. Be careful, now. I bid you good night.' He took her hand, kissed it, and departed, closing the door behind him.

Carrie collapsed against her side of the door, not knowing whether to laugh or cry. She didn't want him to leave, but she didn't want him to stay on old Hewson's terms. And now he'd gone, she had no idea if she'd ever see him again, this handsome, charming, free-spending man. In an out-of-the-way place like this, he seemed too good to be true.

7. The Prodigal Returns

With all the reverence due a good vintage, David Rossini held the long-necked bottle of *Rigoletto* chardonnay up to the sunlight for everyone to admire.

'That was a very good year, Manfred. We did well with *Rigoletto*,' he said.

'Nearly all gone now,' the proud wine-maker replied. He was almost preening.

'Just look at that colour,' David said, gazing through the bottle. The pale yellow wine sparkled in the strong mid-day sun.

'Straw gold and crystal clear,' Manfred said, eyes also fixed on the bottle held high in David's hand. 'A work of art.'

There was a brief silence. Almost like a ritual of respect, Alex thought.

'Come, come, you two,' Anna interrupted their worship. 'Don't stand there staring at it all day. We're here to drink it. The meal is getting cold.' She pointed at the array of dishes on the green striped cloth spread over the big trestle table in the courtyard. Pasta, meat sauce, salads, ciabatta bread, olives, cold meats, cheeses – the dishes filled the table under the shade of the gnarled old olive tree, one of many the family had grown commercially until the wine started to turn a profit again.

David jolted back to reality, deftly uncorked the wine and poured – first for their guest Alex, then for the family – Mamma first.

'*Salute*, Mama,' he said as he handed her a glass.

David and Manfred had buried their noses in their glasses, sniffing the wine.

'Ahhh, that's good. *Salute*,' David said raising his glass to Alex. His family joined in.

'*Salute*,' said Pietro and Mamma Madelena.

'*Salute*, Alex,' said Anna, and clinked her glass against Alex's.

'Why, thank you,' Alex replied, touched. The old-world charm and fine manners of the Rossini family had always impressed her. Even when the chips were down and the media were howling at the door after the landfill announcement, David and his father were hospitable and polite to the reporters, no matter how rude or revoltingly they'd behaved. She'd seen David working hard to control his temper, though.

'And I've a toast too,' she said. 'To Rossini's good name. Now honour is restored, long may it remain.'

They all drank to that.

Alex breathed in the wonderful aroma of one of Rossinis' prize-winning wines and sipped expectantly. Manfred was right. It was a work of art. And of his own making. David delivered him superb grapes and Manfred made them into heavenly nectar. Bottled poetry, they called it in the Napa, after that famous quote of Robert Louis Stevenson's when he was living in the valley with his new wife in 1880.

From the house behind her came the sound of Carreras singing 'Che gelida manina' from Puccini's *La Bohème*. She gazed out past the courtyard at the sunlight catching the dark red maple leaves on the distant hills, and below to the romantic haze across the vine-filled valley. The warm sun on her skin, the mellow wine inside her, the music making her spirit soar. This was the life! This was bliss.

Pietro sang along, his fine baritone an octave lower than Carreras', but his pitch was perfect and his voice, thinner than it would have been in his youth, rang out with confidence and warm resonance. He followed Carreras until he hit a particularly high note – top G, Alex suspected – and Pietro stopped singing abruptly with an embarrassing croak.

'Oh, give it up, *ma che matto che sei*,' Madelena said. 'You can't cut it with Carreras at your age.'

Pietro looked sheepish. 'Just that one note and she's complaining. You didn't complain when I was courting you, *Amore mio*. I used to be able to sing it, you know.'

'Yes, I know, Papa,' David said soothingly. 'Don't you take any notice of Mama. We love to listen to you singing. I remember when I was little, hearing your voice ringing out of the middle of the vines somewhere. It always made it easy to find you.'

'You could have gone on the stage,' Alex said.

'You people wouldn't let me,' Pietro replied with a mischievous twinkle in his eye. 'I offered to sing at your *Opera in the Vines*, but you wouldn't let me.'

'Take no notice of him. He's just baiting you. He does it to me all the time,' Madelena said.

'We couldn't, Papa, you know that. It's not a family show. Even for that first one, we had some of the biggest names in opera on the West Coast as well as those two from the Met.'

'And what a line-up this time,' Alex said, helping David to shift the subject.

'It certainly was something,' Anna agreed. 'I got so carried away when Lesley Garrett was singing, I forgot myself and spilled the wine I was pouring all over the table.'

'We were lucky with the weather,' Alex said.

'A perfect evening,' Anna said, 'and a great crowd.'

'I'll never forget the sight of all those people with their picnics in the setting sun,' Alex said.

'There were so many this year, they were spilling into the vineyard,' David said. 'I was a bit worried at first, but they didn't touch a thing.'

'It's certainly got a good name now,' Alex said.

'Of course,' Madelena agreed. 'What would you expect from the Rossinis. Now, let's eat.' She led the way to the table of food. 'Here, Alex, you're the guest of honour today. You first.' She held out an empty plate.

'You're all skin and bone, *cara mia*, you must eat,' Anna said, taking her by the arm and leading her to the table, her brown rounded face contrasting with Alex's pale thin one.

Patting her hips deprecatingly, Alex laughed. 'Not with these I'm not. Your wonderful cooking, Anna and Mamma Madelena, will be the ruin of me.' She got up from the sunlit table and went to fill her plate, pushing her sunglasses on top of her head as she reached the shade of the olive tree. 'This looks divine. You've been so good to me, taking me under your wing like this. You didn't have to, you know. I could look after myself.'

'Nonsense, *cara*. You don't eat when you're on your own. I know you of old. Just coffee and cigarettes all day long. No wonder you're so thin,' Anna said.

'No cigarettes now, Anna. I've given up.'

'Well good for you,' Anna said. 'I'm proud of you. How long ago did you do that?'

'Exactly one month, one week and two days ago,' Alex said. 'It's not been easy, but I'm determined to stay off them. I started to wake up coughing. That gave me a fright.'

'Well you don't seem to have replaced the cigarettes with food, like a lot of people seem to do. You're still far too thin. Help yourself to as much as you can eat.'

'You deserve all the pampering Anna can give you,' David added.

'You've been a godsend to us this week, Alex. You've saved the good name of Rossini and got those terrible television people off my back. I owe you a great deal.'

'Indeed, Alex. From the moment you got to work, it was like a great burden had been lifted off this big son of mine. You could see his shoulders straighten and his heart lift,' Pietro added.

'And it worked,' Anna said smiling. 'The old Alex magic did the trick once again.'

Alex felt embarrassed at such praise. She wasn't used to it. Mostly her clients just accepted it when she delivered the goods. But the Rossinis were different. She loved her visits up here. She didn't relish the thought of having to go back to deal with Lucian and the mess her apartment – and her relationship – was now in. But the wine-blending issue was dealt with now, the crisis averted, and despite the Rossinis' wonderful hospitality, she'd soon get bored.

'You're too kind,' she said, at a loss how to express her gratitude.

'No, Alex, it's you who's been kind to us,' Madelena said quietly. 'You made sure all those TV and newspaper reporters knew that nasty young man had been arrested for doctoring our wine, and that we'd withdrawn the rest of the *Don Giovanni* from sale. I don't think I've ever seen so many clippings from so many papers. It was absolutely everywhere. But what was really spectacular was the sympathy all those newspaper stories showed to us. You managed to portray Rossinis' as a victim of something beyond our control, and as a result almost every single one of them had something good to say about our wine.'

'We've never had so many orders,' David said.

'If it keeps up at this rate, we'll sell out last year's vintage quite soon.' Pietro added.

'Maybe we can sell the recalled *Don Giovanni* at a premium then!' David laughed.

'The Rossini reputation is restored. That's the main thing,' Pietro said.

'And, we're having the last laugh over Spargo,' Anna said. 'He's in prison awaiting trial while we've never had it so good.'

She raised her glass to Alex and took a sip.

They sat in the dappled sunlight filtering through the vines overhead and shared memories and laughter, recalling the days when Alex had put in long hours and intense effort to keep the media and environmentalists at bay over the landfill proposal.

'Guido's doing so well up there now. He won an award for the recycling work he's doing,' David said, referring to his nephew, Guido

Parigi, whom he'd persuaded to take over the business as soon as David had weathered the protest storm.

'Those greenies have changed their tune now, of course. Now that Guido's recycling the vine cuttings and grape mulch, they write stories saying how wonderful we are. Hunh!' Pietro threw up his hands in mock exasperation and rolled his eyes.

'Oh, come on, *ma che mattochesei*, you loved it when all the fuss was going on,' Madelena poked Pietro on the forearm.

'I loved watching you getting angry at them, that's what I loved,' Pietro rejoined.

'They were interesting times, that's for sure,' Alex said, deliberately diverting them. Pietro and Madelena were always bantering. 'I learned a lot about recycling and sustainability.'

'That's what turned it around, in the end,' Madelena said with acuity. She didn't speak often, except when badgering Pietro, but when she did have something to say, it was usually astute. 'The environmentalists couldn't argue with a recycling plant.'

Manfred pushed his plate away, finished the wine in his glass and wiped his mouth with the big white napkin Anna had provided.

'I must be away now,' he said. 'I have to be in town by three.'

'Surely you'll have a bit more before you go,' Anna said. 'There's coffee and fruit to follow soon, and I've made your favourite tiramisu.'

'I'd love to Anna, you know how I love your tiramisu. But I really must go.'

'You can't hold him up, Anna,' David said laughing. 'He's off to meet his *liebchen*.'

'Oh, I see,' Anna replied, laughing with him. 'We mustn't keep Diana waiting.'

'You've been keeping Diana waiting far too long,' Madelena said. 'You two should have been up the aisle years ago.'

'Hey, Signora Madelena, that's not fair,' Manfred replied, holding his hands up of front of him to indicate she should stop hassling him. 'Diana isn't in any hurry.'

'It's just as well for her,' Madelena said. 'You two have been going out for something like nine years now and you're still only engaged. You Germans always were a bit slow off the mark.'

'Well, we *are* going to get married, soon.'

'*Soon!*' Madelena snorted in disgust. 'What decade might that be, then?'

'Next year, Signora Madelena, next year. I promise.'

'Next year? Well, I shall hold you to that, young man. I won't let it go.'

'I know. I know you won't. You never let anything pass you by.'

'Give him a break, Mama. He'll get around to it in his own good time.' David didn't like seeing his winemaker embarrassed.

'So when's the happy day, Manfred?' Anna asked.

'Er… I'll get Diana to tell you that,' he replied. 'I'm sure she'd want to be the first to tell you the news.'

'Well you be sure to bring her home to tell us,' Anna said. 'How about dinner here next Tuesday. Do you think she'd like that?'

'I'll ask her when I see her,' Manfred promised. 'I'd better be going. There's one of those regular wine-tastings for the Napa Winemakers' Society and it's at Sterling's this time. I said I'd take her up on Sterling's gondola for the view of the valley. She's lived here four years now, and she still hasn't been up on it.'

'How romantic,' Anna said.

'You make sure you name the day, young man. That fancy sky ride will be just the place to talk weddings.'

'Okay, Signora Madelena. I will, I promise.' He was half way out the door.

'Well, Manfred, safe journey,' Anna said.

'Thank you Anna, David. That was a great meal. I'll see you at work in the morning.' Manfred nodded his head slightly and departed.

'Alex, please, have some more,' Anna said, indicating the table where there was still plenty of food left over.

'I couldn't, thank you Anna. But it was lovely.'

'Some wine then,' David said and started to fill her glass, then hesitated. In the distance was the reverberating engine roar of an approaching sports car. From the screech of tyres, it was obviously taking the corners too fast.

'Who the hell's that?' David said. 'It sounds fast and flashy. Must be at least a four litre engine on that one.' David knew his cars. He kept a classic Ferrari in his big garage and a vintage Alfa Romeo beside it, although from what Alex had seen of it, it was permanently up on blocks.

'Can't be a tour party, with a sound like that,' Anna said.

'Don't they know it's Sunday,' Pietro grumbled. 'Madonna! People shouldn't be allowed to make that much noise on the Sabbath.'

The intruder was getting closer, the engine now gunning the corners and filling the valley with an echoing scream. As it came closer, there was a grinding of gears changing down. Suddenly, right at the winery gate, it stopped. The silence was palpable.

'I expect they'll go to the winery for a tasting,' Anna said. 'We don't know anyone who'd drive anything like that.'

But then they heard the house gate click.

David stood up and went to the entrance to see who it was. Moments later, he arrived back with a young man at his side, tall, dark-haired, wearing a city jacket and an open-necked shirt. Alex couldn't see his face because of the sun shining in her eyes.

'Someone to see you,' David said to her.

'Hiya, doll,' the familiar gravelly smoker's voice said.

'Lucian!' she could hardly speak his name. It came out as a pathetic squeak. 'What are you doing here?'

Only last night, lying in bed awaiting sleep, she'd been thinking perhaps it was time to call it quits with him. How had Lucian found her? And why now? And how dare he look like that? His midday stubble made his handsome face even more rugged and desirable. The tight Levis over Gucci loafers, the gold Rolex, black Versace polo revealing a thick gold chain over the thick black hairs of his chest. Alex was overcome at the sight of the chain. She remembered weaving it around her fingers, feeling the soft hairs underneath, as they lay in bed after making love. She could feel her desire for him rising. Yet he was bad news, she told herself firmly.

'Couldn't do without you, doll. I drove the Carrera up from 'Frisco. Did it in an hour almost. Not bad, huh? Had to track you down. Had a feeling I'd find you here.' Casually, Lucian draped the black leather faux World War II bomber jacket he'd had slung across his shoulder over the back of a nearby chair, then held out his hand to her in greeting. Briefly, their hands touched and she felt a charge shoot through her. She was on fire. She hoped nobody would notice the flush she could feel spreading across her face.

'Why didn't you phone?' she gulped.

'Wanted to give you a nice surprise. I knew you'd be pleased to see me.'

Alex swallowed. She was damned if she was going to agree. Even though she could feel lust churning away inside her, she would never let him know.

'I've been very busy,' she said lamely.

'I figured that,' Lucian smiled knowingly at David. 'Saw all that stuff on CBS news.'

'Yes, well it's over now, thanks to Alex,' David said brusquely. He clearly wasn't taking to Lucian.

She fought down a growing urge to fling her arms around his sexy shoulders and turned to David and his family, still sitting around the table. Anna was looking at her with that knowing, quizzical expression she had whenever one of Alex's boyfriends had showed up. David was looking at her protectively. She only had to say the word and David would evict Lucian off his property without any trouble at all. But she hated scenes. She needed to smooth over Lucian's arrival then ease him out gently.

'I'm sorry, I should have introduced you,' she said. 'David Rossini and his wife Anna, his father Pietro and Pietro's wife Madelena,' she said, indicating each one in turn, 'this is Lucian Tate. I met him in San Francisco when he was working for one of my clients managing their database. He's very good with computers and that sort of thing.' She could feel herself gabbling, trying to hide her embarrassment. How dare he do this to her, she fumed inwardly.

'Would you care to join us in a glass of wine?' David asked. 'And please, do have something to eat. We've just finished, but as you can see, there's plenty left.'

Lucian strode over to the table.

'Ah, the famous Rossini's *Rigoletto*,' Lucian said picking up the second bottle, which was still half full. 'Can I have a taste?'

The man has no shame, Alex thought.

'Of course,' David said, and went to fetch a clean glass off the other table. Returning, he poured Lucian some wine and handed it to him.

'Thank you, Maestro,' Lucian said with what Alex thought was far too much bonhomie for a first meeting. But then Lucian had never really known how to pull back. He always went over the top.

'Ahhh,' Lucian sighed, holding the glass up to the sunlight. 'Magnifico. Perfecto. The colour is fields of wheat bending in the wind.' He swirled the glass and sniffed in the aroma. 'The nose is freshly picked nectarines and peaches.' Then he took a swig, held it briefly in his mouth, and swallowed. 'The flavours are so intense. What a chardonnay! My palate has died and gone to heaven.'

Alex thought she was going to throw up. The sycophantic greaseball. She didn't dare look at David. She was sure he would be suppressing a laugh. She wished the ground would swallow her up before she died of embarrassment.

'Thank you,' David said, without a trace of irony or laughter in his voice. 'We're very proud of it. It's done very well.'

'It's scarce as hen's teeth in the liquor stores,' Lucian said. 'Haven't been able to find any in San Francisco for a while.'

'We're nearly out of it now. That's the trouble with a good vintage,' David said.

'Better than it going the other way,' Anna laughed. David and Lucian laughed with her.

'Please join us, Lucian,' Anna repeated. 'Please have something to eat.' She got up from the table and handed him a plate, indicating the table under the olive tree still laden with food, and guiding him over to it. 'You just help yourself. There's plenty.'

'You're very kind, Anna, thank you.' Lucian said, taking a spoonful from each platter and then joining them back at the table.

'Good timing,' he grinned at Alex. That smile again. She felt weak at the knees and sat down opposite him. She took a large swig of wine to calm her nerves. Her insides were pleading with her to forgive him and take him back; but her senses told her to send him packing. She could feel herself getting upset. The sound of the tenor in the background now seemed hollow and empty. The sun's rays no longer warmed her. The wine tasted slightly sour.

'This is lovely food,' Lucian said to Anna and Madelena, 'Thank you for letting me share it. Tell me, did you make the pasta yourself? I've never tasted any as good as this before.'

Anna smiled. 'Yes,' she said. 'I make it almost every day. It's second nature to me now.'

You had to hand it to Lucian, Alex thought. He'd always been good at first impressions. She'd been bowled over the first time she'd met him. So had her friends. It was only after they'd gotten to know him better that the halo had fallen off. She watched him as he chatted to Anna and David, then Pietro. He even managed to get the normally quiet Madelena engaged in conversation. He was positively fizzing. And every time he smiled, she could feel an electric charge around her navel. Those beautiful, even, white teeth. And those deep brown eyes, almost black at times; often he'd gaze into her eyes with such intensity that she almost drowned.

He caught her looking at him and smiled again. She could feel herself sinking.

She could see another side of him that she hadn't seen before. He genuinely did know about the wine. He even seemed to know about pasta and olives and Italian food. She'd always thought it was a big front. But Anna and David would have detected any falseness in an instant and they seemed to have warmed to him.

She remembered the last time they'd been to an Italian restaurant together and she'd accused him of big-noting and pretentiousness when he'd rabbited on about the food and wine. It was the arrogant way he said things. Even if he did know everything, he didn't have to be so cocksure about it.

And she always ended up paying the bill every time they went out anyway. It had been exactly the same with Pete. And look how long she'd let that go on. She could see the similarities between him and Lucian. And each had an equally bad influence on her. Pete, with his Harley Davidson roaring down the coast towards LA, had been just as much of a speed freak and a poseur as Lucian. And she'd gone right along with the charade, dressing up in leathers and slamming back the tequila with all the other lawyers and airline pilots behaving badly on their weekends off. She should have gotten rid of Pete long before she did. She was a fool to make the same mistake with Lucian all over again. Best to split while the relationship was still in its early days.

As she watched him charming her hosts, Alex decided she would be firm and tell him he had to move out of the flat. She would leave Rossinis' tomorrow most probably, or the next day at the latest. Back in San Francisco she would give Lucian his marching orders. There was no way she was going to put up with this sponging, arrogant man any longer.

The next morning, she awoke to the smell of fresh coffee and stale cigarettes. Lucian was in the tiny kitchen across the hallway singing along to some unknown radio station, presumably brewing coffee. She recoiled at the pile of stubs in the ashtray beside the bed. Some of those were hers. And it was all Lucian's fault.

She butted her head into the pillow and groaned. It hurt. She'd drunk far too much last night and look at the consequences. A throbbing head, a mouth furry with alcohol and cigarettes, a return to her nicotine habit, and a return to Lucian, her worst habit of all. How on earth was she going to get rid of him?

Her throat was killing her. She needed water. Groggily, she lifted up her head and propped herself on one elbow to grab at the glass of water by the bed. She missed, and knocked the glass over, spilling water on the books on her bedside table. Now she had to sit up, which hurt even more. Wildly dabbing at the dustjacket with the bedside tissues, she noticed it was the copy of *Women Who Love Too Much* that one of her girlfriends had given her after a tirade about Lucian. She stopped trying to wipe it dry and threw it at the wall instead.

'Fat lot of good you did me!' she wailed at the book, and sank her aching head back into the pillow.

'Hiya doll. You awake?' he greeted her as if he'd been here all his life. She hated being called doll now but hadn't plucked up the courage to tell him. She'd liked it at first. Nobody had ever called her that before and it had been fun for a while. Now it was irritating.

'I've brought you a nice cup of coffee. No milk. No sugar, Y'see – I remembered!'

'Thank you Lucian. Just what I need.' He must be trying to impress her and win her over. He'd never brought her coffee in bed before. He was smiling that stomach-wrenching smile of his, and she could feel that damnable desire for him starting again.

She blew on the coffee then sipped. It burned her tongue. There was probably a lesson in that.

8. Roughing It

Richard peered out through the tent flaps, checking for the hundredth time that there was no-one in the vicinity. There was a strong musty smell of wet bracken and sodden earth. The rain was still pouring down outside, forming muddy puddles and overflowing the small trench he'd dug around the bottom of the canvas. He watched it flowing off down the hillside, down towards the road several hundred yards below his campsite. He knew he was well hidden; he'd camped here before. He wanted to become invisible for a few days and this was the perfect spot – far enough from the main road between Hokitika and the Grey to be safe from discovery yet not so far that he couldn't waylay the occasional passing digger and relieve them of their gold. He and Tom Kelly had used the spot once before to evade capture.

All he could see was the bush around him, rising away from the small clearing to a towering totara and beech forest. Satisfied he was alone, he pulled the flaps shut and tied them tightly together to keep out the incessant rain.

Christ he was hungry. He could feel his stomach rumbling and gripping with hunger. He hadn't eaten since his hurried meal with Tom in the Rosstown Hotel two nights ago. He could taste it now, that juicy roast beef and Yorkshire pudding, covered in gravy. He tried to push it from his mind, but it kept coming back, making him salivate and his stomach grumble even more loudly. There was no point thinking about food, he kept telling himself, because he didn't have a thing to eat. His swag, containing all his food and a change of clothes, had been ripped off him by a young man, far too clever for his own good, as he'd made his getaway from robbing one of the tents in the digger's camp not far from the town. He'd considered going back and dealing to the scoundrel so he could retrieve his bag, but thought better of it. The blackguard deserved to die for taking his swag, but it wasn't worth the risk of being caught over something so insignificant.

Richard felt tremendously proud of the robbery, which had been a particularly cunning ruse. He had to hand it to Tom Kelly, he was an ingenious bushranger all right. It had been his idea to quietly slash the digger's tent around the bottom with his knife then reach in, quick as you please, feel around for the gold and banknotes inside his swag, and extract them while the poor devil was still sleeping. The pair of them had managed to do that to four of the tents in the camp before someone saw them and raised the alarm.

He and Kelly had split up, as they always did, to make their escape. That was when that whipper-snapper had snatched his bag off him. At least he'd kept the night's takings – and a tidy amount of gold it was too. The swag was a small sacrifice for his freedom. He'd circled around the camp until he came to his stash – the place where he'd hidden his tent and a few other belongings. He'd grabbed everything and kept on running, heading along a track through the bush that he knew would take him to the main road, far enough away from the town to be out of danger of capture. He'd expected to hear Kelly somewhere along the way – it was far too dark to see him. But without coming across him, he'd set off on his own. After travelling what he reckoned must be three or four miles along the highway, he'd turned off and made his way up the hill to his present campsite. He wondered if Kelly would remember it and find him. He hoped to Christ that he would. Kelly, by rights, should still have his swag and if he wanted to look after his old friend, then he'd save him a bite to eat. Otherwise, Richard reckoned, he'd starve to death.

He tried to think of something that would take his mind off his stomach.

Carrie! Now there was food for thought.

He opened out the canvas bag in which the tent and his other belongings had been stowed in and spread it on the ground, made a pillow for his head from his small swag of spare clothing, wrapped his greatcoat around him tightly and settled down, hoping to sleep until nightfall, when he could safely move up the road to the next camp and steal himself something to eat – and perhaps a few more ounces of gold. It must be early afternoon by now. With nothing to eat or drink but water from the nearby stream – and he'd already had his fill of that – the best thing he could do was sleep.

He let his thoughts drift back to Carrie. He had a weakness for flame-haired beauties like her. He could picture her now, her hair springing out of its pins and tumbling down the pale skin of her slender neck, her blue eyes appraising him as she sat beside him at cards. Her young, fair heart-shaped face had turned up so prettily to his when he'd asked her if she'd like to go dancing.

That snivelling boss of hers, Hewson, had made a big fuss over getting his cut from Carrie and he'd gone along with it. But he would be foolish to go on forking out money like that every time he wanted to talk to the girl, for heaven's sake. Besides, it was obvious Carrie had no intention of charging him for her attentions, so why should old Hewson make something out of it?

Richard wasn't bothered that Carrie had occasionally accepted payment for her favours. He was used to that. Lord knows how many girls he'd paid for over the years. But there was something about Carrie that was different. That look when he'd asked to take her dancing – it was as if she'd never been dancing before. Even though he knew she was not, she looked so innocent. And she trusted him. It was so rare for someone to trust him as she seemed to, or to look up to him with respect, that his heart felt moved to do something to reciprocate that trust. He could see in her a need as strong as his own for the affection and trust of another.

He wondered if he might be able to change, give her the assurance she deserved and teach her to believe in herself rather than be so subservient and seemingly shy to others. He sighed. He knew he should not give his heart to any woman. He could never stay in one place for very long, because the police would inevitably catch up with him. If he cared too much for someone, that would get in the way of him making important decisions, such as when it was time to leave town permanently or at the very least disappear for a while. And if she ever found out who he was or how he came by so much money, she would turn on him, screaming for justice, or beg him to renounce his wicked ways and settle down and raise a family instead.

Aggie, in Australia, had been like that. She'd hounded him for days to give up bushranging and turn his hand to stonemasonry once more.

'I cannot understand you,' she'd say. 'You shower me with gifts and you take me out dancing and to the theatre. How can you be so good to me, so kind and considerate one day and such a cold-blooded killer the next?'

He'd never thought of that before. He couldn't answer her at first. But then he'd realised how he did it. He put his life into compartments. It was probably something he'd learned to do during all those soul-destroying years on the hulks or in Pentridge Gaol. If you put different bits of your life into boxes, you could close the lid on one part and open another, without letting yourself get upset or grieve for what you'd left behind. It was neat and tidy, and it had saved him many times from tipping over the edge into insanity.

Maybe if he put Carrie into one of his watertight compartments, he'd be able to hold onto his cool reasoning and not lose sight of when it was time to flee.

Suddenly, a twig snapped outside and he sat up with a jolt. It was pitch black all around him. He fumbled for the tent flap, opened it a crack and peered out. All he could see was the surrounding bush and the stars clustered in the sky above him. It had stopped raining and was a typical summer's night, with a chill in the air and a slight breeze. He drew his coat around him, still looking out into the night.

He nearly jumped out of his skin when a voice cried out of the darkness, 'Richard, Richard, it's me, Tom. Are you in there?'

'Praise the Lord, Tom Kelly, I am. Where the devil are you?'

Thomas emerged from the bush to the left of the clearing and strode over to the tent, dumping his swag on the damp ground.

'Thought I'd never find you. It's been a long day, that's for sure.'

'What happened?'

Thomas described how he'd ended up on the wrong side of the diggers' camp and had to hide in the bush until all the fuss had died down. It was almost dawn before he could get to his stash, and then he'd had to run for it when he heard someone coming. He'd stayed in the hills behind the camp all day and had only managed to head towards their secret campsite after dusk.

'Well I'm mightily glad to see you, Tom Kelly. I've not had a thing to eat since dinner two nights ago and I'm absolutely starving.'

The following afternoon, Richard and his friend found themselves hiding in bushes at the side of the road awaiting the arrival of Mr Kerr, the banker from Rosstown. The pair had spent the morning in Rosstown, disguised to avoid recognition, checking out Mr Kerr's movements and listening for word of when he might be on his way. On observing Mr Kerr saddling his horse in preparation for departure, Richard had hurried back down the street to where Tom was waiting and they had made their way out of town along the main road towards Hokitika. Picking up their pistols and knives, hidden behind a rock just outside the town, they had run for much of the way until they reached their hiding spot. It was well located, with a good view of the road to the south and the north, so they could see the victim coming for some distance, as well as get warning of the approach of wayfarers from the other direction. It was several minutes before Richard got his breath back. He wasn't as fit as he used to be. Time was, he could outrun all the police in the Australian outback, in the hills and ranges and in the bush. He cursed the three long years he'd wasted in Dunedin gaol. Since his release some five months ago, he'd been as active as he could be, but his wretched leg was giving him more and more trouble now. Every time they clapped him in irons, it made his old wounds worse, with the result that even a short run would leave him breathless.

'Here he comes,' Kelly said, pointing up the road towards Rosstown. 'Damn! He's got a trooper with him.'

'Maybe he suspects something is up,' Richard said.

'No more than usual, I'd wager,' Kelly said. 'There've been so many stick-ups along this road.'

'Are we still game for it?'

'Might as well give it a try.'

'I'll cover the trooper and you look after the banker.'

They pulled neckerchiefs up under their eyes and waited in tense silence until the two men drew almost level with them. Richard leapt from behind their rock and jumped down the bank, landing on the road a few yards in front of the horses, his recently stolen Colt pistol pointed directly at the head of the armed guard.

'Bale up!' he shouted.

Kelly stood in front of the rock at the top of the bank, pointing his pistol at Mr Kerr.

The horses stopped. The trooper reached for his gun.

'Stop right there!' Richard shouted. 'Or I'll shoot.'

The trooper hesitated then put his hand back on the reins of his horse. Richard saw him say something to the banker but couldn't hear what it was.

'Now throw your gun down on the road over by the bank there,' Kelly said. 'You too,' he indicated to the banker to do the same.

The guard's hand hovered for a moment near his gun, which Richard could see protruding from his belt.

'And don't try anything clever,' he said, anticipating trouble.

The man threw his pistol on the road where Kelly had ordered.

'You have no right to stop us,' Mr Kerr said. 'We are on official business.'

'That's too bad, I'm afraid,' Richard said. 'Because stop you we have.

Now throw down your weapon.'

The banker made no move.

'I don't have one,' he said.

'We'll see about that,' Richard said.

'Hands above your heads,' Kelly said.

The men slowly raised their hands.

'You scoundrels. I'll see you swing for this,' the trooper said.

'No need to be rude,' Richard said with a half-smile. 'All we want is your money, not your life.'

'Now, I want you both to get slowly down off your horses and stand over to the side of the road.'

After some hesitation, the men dismounted. Richard seized the reins of both horses from them and led them further away where he could search the saddlebags unhindered.

'Good,' Kelly continued. 'Remember, I've got both of you covered. One move, and you'll be dancing on bullets.'

Richard tied the horses to two trees at the side of the road and returned to frisk the banker. He didn't believe he was unarmed. He made him take off his coat and jacket, searched the pockets and retrieved a few coins and notes, a bank draft which was of no use, and a silver cigarette case, which he pocketed. But there was no gun.

'Lift up your trouser legs, then,' he said. The banker obliged, showing the tops of his boots. Still no gun.

'Seems you were telling the truth,' Richard said. 'But I shall be keeping a close eye on you, just the same.'

He proceeded to rifle through the saddlebags until he found a wad of banknotes and, beneath them, a heavy bag presumably filled with gold. He pulled it out in triumph

'Aha, that's what we're looking for,' Tom called out to him.

'Here, Richard said, tossing everything up the bank to land at Kelly's feet. 'Keep an eye on those while I see if there's any more.' He continued to pull everything out of the saddlebags, but there was nothing else to take his fancy. 'Right, you two. I want you to empty out your pockets and throw everything down on the road over here.' He indicated a spot in the dirt where he thought he would be safe from their reach should they want to try anything tricky. He trained his pistol back on them, holding it steady as, reluctantly and hesitantly, they tossed a few small items in the road – a silver fob watch and chain from the banker, a pipe and some tobacco from the trooper, a few coins and notes from both, and very little else of value.

'Now then, down the bank with you. I'm going to tie you up and leave you there.'

'But you cannot, sir. This is preposterous,' Mr Kerr said.

'Oh, yes I can, and what's more, I will,' Richard said, and indicated with his pistol that they should start moving.

'No, leave it for now,' Tom cried, leaping down the bank, pistol in one hand and booty in the other, hurriedly stuffing the notes and bag of gold into his jacket pocket. Keeping his gun trained steadily on both men, Tom came up behind Richard and whispered in his ear, 'There's a posse of riders heading our way from Rosstown, just come into view. These two won't have heard them yet, but we need to make our getaway. I'll keep 'em covered. You get the horses.'

Richard took Tom at his word. He didn't dare focus along the road; it might alert the pair that help was at hand. He hurried over to the horses and brought them forward. As he was doing so, Tom said, 'Take your braces off, both of you.'

Neither man made a move.

'Come on now, your braces. Fast. Then put up your hands again'.

Still they didn't move.

'Damn,' Tom said, and fired into the dirt at their feet.

With sudden alacrity, the men undid their braces and threw them onto the road. As they did so, their trousers slowly dropped around their ankles, which would slow them down if they attempted pursuit. Richard smiled at the sight of the long woollen longjohns over their spindly legs and knobbly knees. He would have loved to linger on and tease them, but there was no time to lose. He and Tom clambered up into the two recently vacated saddles and took the reins, turning their stolen horses towards Hokitika. All the while they kept their pistols trained on the two men, standing there helplessly with their trousers at their feet.

'Change of plan, gentlemen. I'm sorry to say we must leave you,' Richard cried out as they spurred the horses to get moving. He felt the big black horse pull away underneath him and spurred her on again.

But no sooner had they turned their backs on the two trouserless victims than a shot rang out, then a volley of them. Richard felt a bullet whiz past his ear and another nearly took his hat off.

'What the…' He turned round to see the trooper firing a small lady's pistol at him. The bastard must have had it hidden somewhere clever. He took aim and fired.

He heard Tom doing the same.

Miraculously, the trooper fell to the ground. What a shot! Either he or Kelly must have felled him.

He spurred the horse on to go even faster, catching sight of the strangers speedily approaching along the dirt road. They were getting uncomfortably close.

'Come on you beauty, go for me,' he called to the black mare as he urged her on. 'Only you can save me now.'

He and Kelly were flying along. The wind was whistling around his ears, the trees and branches a blur as they flashed by. He loved this feeling. The thrill of the chase, plenty of money in their pockets, and the sensation of freedom as the willing horse galloped along the route. After a while, the sound of their pursuers dropped away then disappeared. He reined in his horse and turned to look at Kelly, who matched his slower pace. He was smiling broadly, laughing almost.

'We did it again Tom, we did it!' he cried out, laughing

Tom looked at him and cheered.

'We're a good team, Richard. We're the best bushrangers on the Coast.'

'We are, Tom. We are. But we'll be wanted men now. We'll have to lie low for a while.'

'Did we kill him then?'

'Hard to tell,' Richard called back as the horse slowed to a trot.

'We should have killed them both. They'll identify us to the police.'

'If we hadn't been in such a hurry to escape, I would have finished them both off. That's what Charlie Power always told me to do. Dead men tell no tales.'

9. Dreams Can Come True

Three weeks after their first meeting, when Carrie was working behind the bar one afternoon, Richard walked in through the door, banging it wide open, just like the first time she'd seen him. Her heart started pounding, her palms moistened, and she didn't know whether to pretend she hadn't seen him and ignore him, or follow her impulses and rush to his side. He'd disappeared over a week ago and she'd missed him terribly. She'd tried to find out where he'd gone but nobody seemed to know.

'Kiss me, Carrie, I'm back,' Richard cried as he approached the bar, pointing to his right cheek where she was expected to plant a kiss.

'Get on with you,' she said laughing, 'I've forgotten who you are, you've been away so long this time. What did you say your name was?'

'Now, none of your cheek, Miss. You'll look after your old friend Richard if you know what's good for you.'

And indeed she did. Whenever he returned from his sojourns, he always came back with a pocketful of money and a craving for good wine, sprightly music, and Carrie beside him.

'What'll it be then?' she asked, turning round towards the array of bottles behind the bar.

'Nothing just yet, my little chick. I've something I want to show you. It's a short walk from here, so you'll need your hat and coat.'

'A short walk? Whereabouts? What is it?'

'It's a place you'll want to call your own. Come, Carrie, let me show you the place of your dreams.'

Carrie was flustered.

'What do you mean, the place of my dreams?'

'You'll have to wait and see. It's a surprise.'

'But I want to know now!'

'No Carrie, then it won't be a surprise. You go get your things, and I'll tell Mr Hewson we're going out for a while.'

She met him a few minutes later at the hotel's front door, where he was pacing impatiently and looking at his expensive silver fob watch.

'Ah, at last,' he said, and steered her quickly out the door. 'I don't know what you ladies get up to, you take such a long time.'

They walked along the main street at a breathless pace, with Richard firmly pressing her on faster than she would normally have dared to go. The footpath in front of the shops and hotels lining the street was crowded with people, but they seemed to melt away in front of his purposeful stride. Carrie had to run to keep up with him, her sturdy black boots pattering across the rough pavement. When he crossed the street, she nearly slipped over in the muddy carriage tracks and cried out in alarm when she thought they were going to be run over by the huge Cobb and Co coach as it swept by, splashing mud over the hem of her skirt.

'Oh, heavens, we'll get run over. Please slow down for a minute,' she pleaded. 'You're just too fast for me.'

He gave her a look of complete incomprehension, but slowed down nevertheless.

After what seemed an endless criss-cross of streets and pavements, they finally stopped near the end of a street on the outskirts of town in front of a little cream cottage with a green door and a wide verandah at the end of a stone path. On either side were rose bushes in full bloom, deep reds and pinks and yellows, filling the air with a heavenly scent.

'Well, my little chick, what do you think? Do you like it?' he asked, smiling broadly.

'It's a lovely place,' she said, not sure what she was supposed to do next or why he was showing her someone else's house with such enthusiasm.

'It's yours, Carrie. I've bought it for you and me to share our joys together under the one roof. I want to see you comfortably off, in a home of your own.'

Carrie was speechless.

'What's the matter? Don't gawp at me like that. Come on, now,' he said taking her arm. 'Let's go inside and have a look.'

He propelled her through the gate, up the path past the scented roses, onto the verandah and through the big green panelled front door, which he opened with a key from his breast pocket.

They entered an oak-panelled parlour furnished with big comfortable wing-backed armchairs in a burgundy brocade, a nest of side tables, a mahogany table and dining chairs, all shining brightly in the sun streaming through the lace-curtained window. On either side, heavy green and burgundy floral curtains hung from floor to ceiling, gathered in the middle with a gold tasselled rope. The wooden floor was covered with a patterned, multi-coloured rug.

'Oh, this is lovely,' she said. 'I had no idea…'

'And now the kitchen,' he said and steered her through a far door into a small but practical kitchen with a coal range – cold at present – and a sink and a larder, a green-painted dresser containing an expensive-looking dinner set, and shelves everywhere.

'Oh,' she said again. 'It's wonderful.'

'And there are two bedrooms through here,' he continued, keeping the momentum going before she had time to catch her breath or her senses.

The first bedroom was empty. The second contained a double bed, with a big feather eiderdown on top and two big white downy pillows resting against the oak slatted bedhead. There was also a wardrobe and a dressing table with a mirror.

Carrie burst into tears.

'What's the matter, little chick? Why are you crying? I thought this would make you happy.'

'Oh, it's lovely,' Carrie said between sobs. 'You're right. It *is* the place of my dreams.'

'Well dry your eyes and enjoy it. Here,' he said, offering her a big white linen handkerchief.

She blew her nose and wiped her eyes, pocketing the hanky because it didn't seem right to give it back.

'It's what I've always wanted,' she was able to say at last without sniffing or snuffling 'A place of my own, a place just like this, with a parlour and a kitchen and a garden of roses.'

'So why are you upset, you funny wee thing?'

'Because… because,' she had to force herself to say it, 'because we're not married.'

'Oh, that,' he said.

'Yes, that,' she said.

Now it was his turn to feel at a loss for words. Buying a cottage for Carrie with just a small portion of all the money he'd made in the last two months seemed like a gentlemanly thing to do. He hadn't thought for one minute about marrying her, though. Setting up house was one thing. He'd done it a couple of times before with young ladies. But getting married was out of the question. In his line of work, he could never contemplate settling down. He had a gut feeling that already things were hotting up for him and Tom and the police were onto them. He'd have to be on his way before too long, and what sort of introduction to marriage would that be for a naïve young woman like Carrie? He might be a bounder, he might be able to shoot people and leave them for dead on the highway, but he couldn't lead Carrie on to think she was getting a husband and then walk out on her soon afterwards. Poor creature, she deserved better than that. He realised he would have to tell her the truth about himself sooner or later – but preferably later. Much later. He took her hands in his and looked into her eyes.

'I suppose you're worried what people will say,' he said.

'I *know* what they'll say,' she said. 'It doesn't take much imagination to work that out. But that's not the point. I don't care a fig for what people say. I've already got myself what that doctor's wife would call a bad reputation, by working in the saloon and having a bit of fun now and then. A girl can have a bit of fun. That's one thing. But living with a man… I've never done *this* before,' she said, indicating the bedroom and then the whole cottage with a sweep of her arm. 'It's not what other people see that upsets me. It's the eyes of the Lord that matter. My mother brought me up to believe in the holiness of matrimony.'

'Well, I'll think about it, Carrie, but I can't promise you. I'm away so often, you'd hardly see me, and the neighbours would think you were on your own anyway. Come on, my little chick. I've bought it just for you. Surely you're not going to say no to the place of your dreams.'

Carrie wrestled with her slowly receding principles.

'Well, I suppose I'd be a fool to throw away such a wonderful opportunity as this.' She looked around the room again. 'Maybe…'

'Tell you what, I'll only come out in the dead of night,' he laughed, bending his arm up to the tip of his nose in an imitation of a cloaked highwayman.

'Oh, Richard, you're so thoughtful and kind. This is the nicest thing that anyone has ever done for me. It would be churlish of me to turn you down, even without the prospect of a marriage licence.'

'I was hoping you'd say that,' he said, and kissed her full on the mouth.

'But don't you think I'll give up on the idea,' she said pulling herself away from his kiss. 'I don't give up easily.'

'And don't I know it, my little chick,' he said, and this time he covered her mouth with another, more lasting kiss, not giving her a chance to wriggle away.

Not that she wanted to. She relaxed into the kiss, pulling him closer with her small white hands, encased in fingerless cream lace gloves. For the past three weeks, Richard had treated her with the utmost decorum, not once suggesting that she should do any more for him than receive a companionable but chaste kiss, or a brotherly arm around her shoulder as he guided her somewhere or consulted her on her taste in entertainments or what she would like him to buy her to wear.

He'd been lavish with his gifts – a new shawl, soft leather evening shoes to match the gown he'd bought her at the most expensive dressmaker's in town, a fine cameo brooch edged with pearls, which now sat at her throat atop the high collar of a white lace blouse, another example of his generosity. Carrie had still not been able to find out where his seemingly unending supply of money came from, nor that of his brother Thomas, but since he appeared to lead an orderly life and never attracted the attention of the local constabulary, she assumed whatever he did was legal and derived from the prosperity of the nearby Kaniere diggings. She imagined him an insurance agent or a banker's representative, protecting innocent wayfarers from harm.

Whatever his work, his earnings were sufficient to buy this cottage. He was right: it was the place of her dreams. Realising her luck, she turned her focus back onto her benefactor, whose attentions were now more amorous than before.

'Look, here's another little surprise,' Richard said, disengaging himself from his passionate kiss and turning towards the bedroom window and the dressing table, where she noticed for the first time a bottle of champagne. He swept up the bottle and, with an exaggerated flourish, popped the cork. A few drops spilled over the lip and he licked the side of the bottle lasciviously, his long tongue lingering on the arching neck.

A further sensuous flourish produced two champagne glasses and he proceeded to pour the sparkling pale yellow liquid. He handed her a glass.

'A toast!' he said, raising his glass. His voice was throaty, dusky almost, as if he was finding it hard to speak. 'A toast to the place of your dreams!'

'The place of my dreams,' she rejoined, raising her glass and taking a sip. The bubbles made her mouth tingle. It was delicious. She licked her lips and returned his smile. She was standing beside him at the bedroom window and outside she could see, in the intense light of the late summer afternoon, a huge bush covered in red roses. Beyond, clearly visible, was the neighbouring house, its parlour bay window jutting out far enough for her to see a window seat covered in plump embroidered cushions. She laughed.

'I hope you people next door don't shock too easily,' she cried out to the closed bedroom window. 'Because you're going to have some interesting neighbours!' Then she danced around the room, returning to Richard smiling, her eyes sparkling with gratitude.

'Oh, thank you Richard. I don't think I've ever been happier than this.' And this time she reached up to his lips and kissed him in a long, passionate kiss that she felt reverberate throughout her entire body, even down to her knees and the arches of her feet.

'My little chick,' he said softly, and picked her up, her small frame lifting easily into his arms. He carried her over to the bed and let her down into the plump white eiderdown so that it billowed up beside her. She held up her arms to him, inviting him at last.

He knelt beside her on the edge of the bed, with one leg on the floor, and caressed her on the cheeks at first, moving his hand slowly down to her shoulders and then her breasts. She could feel them tingle and a wave of desire washed through her.

'My lover,' she breathed.

Afterwards, she lay on the eiderdown and stared into his iridescent blue eyes.

'What is it, Carrie? Why are you staring like that? What's the matter?' he said.

'Who *are* you?' she said. 'Who *is* Richard Davies?'

Richard propped himself up on his elbow. He was still wearing his shirt, but very little else. 'Lord, you women are a strange breed. Here we are, in the afterglow of our first passionate love-making and you ask me that?'

It had indeed been passionate. Once unburdened of their cumbersome clothes and undergarments, Carrie had found him a sympathetic but also an ardent lover. She'd only a handful of others to compare him with, but she could tell that he was the one for her. He'd been selfless, waiting for her own desire to be aroused to match his, caressing her until she was crying out for him to take her. She wasn't accustomed to such consideration.

'I just want to know a bit about you. I expect it makes you all the more fascinating, the air of mystery that surrounds you. But now that we're going to live together, don't you think I should be allowed in on your secrets?'

'Not now, my little chick. I can't tell you now. But I will, in good time,' was all he replied.

10. Sprung

Y ou can't do this to me, Lucian. You can't stay here,' Alex wailed. He was showing no signs of leaving on his own account. She was trying to persuade him to leave this afternoon and drive back to the apartment in San Francisco. 'I'll be back there tomorrow, as soon as I'm finished here.'

Lucian held up the palms of his hands as if to stop the flow of her words.

'Come on doll, don't mess me around. I don't want to go back now. I like it here with you. Besides, I don't want to wait until tomorrow, I want you now.'

He pulled her to him, wrapping his arms round her waist and enfolding her in the heady smell of his *Polo* aftershave mixed with his salty body heat. All of Alex's resolve crumbled along with her knees. They fell on the bed together, wrestling off their clothes, hot with desire. It was a short, sweaty, thrusting interlude, with no time for any preparatory pleasure, leaving her unsatisfied for once. She was just wondering whether she would be able to arouse him again for a second chance at it, when she felt the bed jolt suddenly to one side, then back again, and a deep rumbling came from under the ground.

'Earthquake!' she cried. She hated that feeling. You never could tell how long it would last, whether you should rush outside, or hide under a desk or a doorway. The jarring and jolting stopped. She lay perfectly still, hoping there was no aftershock coming.

Lucian appeared unconcerned. He didn't move off her, but gave her a languid, lazy smile, his eyes half closed.

'Hey, doll,' he said. 'I hope the earth moved for you too!'

Alex got the giggles. She was terrified of earthquakes and the relief that it had gone combined with Lucian's silly joke set her off into uncontrollable laughter. Then, in the middle of her fit of giggles, her mobile rang.

'Sorry Lucian, I'm going to have to answer it.'

He didn't move off her. Just kept smiling and laughing with her. That wonderful smile.

She stretched out her arm and just managed to grab the phone, which she'd left on the bedside table.

'Alex Zerakowski,' she said. But there was no-one there. She pressed the caller ID number, but didn't recognise it other than it belonged to someone in the Napa Valley. There was no message. But it brought her back to reality. She stopped laughing.

'Lucian, this is absolutely terrible. I shouldn't be doing this at this time of the day. I've got a job to do. Come on, we'd better get up.'

Lucian still made no attempt to move. He continued to smile. As if he knew it made her weak and defenceless.

'Lucian, come on…'

There was a knock at the door.

'Alex, Alex, are you in there?'

It was Anna. Alex made a superhuman effort with her arms and managed to roll Lucian off her at last. She felt very embarrassed, caught like this in mid-afternoon when she should be over at the winery office.

'Yes, I'm here, I'll be with you in a minute,' Alex said, sitting up and gathering her clothes strewn around the bed in their haste to get undressed.

'David says can you both come to his office right away. He says it's urgent.'

'Sure. I won't be long,' she said and waited for Anna's soft tread to depart back down the hallway.

'Wonder what he wants,' Alex said.

'Probably wants to ask me if my intentions towards you are honourable,' Lucian said and winked at her. He lit a cigarette. She grabbed it off him and took a puff.

'Come on, Lucian. You've got to get up and dressed. You heard what Anna said.'

Alex ran into the ensuite, had a quick douche and wash and sprayed some of her favourite *Gautier* perfume on her arms and neck. She really wanted to take a shower, but there was no time.

Back in the bedroom, Lucian had risen and was dressing at a leisurely pace, pulling on his Levis with studied casualness.

'Hope this doesn't take too long,' he said. 'I want to get you back in here and see if I can make the earth move for you one more time!'

The minute she pushed open the door to David's office, Alex could tell something was wrong. David was standing behind his desk, pacing, looking furious. And there were two strangers in the room seated in front of the desk – two men with almost identical dark suits and sombre ties, who were looking very grave. As soon as she and Lucian came into the room, one of the men leapt up from his chair, closed the door behind them and stayed in front of it, as if he was guarding the entrance. A chill of fear went through her even before David spoke.

'Alex, Lucian, these gentlemen are from the FBI. Agent Devlin O'Malley and Agent Trevor Denehew,' David said, indicating each man as he spoke. 'They want to ask Lucian a few questions.'

O'Malley stepped forward from the desk and confronted Lucian.

'Lucian Tate,' he said. 'Were you employed by the Abacus Pacific Computer Company until eight days ago?'

'I could have been, why?' Lucian said.

'And were you working on communication systems for a big oil exploration company, the US Western Pacific Consortium?'

'I think that was one of their clients, why?'

'We have reason to believe you may have been responsible for planting a computer time bomb inside their system. It's been down for several days. One of their main clients was US Western Pacific Consortium, and all their ships have lost their exploration data. It'll take weeks to get them back on track again. It's costing them millions of dollars in lost time and repairs.' The agent narrowed his eyes and bored in on Lucian. 'There's some quite conclusive evidence that you planted that computer time bomb to go off after you'd been fired.'

'Hey, I wouldn't do a thing like that! You've got the wrong guy.'

Alex was stunned. She was staring hard at Lucian, trying to detect any sign of guilt on his face, but it remained impassive and expressionless.

The FBI man asked him a few more questions, but Lucian wasn't giving anything away.

'I think I'd better phone my lawyer, if you don't mind,' he said, walking over to the window. He flipped open his cellphone and pressed an autodial number. Alex couldn't hear what he was saying. She sank into one of David's visitor chairs, feeling dazed. Could Lucian have done such a terrible thing? She found it hard to believe he'd go that far. He never talked about his work, probably because it was quite beyond her, but she knew he was pretty good at all that computer stuff. He hadn't said anything about leaving the company he'd been working for this past year. But then he hadn't come up with any explanation why he was at home last Monday, or how he could have been with her today when he should have been at work.

The other agent, Denehew, came away from the door and stood in front of her.

'Miss Zerakowski, I'd like to have a few words with you in private, please. We'd like to know what Mr Tate has told you.'

'Nothing.' She could hear her voice come out in a hoarse squeak and cleared her throat. 'He's told me nothing.'

'Yes, that may be so,' Denehew said. 'But nevertheless I'd like to ask you a few questions and take a statement from you in writing.'

Alex gulped. This was serious. She looked across at David, but he was looking at Lucian, his face thunderous.

'I suppose so,' she said and followed the agent out the door. When he asked if there was somewhere they could go, she showed him into her office across the corridor. She sat at her desk, thinking it might make her feel a little more in control.

Agent Denehew asked her all about her living arrangements with Lucian, how much she knew about his work, whether he told her much about it, and where she'd been on Friday August the ninth. Had she been with Lucian, and had she seen him any time that day? He asked her for alibis, and for the name, address and phone number of her friend Magda who she said she'd had a long lunch with.

Then he wrote everything down, laboriously, in capital letters. It seemed to take forever. When he finally finished he asked her to read it through and sign at the bottom, with the date. She signed.

'Thank you Miss Zerakowski,' Denehew said. 'Now I'd like to search this room and your bedroom. I'll get Mr Rossini to come with us and show us the way.'

Alex was mortified. Her room was a mess, the bed unmade and probably reeking of sex. There were wet towels all over the bathroom floor and her underwear and clothes were strewn everywhere. David would be horrified. And she didn't want this awful automaton from the FBI rifling through her things. Denehew stood up and showed her a search warrant. She then watched in horror as he searched through her desk, her drawers, briefcase and even the bookcase. He picked up her diary off the desk.

'I'll be taking this with me, Miss Zerakowski. To check for evidence. I'll see that you get it back as soon as possible. And I'll require the laptop and these spare disks of yours. Could you please pack it up for me now so that I can take it away. I promise we'll be very careful not to lose any of your files or your work.'

'Good God, you can't do that to me,' she cried. 'I can't do without it for even a day. It's my work.'

'I'm afraid I can do it and I will,' the agent said, waving his warrant again. 'Now, will you disconnect it and pack it up for me, or shall I?'

Alex clamped her teeth together and tried to contain her fury as she reached under the desk and disconnected the phone, power and printer cords, before slamming the machine into its leather carry case. She pulled the zip closed with such fury that it caught and wouldn't budge.

'Here, let me,' the agent said, and moved to the desk, to assist.

'It's quite all right, thank you,' Alex said crisply and with a final tug, managed to close the case.

'Here,' she said, and thrust the case at the agent, who she was growing to dislike intensely.

'Thank you. Now perhaps we can ask Mr Rossini to show us the way to your room.'

David was still in his office with Agent O'Malley and Lucian, who was sitting sullenly in one of the chairs, saying nothing. At Denehew's request, David got up from his desk and left the room, closing the door behind him.

David led the way to the house and Alex's room, with Alex close behind. The agent was just out of earshot. 'Whew, glad to get out of there,' David whispered, smiling wryly at Alex. 'What a fine pickle you've got us all in now, Alexandra Zerakowski. You certainly know how to pick 'em!'

'Oh David, I'm so sorry. I had no idea about this,' she said.

'I know, I believe you,' David said. 'You know, Alex, I thought he was a scoundrel from the moment he arrived. And it looks as though I was right.'

Alex thought the better of sticking up for Lucian. It was not the right time.

'I seem to have a knack for finding Mr Wrong every time.'

They arrived at Alex's room. David indicated the door to the agent, who opened it and went inside. Alex looked at the floor to hide her embarrassment. The room was indeed the pigsty she'd imagined, with clothes all over the floor and the recently used unmade bed like a beacon, its rumpled sheets announcing to the world what she'd been up to less than an hour ago.

'Sorry about the mess,' she said to David. 'If I'd known…' she trailed off.

David said nothing. The agent commenced a methodical search, picking out Lucian's belongings and gathering them in a neat pile on the bed. Alex expected him to behave like the cops you saw on TV, who completely ransacked every room they searched. But he wasn't at all like that. He was very circumspect and tidy, putting things back in drawers and on shelves after he'd finished. There wasn't all that much to search, anyway. She'd left most of her clothes and almost all of her books and belongings back in the flat with Lucian. It dawned on her then that they would probably search the flat too. Lucian could be guaranteed to have left it looking like a tip after over a week on his own.

'He only brought clothes and cigarettes with him,' she said feebly. 'I don't think you'll find much to help you.'

The agent picked up a set of keys.

'Yours? Or his?' he asked.

'His,' she replied.

'I'll be taking these too, then. We'll be seizing his car.' He turned to David. 'Someone will come with a truck and take it away,' he added.

With a curt nod, the agent left the room, carrying Lucian's few belongings and the keys. She and David followed him outside and across the courtyard to the office. Denehew then motioned David to follow him into his room.

'Thank you, Miss Zerakowski. We won't be needing you any more today. You will find that the flat you share with Mr Tate has also been subjected to a search, but our agents will do their best to see that it is left as they found it. Good day, Miss Zerakowski.'

And with that, he disappeared into David's office with David, closing the door behind him.

Gloomily, Alex crossed the corridor into her office and stared out the window at the ripening vines running away towards the hills in their orderly rows. The pinot leaves had already started to turn yellow. How she'd like to run to the hills too, she thought. Movement in the courtyard beneath caught her eye. She looked more closely and, to her horror, saw Lucian being led away, handcuffed to Agent O'Malley. She watched with mounting fear as they got into the back of a waiting sedan and drove away.

When the car containing Lucian reached the main road and finally disappeared, she plumped herself down at her desk, head in hands. What a disaster! Trust Lucian to land her in it. She wanted to run away and hide, she was so ashamed of the embarrassment and worry she'd caused the Rossinis. Suddenly that contract offer in New Zealand to help with that landfill problem seemed very attractive.

11. Brush with the Law

The weeks after moving into her new house were the most hectic and most pleasurable Carrie had known in all her twenty-eight years. She was used to living her own life, doing more or less as she pleased, in between working day and night for Mr Hewson. She had no parents to worry about; they'd died many years ago in the Grey. Her father had died in an accident on the wharf, her mother of exhaustion after bringing up six children on her own with hardly a penny, save for what she'd earned taking in mending and darning work from the single men who'd worked with her husband.

But now Carrie had to fit in with another's needs and wishes. She'd quit her job at the Golden Age, making sure she left in good standing with Mr Hewson, who'd been unusually magnanimous and congratulated her warmly on her good fortune. Richard had warned her she might need her job again if he had to go away for any length of time and had talked Hewson into letting her go early without having to work out her notice. Since Richard had recently become one of the Golden Age's best customers, Mr Hewson had been easy to persuade, his decision made easier by Richard offering the services of another young lady he seemed to know. Carrie was initially suspicious of this arrangement, convinced the lady had been having an affair with Richard, but he'd denied it vigorously and she'd kept him so preoccupied with setting up the house and catering to his every whim that he wouldn't have had a spare moment to pay her any attention.

He would still disappear for several days at a time, but she knew better than to quiz him as to where he'd been or what he'd been doing. She'd realised at last that she wasn't going to pry any information out of him until he was ready to tell her himself.

Instead, she concentrated on creating a domestic haven for him, making sure his clothes were washed and pressed, his collars stiff and spotlessly white, and his meals tasty and ready whenever he wanted them

– and that could sometimes be at very odd hours indeed.

If she noticed anything amiss – such as the blood and gashes in his trousers after he returned from one of his mysterious sojourns – she simply washed and mended them and kept her anxieties to herself. If she was surprised when he wanted his breakfast at two o'clock in the morning before going out somewhere with Thomas and not returning for three days, she busied herself with cooking the bacon and eggs and making sure his tea was hot and sweet. If she felt concerned when he and Thomas got roaring drunk on the nights they came home after their trips away, she would take off their boots and cover them with blankets after they'd passed out.

She was surprised at the ease with which she settled into domesticity. It had been years since she'd helped her mother with the mending and ironing for the men, or turned her hand to making dinner for seven out of a few carrots and potatoes. She never thought she'd see the day she'd be grateful for all that hard work at home, as the eldest taking responsibility for most of the cooking and mending. But all those lessons learnt in her mother's kitchen were coming in very handy – from lighting the coal range (after a couple of false starts when she'd forgotten to open the flue), to kneading and rising bread, and being able to mend Richard's clothes almost invisibly so that he had difficulty seeing where the holes and gashes had been.

Of course, now that she had as much money as she wanted to spend at the greengrocer's or the butcher, she could choose special cuts of meat to please Richard's demanding appetite, and she could even ask to have things delivered.

One late summer's day, she'd bought him several treats – some American dried apricots, Moir's fresh herrings, Hennessey's pale brandy, some Port Cooper cheese and a packet of Huntley and Palmer's Reading biscuits to put it on. There'd also been some Canterbury butter at a marked-down price, which she'd brought home and put in the larder. With Richard's seemingly never-ending supply of money, they were living very well indeed. That evening, after dinner, when Richard was sitting out on a bentwood rocking chair on the wide verandah that stretched across the front of the house, Carrie brought him out a plate of the cheese and biscuits and a glass of brandy.

'You know how to spoil a man,' Richard said, grabbing her around the waist as she put the plate down in front of him and handed him the brandy balloon.

Out of the corner of her eye, Carrie could see their nosey neighbour,

Mrs McNamara, peering at her through the bay window. Although they were on speaking terms with the McNamaras, Sybil had a habit of pursing her lips whenever Carrie was around, which annoyed her intensely.

I'll give her something to pout about, Carrie thought. She sat down on Richard's lap and provocatively licked his ear at an angle old Mrs McNamara would be sure to see.

'I say, Carrie, you really do know how to spoil a man,' Richard said, pulling her to him with his free hand and kissing her.

One cold, windy April night, she was sitting by the fire in the parlour hemming a new slate blue silk dress when the door burst open and Richard ran in with Thomas in hot pursuit. As soon as they were inside, they slammed the door shut, threw off their jackets and pegged them on the hook by the door, pulled off their boots and flung themselves on the two armchairs beside the fire. Carrie had been sitting in the small, armless sewing chair directly underneath the light. She looked up, startled.

'Richard, what's…'

'Hush, not a word,' Richard said. 'If anybody asks, we've been here with you all evening.'

They then started talking and joking with each other, as if nothing had happened, although Carrie noticed that their voices were unusually loud and their laughter excessively hearty. She couldn't see what the fuss was about. There was nobody else around. All she could hear, besides them, was the sound of the wind beating against the weatherboards and rattling the front door.

The clock struck the hour. It got to seven chimes when she heard heavy footsteps clumping onto the verandah and a loud knock at the door.

'We've been here all night,' Richard reminded her as he stood up to answer the door. Carrie was horrified to see two policemen standing there, one of them the sergeant who used to come in to the Golden Age from time to time.

'Good evening, sir, Miss O'Neill, Mr Kelly,' Sergeant Griffiths said, taking off his hat and coming in uninvited. 'I hope you'll excuse my intrusion Miss O'Neill, but I would like to have a few words with these gentlemen here. You might care to step into another room for a few minutes. I'm sure you don't want to hear my business.'

'I'm perfectly…'

'You'd better do as the sergeant says, Carrie,' Richard said, looking so fiercely at her that she froze. Those eyes could be a very steely shade of blue when he was on guard, she realised.

'I'll make you all a pot of tea,' she said firmly, though quaking inwardly, as she went to leave the room.

'One moment, Miss O'Neill,' the sergeant said. 'I wonder if you would be so good as to inform me how long these two gentlemen have been with you tonight?'

Carrie gulped and tried to hide her nerves.

'Oh, all evening,' she said. 'We all had dinner together.'

'And they've been here ever since?'

'They have,' she said quietly, trying her best to look as if she was telling the truth.

'Thank you, Miss O'Neill. That will be all.'

She'd never made tea as hastily or with as little concentration as she did that night. Her hands were shaking so much that, while pouring the hot water from the kettle into the silver teapot, she missed the opening, splashing boiling water onto her skirts. Carrying the tray back into the parlour, she could hear the cups rattling in their saucers. Her mind was racing. What if Richard had done something wrong? What would become of her? And what could he have done? This was the first time Richard had been interrogated by the police, but all the same, it didn't look as if they were pursuing him over some minor misdemeanour. Richard and his brother had looked desperate when they'd rushed in the door, then very guilty and sheepish in those few brief moments while they were sitting by the fire with her before the police arrived. And the sergeant had called Thomas Mr Kelly. If that was really his name, he couldn't be Richard's brother – his name was Davies.

Carrie knocked on the parlour door before entering. The sergeant opened it.

'Ah, Miss O'Neill,' he said. 'Let me take that. And thank you so much for going to the trouble.' With that, he took the tray and elbowed the door closed behind him.

She stood there for a few moments, almost crying with fear and frustration. She wanted to help Richard, but save lying about his presence at home, she could do no more.

The wait seemed like an eternity. She'd left her needlework in the parlour in her haste to depart and there was nothing to do in the kitchen now the tea was made. The dinner dishes were washed and put away, which was just as well if the sergeant came prying to check out her alibi. The ironing was done. The only thing to read was an old copy of the

West Coast Times in the coalscuttle. She pulled it out and sat down in front of the kerosene lamp on the table by the curtained window.

It was dated Tuesday, April the twenty-fourth, which made it four days old. She remembered Richard bringing it home and reading it, his wet socks steaming as he rested his feet on the coal range. Whatever he'd been reading had amused him mightily.

She held up the thin cream newspaper and started to read. The front page was filled with advertisements from tradesmen, shopkeepers, English agents persuading people to order directly from London, selling everything from Colt revolvers to cures for almost anything that could ail you.

'FRAMPTON'S PILL OF HEALTH,' one column was headed. It purported to have 'long-tried efficacy for purifying the blood and correcting all disorders of the stomach and bowels,'

'BEST REMEDIES FOR INDIGESTION,' the same column proclaimed further down the page.

'Norton's camomile pills – a powerful tonic and gentle aperient. 2s a bottle.'

And underneath that, another cure-all:

'DINNEFORD'S FLUID MAGNESIA,' it said.

'For sour eructations and bilious affectations,' it was supposed to be able to cure 'gout, complaints of the bladder, rashes, and sickness of pregnancy.'

She read on. There was nothing else to do. She turned the page and studied the long, spidery columns of type. On the left, three columns were devoted to the shipping news. Then came the news of the day before. She was confused at first, wondering what the latest presentation at the Corinthian Hall had to do with a fight between two bill-stickers over whose bill was pasted on the lamppost first. There were no headings or breaks between stories – each item of news was presented in one long continuous story, with only a paragraph break between items. Once she'd worked that out, it became easier to follow.

An item at the bottom of the page caught her eye:

A daring attempt was made last night to "stick up" a bootmaker, who lives in one of the side streets off from the upper end of Revell-street. Just before retiring to rest, his attention was aroused by some person knocking at the door, which he at once opened and was immediately set upon by a man who attempted to throttle him. A desperate struggle ensued between them but the resistance offered by the disciple of St Crispian was so effectual that the rogue was glad to make his escape leaving, as a trophy of victory, his hat behind him. The darkness of the night facilitated his escape and although the police were called, no trace of him could be discovered.

That, Carrie realised, was the same night Richard had come home after a two-day absence with holes in his jacket and blood on his shirt cuffs, complaining that he'd lost his hat and would have to buy a new one. Could it have been this piece of news that he was chuckling about? Could he have committed this crime? She didn't believe it possible.

She read on, through several other items of news, until she found another alarming piece:

'George Cameron, who runs the mail between Hokitika and Rosstown was stuck up by two men on the morning of April 20th. It appears he left Rosstown en route for Hokitika and, when about three miles along the road, was met by two men wearing masks, who covered him with their revolvers and ordered him to "bale up" in the most approved style of bushranging.' The story went on to describe, in picturesque detail, how the robbers then allowed Mr Cameron to keep most of the money he'd been carrying after he'd pleaded poverty. It concluded: 'Two troopers were immediately dispatched in pursuit of the bushrangers, who have not been discovered. The police said they had reason to believe that the two bushrangers were the very same rogues that held up the Rosstown Bank the week before.'

The morning of April the twentieth – Richard had been away then too. She remembered it well because it was the day she had an appointment to see Doctor Rosetti in Revell Street. Richard had come home that night after a two-day absence and made some comment about not earning as much money these past couple of days as he should have. Whereas the week previously – the week the bank had been robbed – he'd been rolling in money and had spent lavishly on luxuries, taking her out to dinner at the expensive dining room near the waterfront, buying her an exquisite pearl necklace and drop earrings and going on a bender with Thomas that had ended with them both coming home drunk and disorderly at four in the morning.

She believed Richard to be involved in something related to law and order. She knew he sometimes carried a gun and he was always intensely secretive about his out-of-town activities. But she thought he needed a gun because he was in some way upholding the law, protecting miners and travellers from being robbed, like the men the insurance companies hired. Never for one minute would she have picked him as the robber.

She felt a thrill of both fear and excitement. If Richard held up mail carriages and banks for a living, that would explain why he always had so much money. She could just see him swashbuckling his way to the safe and extracting piles of banknotes and gold. She'd heard about men like that, who blew safes open with sticks of dynamite and got away with hundreds of pounds. But they did seem to get caught eventually. She'd read of one gang that'd been pursued by the police for months until one night they'd finally run them down, camped by a river, deep in the bush.

She threw down the paper and jumped up from the table, trembling. She'd only just settled down with Richard and, despite his wanderings, she felt very happy. There was the small matter of the missing marriage certificate, but she was sure she would be able to engineer that before too long.

Her thoughts were interrupted by a clomping of heavy boots and the bang of the front door, followed by an eerie silence. Cautiously, she stood up from the table and approached the parlour door, pausing behind it to listen. Not a sound could be heard from within. She knocked, softly at first, then more loudly. Still nothing. With trepidation, she turned the handle and peered round the door. The room was empty. The tea tray was on the table, with just one cup poured and only half consumed. The other cups, the biscuits, were untouched. Her sewing was still lying discarded on the floor where she'd left it. Both Richard and Thomas must have departed with the police, which worried her even more.

She busied herself with the tea things, tidying the parlour, washing the few dirty dishes, and fussing over her sewing. Still no sign of Richard.

Eventually, tired of waiting up for him, she took herself off to bed, where she tossed and turned, unable to sleep properly while feeling sick with worry about him.

It was the following afternoon, a Sunday, before he returned home, morose and grumpy, quite unlike his usual cheerful self. Normally he would try to make a joke out of anything that might be bothering him. But whatever was troubling him this time was far too weighty for him to make light of.

She made up a tea tray with her the grocer's special Twinings blend and a citrus cake she'd baked after church that morning in the hope of his return.

'Are you all right, Richard?' she asked as she handed him his cup of tea. 'Is there anything I can do to help you?'

His face seemed to lighten a little when he saw her and the tea tray. He smiled, although he still looked distracted, as if he wasn't quite there. He helped himself to a slice of cake.

'Delicious, as always,' he said then looked serious again. 'You've done enough already to help me, my little chick. You lied to protect me last night, and I will always be indebted to you for that.'

'You know I'd do anything for you, Richard.'

He was looking away as he ate, so she couldn't catch his eye and try to gauge what he was thinking.

'I'm sorry it's come to this, Carrie,' he said, still facing the window, which was letting in dappled afternoon light through the lace curtains. 'I've tried to protect you, but I've failed. I'm sorry you had to go through it all, with the police coming for us and taking us away.' He glanced up at her with quite the strangest look in those impenetrable blue eyes. She realised at that moment she hardly knew him.

'I just wish I had some idea what was going on,' she said. 'I hate all this secrecy.'

'It's best that you don't know,' he said. 'The less you know, the less trouble you can get into.'

'Richard, I was reading the *Times* you brought home the other day and I couldn't help but wonder if... if it was you and Thomas they were talking about robbing that bank in Rosstown, because...'

'Hush, Carrie,' he said, pressing his finger to her lips. 'No more. Now, how'd you like to come with me to the Grand Ball at the Union Hotel at the end of next week. Tom and I have purchased some tickets and I would very much like you to be my partner.'

He was very good at changing the subject like that, at diverting her away from what she really wanted to know. She'd had to leave it there; it would be impossible to get anything further out of him. Whatever had happened at the police station – assuming that was where they had gone with the sergeant that night – would have to remain a mystery. Besides, even though she knew it to be a deliberate ploy to distract her from his brush with the police, she was mightily attracted to going to the Grand Ball. She'd never been to one before, never known any gentlemen wealthy enough or who liked her enough to ask.

'Oh Richard, you're impossible!' she cried, stamping her foot in frustration at his clever diversionary tactics. 'You know I'd love to go.'

12. Long Way from Home

The tiny plane was bouncing around over the dark blue ocean. Although Alex was accustomed to flying, this turbulence was worse than she'd experienced before and the plane was like a flying pencil, it was so small. She tucked the Maria Callas biography she'd just finished reading into the seat pocket and gripped the side of her seat. The captain had warned them it would be a bumpy flight. Something about strong northwest winds over Cook Strait, which was presumably this stretch of water beneath them. If it weren't such a hail-Mary-heartstopper flight, she'd have been in raptures over the view. The unbroken expanse of sea was now giving way to a myriad dark green islands and peninsulas, each cradling a bay of golden or white sand. She wished she were down there instead of being tossed around at the mercy of this infernal wind.

For a moment, she even wished she were back home in San Francisco. But then it all came back to her. She shuddered involuntarily at the memory of Lucian being led away, of leaving Rossini's feeling she was under a cloud despite the family's protestations, and of going back to the flat to pack up and leave. It had been a no-brainer, accepting this job in New Zealand. It was a short-term contract, and it would give her time to get over the fiasco her life had become. She'd not heard a word from Lucian, although that was hardly surprising, since she'd heard on the news that he'd been arrested and charged with sabotage. She'd parcelled up his stuff and couriered it off to his sister in San Diego, certain that would be the last she would have to do with him. The new world, down under, had suddenly seemed very attractive. It would give her the opportunity for a fresh start, even if just for a few months, and she could escape the shame and humiliation of Lucian's arrest.

The captain announced that you could see the Marlborough Sounds to the left of the plane, which was Alex's side, and the rest of Tasman Bay to the right, and that they would be landing in Nelson in ten minutes, so please fasten seat belts etcetera. Thankfully it was a short flight, and would soon be over, Alex thought, still gripping the armrest as the plane continued to give the impression it was dropping out of the sky.

Below, now, she could see a tiny city sprawling across dark green hills and a patchwork plain to a deep blue sea. She felt an unaccustomed pang of homesickness. The scene below was quite different from any she'd seen at home and suddenly she wished she were back in her comfort-zone – her pint-sized little office tucked away in a commercial block off J Street with Lacey standing guard at reception and Sharon on hand in the next office to help out with anything tricky. She wondered how they were getting on without her. She would gladly have caught the next plane home at that moment. Funny, she thought, she hadn't felt homesick in years.

But she was brought back to reality by the ping of the seat belt warning and its sign flashing above her head.

She braced herself as they came into land, finding it hard to believe that this tiny aircraft would be able to land safely in such a crosswind. The wings were tipping fearsomely from side to side as the wind caught them, and the engines were revving full throttle. She shut her eyes and prayed, although she wasn't terribly religious at the best of times. But somehow this called for the intercession of a higher power.

The landing, when it came, was something of an anticlimax, with just one heavy thump as they touched down. In no time they'd taxied to the tiny terminal and Alex started to scan the groups of people waiting outside in front of the building to see if she could recognise her new employers – Oliver and Geneviève Darby.

She spotted them as soon as she'd negotiated a narrow stairway down from the plane and stepped onto the tarmac. They were just as they'd described themselves in their last email: a tall fair man and a shorter woman, her long red curly hair escaping from its bands and blowing in the wind. She was standing behind a pushchair and clutching the hand of a small red-haired girl, who was bouncing up and down and waving excitedly. Alex waved back as she drew closer, passing through the terminal gate before walking over to them and holding out her hand.

'Hi there, I'm Alex,' she said, shaking Oliver's hand, then his wife's. 'It was easy to recognise you from your description.'

'Welcome, welcome,' the young man said, trying to brush his long sandy hair out of his eyes with one hand while shaking hers with the other. The wind was blowing a gale. 'I'm Oliver, as you will have guessed. Welcome to New Zealand.'

'And I'm Gen – short for Genevieve,' the young woman added,

taking her hand then giving her a hug. 'We're both so thrilled you could come. It's just great to have you here. And this,' she said in response to a fierce tugging on the hem of her shirt, 'is Isobel.'

'Hello Isobel,' Alex said, bending down and holding out her hand to the little girl. 'I'm Alex Zerakowski. Thank you for coming to meet me.'

'That's okay,' Isobel said, taking her hand timidly before looking up at her mother for approval.

'And is this your baby sister?' Alex said, indicating the wriggling baby in the pushchair.

'Her name's Claudia,' Isobel said.

'Hello Claudia,' Alex said to the pushchair. She wasn't very good with babies, didn't know how to relate to them. Claudia looked like a very happy baby, which was in her favour. She didn't like them when they cried. This one was gurgling and smiling merrily. 'How old is she?"

'Eighteen months,' Gen replied. 'A lovely age.'

Alex wasn't so sure. The only babies she knew made a lot of noise and took up a lot of their parents' time. She'd watched her brother and sister and several of her friends get taken over by babydom and you could never have an uninterrupted conversation with them.

'Right, let's get out of this wind and go find Alex's luggage, and then we'll head for home,' Oliver said, taking the pushchair handles and starting to steer it towards baggage claim.

Alex was surprised to discover the bags were brought to you outside – a bit like on Maui. She went to grab her black Samsonite when it was seized by a big brown masculine hand. She was just about to protest when she realised it was Oliver, who then manoeuvred both pushchair and suitcase along the pavement, across the road and into the back of a Range Rover at such lightning speed she was left standing.

'Come on, we'd better catch up,' Gen said laughing. 'He's not one to wait around, our Ollie.'

Luggage stowed, Oliver offered Alex a hand up into the front seat then turned to help Gen strap the children into their car seats.

'Wouldn't you like to sit in the front?' Alex asked her.

'No, I prefer it in the back. That way I can keep an eye on both of them at once.'

Gen had perched in the middle between the two child safety seats, and was handing the baby a toy, rattling it and waving it temptingly.

'We'll be home in just a few minutes. It's not far at all,' Oliver said as he negotiated the car park and fed some coins into the machine to activate the barrier arm.

'I hope you like it at the farm,' Oliver continued. 'We've cleaned out the cottage for you and it's looking really great now, with the wisteria out and the cherry blossom in the front yard. Gen's painted all the walls white to lighten it up and it should be really comfortable.'

'Thank you,' Alex said, turning to Genevieve, who was entertaining Claudia with a small fat picture book. 'I'm sure I'll love it here, it's…'

'And the vineyard is coming to life again after the winter, with buds bursting just at the right time and no sign of frost. It's a great time to be here, the spring.'

Alex felt a twinge of longing for Rossini's, where it was almost fall and harvest would begin in a month or two. She could just picture the big green and gold leaves, the ripe fruit glistening with that sugary yeasty powder that made it look like something out of a candy store, and the maples red and yellow up on the hills. Somehow, she'd skipped a couple of seasons in a day, and now it was spring again.

'…and this nor'-wester will be melting all the snow up in the mountains. The skiers won't like that. D'you ski where you come from?' Oliver paused at last.

'Oh yes, a bit. But I'm not very good. I never seem to have time.'

'Well, New Zealand's a great place for skiing,' Oliver continued, probably without hearing her, she thought. He was a veritable babbling brook. 'Lots of Americans come here every winter to ski – in your summer, of course. There's a skifield near Nelson, but the big ones are further south. Nelson's best known for its summers, for sunshine, and for its art. We've got some of the best potteries in the world here. Gen'll show you sometime. And there's all sorts of other famous arts and crafts. The galleries around Nelson are legendary. And so are the cafés. We'll have to take you into town and give you a taste of Nelson and its artists. There are a couple of restaurants that are world-class. You could eat somewhere different every day.'

'And believe me, he tries to,' Gen interrupted from the back seat. 'You can tell from his waistline that Ollie's a bit of a bon vivant!'

'I know, it's a shocker. It's getting harder and harder to do up my belt. I'm going to have to start going to the gym, there's nothing else for it.'

'Hah!' Gen cried. 'That'd be the day. You've been saying that for years.'

'I bought a gym membership once,' Ollie protested.

'Yes, but you only went once for the assessment then fled in fright when you got the results. Any sign of hard labour and you run a mile!'

'Hey, that's not fair,' Ollie said. 'I work like a slave in the vineyard.'

'That's different,' Gen said. 'Those grapes are your passion. You couldn't bear to leave them alone, not even for a day.'

'Look, there's the turnoff to Mac's Brewery,' Ollie said to change the subject. 'It makes world class ale and cider. Not so keen on their wine though. It's not nearly as good as ours. But then I would say that, wouldn't I! You'll have to try their Summer Ale when it comes out before Christmas. It's out of this world. Spicy and tangy-sweet. And…'

'Slow down, Ollie,' Gen said from the back seat. 'You'll overwhelm the poor girl on her first day.'

'Yes, sorry, Alex. Gen's always telling me I talk too much.'

'Mummy, what's this lady going to do when we get home?' Isobel's voice chimed in.

'It's Alex, darling. I'm sure you can call her Alex?'

'Of course,' Alex replied. 'We don't stand on formality where I come from. Call me Alex, please.'

'But what's she going to do?'

'I expect she'll want to unpack and settle in at the cottage first, then perhaps she'll have dinner with us up at the house, if she'd like to.'

'That'd be great,' Alex said. 'Thank you.'

'But what is she going to *do*?' Isobel was becoming insistent.

'I told you darling, she's going to handle all those reporters that've been bugging us lately, and see if we can get rid of some of those protesters that've been hanging around the gate.'

'How will she make them go away?'

Alex laughed. 'By finding something else for them to protest about,' she said.

'That'd be something,' Oliver said. 'They've been making life very difficult for us lately. They were there this morning when we left for the airport, and I'll bet they'll be still there now.'

Alex looked outside. They were approaching a small town. She could see its name – Hope – on the side of the road. Perhaps that was an omen, she thought. Silently, she hoped for a man who would be better for her than Lucian – a man that Anna would call Mr Right. But she didn't like to say anything. She hardly knew the Darbys and it was far too soon to be talking about her hopes and dreams.

Instead she asked, 'How's the landfill going?'

'It would be going just fine if it weren't for the greenies,' Oliver said. 'We've got the resource consent, and the contractors are ready to move on to the site to carry out the earthworks and get it ready to open. But the protesters won't let them through the gate.'

'Lying down in front of the bulldozers I suppose?' Alex said.

'You've got it. That and more. You'll see. It's a real mess,' Oliver said.

'And it's especially awful with the children there,' Gen said. 'The protesters know they can't come on our land without getting arrested, but just the same I don't feel the children are safe.'

'Duh Duh Duh Duh,' Claudia called from her carseat. Alex turned to see her pointing at a picture book.

'No. You never know what they're going to try next,' Oliver said. 'David was telling me that things got pretty heated up in the Napa Valley too for a while.'

'Duh Duh Duh,' Claudia continued.

'Yes, it's a dog. Good girl,' Gen encouraged.

'For a short time, yes. But it could have been a lot worse,' Alex said, finding it hard to keep her thread of the conversation.

'Probably because *you* were there,' Gen chuckled. She seemed able to switch from baby talk to burning issues with no trouble at all. Alex was getting distracted as Claudia's animal identity parade got louder.

'Muh Muh Muh,' she was now shouting.

'Yes, a cow, Moo,' Gen agreed.

Where was she? Alex's mind seemed to be deserting her. Oh, yes. Protesters in the Napa.

'I don't know about that. I'd like to think I helped. But the greenies could see there were a lot of benefits environmentally, with the recycling and everything.'

'Guh, guh, guh, guh,' from the back seat. Alex closed her eyes. She couldn't begin to guess what this creature could be.

'Goat,' Gen said approvingly. 'Goat. Ow! No Claudia, don't hit me with the book. It's cardboard and it hurts.' Alex heard a thud as the offending book hit the floor behind her. She silently thanked the Lord for small mercies.

The Range Rover lurched to the left and Alex gripped the armrest in the passenger door as they turned off the main road. Out the window flashing by were orchards – apples and pears, she could see, then a field of rambling vines she didn't recognise.

'Kiwifruit,' Ollie said as they passed. 'It grows really well here. They export almost all of it. But it's been a bit boom and bust lately. It's back on track now, but a lot of orchardists got out of it in the bad years,'

Ahead were high bare brown hills curving gradually upwards until they joined a steeper slope rising high above them. In places, there were green thickets of trees. It reminded her of parts of the Napa. And now, to the left and to the right, familiar rows of vines – hard-pruned, bare grey-brown sticks poised to shoot new stems in the spring along the miles of wire – marched away in soldierly lines up a gentle slope basking in the early afternoon sunshine. And what strong sunshine it was. Even with her Oakleys on, Alex didn't think she'd ever seen a sky so blue or a glare so bright. She'd heard about the ultraviolet rays in New Zealand, been warned to take plenty of sunblock, and now she could see why. Between the rows was a metre-wide strip of neatly mown green grass. For a moment she felt nostalgia for the bright yellow flowering mustard of the Napa, reaching as tall as the highest canes in the spring. There, they grew it as ground cover between the vines. Here it was quite different, with neat lines of bare earth under the vines interspersed with the manicured grass, stretching up to the dun-coloured hills and the azure sky beyond. It was stark but beautiful.

'Wow!' she said involuntarily.

'Yup. This is ours,' Ollie said. 'The big peak in front of us now is Hangman's Hill and that's our vineyard on the right. There's quite a history to it all. I'll tell you about it when we've more time. This slope,' he indicated with a sweep of his arm to the right of the Range Rover, 'is all pinot noir. Four hectares of it. Further on up the road, you'll see the chardonnay and riesling. We've had three great vintages out of the pinot so far. And several more out of the chardonnay and riesling. Last year's pinot won an award at the International Wine Challenge in London. There've been a few New Zealand reds winning awards lately. And now we're right up there with them.'

He turned round excitedly. Alex wished he would keep his eyes on the narrow road.

'I know. I read about it,' Alex said. 'The world is waking up to the fact that you make good wines here now. And not just sav. blancs and chardonnays either.'

'It took us Kiwis a long time to get the reds right,' Gen said. 'Our wine industry is still relatively young, even compared to the Napa Valley. And it's still quite small. But because our industry is so young, we can learn from the mistakes and experiences of everyone else. We're getting better every year. We're finally growing the right grapes for the climate.'

'Yeah, but it's still hard to get it right. That pinot can be a real minx of a grape. It's like a temperamental woman.'

Gen laughed. 'He loves that pinot out there. Sometimes I think he loves it more than he loves me. He spends more time looking after it!'

'Hey, that's not fair,' Ollie said, laughing too. 'Look there's the chardonnay. And behind it, you can just see the house.'

As he spoke, Alex spotted a large, white plastered house with a charcoal iron roof in the middle of the rows of vines. It looked almost new.

'Uh-oh,' Ollie groaned. 'You've got a welcoming party, Alex. The protesters are still with us.'

'Damn, I thought they'd go away without us there,' Gen said.

'They must have guessed Alex wanted to meet them,' Ollie said.

'Well, at least I'll know what I'm in for,' Alex said.

'I'll slow right down to go through them,' Ollie said. 'But don't say anything anyone. Just keep looking straight ahead.

He locked his door and Alex could hear all the doors click locked in unison.

13. Belle of the Ball

Richard was sitting by the fire in the parlour, curtains drawn against the cold May evening, waiting for Carrie to come out from the bedroom in her new ball finery. He was cradling a madeira and anticipating a tremendous night's entertainment. There was just one thing troubling him. He knew that he would be leaving town for good before the winter and, much as he liked Carrie, her lively company and her homely ways, he didn't see how she could accompany him. It was a dilemma – whether to tell her; how soon he would have to go – and it was hanging over him like the sword of Damocles. He imagined she would plead with him to stay. Then she would beg to go with him. But what sort of life would it be for a woman, traipsing from one town to the next, never being able to call one place home for more than a few weeks? Much as he would like to have a warm and comfortable home to retreat to wherever he went, he could see it wouldn't be fair on his poor beloved.

Carrie had taken his heart, that was for sure. He had never been captured like this before. He'd known a few women in his time, but Carrie was different, more vulnerable somehow, and more trusting. Despite working behind the bar at the Golden Age, where she must have seen the rougher side of life more than most women did, she remained innocent of the wicked ways of the world. The Golden Age had been her first job since leaving home; her whole world was confined to Mr Hewson's almost genteel hotel and, prior to that, her mother's impoverished home up at the Grey. It never seemed to have occurred to her that he might be engaged in illicit activities, that the ready money supply might come from ill-gotten gains.

'Oh, Carrie, what is to become of us?' he sighed, staring into the glowing embers in the grate.

He contemplated putting another log on the fire, but the carriage was due any minute and the house would be empty. He leaned forward from his chair and stirred the embers with the poker and tiny flames licked back to life.

He could see no solution to his problem. He would have to leave Carrie behind. And that raised again for him the problem of when to break the news to her. Not tonight, anyway, that much he knew. Tonight was Carrie's special night. But soon. He was running out of time.

He and Tom Kelly needed to get away from Hokitika. The police were becoming increasingly suspicious of their activities and he knew they'd been under surveillance ever since that close shave the other night when they'd been followed right to Carrie's door. It was difficult now to give them the slip and it would be impossible to carry out any further robberies under these circumstances. It was a damnable thing, he'd said to Kelly earlier that day, but they would just have to sit tight until either the police turned their attentions to somebody else or they got out of town.

'It's not as if we haven't got a pile of money to play with, Tommy boy,' he'd said. 'We might as well sit back and enjoy it for a change.'

'Nothing quite as rewarding as living off your ill-gotten gains, is there?' Kelly had replied.

'Indeed,' he'd said. 'And that bank won't miss what we've got. Why, with all the money the diggers are depositing these days, the few hundred pounds we got away with are just a drop in the ocean.'

But the night's takings from the diggers' camp were trivial compared with what they got from the Rosstown bank. A comparatively easy target, after all their planning and preparation, it had produced a fine reward, earning them some five hundred pounds in all.

The bank, in fact, had been a godsend. Until then, they'd had very lean pickings indeed. The pair had robbed some twenty people over the summer, but luck had been against them. It seemed everybody they'd held up had either just been to the bank and deposited their money and gold, or been down on their luck. The one exception was that hold-up of Mr Kerr on the road north of Rosstown. That had produced over two hundred pounds, once the gold had been cashed in. He'd had to wait a couple of weeks though before he dared approach a bank with it. There had been the usual fuss around town about poor Mr Kerr being robbed again, even with a trooper to protect him. The trooper had come to little harm, it turned out, which Richard realised was just as well. Much as he would have liked to finish the blackguard off for his impertinence, he knew it would have led to an enormous manhunt for the killers, whereas the robbery was just one of many that happened every week around the gold camps on the Coast.

That trick Tom had shown him at the diggers' camp, of slashing the bottom of each tent to get at the gold within, was a mighty fine ruse. They'd got away with it twice already, and would try it again before too long. It was risky, for sure. There was always the chance that the digger inside wasn't asleep, or that their fumbling hands would disturb and waken him. That first time, someone had seen them and raised the alarm. But the last time, there'd been no trouble. They'd escaped with ease. It was only when they stopped some distance from the camp to count their booty that they found the bags of gold contained more rocks than nuggets. He'd cursed mightily at the discovery.

'I reckon the diggers around here are getting cagey,' Kelly had said. 'There's a lot of bushrangers like us around. You always find people like us hanging around when there's gold being discovered in such quantities.'

He and Kelly, of course, were by no means the only ones, but he was proud of their record. Between them, they must have robbed more people than anyone else in the vicinity.

He smiled as he recalled their hold-up of the coach on the road several miles south of Hokitika. Kelly had given him a hard time over that pretty young lady he'd let keep her purse. But she'd put up such a compelling story about how it was all she had in the world because her parents were both dead and this was all they'd left her. Tom hadn't believed her for a minute, but something about the way she pleaded with them had softened Richard's heart and he'd let her away with it.

He'd had to make up for it at the next robbery, by being particularly hard on a hugely fat gentleman who had foul breath and behaved like a coward, hiding behind two of the ladies in the coach and trying to pretend he wasn't there.

His thoughts were disturbed by the clatter of horse hooves on the road outside. He stood and pulled back the heavy velvet parlour curtains to look out the window. The carriage had arrived, at precisely seven o'clock, to take them to the ball. It was a comparatively humble horse and dray, but Richard knew that to Carrie it would be a carriage nevertheless. He wanted tonight to be really special for her. He had remained at home all week, playing the dutiful partner, accompanying her on her mission to buy a ball gown and a new pair of satin shoes. He'd happily paid up nearly twenty pounds to make sure she looked the part.

'Carrie, your carriage is here,' he called towards the bedroom. She'd been in there for ages and he'd been ordered out long since.

She appeared at last, sailing though the door in quite the most fetching gown he'd ever seen on her. It was powder blue, with frills of darker blue material inlaid with peach-coloured roses and pearls. The slightly plunging neckline rose to reveal her pale, bare shoulders and around her throat was the triple row of large cream pearls he'd given her. She'd managed to fix her luscious red hair up on top of her head, with fronds of red curls escaping down the back and framing each side of her face. Her smile was radiant. Her eyes were sparkling.

'My goodness, Carrie. You look absolutely beautiful.' He was completely bowled over. He must be mad to contemplate leaving such a beautiful woman as this, he thought.

'Thank you, Richard. I'm feeling quite pleased myself with the result. I didn't know I had it in me! Do you know, this is the first time I've been able to get my hair to stay up like this. And the gown you bought me is divine. I feel like a princess tonight.'

He played the gallant gentleman and planned to make sure she would have the best night of her life. If he could do nothing else for her before he left, he could at least know that he'd given her a night to dream about when the cold winter set in and he was far away.

He hardly recognised the Union Hotel, they'd done such a good job of decorating it for the occasion. He'd heard that the wives of the volunteer firemen – whose brigade was to benefit from the money raised that night – had been working for months on theming and transforming the big high-ceilinged ballroom into a magical experience. Blue and gold streamers poured from the rafters, dazzling under the bright lights of myriad gas lamps. Gas lighting was comparatively new in Hokitika, and he was most impressed with the effect. In the middle of the room, in front of the dance floor, was an enormous silver fountain, with water cascading down into a little circular pool and sparkling under the bright lights.

'My, Carrie, this really is something,' he said.

Carrie was standing in one spot and staring around her, eyes wide open.

'I've never seen anything as fabulous as this before,' she said at last.

The orchestra was striking up a waltz.

'May I have the pleasure of this dance, Miss O'Neill?' he said formally, bowing to her.

She took his arm and they were off. One-two-three, he counted to himself, one-two-three. He was determined that Carrie would enjoy this last night out together, and that meant he would have to overcome that damnable limp in his left leg.

He managed to stay on the dance floor for the next three dances – a caledonian, a schottische and a quadrille, but when they swung into the lancers, he knew he'd have to bow out.

'Phew!' he said, mopping his brow with his handkerchief. 'I think I shall have to sit this one out, Carrie. I don't think I could keep up with the lancers.'

He'd spotted Kelly near the bar and brought him back to their seats, along with a drink of punch for Carrie and a beer for himself. With Tom and his latest paramour to entertain them, Richard managed to stay away from the dance floor until supper time. Kelly had proved an able and companionable accomplice, who'd mirrored Burgess's own sense of excitement and complete lack of fear at the prospect of a robbery. At first, he'd thought him related to that young Ned Kelly he'd heard Harry Power talk of in Glenrowan. But Tom was from a different Kelly family and had not long been out from England. He smiled as he watched him sweep Fanny around the dance floor, a much better dancer than he, unhindered by the injuries of leg-irons.

'Don't they make a handsome pair?' he said to Carrie, promising her the first dance after supper. When the dance floor was cleared, he escorted Carrie to a line of tables groaning with plate after plate piled with chickens and hams, breads, cheeses, chutneys, herrings and every savoury delicacy you could want. By the time they'd drunk their tea and consumed a delicately iced queen cake and Carrie had absented herself to go with the other ladies to powder her nose, he was relieved to see there were just a few dances left on the card.

True to his promise, Richard invited Carrie once again to the dance floor and led her in a varsoviana and an albert, doing his utmost to give the impression that he was an old hand at such things, when in fact his experience on the dance-floor was almost zero. The sort of fancy footwork he was good at was more suited to escaping from prison. There had been times in between his far too frequent visits to gaol when he'd lived the high life and managed to brush up on such niceties as dancing steps and table etiquette, but his last lessons – from an extremely charming young prostitute in Melbourne – seemed a long time ago as he struggled to remember where to put his feet as each dance put new demands on his memory.

When it came to the final waltz of the night, he pressed Carrie to him and swept her around the floor. She hadn't seemed to notice his discomfort or his struggles to remember the right moves. She was whirling around beside him in a dream, smiling happily as she had all night. It was going to be awfully hard to break it to her that he would soon have to go.

He managed to get another carriage to take them home after the ball and, as it drew up at their gate, he leapt out and helped Carrie down, catching her as she tripped on the high bottom step and fell into his arms.

'Careful, my little chick,' he said and, picking her up, carried her up the path, somehow managing to open the front door with her still in his arms. He swept her over the threshold, kicking the door shut behind him and continuing on into the bedroom where he deposited her gently on the bed with her head resting on the pillow.

'My lover,' he said, and bent down over her, caressing her breasts and slipping his other hand behind her neck, cradling her head. The red curls were tumbling victoriously out of their pins now, cascading around her shoulders. He could feel desire surge through him. He started to kiss her passionately, urgently.

'Oh, Richard, stop for a minute,' she said, pushing him away gently but assertively. 'There's something I need to tell you.'

There was something about the look on her face that was ominous. He could feel his ardour drain away at her words. He stopped what he was doing, withdrew his hands and sat on the side of the bed, waiting for her to continue. She pushed herself up on the pillow and faced him, resting on one elbow.

'I'm going to have your baby, Richard. I'm pregnant,' she said, her eyes shining with excitement.

'Good God,' was all he could say.

'I've suspected as much for a little while, but now I'm sure. I started feeling sick yesterday morning. And I haven't had my bleeding for two months now. I've seen the doctor twice and he confirmed it. Isn't it wonderful news?'

He didn't know what to say. It would be terrible for poor Carrie to have to bring up a baby on her own. He couldn't possibly stay with her. He had to leave town before the police worked out who he was and he was arrested and sent to gaol again. And it would be impossible for Carrie, especially in her newly delicate condition, to follow him all the way to Nelson, where he and Kelly planned to go. But of course, she didn't know any of this yet. And now would not be a good time to tell her. So he lied and did his best to cover up his true feelings and told her yes, of course he was delighted and how nice it would be to have a baby in the summer. She told him she thought the baby would be born in early November and she hoped it would be a boy and then she could call it Richard after his father. He could see it was turning into a flood of hopes and dreams and he could bear it no longer.

'Stop, Carrie,' he said, pressing his finger to her lips to stem the river of words, 'enough. We can talk about it in the morning. It's been a wonderful night, but I need to rest. I'm exhausted after all that dancing.'

His desire now quite gone, he stood up and started to undress.

'I knew you'd be annoyed,' she said quietly as his back was turned.

'Nonsense, my little chick,' he said, turning, trying to sound as if he meant it. 'I'm not annoyed. I'm pleased we're going to have a baby. But I'm tired. Let's talk about it tomorrow.'

After that bombshell, he'd not had the heart to tell her of their impending departure. And so it was, a few days later, that he and Tom had met Joseph Sullivan. They'd run into him in the main street of Hokitika, Tom recognising him from his old school days in London some twenty years previously. Kelly had introduced Richard as his brother, playing on their uncanny likeness and, as usual, getting away with it. The three had gone to the Rising Sun Hotel and played a few games of cribbage. Sullivan began losing heavily, and Richard noticed him starting to cheat. He'd wondered how long it would go unnoticed. Hokitika was no backwater when it came to cards. And sure enough, one of the people Sullivan was playing suddenly threw down his cards and accused him of cheating. Sullivan had grabbed the man by the collar and punched him, leading to a most unseemly brawl which had resulted in the three of them getting thrown out and told never to darken the doors of the Rising Sun ever again.

Richard had been furious. Not only did he dislike fighting like that in a hotel barroom, but he hated drawing attention to himself and Kelly. They were in enough danger of discovery as it was, without being arrested for disturbing the peace.

To make matters worse, he found out the next day that Sullivan had dobbed some other poor bastard in for his brawl, so that the innocent party had been arrested and held for two days until the charges were dropped for lack of evidence. Richard had a feeling that there was something about Joseph Sullivan that didn't bode well.

The Prince of Wales Opera House, in the heart of Hokitika, had been open for just two months and tonight Richard and Carrie were to occupy two seats in the dress circle to watch the special performance on Wednesday, May 23rd – the eve of the celebration of Queen Victoria's birthday. In honour of her birthday, the new gas lights in the Opera House would be turned on for the first time. Richard had read out from the *Times* that morning that the theatre was also going to unveil that night its new saloon, billiards and reading rooms attached to the dress circle, as well as its Cigar Divan, selling the finest Havana cigars. Richard was not a cigarette smoker, but in keeping with the image he'd adopted to match all the money he'd been dispensing, cigars were currently in vogue with him.

Tomorrow would be a holiday. All the shops would be shut, but there had been talk of a pleasure trip on a boat to the Grey, which Carrie thought sounded a lovely idea. Later in the evening, she planned to ask Richard if they could go.

She looked around her in awe. Before she'd met him, she realised, she would never have dreamed of coming to such a fancy place as this. She stood next to him in the large chandeliered foyer, sipping champagne like all the other couples and studying the beautiful gowns. She found it hard to accept this was really happening.

Suddenly, from somewhere overhead, a bell started ringing. It stopped after a few seconds, then started again, on and off, on and off.

'That must be telling us we're supposed to take our seats,' Richard said. She handed him her glass so he could return it to a nearby table, then he led her across the thick blue and gold carpet and through the doors of the dress circle.

Once inside the theatre, she gasped in disbelief. It was the most beautiful building she had ever been in. In front of her, deep blue velvet curtains hung down in front of the stage, over which stretched a high, gilded proscenium arch. Stretching back from the stage was a horseshoe-shaped circle, with royal boxes at either side. Already she could see the dignitaries of the town gathered in a box, looking very grand and behaving very self-consciously, no doubt aware that everyone was looking at them. As they walked forward and down the stairs to their seats, she could see the pit below, where all the ordinary people – like her, before she met Richard – would stand during the performance. It was filling up already, with the area in front of the stage completely packed out. The ceiling, high above her, held an enormous chandelier of gas lights and around its perimeter, painted on the moulded plaster, was a motif of a scene from Shakespeare's *A Midsummer Night's Dream*. Richard had told her about it while reading the paper this morning.

'Isn't it grand?' she said.

'Not bad for a little town in the colonies at the bottom of the world,' he said, smiling.

The evening's entertainment started with a special singing of the National Anthem, to mark the Queen's birthday, followed by a birthday tableau of Albion, Queen of the Sea. Carrie knew it was in honour of Queen Victoria and thought the costumes and poses very pretty, but couldn't fathom it at all. She'd not seen a tableau before. She looked at Richard for an explanation, but he was similarly perplexed. He caught her eye and shrugged his shoulders.

The main play of the evening was a performance of Alexander Dumas' *Catherine Howard* – a tragedy Carrie found gripping, if somewhat sensational. The well-known actress, Rosa Cooper – who Carrie had served on two occasions at the Golden Age – was equally convincing as Catherine the country girl, the loving wife and the ambitious young queen. In the second act, when the heroine awakened in the tomb and found she had been buried alive in the Vault of the Northumberlands, Carrie had to pull her handkerchief out of her reticule and wipe tears from her eyes, she was so moved. The final scene, in the Tower of London, was almost more than she could bear.

As the curtain fell, everybody clapped and cheered and called out for more. But the curtains remained closed and the lights on the chandelier were illuminated again. She declined another drink at interval, choosing instead to remain in her seat and watch, fascinated, all the people – above her in the gallery, or the gods as they called them, below in the pit, and in front in the fancy boxes. Richard excused himself and said he'd just pop out for a few moments and inspect the new Cigar Divan and billiards room.

The second half of the evening's entertainment was a light comedy called *The Honeymoon*. The English actors who'd taken the lead roles just moments before in the tragedy were now transformed into romantic comedy figures, with Rosa Cooper playing Julia, the love-smitten maiden this time. Carrie was impressed that she could make the transition so effortlessly, and indeed that she could remember her lines for one and sometimes two different parts in different plays every night. When the performance concluded, Carrie clapped and stamped her feet along with everyone else.

'I'm glad you've enjoyed the evening,' Richard said, as her helped her out of her seat and up the stairs.

'It's been as good as the night of the ball,' she said happily. 'You've been so good to me, Richard. I've never been so happy.'

There was a long queue to collect their coats, such was the crowd at the theatre. And then there was an even longer queue for a ride home, so they walked instead, with Richard putting his hand under Carrie's arm, their breath making small pockets of steam in the cold night air.

Carrie waltzed through the front door humming one of the haunting melodies the orchestra had played during the interval, feeling as if she could float on air.

'Thank you, Richard,' she said turning back to see if he was coming in and closing the door. Now that it was nearing the end of May, the nights could get below freezing, and it felt as if it were close to zero tonight. 'It's bitterly cold out there. Let's see if I can stir up the fire and warm the room again.'

'Don't do it on account of me, my little chick,' Richard said. 'I've to be going out again soon, to meet with Tom Kelly.'

'What? You can't go out now! It's past midnight. What on earth can you hope to achieve out there at this time of night?'

'Nothing you need concern yourself about. I shan't be gone long.' He locked the front door and headed through the parlour door to the bedroom. 'I must get changed out of these fancy clothes.'

Carrie shrugged at his departing back. She'd long since stopped trying to prevent him going out on his missions. She knew he wouldn't take the slightest notice of her protestations. Instead, she went through to the kitchen, where the coal range could be easily stirred back to life, to make a cup of tea and warm her toes. These tight, high evening pumps were all very well for making your feet look dainty and fashionable, but they pinched your toes terribly. Her feet were cramped and freezing. She dug a shovel full of coal out of the scuttle, opened the damper and then the lid on the firebox, stirred the embers with the poker, and tossed the coal in, wiping her hands together to get rid of the dust from the handle.

'There, that should fix you,' she said to the range. Using the thick sacking heatproof cloth, she pulled the kettle forward on the hob, then sat down with a grateful sigh and removed her shoes. 'Aaaah, that's better,' she said, rubbing her aching feet. It occurred to her that Richard might want a hot drink before he departed, so she reluctantly pushed herself up out of the chair and opened the door to the bedroom.

'Fancy a hot drink before you go, Richard?' she said as she popped her head around the door, then shrieked in dismay when she saw him in his rough trousers. He was just about to put on his shirt and she could see two handguns tucked into the back of his belt – one on each side. But it wasn't the guns that caused Carrie to cry out. For the first time, she'd been able to see his back. Normally he'd kept it covered, even when making love. But now she could see lines of deep scars criss-crossed on his back, ugly testament to what must have been many, many lashes from a switch, and to one side another old wound making a deep gouge in his badly marked flesh.

'What is it?' he asked impatiently.

'Your back! Those scars!' she gasped.

'Oh, that. That's what they do to you at sea,' he said. 'That happened on the ship on my way out from England. I prefer to forget about it.' He turned away from her and continued dressing. Carrie could see that the subject was closed.

'And you've got *two* guns in your belt.'

'Very observant, my little chick. And what's the matter with that? Haven't you seen a gun before?'

'Yes, yes of course… But two… But I didn't think…'

'You didn't think I'd carry guns? Why ever not? You're being very naïve, my sweet, if you think a man can be safe out at night without some means of protection.'

'But most men don't go out at night,' she protested. 'At least not at this Godforsaken hour. Most men are tucked up in bed asleep by now.'

'Well, I'm not *most* men,' he said, continuing to get dressed. 'I've promised to meet Kelly in town in ten minutes, and meet him I shall.'

'Have you ever shot anyone with a gun?' She couldn't help but blurt it out.

He put his coat on, covering the offending weapons, and turned to her with a look of condescension.

'Now really, Carrie, why do you ask me that? Do you really want to know?' He walked up to her and rested his hands on her shoulders. 'What would you do if I said yes, now? Would you cry out in alarm and faint away? And if I said no, you probably wouldn't believe me. There's no point in answering it.'

She looked into his eyes, steely blue behind his half smile.

'I suppose so,' she conceded, 'but I do worry about you so.'

'I know you do, my little chick, I know you do, and I love you for it.'

And with that astonishing remark, he kissed her lightly on the cheek and went out the door. Carrie stood rooted to the spot for a second, touching her cheek, unable to believe what he'd just said. He'd never mentioned the word 'love' before. Did this mean he was coming around to the idea of marriage? She heard a chair scrape in the kitchen. He would be putting on his boots, which had been drying on the rack above the range. She realised she'd better go to him if she wanted to catch one last glimpse of him before he left.

'Oh, Richard,' she said as she came into the room, which was warmer already, now that the fire had revived. He finished tying his last shoelace, stood and walked to the door, picking up his hat from the peg. 'Oh, Richard,' she said, plucking up the courage to say it, 'I love you too.'

He laughed. *He laughed!*

'You're a funny little thing,' he said and, with a farewell kiss – this time a proper one, full on the mouth and with some passion, albeit brief. Then he opened the door, put on his hat, and was gone.

The next day, the Queen's Birthday holiday that she had been hoping to spend with Richard on a pleasure trip to the Grey, she spent instead on her own, with nothing to do but amuse herself. Everything was shut, and the public amusements would have been abominable without a partner. She felt unusually lonely, as if this time Richard had really left.

Two mornings later, there was still no sign of him – a fact that did not at first distress her, as she was used to his lengthy trips away.

Early in the afternoon, she walked into town and picked up a small piece of meat for her dinner (with enough for Richard just in case he returned), some butter and some freshly baked bread. As she passed the bookseller's that morning's *Times* billboard caught her eye.

'EARLY MORNING ROBBERY OF DIGGERS' CAMPSITE,' it said. She went in and bought a paper then, once out in the street, opened it up and searched for the story. She found it on Page Three, halfway down the page, under *The West Coast Times* banner line. It said:

Dwellers in tents situated on the outskirts of the town may take warning from the following daring robbery committed the night before last at a tent close to Gibsons Tramway. There were at the time two men asleep inside and one of them was awakened by feeling a sharp jerk at the head of his stretcher, but as it was not repeated, he took no further notice and went to sleep again. In the morning however, the tent presented a very sorry spectacle as it was cut half round the bottom and up one of the sides; and when Kenney, one of the inmates, proceeded to dress himself, he found that his trousers were missing. This was more serious, as his purse happened to be in one of the pockets and it was very evident that both had been burglariously abstracted. The Camp, of course, was visited by the Police and information given but no trace of the thieves has been discovered. However, the modus operandi of the robbers encourages the Police to believe that they are the very same pair of armed rogues who held up the Rosstown Bank last month.

The Police now have a fair idea who these men are and are pursuing a line of inquiry.

The evidence was gathering enough force to be conclusive, she admitted to herself. Richard and Thomas were outlaws who robbed banks and people of money and gold, and who were now wanted by the police. That could well mean she might never see him again. She felt like crying with shame and desperation, but willed herself to be strong. She could feel the eyes of everyone in the street upon her. She must not show how upset she was, especially after reading about the robbery; people might suspect. Folding the newspaper with some haste, she thrust it into her bag and returned home.

She'd only just had time to remove her coat and hat and light the parlour fire when there was a knock at the door. An urchin she did not recognise as being a local lad was standing there with a letter in his hand. She took it from him and was just about to ask how he'd come by it when he took off at such speed she had no chance of catching him.

Closing the door behind her, she went over to the fire and, settling in one of the big wing chairs, studied the hand. It was not Richard's. Turning it over, she slipped her finger under the flap on the thick creamy envelope, breaking the red, waxy seal.

'Dear Miss O'Neill,' she read.

'I have been asked by my client, Mr Richard Burgess, to furnish you with the enclosed bank draft for three hundred and seventy pounds.'

She nearly dropped the letter in surprise. She looked inside the envelope and there, sure enough, was another piece of paper – a large, thick, official looking document, stating that as the bearer of this bank draft she, Miss Caroline O'Neill, was entitled to cash it for the sum of three hundred and seventy pounds. It took her a moment or two for this to sink in. She read it again. It seemed an astronomical amount of money, more than she'd ever dreamt of having. But, back to the letter:

'Mr Burgess has asked me to tell you that he regrets he will be unable to rejoin you in Hokitika again as he has had to leave with Mr Thomas Kelly to attend to some urgent business in Nelson. He hopes that you will be able to join him there as soon as possible.

'In the event that you are able to sell the house in Hokitika and move north, he has asked that you bring several items with you that he has left behind. He says you will know which items of clothing to bring, but he has specifically mentioned he would like you to bring his greatcoat and the photograph he had taken of you with him at the Grand Ball.'

'On behalf of Mr Burgess, I remain your humble servant,

'Arthur Hackett, Attorney at Law.'

14. Protest

At the entrance to the Darbys' vineyard, on either side of a pair of ornate charcoal wrought iron gates – inset with patterns of bunches of grapes and surrounded by a curving white plastered fence – was a crowd of protesters. Alex could see about twenty men and women of all ages, some of them with children and pushchairs. Several carried placards saying 'Dump the Dump' and 'No Landfill in our Valley.'

'There are several more wine-growers up the road, some of them with quite big wineries,' Ollie said as he slowed down to a crawl, careful to avoid the throng, which was now surging forward towards the car. Alex felt a tiny grip of fear in her stomach. 'They think that having a landfill here will put people off buying their wines or their grapes. We've tried to talk to them, but they just won't listen.'

Suddenly there was a loud bang on her passenger door and Alex only just stopped herself from swearing at the shock of it. Ignoring Ollie's warning to keep her eyes straight ahead, she looked out her window and saw a young man, probably the same age as herself, with a look of absolute outrage twisting his face as he thumped the door.

'We don't want your dump here,' he was shouting in between thumps.

The noise woke Claudia, who started wailing loudly in fright.

'Sorry,' Ollie said quietly as he manoeuvred through the crowd. 'Be over in a minute.'

They inched forward without speaking further. Even Isobel was scared into silence. Claudia's crying crescendoed as the thumping continued.

Once through the gates, Ollie picked up a remote control and aimed it at a box on the side of the drive. Slowly the gates closed behind them.

'Thank God that's over,' Gen said. Alex turned and noticed that she was clutching Isobel's hand tightly with one hand and was stroking Claudia's hair with the other, trying to soothe her with words that were drowned out by the baby's deafening bellowing. Alex winced. Babies sure could make a lot of noise. Not that she could blame Claudia for it. She'd felt a bit like bellowing herself when the young man had banged on her door.

'I hope you can do something, Alex,' Ollie said loudly over the din. 'We're at our wits' end.'

'It's scary, isn't it,' Alex said as the car sped away from the noisy protest towards the house. 'It's not easy to get them to understand, but I'll give it my best shot.'

She looked behind as the protesters diminished into the distance, small blurry stick figures dancing around the closed iron gate. Ollie glanced at her.

'They'll probably go home now they've confronted us,' he said. 'They like to make their point to us at least once a day. But they're not obsessive. They don't spend all day there.'

Outside, the neat rows of winter canes had given way to a wide, circular entranceway and they pulled up in front of the house with its square-columned portico. The glimpse she'd seen of it up the road was now magnified into a two-storey, startlingly white, sprawling family home. An eight-foot-high panelled wooden door was flanked by tall terracotta pots containing small orange trees set on ochre tiles. On each side of the terrace were borders of rose bushes and lavender, emerging from their winter slumber with new green shoots. But the neat architectural lines were sharply broken by a clutter of children's toys – a red and yellow plastic trike, a white cane dolls' pram spilling over with bright pink quilts and dolls' clothes, and beside it a half-dressed Barbie doll, its hair cut ragged, its semi-naked torso lying on the paving stones with its legs at a dislocated angle.

'Home sweet home,' Gen announced, climbing over the crying Claudia and starting to unbuckle car seats. Claudia seemed to recognise the familiarity or at least the general feeling of security regained and consequently, Alex was pleased to observe, cut down on the wailing, subsiding into intermittent sniffling.

Alex jumped down from her seat and went to help Ollie with her bags, grabbing her laptop, carpetbag and suit-carrier. With her suitcase in one hand and Isobel's hand in the other, Ollie managed to open the front door and Alex was besieged by a small, white, fluffy, barking dog.

'That's Tess,' he called to Alex as he disappeared through the door then stuck his head out again. 'Do come in,' he added.

'Can I help with something?' Alex asked Gen.

'No thanks, we're all sorted here,' she replied, clutching Claudia under one arm and a carrybag in the other hand.

The dog was running around her ankles, still barking, but Alex couldn't see how she could deliver a swift kick without Gen noticing, so concentrated on picking her way across the tiles to avoid standing on the snapping, yapping terrier. Dogs, children, babies, protesters – what next? she wondered. As long as there weren't any birds. She hated feathered creatures. They gave her the creeps.

'I'll show you to your lodgings. Caroline Cottage, it's called,' Ollie said, leading the way with her big heavy case as if it were no weight at all. 'I hope you don't mind. But Gen has her hands full now.' She followed him down a long hallway, hung with a glimpse of beautiful paintings, until he stopped at a cream doorway and pushed it open with his toe. It opened onto a wide, sunny courtyard which they crossed. At one end of the yard Alex could see a row of toolsheds and open-doored garages, one housing a tractor and large sprayer resembling the one in David's toolshed, as well as another funny-looking machine she didn't recognise. There was also a single row of small vats for making wine. She followed Ollie through an old iron gate and up a narrow gravel pathway, where he stopped and put down her bag.

'This is Caroline Cottage,' he said. 'It used to be Gen's grandparents' home. Gen's family has owned this land for five generations. It wasn't until her mum and dad built a new house up the road that the cottage stopped being the family home. Her Mum and Dad are still in their new house. We'll take you to meet them tomorrow. We've just finished building the big house next door, me and Gen and the girls. But we didn't want the cottage to fall into disrepair like so many other old farmhouses, so we've done it up and use it for farmstays, for guests and for special people like you.'

Alex had never seen anything so romantic and quaint. It was a very small, square, white two-storey weatherboard house in immaculate condition, with a verandah in front and a flowering blue wisteria stretching across its porch. The door was painted the same colour as the wisteria, and its coloured leadlight windows drew her forward to see in. To either side of her, as she walked, were beds of rose bushes. A magnolia tree was in bloom above the path, its petals sending down a strong heady perfume. It looked just like one of those pictures on a schmaltzy greeting card. The only thing missing was the cat on the doorstep.

Ollie had picked up her bag and was now on the verandah, opening the front door.

'Please come in,' he called, waiting for her to catch up. 'It's all yours now. I hope you like it.'

Alex followed him across creaking floorboards through the front door and nearly tripped up over her bag, deposited just inside.

The door opened straight into a living room, which was surprisingly large given the size of the cottage. Its cream walls were hung – like the hallway in the modern house – with intriguing works of art. In front of her, on the far wall, was an old marble fireplace with a new gas fire installed. On either side of the fire were two plump sofas, covered in a striking mauve and green floral pattern, with mauve braided cushions. In the middle was a glass coffee table on which stood a vase of fat mauve-pink peonies. The floor was a light polished wood, covered with rugs, some of them Persian. There were a couple of antique chairs, an old writing desk, and a large bookcase. In one corner she spotted a mahogany console, which she suspected housed the TV and video she'd been promised. She'd need them to follow the news.

'Through here is the kitchen – a gas cooker, microwave, dishwasher, all you could need. And Gen's put a few things in the cupboards for you, to keep you going.'

Alex crossed the lounge and entered the kitchen behind Ollie. It was, indeed, everything she could wish for and looked remarkably modern for such an old house. The only sign of its age was a high arching fire surround over the gas cooker. Alex figured that must have been where the old coal range would have burned night and day to keep the water hot and the bread baked.

'The main bedroom is upstairs,' Ollie said, ducking back into the lounge. He retrieved the suitcase from beside the front door and headed for a narrow wooden staircase to the side of the room. She climbed the steep limewashed and lacquered steps behind him. At the top, she turned sharp right and entered the room to the left that Ollie was indicating with a sweep of his hand.

It was very spacious and designer-looking, with a high arched cathedral ceiling sloping half-way down to the floor. The walls, ceiling and furniture were painted cream, including the bedhead, bedside table, lampshades, armchair and coffee table. In the corner, across at an angle and in the same place as the one downstairs in the lounge, stood an old fireplace. It was quite small, with pale green and blue tiles all around it and a narrow black iron grate over clean white tiles that had clearly not seen a fire for many years. To her left was a big double iron-headed bed covered with a heavily patterned floral bedspread in shades of wisteria and cornflower blue. To her right, matching curtains framed a gabled window with a view to die for. As far as the eye could see was a panorama of vines leading upwards to a circle of variegated hills, misty and vaguely defined in the afternoon haze. It looked just like the label she'd seen on the Cloudy Bay chardonnay in that restaurant in San Francisco.

'This must be one of the best views I've seen from any room that I've stayed in,' she said, depositing her bags on the floor and walking to the window.

'It's pretty amazing, isn't it,' Ollie agreed, lifting her heavy case onto a low table in the corner next to an old-fashioned free-standing wardrobe. In the oval mirror attached to its single cream door Alex could see Ollie's reflection. 'I sometimes have to pinch myself that it's real. Although Gen's family has owned this land for over a hundred and thirty years, it's only in the last ten years that there's been anything other than sheep and cattle. We bought twelve hectares off them ten years ago and planted grapes. They all told Gen she was mad. They said she'd be pulling out the vines and bringing back the cattle in five years. But we're still going strong. It's not going to make us rich – until we sell the land – but it's a good living and it's the most wonderful thing, to know that your grapes have made one of the best wines in the world.'

'It's a rare gift,' Alex said quietly, savouring the view and thinking of the award-winning wines the insignificant-looking vines in front of her might soon produce.

'We've both taken it very seriously,' Ollie said. 'I studied oenology in New Zealand and Gen studied it at Charles Sturt University in Sydney. We both come from this part of the world, but we never met until we were both working at wineries in France, of all places.'

'What about the Napa? Did you ever go there?'

'No, we've never made it to the States. We'd love to go though. And now the money's not so tight, we might be able to, although I don't know that we could take Claudia and Isobel yet – at least not if we wanted to see anything!'

After the assault on her ears in the car earlier on, Alex knew exactly what he meant. But she thought it prudent not to say so.

'So you're growing pinot and chardonnay and a bit of riesling?' she said instead.

'Yes, that's what grows best in this area. But it's the pinot I love the best. We're trying champagne this year. From pinot noir. We don't make it here. As you know, we sell almost all of our grapes to the top wineries in Nelson. We only keep enough to make a bit for ourselves and to keep our hand in. But there's a French winery not far away that makes beautiful champenoise, and they're letting me in on the process with wine made from our grapes. I go down there every week to turn the bottles. I'll take you there one day.'

'That'd be great. But first we have to sort out the little problem at your gate. Not to mention the wider problem of what the locals think about you.'

'I do so hope you can,' Ollie said. 'Anyway, I'd better finish the guided tour. There's an ensuite through there,' Ollie said, pointing at a closed door. 'And around the corner here is a computer desk and office set up for you. Feel free to log in to our system any time. I'll show you how. You can make calls and work from here whenever you like.'

Alex followed him to the far side of the room where a plain cream shelf had been strung across the gap between window and wall to make a wide desk. On it sat a laptop, a printer and a pile of papers.

'The laptop works off the network and, of course, is also perfectly portable so you can keep in touch wherever you are,' Ollie continued. 'The main office is across the yard in another building. There's a spare desk there you can use too. Just take your pick.'

'It's fabulous,' Alex said. 'Thank you so much. You've thought of everything. And I just love the house. I've always wanted to live in a little cottage with roses in the garden. But they're not exactly two-a-penny in California.

'It's nice, isn't it? A lot better than when Gen's family used to live here. This whole upstairs area was three bedrooms, so you can imagine how cramped it was with four children. But Gen's done a great job. She got the same architect who did the big house to do the make-over. And Gen chose the fabrics. She wanted it to be in keeping with the old-world charm of the place.

'I love the old fire surround.'

'It's an original. It belongs to the cottage,' Ollie replied. 'You'd pay a fortune for something in such good condition nowadays. But don't try to light a fire. We've blocked up the chimney to prevent draughts. It's just for ornamentation now. There's a wall heater over there, and a heater in the bathroom too, so you won't have to worry about the cold. It can get quite chilly at night here.'

'D'you get frosts here?'

'Unfortunately, yes. Bud burst is usually in September and, if we get a frost then, it can wreck the whole season,' he said.

'They were the bane of David's life in the Napa every spring,' Alex said. 'He used to turn the irrigators on at night if a frost was in the air. Mostly it seemed to work.'

'We've been pretty lucky so far. The frosts tend to come at the end of the growing season rather than the beginning, which doesn't really matter. In fact, we got a really lovely botrytised riesling one year after a frost. Remind me to give you a taste sometime.' Ollie paused. 'I must stop waffling on. Gen's always telling me I talk too much. And you'll be wanting to unpack.' He turned away from the window and its view of the vineyard. Alex could detect in him the same passion for the vines that David had.

'Not at all. I love hearing about your craft. The more I know, the more help I'll be.'

'That's true.' Ollie was now standing in the doorway, facing her. He raised his arm in a wave. 'You should have everything you need now to be reasonably self-contained. You'll be able to cook for yourself if you want. But we do hope that you'll dine with us whenever you feel like it. We want you to feel one of the family. Please join us for dinner tonight. The girls will have eaten early and will be in bed by dinnertime, so you might be able to get a word in!'

'I'll look forward to that.' Alex laughed at the recollection of the three-way conversation on the way here. 'You're very welcoming. You're making me feel right at home.'

Ollie departed downstairs and she heard the click of the front door as he left, followed by the crunch of his footsteps on the gravel path. Alex looked at her watch. It was four o'clock New Zealand time. A couple of hours before dinner. Back home it would be yesterday morning. She wondered what Lucian would be doing now and if he was still in prison awaiting trial. Would he be thinking of her as he awoke to face another day behind bars? She doubted it somehow.

'Stop it,' she told herself sharply. 'He's history.'

She turned away from the window to unpack, carrying her toiletries through to the bathroom, which resembled the ensuite of a five-star hotel with an enormous marble spa bath, a separate glass-walled shower, a double vanity and wide expanse of marble floor. The sight of the shower reminded her that she badly needed one after spending the best part of twenty-four hours travelling. Not particularly fastidious about her toilet or appearance, Alex could at least see she'd be more appealing to her hosts at dinnertime if she'd had a shower. And what a shower it was, with gleaming sliver jets lined up in two corners, an array of expensive brand shampoo, conditioner and body wash on the shelf, and thick

Egyptian cotton cornflower blue and deep purple towels hung over the cream heated towel rail.

The cottage renovation must have cost a small fortune, she realised, even in New Zealand dollars. She wondered where Gen and Ollie got all the money – for doing up the cottage, for the enormous new architect-designed house they lived in, for all the new gear she'd seen in the shed, not to mention the acres and acres of neat staked vines stretching out from her bedroom window as far as she could see and snaking up the base of Hangman's Hill. She was intrigued by at the name. She must ask Ollie what the history was that he'd alluded to.

She caught her reflection in the Hollywood-style bathroom mirror, surrounded by lights, and did an impromptu twirl, imagining herself as a movie star on location. But she had to laugh at herself for being so silly. Her hair was a mess, like she'd just got out of bed, and her clothes were totally rumpled. She must get into that shower. As she laid down her things on the vanity, she gave herself a squirt of Issy Miyake in a vain attempt to remove the odours of long-distance travel, then returned to the bedroom to hang up her clothes in the little old-fashioned wardrobe, finding it hard to see properly inside. She shivered involuntarily. It felt weird, as if it belonged to another era and another person. Which it did, really. She must ask Gen where it had come from. It was quaint, but it wasn't terribly practical.

Her innate desire to make a home wherever she went – and she knew there had been far too many nests to build in far too many hotels and guest rooms – drove her to unpack her bag, put her clothes away in the wardrobe and drawers, and arrange all her other things around the room, to give it some semblance of familiarity. Then she would usually ring room service – not because she was hungry or particularly needed anything, but because she liked the ritual of it all and having someone to talk to, albeit briefly. But there was no room service here – not unless she wanted to do it herself.

The Barbara Kingsolver novel she planned to read next, she placed on the bedside table beside a bud vase filled with pansies. The motivational PR book she was reading – *Shameless Marketing for Brazen Hussies* – she tucked underneath the Kingsolver. It was good, but she needed something lighter, and *The Prodigal Summer* was gripping. The slinky blue star-covered PJs, still neatly folded, that had cost so much money last year at Bloomingdales, she slipped under the crisply ironed pillowcase. She might be disorganised and messy in her personal appearance, but her things were always immaculately tidy, which gave her a feeling of security and belonging, no matter where she was or whose place she slept in.

Her large collection of shoes – she never seemed to be able to leave many out – she arranged neatly in the bottom of the little wardrobe, finding she needed to lay one set of pairs upon the other, there was so little room. She counted them – walking shoes for getting around the vineyard, sandals for the Nelson beaches she'd read about and three pairs of heels for the night life she planned to enjoy, including the spiky-heeled black pumps she'd bought a year ago for almost a week's pay, two pairs of court shoes for work, a pair of medium-heeled ankle-high winter boots for when it was cold, two pairs of flatties in startlingly bright colours (hot pink and lime green for one, bright blue, red, yellow and orange flowers on the other) and two pairs of slides, one black, the other tan. Twelve, she counted. Better than last time she'd travelled overseas and found herself unpacking fifteen pairs. Mind you, she'd worn them all. You could never have too many shoes, she told herself, as she shut the wardrobe door for the second time after rearranging the shoes again so it could close.

Unpacking had only taken ten minutes. Showering – if she could manipulate the faucets on that fearsome-looking shower – would take another ten. But she had a whole two hours before dinner. What would be the best use of her time? A spa bath instead of a shower? Phone home on the cell phone? A sleep? She decided instead to catch up on all the reading material about the Nelson area and the pile of press clippings she'd seen smudging the otherwise pristine desk, and see if there were any emails in her mailbox. The spa bath could wait. Maybe while she was here she'd be lucky enough to find someone good enough to share it with.

'Fat chance,' she told herself and, picking up her towelling bathrobe, which she'd left draped on the bed, she headed for the bathroom to tame the multi-headed monster shower.

Half an hour later, refreshed and clean, all traces of planes and airline food scrubbed away, Alex set up her laptop on the smooth cream desk and clicked onto Outlook Express. There was an email from Lacey about client stuff – that could wait a bit – and a longer one from Magda.

'Another one bites the dust,' it was headed. She could imagine what that was about. Magda tended to be blunt. She opened it up.

'Lover boy has gone to jail,' Magda wrote. 'How sad!'

Magda never did like Lucian. She was the one who had led the chorus of calls for Alex to get rid of him after he'd moved in.

'This morning's *LA Times* says Lucian James Gray was sentenced to six years in prison after pleading guilty to malicious damage of computer equipment. Word has it he plea bargained his way into a lighter sentence by pleading guilty. They were ready to throw the book at him. Six years is getting off lightly for what he did. It's not long enough, if you ask me. Mind you, the company whose system he planted the worm in can still sue him for damages. Apparently it cut off all their oil exploration ships, putting them out of action for upwards of two weeks. One of them even lost power in a storm. It got pretty dangerous, according to the *Times*.

'So you've had a lucky escape, sweetie. Count yourself lucky.'

Magda would know what Lucian could have expected as a sentence, as most of her clients were in the hi-tech/IT area and computer crime was rife. Whether it was accessing porn over the internet at work or something more far-reaching, like planting a time bomb in the system as Lucian had done, Magda seemed to come across it almost every day. The email went on to gossip about friends in common and client headaches she was having.

Alex finished reading and closed it. She'd reply to them all later. Then she noticed one from Kate. It was a short one, so there would just be enough time to read it before she was due at the house.

Kate had forgiven her – just – for abandoning her on her father's birthday. Now she was reporting back about another family gathering, this time at her place, when Max had come round with Trish and Annelise for dinner after church on Sunday. Kate had pulled out all the stops.

'I was determined to turn on the sort of designer meal that "Patrice" would expect,' Kate wrote, describing the dishes she'd spent the day preparing all Saturday – in between taking the kids to sports and to their friends. 'Of course, she turned her nose up at the marinated barbecued lamb. "Oh, I don't eat lamb nowadays," she sniffed. I could have killed her. Then after we'd eaten, Georgia took Annelise up to her room to play CDs. That Lise, she's only a year older than Georgia, but she's 12 going on 20. She scoffed at Georgia's taste. "Oh, I don't like those," she sniffed, just like her mother. "They're for little kids." Georgia was so upset. By the time they left to go home, I was ready to push them out the door.'

Poor Kate. She'd always been tolerant of other people's foibles. But it would take the patience of a saint to put up with Patrice's rudeness.

Alex closed down the laptop and returned to the bedroom to get ready for an evening with the Darbys.

15. Setting up House

With an extra shove, Carrie managed to push open the heavy front door to the cottage she'd just purchased. Ninety pounds she'd paid at the Nelson solicitor's office, where she'd collected the title and keys, along with directions for finding the place, then returned to the coach depot where she'd left her three big trunks and caught the midday mail carriage south towards Hope. The cottage was bigger than she'd expected – of cream weatherboard, two storeys high, with wide sash windows set in dark green frames and a garden as yet unformed and only sparsely planted. But it was far enough out of town, at the end of a long country road with only a handful of neighbours; she hoped nobody would notice Richard's frequent absences and nocturnal comings and goings. She was sure that he would rejoin her once she managed to find him – hadn't she brought his greatcoat and boots and other belongings, as he'd asked? As soon as she was settled in, she resolved, she would return to Nelson and resume her search.

'Anybody here?' she called uncertainly. The solicitor had told her the tenants should be out by midday and she wasn't sure if they'd got the message. But there was only the sound of the wind whistling around the gables and rattling the windows.

'Where do you want your trunks left, *Frau* O'Neill?' the countryman asked with a thick German accent. Carrie had hired a local farmer to bring her and her luggage the three-mile journey from Hope to her new home. It hadn't taken her long to find out that a large number of the farmers around the district were from Germany.

'Inside please,' she said. 'Just here in the front room will do.'

The farmer and his lanky blond son puffed and heaved at her three big trunks, the receptacles of all she held dear in the world. The wealth of crockery and china, cutlery and silver, bedlinen and kitchenware – everything she'd had in the house Richard had bought for her in Hokitika just a few months ago – she'd wrapped carefully in newspaper and brought with her on the coach. The furniture had been sold. With the proceeds of that and the house she would have plenty of money left over to buy more once she'd settled in. In the meantime, she'd arranged with the solicitor for the vendor to leave some bedding.

'Thank you, Mr Mueller,' she said when the now sweating farmer and his son had deposited the third and last trunk on the floor. She handed him an envelope containing enough money for the journey and his labours.

'*Frau* O'Neill,' he said again, '*Guten tag.*' He tipped his cap before clambering up on the cart with his son and prodding the carthorse into motion.

Carrie stood still for a moment, watching them depart, captivated by the view. For miles and miles, as far as she could see, stretched a large, green plain, patched in places with pasture and crops, in others with thick bush and trees. And far away, across the other side, a range of dark green mountains filled the horizon, shrouded in rain cloud. To her right in the distance she could see the sea, sparkling in the early afternoon sunshine. She took in a deep breath and smiled. The air smelled sweet and dry after the damp mustiness of Hokitika and the brisk wind and bright sunshine was a tonic after a day and a night travelling on a cramped steamer. The entire journey she'd been sick, until it felt as though there was nothing left inside her to bring up. She didn't know if it was the last vestiges of morning sickness or the swollen sea that had made her so ill, but she could put all that behind her now she'd arrived at her new home. With one last deep breath, she soaked up the sunshine and the view, then turned inside and shut the door behind her. It was time to investigate the house and get it ready for her beloved.

As her eyes gradually became accustomed to the dimness of the room after the bright light outside, she could make out a parlour with a fireplace directly in front and a polished wooden floor. The walls were covered in a heavily patterned wallpaper and the door surrounds, picture rail and skirting were of a rich lacquered oak. Above her was a kerosene lamp hanging beneath a frosted glass cover. To her left was a narrow wooden staircase following the far wall upward to the top floor, where she knew there were three bedrooms. To her right, a big polished wooden door led to another room.

She opened it to reveal a kitchen, taking up the depth of the house and dominated by a large coal range set into a high arched fire surround. For the first time she noticed the cold. There was only a small window facing west. Away from the sun's warmth, the kitchen was chilly. She would have to light the fire anyway to heat the water and cook some food. In search of coal and firewood, Carrie opened the back door and was again overawed by the view, this time behind the house. The land sloped gradually at first and then more steeply up a high hill, most of it covered in bush. Her land, she'd been told and had seen marked on the title, extended about twenty yards uphill, as far as the clearing, and then for several acres on either side of the house around the brow of the hill into a valley. A few yards to her right was the outhouse and nearby, a hand pump and a shed which, on closer investigation, housed a coal bin containing enough coal to last her a week or two. Next to it was stacked a pile of neatly chopped wood. She silently thanked the previous residents for their kindness, gathered an armful and carried it inside, returning with the coalscuttle and shovel to collect the coal.

'There, that should warm things up a bit,' she said as she shut the lid and checked the damper was fully open. Sure enough, in a few moments, it was burning brightly. Hoping that she'd timed it right, she opened the lid again, shook on a load of coal from the scuttle, stirred it around with the poker, then shut it again and crossed her fingers for luck. You never knew with those pesky things.

While waiting for it to make up its mind if it would go, she picked up the old black iron kettle that had been left behind on the hob and went outside to fill it from the water pump. It was stiffer and heavier to lift than the pump she'd been used to at Hokitika. For a moment, she wished Richard was with her to help her with such things. All in good time, she told herself, as she returned inside and set the kettle on the hob.

That morning, she'd inquired in several hotels and emporiums in Nelson for Richard but had not been able to gather any intelligence as to whether he was there. Besides, she realised, he may well have entered the town under an assumed name, as he had in Hokitika.

She'd stopped to take tea at a small hotel not far from the waterfront and learned that the town was preoccupied with the fate of four missing men.

'Did you see the report in the paper this morning about the men from Canvastown?' the waitress had asked her when she'd ordered morning tea with a buttered currant scone.

'Canvastown?' Carrie had repeated. She'd not heard of it before.

'Oh, surely you've heard?' the waitress said. 'Them that's disappeared on the Maungatapu Saddle? The whole of Nelson's talking about it.'

'No. I've just arrived on the boat from Hokitika,' Carrie said, hoping that Richard wasn't one of the missing. It would be just like him to go bush and she was desperate to see him now that she'd come all this way.

'Four men and their horse, just disappeared without a trace,' the waitress said. 'Along with a whole pile of cash and gold they was bringing over to start up a business. You should read the papers. The *Mail* and the *Examiner* are full of it.'

'Oh, thank you,' Carrie said, only half listening to the story. 'I will. But may I please have some tea. I'm absolutely parched.'

She'd eventually purchased a copy of that morning's Nelson *Examiner* on the way to the solicitor's and read it while waiting for him to see her. She'd scanned the front page advertisements with some interest: a shipment of furs – ermine, sable, badger, African monkey – had arrived at Wilson and Richardson, Bridge Street, along with an array of winter fashions, "imported fabric, with garments made to order from models designed by Parisian artists." It sounded very grand – much more fashionable than the little backwater she'd just come from. But she wasn't going to allow herself to be distracted from her main purpose in being here: to find Richard and settle down together again in their own house. Idly, she turned to page two and found the news of the day:

'MONDAY, JUNE 18th, 1866,' the column was headed.

A SUPPOSED CASE OF STICKING UP.
'A very considerable amount of apprehension is felt in Nelson for the fate of four men who, on Tuesday last, left Canvas Town for the purpose of coming to Nelson and who have not yet reached this town… Some say four suspicious characters left Canvas Town too with double-barrelled shotguns and they haven't been seen again either.

'Mrs O'Neill,' a man's sharp voice had interrupted her thoughts. 'Would you come this way please.'

She stood and followed him down a dark, wood-panelled corridor to an opaque glass door stencilled with the name 'William Hardacre, LLB. Solicitor.' He opened the door, motioned for her to follow then indicated a large leather cushioned chair.

'Please sit down, Mrs O'Neill.'

The rest of the interview had passed in a blur. The cottage transaction had taken place and she'd handed over a bank draft sufficient to cover the purchase of the property as well as Mr Hardacre's conveyancing fees and to ensure his services were available for future needs. She'd resisted any inquiries about her personal circumstances or where her money had come from, despite the solicitor's persistent niggling. But if she hadn't come away with the house details written down, she realised she wouldn't have had the slightest notion as to its whereabouts or title. The news of the missing men – the ones purported to be carrying gold and large sums of money as well as the others armed with shotguns – had disturbed her thoughts significantly and had obliterated much else from permeating her brain.

16. Visitors

The whistling of the kettle brought her back to reality. She was dying for a cup of tea but would need to unpack her tea set and the box of tea she'd bought, along with several boxes full of provisions after alighting from the mail coach at the Hope general store. Pushing the kettle to the back of the hob with the poker, Carrie damped down the now fiercely burning range and headed back to the parlour to unpack. She opened the biggest trunk first – the brown leather one containing all the things she would need in the kitchen. It was a pleasure unwrapping each piece and finding a place for it in the ample blue and white cupboards and shelves. The new willow pattern dinner set with the big carving plates and beautifully shaped sauceboat she and Richard had bought together, fitted neatly in the built-in dresser. She arranged some of the smaller plates carefully across the middle and upper shelf and left the sauceboat out on the lower shelf, along with her lily-of-the-valley-patterned water pitcher and bowl, which she would take upstairs when she'd purchased some bedroom furniture. By the time she reached the bottom of the chest, the kitchen was looking almost homely, filled with familiar things. She'd even hung up the large photograph she'd had framed of her and Richard at the grand ball in Hokitika. A handy nail left behind on the wall had proved just the place to show it off to advantage. She stood in front of it for a moment, overtaken by sadness that Richard wasn't here with her and, if he was in hiding or among the missing men, was unlikely to be joining her for some time. It seemed as if her dream of living with Richard in this remote country cottage would come to nothing. But she was prepared to wait for him, she told herself. He would come back to her eventually. She was certain of it.

Her reverie was interrupted by a knock on the door. She opened it to reveal two older ladies – one tall and thin, wearing widow's black, the other short and dumpy, carrying something wrapped in a tea towel.

Behind them, Carrie noticed, the sun was low in the sky and would soon set. She'd been so engrossed in unpacking she hadn't noticed the time.

'Oh, good afternoon, Mrs O'Neill,' the plump one was saying. 'I'm Miss Shaw. Mary Anne Shaw. And this is my sister Mrs Catherine Donaldson. We live just a short distance away up Clover Road and we wanted to make sure you're made welcome. So we came visiting in the trap and brought you this.' She handed over the parcel, which Carrie could feel was an earthenware dish, still warm.

'Oh, that's very kind of you,' Carrie said, lifting the cloth slightly to peek underneath. The dish contained a crisp, golden pie, topped with a leaf-shaped pastry decoration. 'I've been so busy since I arrived, I haven't had time to think about making anything to eat. Please come in.' She ushered them into the parlour. 'I'm afraid there's nowhere to sit just yet except on the trunks. I'm so sorry. I was going to buy some furniture tomorrow. But do sit down, please,' she said, covering the trunks with some of the red velvet cushions she'd unpacked. The trunks were fortuitously grouped around the big bay window, catching the rays of the slowly sinking sun. 'I'll just pop this in the kitchen and put the kettle back on the hob.'

'Oh don't go to any trouble on our account,' Mary Anne Shaw said.

'No trouble at all, honestly,' Carrie said. 'I've been dying for a cup of tea all afternoon, but even though I unpacked the tea and all my provisions ages ago, I've only just found the teapot and cups.'

Returning from putting on the kettle, she found the two sisters leaning forward, talking to each other in hushed tones, as if they were saying something they did not wish her to hear. They both sat up straight when they saw her coming back into the room. It was then that Carrie noticed her white porcelain chamber pot sitting at the foot of the stairs, in full view, along with Richard's bedside pisspot. Well, at least that'll show them there's a man around, she thought to herself, turning away momentarily to hide her embarrassment.

'The kettle shouldn't take long to heat up,' she said, looking down at the third trunk, as yet unlocked and unpacked. She perched on top of it. 'I hope you can tell me about Hope,' she continued then laughed at how silly it sounded 'Hope about Hope. That's funny, isn't it?' She noticed the sisters were smiling politely but weren't really amused. 'I suppose everybody makes fun of it like that. You must get awfully sick of it.' She felt herself gabbling now to hide her nervousness.

'Hope is a very happy little community,' Mrs Donaldson said. 'There's been a settlement here almost since the first families arrived off the boats from England in 1842.'

'And then a decade or so later, several German families arrived and settled on land purchased by the German Mission,' her sister added.

'Yes, like Hans Busch and the Ranzau farm up the road.'

'And it wasn't long before we needed a school and a store and all the things that make a community.'

'Of course, not everybody sees fit to populate the land and the Hope schoolroom as much as Mr Busch,' Mrs Donaldson said with a disapproving frown.

'Yes, eighteen children is a little excessive, I'd have to agree,' Miss Shaw said. 'They fill an entire schoolroom. It was such a pity you and Alistair couldn't have children before he passed away.'

'Oh tusch, Kittie, you tattle so. I'm sure Mrs O'Neill isn't interested in my affairs.' Mrs Donaldson turned to Carrie. 'Do you and your husband have any children, Mrs O'Neill?'

Carrie had deliberately started the pretence of being a married woman – first with the solicitor, and then with the good people of Hope.

'No, not yet. But there is one on the way,' she said patting her stomach, which was still comparatively flat under her laced bodice and full skirt. However, she reckoned it was best to prepare her neighbours for what would soon be undeniable – a pregnancy without a perpetrator.

'Oh, how lovely,' Miss Shaw said, with a noticeable narrowing of the eyes in her sister's direction. 'And when is it due?'

'November, I think, or possibly December. Mrs Lang, my accoucheuse in Hokitika, said it was most likely to be late November. And of course, I haven't found an accoucheuse here yet. I'll be guided by you if you know anyone?'

'There's a wonderful woman not far from here in Richmond. She attends all the births around these parts. I'll give you her address next time I'm passing,' Mrs Donaldson said.

At the whistling of the kettle, Carrie excused herself and went to the kitchen to make tea. She could imagine the sisters gossiping about her and her condition in her absence and smiled. She suspected they'd pass it on for the whole town to gossip about now. Her long days and nights behind the bar in Hokitika had made her very adept at handling, stimulating or stemming the local grapevines. She would have to use the same resources to work for her here.

She set the tea things on her best tray and carried it through to the parlour.

'Brrrr, it's getting colder now the sun's going down,' she said. 'I shall have to light the fire as soon as I've laid it.' She put the tea tray down on the trunk she'd vacated and started to pour.

'Milk? Sugar?' she asked each of the ladies. 'I'm sorry, I have no lemons as yet. But I do have a slice of some German apple cake they were selling at the store. I've not seen it before and it looked so delicious.'

'No thank you,' Mrs Donaldson said to milk, sugar and apple cake. She took her black tea with a quick smile, not moving from her precarious perch on the cushioned trunk.

'Yes, please,' Miss Shaw said to all three. Carrie carefully passed her a slice of the cake on the deep red rose-covered, gold-edged plates – part of the tea set she'd coveted until she'd persuaded Richard to buy it for her.

'How many plates does a man need to eat off?' he'd joked with her. 'At least you'll never have to wash the dishes. You've so many you won't need to.'

'What lovely cups and saucers,' Mrs Donaldson said, putting her cup back in the saucer, her little finger sticking out at what Carrie thought was a most peculiar angle.

'Aren't they lovely? They're Royal Albert from England. They're my favourites,' Carrie said, pouring herself a cup of tea, with milk no sugar, and finding a space alongside the tea tray to sit.

'You must have found it hard to leave all your furniture behind.' Miss Shaw said.

'Oh I did,' Carrie said. 'I had some really lovely pieces. But it was impossible to bring everything on the steamer. Besides,' she steeled herself to lie a little, 'my husband said we would be able to buy new with the proceeds from their sale and the sale of the house.'

'And where is he, your husband?'

Carrie knew the question would inevitably come and was ready with an answer.

'Oh, he works with the police,' she said carefully. 'He does a lot of work in the goldfields. He had to stay behind when George Dobson went missing, to help find the culprit.'

'Isn't it terrible, all this murder and mayhem going on?' Mrs Donaldson said. 'You can't sleep safe in your beds for worry about what might happen next.'

'And when do you expect he will be able to join you?' Miss Shaw persisted.

'I can't really say,' Carrie demurred. 'He was supposed to be coming with me, what with my condition and all. But it was not to be.' Carrie didn't find it at all difficult to shed a tear and made quite a show of wiping it away. She was genuinely distressed at not being able to find Richard and was anxious now that she might not see him for some time.

'Oh, you poor soul,' Mrs Donaldson said. 'Having to move house all on your own like this.'

'I'm sure everything will be fine,' Carrie said, dabbing at her eye with her handkerchief. 'He's promised to come on by steamer as soon as he can.'

'We'll make sure you're not lonely,' Mrs Donaldson said.

'Yes, there are plenty of kind folk here who will help you. You just have to ask,' Miss Shaw said.

'I was deluged with kindness after Alistair died last year,' Mrs Donaldson said. 'You don't realise how much of a community we are until something like that happens.'

'Mrs de Vries, she was just wonderful. She bakes the best bread this side of Richmond. She was always popping in with a loaf for you, Kittie.'

'And remember how Annie Kempthorne would insist on dropping by with all her children in tow to deliver those baskets full of goodies?' Mrs Donaldson turned to Carrie. 'Mrs Kempthorne and her husband Arthur have the next farm along from yours, down Clover Road. They live almost opposite us.'

'And their children just run wild, Mrs O'Neill. You just wouldn't believe the mischief they get up to.'

'Not like those Busch children up on the Ranzau farm. They're always perfectly behaved.'

'And so they should be, Kittie, with a father like that. He rules them with a leather belt. D'you know, he won't let them go anywhere near the school. Poor uneducated mites. He makes them all work on the farm from dawn 'til dusk.'

'It's his wife I feel sorry for.' Miss Shaw turned to Carrie and leaned forward as if to share a secret. 'When he goes to town for the day,' she said sotto voce, 'he puts his wife Dorothea down the well so she can't entertain anyone in his absence. Did you ever hear such a thing?'

'Good heavens, no!' Carrie said. She wondered if that was a particularly German trait, or if it was something he'd learned in this part of the world. 'Wouldn't she get awfully wet?'

'There's a shelf in the shaft wide enough for the poor woman to sit on. Though I imagine it must be terribly depressing and lonely down there all day.'

'He's tried the same approach with his older daughters. He locks them in the loft when he goes out.'

'But the local lads haven't let it put them off,' Mrs Donaldson said. 'They simply get the ladder and put it against the barn to climb up to the girls.'

'What an unusual man.' Carrie said.

'Oh, there's some strange ones around here, I can tell you,' Miss Shaw said.

'Like the vicar,' added Mrs Donaldson. 'The Rev. Mr Graham. Now he's an odd sort of person to be bringing God's word to earth.'

'Hush, Kittie, you mustn't speak of him like that.'

'But he is a bit unusual, Mary Anne, you must admit.' She turned to Carrie. 'It was the scandal of the whole district, you know, when it happened. He did all the baptisms and marriages for miles around. It was only when the Kempthornes went to him last year to get the birth certificate for one of their children who was applying for a scholarship to Nelson College that they found out he hadn't registered a single birth. Not the Kempthornes', not anybody's!'

'And not only the births, but the marriages too. Everyone who'd had the misfortune to be married in his church was legally,' she lowered her voice and pursed her lips, 'living in sin.'

'Oh!' cried Carrie. 'How terrible.'

'It's still not completely sorted out. There's been an awful to-do up at the diocese office. But they can't get rid of him – there are too few men of the cloth as it is.'

'But they are keeping a much closer eye on his paper work now,' Mrs Donaldson said, sniffing disapprovingly.

'Not that it mattered to Freddie Stratford, up the Aniseed Valley,' Miss Shaw said. 'He's had two wives for as long as I can remember, both living on the same farm but under separate roofs.'

'And the first wife, Louise, looks after her own ten children as well as the child of the second wife, who beavers away like a workhorse on the farm with Freddie, fencing, mustering, shearing…'

'They say she can shear up to thirty sheep a day.'

'Good heavens!' Carrie exclaimed. She didn't know when she'd heard so much tittle-tattle in one sitting. Even the Hope and Anchor, a hotbed of gossip most days, couldn't have unearthed such an incredible amount of bizarre human behaviour in such a short space of time. She was beginning to wonder if there were any normal people in the neighbourhood. Still, she could see the bright side – if everyone was so busy coping with their own problems and difficulties, she might well be left alone.

'Well, we'd better be going,' Miss Shaw said, putting her cup and plate down on the hard tin chest and standing up, shaking crumbs from her skirt.

'Heavens, yes, it's almost dark,' Mrs Donaldson said, standing also. 'We must get away home before it's too hard to see.'

The two departed, taking Carrie's hand at the door and thanking her for the tea and apple cake. She waved goodbye from the porch before returning inside to clear up the tea things.

'Whew, thank goodness that's over,' she said as she closed the door behind her. 'I'll bet they can't wait to spread that around.'

17. Dump the Dump

Here you are,' Ollie said, handing Alex a big tall-stemmed crystal glass of straw-coloured wine. 'It's my riesling from last year. Hangman's Hill riesling, I call it. I'm very proud of it. Riesling's a tricky wine to get right. And you can only taste it here, of course. I've got just two rows of riesling; it's just enough for our own use.'

'I'm very honoured then,' Alex said, taking the glass and raising it in a toast to Ollie. 'Here's to Hangman's Hill.'

'I'll drink to that,' Ollie said, going back to the sideboard and raising his own glass in response, before settling himself in one of the large comfy pale green leather chairs.

Alex ignored the little white dog sniffing enthusiastically at her ankles and relaxed back into the deep, squashy chair, raised the glass to appreciate the nose then took a sip. 'It's really nice. Well done. You should make it commercially.'

'Did I hear the word drink?' Gen asked, coming in from the kitchen with baby Claudia under one arm and Isobel trailing right behind her. 'I'm just about ready to collapse.'

Isobel ran to jump onto her father's knee.

'You smell good enough to eat,' he said nuzzling into her long hair. 'You're so angelic after your bath, aren't you Izzie?'

Isobel giggled and gave her father a peck on the cheek.

Gen had poured herself a glass of wine and toasted both Alex and Ollie before taking a hasty gulp and putting the glass down again.

'I'm going to put Claudia to bed now,' she said as she departed through the hall doorway. 'I'll be back in a minute.'

'She's a good little baby, your sister,' Ollie said to Isobel. 'I wish you'd been as easy to get to sleep when you were little.'

'Didn't I like going to bed?' Isobel asked.

'You most certainly did not,' Ollie replied, tickling her tummy. 'You were a holy terror at bedtime. You used to bellow for hours.'

'Why, Daddy?'

'Blessed if I know,' Ollie said. 'We took you to the doctor, but she said there was nothing wrong with you. We just had to be patient. You were such a social wee baby, I think you just didn't want to be on your own.'

'I'm much better now, aren't I?'

'Thank heavens, yes. In fact, you've been such a good girl, I'll put you to bed tonight and read you your favourite story.'

'*Hairy Maclary*?'

'Of course.' Ollie turned to Alex. 'It'll only be the hundredth time.'

Alex had never heard of *Hairy Maclary*, but then she hadn't encountered any children's books for more than two decades. She had no plans to volunteer to read one now. She took another sip.

'Tell me, why don't you make wine commercially? This would surely sell?'

'It's not bad, is it, even though I say so myself. But for now, I'm happy just to make enough for our use. We make just as much money – more even – by selling our grapes to other winemakers, as we would if we made wine. By the time you put in all the equipment, hire all the expertise, and build up the branding and the marketing, you've spent a small fortune.' He paused and held his wine glass up to the light, before draining it. 'No, we're better off to grow the best quality, high-demand grapes and make our money that way.'

'Do you sell them to the one winery? Or to several?' Alex asked.

'Mainly one, the top one. But sometimes, if the price is right, we'll sell to one or two others. We used to sell to one of the wineries up the valley. But now they're so annoyed about the landfill they won't take our grapes any more. Not that it matters. We're known now for our high quality pinot and chardonnay so our grapes are always in demand. And as I told you before, there's the champenoise maker on the other side of Hope who's taking as much of our pinot as I can give him.'

'I'd like to see how they do it, one day,' Alex said. 'I love champagne.'

'You and Gen both,' Ollie laughed. 'But we're not allowed to call it champagne any more. The French are very strict about protecting their name.'

'He's right. I love a good champenoise,' Gen said coming back into the room, running her hands through her thick hair, rumpling it as she did so. 'And they make some excellent bubbles around here. We'll go on a tour some time.'

'I'd like that. Especially if they do tastings.'

'You bet.'

'Right, young lady, your turn now,' Ollie said, standing up with Isobel still clinging to him. 'Say good night to Mummy.'

'But I don't want to go to bed now. I want to listen,' Isobel protested.

'Plenty of time for that tomorrow, darling,' Gen said. 'Be a good girl, now.'

'Will the lady still be here tomorrow?' Isobel asked.

'Alex. Her name's Alex, darling. She said you're to call her Alex.'

'Will Alex be here tomorrow, then?'

'Sure I will,' Alex said.

'How long will she be here?'

'I don't know the answer to that one, Isobel. As long as it takes, I guess,' Alex said. 'We've got to sort out the problem with all those people at the front gate before I can go home.'

'It could be a month. Could be longer,' Ollie said, holding on to the clinging Isobel as he headed for the door. 'Come on, Izzie. Time to say good night.'

'Good night, Mummy,' she said obediently. 'Good night, er, Alex.'

'Night darling,' Gen said.

'Good night,' Alex added.

Father and daughter disappeared through the door and Alex could hear their tread on the stairs and their voices trailing off.

'Oh, Lord, Alex has forgotten Pooh,' Gen said, picking up a fat yellow stuffed bear wearing a bright red top. 'I'd better take him up to her or she'll never go to sleep. Be back in a second.' Gen followed them upstairs, clutching Pooh, the dog trailing at her heels.

Alex lay back, nestling into the soft leather, took another sip of her riesling and looked around the room.

It was remarkably tidy and uncluttered for a household that seemed to be filled with small children. But then she supposed the children would spend most of their time in the big family room and kitchen she'd come through on the way in here tonight. There had been plenty of evidence of babies and small children there, with toys, picture books, and a child-sized table and chairs covered with crayons and paints taking up most of the available space. In the kitchen next to a wide breakfast bar was a high chair, still smeared with the remains of a recently eaten bowl of baby food, and the breakfast bar still sported the remains of Isobel's dinner. Alex had noted with amusement that there'd been quite a few pieces of broccoli and zucchini left in the bowl, amid gobs of tomato sauce. Gen had been unfazed by all the mess, calmly preparing the adults' dinner, which looked as though it would be roast chicken. It sure smelled good. Alex could detect a whiff of lemon and garlic.

After the kitchen and family room, the lounge was a haven. Acres of pale blue cut pile carpet surrounded her. In front was a gas flame fire flickering warmly over its fake logs. A large, glass-topped, twisted-iron coffee table set with a vase of fat pink peonies and several *House and Garden* magazines, was framed by two long plump sofas in pale green jacquard fabric, brightened by colourful cushions in a rich blue, burgundy and green floral pattern. Behind her, the sea of pale blue carpet reached to the window seat, with the blue, burgundy, pink and green patterned curtains drawn against the winter night. All very designer, Alex thought, very *House and Garden*. She stood and picked up one of the magazines and opened it at a photographic spread showing a house where a couple were growing lavender and olives, the old white renovated farmhouse now dwarfed at the end of row upon row of mid-height olive trees.

Alex had no idea olives grew in New Zealand. But it figured, she supposed. If they grew grapes for wine, then the climate and soil could suit olives too.

'Well, Pooh is snuggled down in bed now, along with Isobel,' Gen said as she returned. 'Let's make the most of it. No kids to interrupt us.' She picked up the wineglass she'd only managed one quick gulp out of so far and plumped herself down on the sofa, crossing her long black-trousered legs revealing bare feet in a pair of elegant low-heeled black pumps with silver buckles.

Always on the look-out for new shoe purchases, and ignoring the excessively large pile jostling for space in her wardrobe, Alex said, 'Nice shoes. Are they made here?'

'Molly N,' Gen replied looking down and studying them, then flicking her head to shift her glossy dark hair out of her eyes as she looked up again. 'You won't have heard of them in the States. But they're well known here. New Zealand makes good quality leather shoes. And clothes too. If you're interested, I'll show you some good shops in town.'

'That'd be great,' Alex said. 'I don't shop often, but when I do I tend to go overboard. It's time I had another binge.'

'I don't get much time myself,' Gen said, 'what with the kids and the vineyard and the landfill and my wine column.'

'You write a wine column?'

'Only for the local paper. But I love doing it. All that training I did in Australia at wine college, and I've been a cellar master for four years now. So it's good to be able to put it all to some use. Apart from the vineyard, of course. Though Ollie tends to do most of it now. I get a bit tied to the kitchen.'

'You don't share the parenting?'

'We used to make a point of it, but it's harder with two. Especially while Claudia's still a baby. In a year or so, I'll be able to take her to childcare. But I don't like to yet. They're only little for such a short time.'

Alex thought she'd have no problem popping a baby into childcare from the day after it was born. But then, she'd read that hormones tended to change all that. Just the same, she couldn't understand why Gen wanted to be a full-time mother. She was sure it wouldn't be her choice.

'So what do you write about in your wine column?'

'Oh, about the different grapes you can grow around here, about the local wines and how well they're doing overseas or in the wine competitions. It's fairly chatty, mostly wine gossip I suppose, but I do tastings too – usually based on what our cellarmaster's club says during blind tastings. That way, there's no bias. Not that I'm likely to be biased anyway – because we don't sell our wine.'

'Yes, Ollie was telling me about that. But you do still make some.'

'Hangman's Hill?' Gen said laughing. 'Yes, and excellent wine it is too. Though with a name like that, it's a wonder. It was Ollie's idea. I'd never have let him call it that if it was going on the commercial market.'

'Why not?' Alex said. 'It's intriguing enough to spark people's curiosity.'

'That's true. But we wouldn't want people to buy it out of curiosity or because it has such a daft name. We'd want to have a name that wasn't so… so… threatening.'

'Why is it called that? The hill, I mean.'

'Didn't Ollie tell you? He usually can't wait to tell our guests.'

Alex shook her head, no.

'He said there was a very interesting history to the place, and that he'd tell me about it later.'

18. Reward

Lying back in the red leather barber's chair in the fashionable American Saloon, Richard closed his eyes and relaxed for a moment while Barber Dupuis applied shampoo and water to his long, tangled hair. He was well overdue for a tidy up, especially if he was going to see Carrie. She would never accept him looking like a digger. Although from comparatively humble beginnings, like himself, Carrie had set herself high standards and her ambition to rise above herself drove her to maintain appearances.

He was feeling warm and tingling still from the saloon's bathhouse where he'd scrubbed himself clean, ridding his body not just of the dirt and dank waters of the trail, but of the traces of blood that he was certain would still be on him. He'd made sure all the clothes were blood-stained and carried other tell-tale signs of a struggle and gunfire had been well buried in the bush on the outskirts of Nelson. But he'd still felt unclean, as though the blood of those five men had stained his soul.

It wasn't the first time he'd killed in cold blood. He'd been party to the slaying of some twenty men already this year. But never so many at the one time. It worried him, nagged at his conscience. He didn't like that one bit. He was used to holding up travellers, relieving them of their booty and then disposing of them so they didn't live to bear witness against him. So he was troubled to find the Maungatapu incident was weighing on his mind. Especially that poor old man James Battle who'd come through at the wrong time and had to be disposed of quickly before their four wealthy intended victims arrived. The old swagger only had three pounds on him – hardly worth taking and certainly not worth dying for. But they couldn't risk having him ruin their planned hold-up. He'd had to go. It niggled at him still.

Sitting in the bath before, with the warm, soapy, sweet-smelling water swirling around him, he'd reflected that it really was about time he gave up his life of crime. If it hadn't been for that swag of money he'd left for

Carrie, he'd be nicely set up now. But his conscience had told him he should leave her and the baby well provided for. He still felt ashamed of himself for abandoning her like that without saying good-bye or even telling her he was going. He longed to see her again and hoped she had been able to sell the house and bring some of his things up here as he'd asked her. He was particularly attached to that woollen greatcoat. It had kept him warm through many a cold night in the bush. That greatcoat had a history; it was an integral part of his life.

It had occurred to him he should ask around and see if Carrie had made it this far north yet. If she had managed to sell the house, she should have plenty of money to set up here and it would be well for her to be away from folk who would know her and would make the connection to him once news of his involvement with the murders was known. He planned to find her.

The poor souls lying in the bush half way up the Maungatapu Mountain had earned him more than one hundred and twenty pounds – enough to get him on the next steamer out of Nelson to the United States of America. He'd seen in the paper that one was due to leave next Wednesday and he planned to be on it. The paper had also reported a "Proclamation from America" signed by President Andrew Johnson that the insurrection in the Southern States had ended and the war was over. That should mean plenty of work. Houses and businesses would have to be rebuilt and he might even turn his hand to his once-learnt trade of stone-cutting to earn a living. A life devoted to crime had reaped him thousands of pounds over time, but where was it now? All spent. Wasted on champagne, gambling and high living with women he'd met in hotels. And the wages of his sin were more years spent in prison than out – the worst of them in those vile floating hells of misery, the Hulks. Not even Pentridge was as bad as the Hulks, where both legs had been in irons for two years on end. No wonder he still bore the scars.

He became aware of a voice trying to penetrate his consciousness.

'Your beard, sir,' the barber was saying impatiently. 'What is it you want done with your beard?'

'Oh, my beard, yes,' Richard said, trying to collect himself. 'Ah, what about shaving it off around my chin? I think that would look smart, don't you?'

'Quite the fashion,' Barber Dupuis said.

'But leave the whiskers on my face. Perhaps just a trim around the sides. But nothing on the chin.'

'And your moustache, sir? It's a fine specimen, that's for sure.'

'Yes, I think we'll leave it as is. Just a trim there too.'

The barber set to work again and Richard relaxed once more. A change in his appearance would help disguise him should the police learn five men were missing and start a search for their killers. He knew that they'd been seen in Canvastown, and Sullivan's behaviour there had been enough to rouse local suspicion. But they'd disposed of the bodies so carefully it would be unlikely that anyone would find them for a long time. He felt sure he'd be safe in Nelson for a couple more days at least. Then he could go bush until the steamer was due to leave for the San Franciscan goldfields.

'There, sir. Is that to your liking?' Richard sat up and looked in the mirror the barber was holding up to see the cut at the back of his head. He studied his shortened locks, avoiding taking any notice of the growing bald spot on the top of his head and turning his attention to his whiskers, which looked very fine indeed, he thought. He was certain Carrie would find him very attractive now, if only he could find her.

'An excellent job, Barber Dupuis,' he said. He paid, donned his new long coat-jacket and strolled out into the weak midwinter sunshine of Bridge Street. Being late morning, it was a busy time of the day, with a bullock train passing at that very moment, ploughing up the muddy street and leaving behind a most unpleasant stench as the cart piled high with large bales of wool retreated slowly. The pavements were crowded with men and women visiting the many shops. He was aware from that morning's paper that Wilson and Richardson had a sale of fine cashmere shawls and furs. He crossed the street to look in their windows. Carrie would like those furs very much indeed. He decided, on an impulse, to buy her a sable wrap.

Coming out of the shop carrying the boxed gift, he turned the corner into Trafalgar Street and saw the display of boots in Peat and Thornton's window. He spied a fine pair of Balmoral boots, as well as some light watertights, which he'd thought for some time would be practical footwear for his frequent bushranging. They'd be just as handy in the United States. Who knows what he'd need them for there. He went inside and was fitted for the watertights, which the bootmaker told him would be ready on the morrow. He fancied a dainty pair of fine kid button boots for Carrie but was unsure of her size. Perhaps he could take her shopping when he found her. She seemed to find more joy in shopping, he'd come to think, than in almost anything else.

He returned to Bridge Street and crossed the road to the Oyster Saloon, where he and Sullivan had been lodging these past two nights, and ordered a large plate of oysters to be shelled for him for his luncheon. They came with a pepper-shaker and several slices of lemon, which he squeezed over the succulent shellfish before scooping them out of their shells and swallowing them whole. Thirsty now, he called for a beer and sat savouring the moment. Life was good, he told himself. Perhaps the wages of sin weren't so bad after all. Hearing a noise behind him, he turned and saw two men sitting down at the table beside him. He nodded a polite greeting and continued to sip at his beer.

'...the sergeant's all stirred up about those missing men,' he overheard one man say.

'Aye, Rob, I heard that the police suspect foul play,' the other replied.

'The sergeant said they're looking for a gang of criminals,' the first one said.

Richard had to rein in his reaction: the last thing he wanted to do was draw attention to himself now. But this was terrible news. He'd not expected the constabulary to be onto them this quickly.

'They're posting a reward around the town this afternoon. I saw one of the bills go up on my way down Bridge Street just now.'

'Did you, by Jove? A reward, eh? Maybe we can find the blackguards and earn something for our efforts.'

'More than something, Rob. They're offering four hundred bloody pounds!'

Richard couldn't help himself. He let out an involuntary gasp. That was a deuce of a lot of money! Luckily, Rob's companion was also taken aback at the amount and had whistled loudly upon hearing the news, drowning out any noise that Richard made. He curbed his initial instinct to rush out the door, run up the road and tear the notices off the windows and walls. Instead, he made himself sit there, outwardly calm, sipping his beer. He waited a good ten minutes before slowly pushing back his chair, standing up and casually walking out the door, as if he had all the time in the world.

Once round the corner in Bridge Street, he quickened his pace considerably until he found one of the posters attached to the inside of the American Saloon, where he'd been pampered by Dubois not an hour ago. He stopped, affecting only mild interest, and read it:

'VR,' it was headed, with the Queen's crest. Victoria Regina.

'Whereas John Kempthorne, Felix Mathieu, James Dudley, and James Pontius, having been missing since the 13th of June instant, and are supposed to have been MURDERED on the Maungatapu Mountain:

'Notice is hereby given, that a Reward of four hundred pounds will be paid by the Provincial Government for information leading to the apprehension within twenty-one days from this date, of any person found guilty of committing such murder.

'The above will not be paid to any person concerned in the murder.'

Well, that would put paid to any designs Sullivan might have on the money, Richard thought. He read on:

'NOTICE!'

'TWO HUNDRED POUNDS REWARD.

'Free pardon for an Accomplice!'

Richard's eyes opened wide at that. It went on to offer a free pardon to anyone implicated in the murder if they gave information leading to the conviction. That set him thinking. Would one of the others betray them all and turn Queen's evidence? He knew Sullivan well enough by now to have his suspicions. He resolved to keep a close eye on him henceforward.

There was every chance the newspaper would carry something of the affair too, he realised, so he crossed the road, doing his best to avoid the muddy splashes from passing drays and carriages, and hurried towards the offices of the *Examiner*, where he purchased a copy and opened it to page two:

'MONDAY, JUNE 18th, 1866," the column was headed.

'A SUPPOSED CASE OF STICKING UP.

'A considerable amount of apprehension is felt in Nelson for the fate of four men who, on Tuesday last, left Canvastown for the purpose of coming to Nelson and who have not yet reached this town…. Some say four suspicious characters left Canvastown too with double-barrelled shotguns and they haven't been seen again either.'

Damn! Richard thought but did not dare speak out loud. This intelligence meant that he should go bush until his ship sailed. It was dangerous to wait around in Nelson town while the police were gathering evidence that would point the finger at him and his con-spirators.

But first, he reasoned, he should try to find Carrie. She could help him keep out of sight for the next two days, and he could ask her forgiveness for his earlier hasty departure. And she should have brought his warm coat and spare clothing. The coat would come in handy in America, and now that the town was suspicious, it would be foolish to go buying further apparel. He might even have to forego those precious watertights he'd wanted for so long. If Carrie had indeed brought his belongings, he would do well to find her.

Besides, he was damnably fond of the girl. She was sensible and she trusted him. He believed that he could also trust her in return and he was a fool not to have done so in Hokitika. He suspected she had ambitions that would ensure she'd ask no questions if her fortunes depended on it.

But how to find her? He could hardly go to the police. He resolved to go down to the port and ask the shipping companies if she'd arrived recently and then to contact that sombre solicitor to see if he knew where she might have gone. Meanwhile, he decided, he would spend one more night in the Oyster Saloon then he'd hire a horse and head south, towards Wakatu and Wakefield, where he'd be well removed from the arm of the law. He might even find Carrie there; it was just the sort of out-of-the-way place she would like to go.

19. Stocking up

It took no more than an hour for Carrie to walk the three miles into Hope. Her stout black button boots were covered with dust and grime from the long dirt road but her feet were warm and her gloved hands tingling from the exercise. She entered the general store with a long list of necessities, ranging from furniture and coal to flour and eggs. She also planned to buy a cow, some hens for laying, a few farm animals, fruit trees and bags of grain. It was time, she knew, to sow seeds and establish her farm, so that she could reap the harvest later on. She had plenty of money for now, but she would need to spend it wisely to make it last. If she could be self-sufficient, she could save the precious pounds. With a baby on the way and no certainty that its father would return, she realised the bounty she'd received from Richard could not be wasted.

'Good morning, Mrs O'Neill,' the storekeeper's wife said. 'Tessie McTavish, at your service. Sure, you won't remember me when you passed through yesterday. I'm the one that filled your hired cart with provisions.'

'Oh, yes, Mrs McTavish. I do remember. That apple cake I bought from you was a godsend, really. I had visitors just after I…'

'That'll be the Shaw sisters for sure. They're so keen to find out the latest gossip they descend on every new arrival, poor souls. I hope they didn't put you off ….'

'Oh, no, not at all. They were absolutely fascinating. I learned so much about the neighbourhood.'

'I'll warrant you did. But whether there's any truth in it…'

'Well, I did wonder at some of it. But it was quite fascinating just the same.'

'You'll have a strange impression of us all then. But I'd have to admit, there are some unusual people around here. Now, what can I get for you?'

Carrie ordered everything she needed to fill her cupboards, her coal box and her empty house. Might as well make the most of it while the money lasts, she thought as she added up the cost of everything as she went. Bed frame and bedhead, dresser with drawers, wardrobe, armchairs, sewing chair, nest of tables, dining table and chairs, kitchen dresser, and a small writing desk as a special treat. She planned to start a daily diary, to record details about Richard and her relationship with him, so she would have something to show her unborn child. She could see that Mrs McTavish was moving from being impressed to overawed to somewhat appalled at the seemingly endless list of goods she was ordering.

'I sold everything before I left Hokitika,' she explained. 'My husband told me that would give us a good start on buying them new after we'd shifted house. That, plus the proceeds of the sale of the house there. So I'm on a buying spree to fill up the house,' Carrie said, hoping to sound ingenuous. 'It's such fun. I expect this'll be the only time in my life I get to do this.'

'My dear, you must be living in an empty shell. Is there anything I can get you in the meantime? Most of the furniture will take at least a week to get here.'

'I'll be fine for now, really. I've got a bed and all my kitchen things. It'll do until the furniture arrives.'

'Some of the items you've chosen we can bring up from Nelson on the freight carriage. But this one,' she pointed at the large wardrobe, 'and these,' she indicated the nest of tables and the writing desk, 'will probably take longer. Several weeks even. They'll have to come from up north. But I can order by telegraph today.'

'Telegraph?' Carrie said bewildered.

'It's the most wonderful thing to happen. Just a few weeks ago, they finished laying the Cook Strait Cable, which contains telegraph lines between the North and the South Islands. And for quite some time now, there's been telegraphic communication between Christchurch and Dunedin and the West Coast. So now we're in touch with the rest of the country – and with the world. We have to go into Nelson to send the messages, but my husband goes in almost daily anyway, so it's no trouble.'

Mrs McTavish promised Carrie a ride back home on the delivery cart if she didn't mind waiting for Mr McTavish to return from town. He'd gone into Nelson to pick up a big order for the Busch farm.

'It's so good to see they're doing well up there on the Ranzau Road,' Mrs McTavish said. 'They've been struggling for so long. Poor dears haven't been able to afford even a bolt of fabric or a pair of shoes. It seems their fortunes are turning at last.'

'Is it hard, making a go of it here?' Carrie asked.

'At first it is, my dear. Especially if you're not used to this life. But you look like a practical young lady. And that husband of yours, he'll turn his hand to fixing things and growing things, for sure. You're arriving at just the right time of year for getting started.'

'My husband, Richard, he's not here yet,' she said lamely. 'He's still on the Coast.'

'So I'd heard, my dear, so I'd heard. But I wouldn't let that worry you. The people here have a strong sense of community,' Mrs McTavish said. 'They got that school going out of nothing. And now look at it, two schoolrooms and a permanent teacher. You'll find there's always someone can give you a hand. You just have to ask.'

'I don't know when he'll arrive. He was supposed to be coming with me, but he had to stay behind to work on a special job.' She did her best to look pathetic.

'You poor dear,' Mrs McTavish said. 'I'll make sure my Angus lets everyone know you're on your own and might be in need of a bit of help. And we'll hurry along those furniture makers so that you'll have a nice place for him when he arrives.'

20. The Ghosts of Hangman's Hill

It's spooky almost. Here, let me refill your glass. This could take a while.' Gen took a swig of her wine, stood up and took her glass and Alex's over to the sideboard and splashed in more riesling. 'The dinner's a roast, so it'll be a while yet.'

Returning to the coffee table, Gen handed Alex her glass and sat down on the sofa, kicking off her shoes and curling her long legs under her.

'Ollie probably told you about Carrie's home – Caroline Cottage?'

'He said it had been *your* family home.'

'It was. For five generations we've lived there. I was born there and so were my brothers. And so was Mum. She lived there all her life with her Mum and Dad. She was an only child,' she added by way of explanation. 'It wasn't until I was about ten that Mum and Dad moved to the brick house up the hill. And then when Ollie and I bought the farm and converted it to grapes, we moved back into the cottage and lived there ourselves. Isobel was born there. So it's always been part of my heritage.'

Alex nodded. 'Five generations is a very long time. It sort of feels as if it still belongs to someone else.'

'You noticed that?' Gen said. Alex nodded. 'That's why we wanted to do it up so thoroughly, why we stripped almost all the old stuff out of it, to get rid of that haunting feeling. It's not haunted, of course,' Gen added, laughing nervously. 'Nobody believes in that stuff these days. No, it was just as if all the people who'd lived there had left something of themselves behind, something that made it feel as if they were still there somehow. We thought we could hear moaning in the middle of the night, like a woman crying out for help. Mum's heard it, and so have I. It was really spooky. So we pulled it apart and stripped it down and got rid of all the spooky feelings. There's nothing left now to worry about. No moaning, no ghosts. It's spirit-free.'

'I see,' Alex nodded again. She had no patience with ghosts and haunted houses and had no intention of encouraging any further talk like this from Gen. It was all nonsense, this spooky stuff.

'But it wasn't my Mum and Dad, or my grandparents who gave the cottage its ghosts. It was way back last century, in the 1860s, when this place became the centre of attention – not unlike it is now, with all the protesters,' Gen gave a hollow laugh. 'It was then that the name Hangman's Hill was given to that stark black mountain up behind the farm. It was then that the cottage harboured the troubled folk who would have given it its ghosts.'

Gen paused and shuddered slightly, as if remembering something unsavoury, then flicked her hair back again.

'So what happened?' By now Alex was on tenterhooks.

'Well, the year was 1866,' Gen said dramatically. 'It was just after the murder of George Dobson, a young surveyor and the son of one of this country's most famous pioneers and original surveyors, Arthur Dudley Dobson. People said he was murdered by the Burgess gang. About that time, a young woman by the name of Caroline – Carrie – O'Neill came to live in the cottage, alone. She had a sizeable sum of money – plenty enough to purchase the house and quite a bit of land around it and to live well enough without any visible means of support. She brought very little with her – a few clothes, her own and those belonging to a man. She used to wear a big grey man's greatcoat.' She paused and took a sip of her wine.

'She kept herself to herself. She was pregnant. You can imagine how that went down, in those days. A woman alone, with child, with no explanation as to where the father might be. You know how it would've been. But she wasn't giving anything away. She had the baby, a little red-haired girl, and called her Christina. But still she kept to herself, never confiding in anyone, so nobody knew who she was, where she came from, nor what had happened to the father of her child.'

Alex heard Ollie pad into the room, his footfall muffled by the deep pile carpet. There was a pause while Gen waited for him to settle.

'Oh, you're telling Alex about the cottage. Good idea,' he said, and sat down after refilling his wine.

'It wasn't until little Christina was four weeks old that the post-mistress at Hope put two and two together and worked out who Carrie was,' Gen continued. 'She was none other than the paramour of Richard Burgess; a barmaid, she'd followed Burgess all the way from Hokitika to Nelson. And by that time Burgess and his gang had been hanged for the Maungatapu Murders and poor little Christina was fatherless.'

'You have to know what it was like then to understand,' Ollie interrupted. 'The Maungatapu Murders were the biggest thing to happen in Nelson for decades. The whole region – no, the whole country – was abuzz with the arrest of the Burgess gang for the Maungatapu Murders. It was all people talked about, all the papers printed for months on end.' He caught Gen's eye and stopped. 'Oops, sorry love. Mustn't interrupt. But I just love telling this story.'

'The Burgess gang was led by the handsome young bushranger Richard Burgess,' Gen continued, giving Ollie a grin. 'He was the very same Burgess that the books say honed his skills with Harry Power and the young Ned Kelly.'

'Ned Kelly?' Alex exclaimed. 'I've heard of him. Wasn't he that famous Australian bushranger? The one with the steel helmet.'

'That's him,' Ollie said.

'So when the good people of Hope found out that our Carrie, the owner of our cottage, was the mistress of one of the monsters responsible for the murders – the ringleader in fact – you can imagine what happened.' Gen paused for effect. Alex felt she was called upon to respond.

'No, I can't, really. But I bet it was awful,' she said.

'You're right. It was terrible. It all came to a head one summer evening, when a lynch mob gathered down at the cross – that's the crossroads a mile or so past here, where the road will go into the landfill. It was awful what they did. But I'll spare you the grisly details. Suffice to say that by morning Carrie and her baby were gone.'

'So that was the end of it?' Alex asked, riveted.

'Not quite, no. She returned two years later with her daughter and a husband – a big, burly, German who was as wide as he was tall. He'd taken over as little Christina's father. The wee girl bore his name. And so did Carrie.

'They lived here for many years, never fully accepted by the people of the valley, but on the surface at least they lived happy enough lives, building up a farm that began to thrive. They had more children and joined in with the local community as much as they could. They went to church in Hope every Sunday. Little Christina went to school there, as did her brothers and sisters. Carrie and her husband farmed sheep that were renowned for their meatiness and dairy cows that produced beautiful creamery butter – churned by Carrie herself.'

'It was as if the terrible events of 1866 had never touched their lives,' Ollie said. 'We've never been able to find out if Carrie's husband ever knew about Burgess and the notoriety of his adopted daughter's birth father. But they certainly behaved as if he'd never existed.'

'So that's the heritage of Caroline's Cottage,' Gen said. 'Quite something, isn't it?'

'And of course it's Gen's heritage too,' Ollie added. 'Although her family has kept it a secret all these years. No-one else knows.'

'Or at least we hope that's the case,' Gen said. 'All the people who were around in those days are long dead, of course, and their families have all moved away from the area. It's not the sort of thing you'd want the neighbours to know.'

'But surely, after all these years...' Alex said.

'You'd think the hostility would have died down. But I wouldn't be so sure.'

'It's not worth the risk,' Ollie added.

'It's certainly an amazing story,' Alex said. 'I can see why you wanted to redo the cottage and obliterate its past. What unhappy memories.'

'It's quite special, in a way, being part of Nelson's history,' Ollie said. 'But unfortunately it's not the sort of history people want to remember constructively. We're convinced that if people knew this was Burgess's mistress's cottage, there'd be some who'd want to burn it down or deface it in some way – even all these years on.'

'So when did it become known as Hangman's Hill?' Alex asked.

'Nobody knows for sure,' Ollie said.

'Grandma used to say it was not long after the lynch mob frightened Carrie away,' Gen said. 'She said the locals were so proud of what they'd done, getting rid of her, that they took on the notoriety of Burgess as a badge of honour.'

'And you think people would still be angry if they knew the cottage had these connections, even all these years on?'

'Yes, it's still a sore festering away in the soft underbelly of Nelson,' Gen said with an ironic chuckle. 'The Maungatapu Murders are remembered around here as a blot on the region's history, for bringing an evil focus on Nelson that its townsfolk felt it didn't deserve.'

'Like the dump,' Alex rejoined.

'Exactly,' Ollie sighed.

'So history repeats itself?'

'Not quite,' he said, 'though the lynch mob at the gate does bear some comparison, I suppose. And it's starting to take up almost as many column inches in the paper as the murders did.'

'It's not so bad we're thinking of leaving though,' Gen said. 'We're not going to let it drive us out of our home, like it did Carrie.'

'That's why you're here,' Ollie said, looking at Alex and raising one eyebrow. 'Sounds a bit of a tall order, I suppose?'

'You'll have to tell me more about it,' Alex said. 'I've read up on all the clippings you left on the desk. I can see where it's been heading. But I'd like to know about it from your point of view.'

'Why don't I finish getting the dinner and you two can talk,' Gen said, standing up. 'Ollie is better at talking about it than me. I tend to get a bit emotional, raking over it again and again.'

'Sure, hon,' Ollie said. 'I understand.' He gave her arm an affectionate pat as she passed by on her way to the kitchen.

'It's started getting to Gen of late,' he said after she'd left the room. 'She's pretty strong on the whole, but I think she's worried about the kids.'

'Understandable,' Alex said, 'with that lot at the gate. Even if some of them are your neighbours, you still don't know what people might do in anger or frustration.'

'I don't think they'd try anything. Hell, I know half of them, have known them for years. I just can't understand why they're so anti. I mean, in the long run, this landfill and its recycling centre will benefit them. They'll be able to recycle their finings and other leftovers from the harvest and get it back a year or two later as good compost for next year's crops.'

'I know. It all sounds so logical to you and me,' Alex said. 'But it's different for them because it's so charged with emotion and misunderstanding. That's why I'm here, as you said, to turn that around so they can understand what you want to achieve and even help you achieve it.'

Ollie whistled appreciatively. 'You think you can do that? Wow! Gen'll be over the moon.'

'It'll take time and patience. And you'll have to do as I say. But, yes, we should be able to turn it around, sooner or later.'

'The sooner the better,' Ollie said. 'Well, I'd better fill you in on it. So you know the full story.'

'Shoot,' Alex said, settling into the soft, comfortable leather and taking a sip of wine.

'Where to begin?' Ollie said, and paused to collect his thoughts. He held his wineglass up to the light and swirled the pale yellow liquid around in it. 'Well, about five years ago, when I was taking another load of grape marc – I think you call it pomace in the States – and finings to the dump, I thought what a waste it was, dumping it like that. I thought it would make such good compost for the vines. So I set up a basic composting system and started saving all the clippings, the leaves, marc, everything that would break down into good soil nutrients. And after a couple of years of this, I was at this winegrowers' seminar and there was this speaker from some ecological organisation who was showing photographs from the Napa where he said there was a special landfill that took *everybody's* waste and separated the organic material for composting. And it set me thinking, why don't we do that? There are heaps of wineries around this region and it seems such a pity to throw all that goodness away.'

'Surely the grape growers would have agreed with that?' Alex said.

'Indeed they did. They were very enthusiastic about the idea. But then it sort of grew. And this big waste firm from outside the valley got involved, and started talking about having a full scale landfill – you know, waste from the city and from all around the region. It turned out that Nelson was looking for a new landfill site, and hadn't been able to find one that was secure. You've got to have the right bedrock, the right geology so that the leachate doesn't escape. And while we were getting our site tested to find out if it would be okay for our winery landfill and recycling centre, one of the geologists introduced me to this guy from GreenWaste International and said he was looking for just the sort of site we've got.'

'Oh, I see,' Alex said. 'So things would've got more complicated then?'

'You're onto it,' Ollie said. 'You see, our land stretches a long way around Hangman's Hill, almost right round to the other side. Here, let me show you.' He jumped up and strode over to the tall bookcase against the far wall, plucked out a tall slim volume and strode back, opening a large map out on the coffee table in front of her. Alex leaned forward to see.

'Look,' Ollie stabbed at a black spot surrounded by lots of red lines. 'This is Hope. And here,' he traced his finger along a red curving line until it straightened out, 'this is where our farm is, at the end of the road and stretching back into this valley. The farms marked along the road here are pretty much all vineyards. Now here,' Ollie pointed at a long side road to the right of the main road, 'here is the road to the landfill. See, just along here a short way is where Gen's Mum and Dad have built their house. It's even higher up than we are, with an even better view that takes in the whole of Nelson and the sea beyond. Anyway, you can see that the side road here is bordered on one side by our vineyard and on the other side by the Davenports' vineyard and winery. Hope River wines, they are. Now old Ivan Davenport's a nice enough bloke, but he's taken this landfill thing very much to heart. He reckons he's going to put in a restaurant as part of his public offerings, and he says the rubbish dump, as he calls it, is going to put paid to that forever.'

'I see,' Alex said when Ollie paused.

'Anyway,' Ollie continued after a gulp of wine, 'I'll tell you about the opposition later. Back to the geography lesson. Now, see how the road winds round the bottom of Hangman's Hill – round here,' he pointed at the spot. 'Well there's a foothill here, and on top of it there's this sort of crater place where apparently it's perfect for a landfill because it's isolated from the aquifer system. And that's where it's going to be.' He sat down again, leaving the map open for Alex.

'So you still own the land?'

'Well, the man from GreenWaste International brought his boss down from Auckland and before I could blink, they'd put an offer on the table. They were so desperate for a landfill site for Nelson that they turned up, contract ready to sign, and a cheque for just under a million dollars. Gen and I couldn't believe our luck.'

No wonder they'd been able to afford a new house, a remodelled cottage and all the trappings of wealth, Alex thought. A million dollars would buy a lot of fancy new equipment for a family vineyard.

She looked at Ollie and noticed that he was waiting for a response.

'I see,' she said again. 'No wonder you were tempted.'

'We didn't have any choice, really. We were over-committed financially. Borrowed more than we could afford to buy the farm off Gen's parents, then borrowed more to put in the vines and the shed and buy a tractor and crop sprayer. And of course, we didn't get any return from the grapes for the first four years, so there was no money coming in to pay it off. I worked my butt off earning as much as I could at the winery we sell our grapes to, and got another job working nights in a bar downtown. And somehow managed to look after our vines in between. Gen was working two jobs too, until she had Isobel. Then it just wasn't possible. We worked out that the cost of running a second car and the childcare would have been more than she could've earned. So we were running ourselves ragged working sixteen-hour days and we didn't seem to be making any headway. The mortgage seemed to be getting bigger rather than diminishing, and things were looking pretty hopeless. Until Mr Greenback came along.'

'It must've been hard,' Alex said.

'Not nearly as hard as making that decision to sell,' Ollie said. 'I'm telling you this because you'll find it out anyway. Everybody around here seems to know the financial pooh we were in. And you can bet your bottom dollar GreenWaste knew it too.' Ollie put his face in his hands, his elbows resting on his knees, and rubbed his eyes.

'You see, Gen and I had this dream of doing something towards a sustainable future for our children. We wanted to provide a recycling and composting service for as many of the vineyards of Nelson that we could. We wanted to put the goodies back into the soil that we were taking out of it, naturally. Sustainably. It all sounded so right. But then temptation intervened, in the form of a million dollars. And now we're the bad guys of the valley. All our neighbours hate us. Half of Nelson hates us. We might not be in the financial crap any more, but we're still in the crap as far as our reputation is concerned. We'll never be able to hold our heads up around here again.'

'I guess that's how poor Carrie must have felt too,' Alex said. 'But she didn't have me to help her. I'm sure I'll be able to get you out of the mire somehow.'

Ollie looked at her as if she was bearing another million.

'Really?' he said.

'I'll do my best.'

'Dinner's ready,' Gen called from the kitchen, then appeared in the doorway with a tea towel over her shoulder. 'I'm going to serve it on the dining table in here. And you two can tell me what you've decided.'

'Not decided exactly,' Ollie said, standing up. 'Just leave your glass, Alex. I'll get us some fresh ones for dinner and open another bottle. A different wine this time. Got to show you what this valley can produce.' He turned to Gen. 'I've just been filling Alex in on where we're at and why. I'm sure she's still got lots of questions before we can even think about making a decision.'

Over dinner – moist roast chicken with a delicious stuffing, accompanied by roast potatoes and broccoli – Alex found herself the focus of attention. She was used to asking all the questions, but this time it was she who was being quizzed.

'I hope you don't mind my asking, but do you do this sort of thing a lot? You know, flying round the world, trouble-shooting?' Gen asked.

Alex laughed. 'No,' she said. 'It sounds very grand, but no this is only the third time I've had an assignment outside America.'

She took a sip of her wine – a slightly spicy, aromatic pinot noir. Ollie had shown her his Hangman's Hill label when he'd poured it. She'd been relieved to see that it didn't sport a picture of a noose or a headless man. It hadn't looked too bad at all really – just a plain dark green and white label, with no graphics and minimal lettering. She'd liked the clean lines of it. 'The name beggars any descriptive design,' Ollie had said when she'd commented on this.

They'd asked her lots of questions – about her education (high school in Sacramento), her degrees in communications and PR (UC Davis and a post-grad period at Berkeley), why she'd gone into it in the first place (started out in business journalism but wanted to be more involved in the businesses she was covering), and what other assignments had she enjoyed, other than at David's (tricky that one, but she'd settled for the touring opera company launch and follow-up, and the big food company merger). Thankfully, they stayed away from her personal life and she was of no mind to enlighten them on that subject. Not that there was much to enlighten them with. She hadn't heard from Lucian of course since that awful day he'd been carted away by the men from the FBI – she hadn't expected to hear from him, though she knew herself well enough to realise that she'd like to.

'You'll have to experience the nightlife here,' Gen said. 'You'd be surprised, but Nelson rocks sometimes.'

'Especially from now on, as we head into summer,' Ollie added. 'And there's the WearableArt Awards coming up soon too. I'll see if we can beg, borrow or steal a ticket for you. You simply can't miss it.'

'WearableArt? Whatever's that?' Alex said.

'It's an annual competition to find the most artistic, the most creative…'

'…and the most outrageous,' Ollie added.

'…costumes,' Gen continued. 'It's world famous now. People come from the States and Asia and Europe to see it. You'll never see anything like it ever again. They theme it, and there are different sections, including children's and luminous and out of this world. Last year there were trapeze artists and fire-eaters. This year… who knows?'

'It sounds fabulous,' Alex agreed. 'I'd love to see it if you can get tickets. I'll give you the money if you let me know how much it is.'

'No problem, I'm sure Gen'll be able to swing it.'

'Yes, there are still some people speaking to me in town.' Gen laughed ruefully. 'I'll see what I can do. Now, who wants coffee?'

21. Homework

Alex flicked on the bedroom light switch and kicked off her shoes. The cottage was now a blaze of light. Since she'd walked in the front door – across an eerily dark verandah because she'd forgotten to leave any lights on when she'd left for dinner – she'd wasted no time in turning a light on in every room. After tonight's tale of Hangman's Hill and lynch mobs and scary happenings, she needed the reassurance of light – and plenty of it. She'd also closed all the curtains, feeling a little silly as she did so. As she was drawing across the bedroom curtains, she glanced briefly at the darkness beyond. To her relief, nothing was visible except the shapes of a few trees in the garden nearby. The bedroom was now bright and welcoming, if a little chilly. Pity she couldn't light the fire. It would have chased away the remaining shadows of unease.

Perching on the edge of the bed, Alex pulled off her shirt, camisole and bra and put on her pyjama top, which she'd extracted from under the pillow. She stood and took off her old beige linen-look pants (linen was hopeless for travelling) and knickers, and drew on the pyjama bottoms. The sight of the pillows had brought on a sudden and inescapable sleepiness. All she wanted to do was collapse into bed. She switched on the bedside light, then stood up and turned off the main light. The room was now full of shadows, climbing down the walls towards her. But she was too tired to care. She picked up her clothes on the way to the bathroom and hung them in the wardrobe, unusually haphazardly for her, and closed the wardrobe door quickly. She'd felt that cold breath of air again – no doubt it was cool and damp from being shut inside that cramped little space. All the same, she didn't like the clammy brush against her skin, like walking through a dewy spiderweb. And there was a faint musty smell, as if an old pair of boots had been left in there for too long. It wasn't her shoes, she knew for sure they were all clean, dry and well polished. If anything, she should be able to smell shoe polish.

Unable to recognise any past-life memories that might be harboured by antique furniture, Alex shrugged and continued on to the bathroom. A quick wash, a flick of the toothbrush, and she was ready to collapse onto the cool, fresh sheets. She knew she'd left most of the lights on downstairs and on the landing, but for her first night, she preferred it that way. No ghosts would come to haunt her with that blaze of light in every room. Not that she believed in ghosts anyway. She turned her head on the pillow, away from the bedside lamp and, with its soft rays offering a reassuring view of an empty room, went straight to sleep.

The next morning, straight after a breakfast of black coffee and a helping of Isobel's sweet, sickly – and therefore utterly delicious – Fruit Loops, Alex went back to the cottage with a copy of GreenWaste's report on the landfill site, switched on the gas fire against the chill morning air, plumped herself down on the sofa and set to reading it, making notes with a pencil she'd extracted from her bag on the table.

GreenWaste, the report said, was a multi-national, environmentally aware group of companies known throughout the Pacific Rim – or so it said – for seeking out safe, tidy and environmentally secure landfill sites that blended in with their surrounding communities, working in harmony with their neighbours and ensuring each community was fully satisfied with their operations.

'Sounds pretty good,' Alex said out loud. 'But then it would, wouldn't it, since they wrote it.' She remained sceptical. GreenWaste was paying for her to be here, to put into practice the community relations they were so proud of. But she suspected it was pragmatism rather than idealism or neighbourliness that was paying her expenses.

She sighed and turned the page. She saw it all too often – companies like GreenWaste calling her in to get them out of a fix. If they'd employed her from the start of the project, from the moment they'd considered applying for a resource consent, she could have laid out a nice, easy, community-friendly communication strategy that would have kept everyone – neighbours, winegrowers, local authorities, mayors, officials and the local media – not just informed, but contented as well. Still, she wasn't going to complain. She could charge a lot more for crisis communications, and she always enjoyed watching a few simple, common-sense tactics turning around what seemed insoluble to everyone else.

Most of the first part of the report was devoted to the lengthy resource consent process, which Alex found interesting, but not particularly helpful as far as her job was concerned. There was talk of a consultation process and meetings with neighbours, but no indication as to how these had gone.

The geology section was detailed and a bit too technical for her level of understanding. She'd seen similar reports before when David was planning his landfill and waste-recycling centre, but she still didn't understand all the jargon. She took in what she could and turned to the community relations page. Here was what she needed to know.

The report outlined no fewer than seven public meetings, individual discussions with those people living closest to the landfill and its access road, and meetings with council officials. A booklet had been printed, and a newsletter started. There'd been a huge amount of activity around the time of the resource consent hearings and approval, but next to nothing since. And in the vacuum had grown a hydra-headed monster that had the neighbours believing their grapes would be polluted by dust and diesel from passing waste trucks, their properties devalued by a messy, smelly rubbish dump, and their wines rejected by association with it all.

Not surprisingly, they'd called their own meetings, rustled up the support of most of the other landowners in the valley, and formed a very vocal, active lobby group that had easily bent the sympathetic ear of the local media and, gathering momentum as its cause became more widely known, had attracted more than a few greenies who revelled in having something new to protest about. Hence the rag-tag element added to the other protesters at the gate. Even in the brief few moments as they'd eased their way through to the gate yesterday, she'd noticed two distinct types of people protesting. There were people her own age or slightly older, people with young children and teenagers. There were quite a few older people, too, well dressed in a country sort of way, wrapped up warm against the cold spring air. And then there was rent-a-crowd – young men with dreads and pierced eyebrows, baggy pants and thick-soled boots; young women with long hair, nose rings, and clothes that would have been more suited to a circus tent.

Later that morning, when she'd finished reading through the report and made notes, as well as summarising the clippings she'd read the night before, she phoned all the people in the valley from a list Gen had given her and made appointments to see them over the next few days. Some she had to call back later until she got hold of them. But by the day's end she'd started to get a good picture of what was going on.

Three days later, when she'd visited all the neighbours and asked them a series of similar questions, she had an even better picture. She'd introduced herself as a researcher, which was at that time true. It helped her get an impartial view of how people were feeling and where the main problem might be. Towards the end of each interview, she'd told everyone who she was and that she doing research for GreenWaste, but by then she'd established a reasonable rapport with them and was able to maintain the momentum. Better than turning up and saying she was from GreenWaste for starters and being shown the door.

Back in the cottage, she made herself a mug of tea and sat down at the kitchen table to work it through. A good old-fashioned SWOT analysis would help. The strengths and weaknesses were obvious, but when she came to list the opportunities it dawned on her that the Davenports and their long-held dream of opening a high-class winery restaurant provided an ideal chance for a win-win solution – the sort she always hoped to find. And if the Davenports were happy, the rest of the valley might also come to realise that the landfill could actually be of benefit to the locals, rather than a threat. From there it would be a simple matter of showing the other winegrowers the good things that the landfill would bring – the recycling, the composting, the community sponsorship and support. She would push the recycling angle for all it was worth. That was what had won the day for Rossinis, and there was no need to reinvent the wheel. The sustainability of the recycling plant should buy them lots of brownie points with the greenies.

And once the neighbours realised that the containerised waste trucks were no different to a covered road train carrying fruit juice or bread, once they grasped that the landfill would be invisible, clean and neighbourly, they might give up protesting and, who knows, even support the project. While she'd been researching the Napa site, Alex had learned of quite a few newly-constructed, regulation-encrusted landfills around the world located on the outskirts of cities or in high-profile tourist or intensively cropped areas like this one and the locals had all come round once they actually seen the comparatively innocuous result. However, most times it had taken years for that to happen, and Gen and Ollie didn't want hostile neighbours for that long.

She fixed herself a sandwich from the bread rolls, brie, ham, salad and chutney she'd bought along with a pile of other groceries the day after she'd arrived, pulled out a dining chair, and sat in the warm spring sunshine to eat her lunch, along with a can of diet Coke. The sun glistened on the fresh green rose buds in front of her, and the musky scent of wisteria filled her nostrils. Birdsong surrounded her – she could hear a nest of squealing baby birds above her in the wisteria and soon witnessed the arrival of a mother thrush bearing a beak full of grubs and worms. Invigorated by the energy of new life all around, Alex climbed down off the verandah and walked around the back of the cottage – the first time she'd had a moment to explore. Behind the freshly painted walls was an orchard bursting with blossom and humming with bees. Feeling like a child again, she ran through the grass under the trees, brushing the low-hanging petals as she passed, dancing round and round like a demented May Queen, before falling exhausted to the ground, lying on her back, panting, relieved there'd been no-one around to see her. Through the pinky-white blooms she could see hyacinth-blue sky – surprisingly blue for this time of year – and a few streaky white clouds. It reminded her of when she was a child, when she'd run outside and fling herself down in the long grass behind their suburban house and gaze up at the sky and the clouds scudding past for what seemed like forever, instead of getting on with her homework or helping her father get dinner. Sometimes Kate or Max would find her and haul her back inside. But mostly she could lie undisturbed for ages. The hard bit was always picking yourself up and dragging yourself back inside to face the reality of a taciturn, preoccupied father who'd hardly had a kind word to say to her since her mother had died. He'd become a changed man after his wife died from breast cancer. Alex was thirteen at the time and eventually found solace from her distant, disapproving father by creating a world of her own, a world where she was her Daddy's girl, and everything she did made him terribly proud of her.

'Oh, Daddy, if only we could have saved her,' she said to the clouds and laughed at herself for being so maudlin. Then, just as she used to do a world and time warp away, she thumped the ground with both palms, forced herself to stand up, and walked slowly back indoors.

Upstairs, the computer was waiting for her to get her thoughts and suggestions down in some semblance of order. Alex switched it on and logged into the network, picking through the menu until she came to the folders specially created for her.

'Hidden Valley Landfill, Communication Strategy,' she typed in big letters, then started on the well-worn track of getting everything down in writing – what the situation was now, what it should ideally be, and how to get there by, once again, noting down who should say what, to whom, when, and how: a simple formula that was, however, incredibly difficult to get right. Hence her popularity with corporates in trouble.

It took the entire afternoon, including the time she took to make a few additional phone calls to check out details and to answer a couple of incoming calls – one from Gen asking her over for a drink ('We've hardly seen you,' said kindly) and one from the geologist to provide a simple explanation for a particularly complicated piece of verbiage. Before closing the laptop, she checked her emails and found one from Lacey and another from Sharon about the same client, who was causing problems. She emailed back some suggestions. There was another email from Kate – a long chatty one, which she could reply to later. And another from Magda, filled with gossip about their PR colleagues, news of clients and past clients, and more than she needed to know about her latest man. Magda was divorced, with no children to cramp her style, and loved to play the field. Even Alex found it hard to keep up with her sometimes. Magda had attached some photos – taken on her battered Pentax SLR and put through the scanner. Magda's weekend passion – apart from men – was taking black and white pictures and developing them herself. There was an arty photo of one of her lovers asleep between rumpled sheets and another photo of Magda and the rest of the Wicked Women – the girls that she and Shimmy would get together with as often as possible to get roaring drunk and swap increasingly hairy stories. Alex felt a pang of homesickness. She missed their sessions. There was nothing like that here, although she was looking forward to going out tonight. Antoinette, the French-born winemaker at the Chantal champenoise winery where Ollie sold his grapes, had asked her to join her for a night on the town and was coming to pick her up.

Not wanting to offend Gen and Ollie, she popped over to the house around six for a quick catch-up over a glass of wine, narrowly missing standing on the fluffy white barking rug. She explained she couldn't stay long because Antoinette would be picking her up soon.

'Here,' Alex said to Gen, handing over a copy of the plan she'd been working on all afternoon. 'This is what I think we need to do. If you're happy with it, I'll email it to the people at GreenWaste and see what they think. But in the meantime, I'd like you and Ollie to work through it, talk it over, and then meet with me some time tomorrow to discuss it.'

'Hey, well done,' Gen said, taking the plan, opening it gingerly, then closing it again and putting it down on the breakfast bar, away from the children's detritus. 'I'll read it thoroughly straight after dinner, and so will Ollie. Now, you be careful tonight. Those French girls have a rep for letting their hair down.'

'You sound like my Mum,' Alex laughed. 'It's nice to have someone keeping a watch on me again. That should stop me going off the rails, knowing you'll hear me come in.'

22. Dark and Handsome

Jackie the art director raised her glass.

'To a successful show,' she said.

'With no glitches,' said Skye the designer, holding up her tequila.

'And pray to God the trapeze act doesn't fall down,' said Sylvia the choreographer, clinking her Mac's against the other glasses.

'And the costumes don't crumble,' said Gretchen the costumier.

'And the sound system doesn't play up,' said Scott the soundman.

'Down the hatch,' said Skye, tossing the tequila down her throat then pulling a face as it hit the spot. 'Aaah, that's good.'

'To listen to you guys, you'd think the show was disaster prone,' Rick said, cradling his Steinlager. 'But every year, you manage to pull it off without a hitch.'

'Well, at least that's what it looks like,' Jackie said. 'It's like the duck swimming upstream – calm and serene on the surface, but paddling like fury underneath.'

'Yeah, you should see what it's like out the back,' Gretchen said. 'All those crazy costumes, some of them with dozens of different bits, some of them so fragile they look as if they'd fall apart in your hands.'

'And you have to get them onto some poor sod…' Jackie said.

'Who has to make it look as if it's a breeze to wear…' Scott said.

'When really they're just about to collapse under the weight of it …' Gretchen said.

'Or they're so hobbled they can hardly walk.' Jackie said, finishing her pinot. 'Here, my round.' She went up to the bar to buy the drinks.

She was drinking in the Victoria Rose pub with her workmates from the *Montana World of WearableArt Awards* show at the end of a very long day. She'd started work just after seven, going in to the big old warehouse early to work on one of the set pieces she'd been having trouble with. The colours hadn't looked right, but after this morning's efforts she was feeling much more satisfied with it – the sea greens and blues now dark and muted to provide a better backdrop for the fluorescent underwater creatures Skye had created. There'd been meetings, problems to sort out, people wanting her to help with this and that until the day had gone and there was just enough time for a Thai takeaway – again – and a Red Bull before rehearsal. With that over for another day, she'd come down to the Vic Rose with the crew – again.

'Whadd'ya have to do to get a drink around here?' drawled an American voice next to her, making her start. It took a moment before Jackie realised the drawler was talking to her. The voice belonged to a tall, slim slightly dishevelled-looking woman, about the same age as herself, who was wearing a hideously conservative crumpled beige jacket that had clearly seen better days and classic long-line pants like her mother used to wear. Not her type at all. The only indication of anything interesting behind the beige façade was a hot-pink, long-tasselled scarf around her neck.

'Oh, yeah,' Jackie said, startled at being addressed. 'They're slow tonight. It's Monday. They're probably short staffed.' She didn't want to sound like she was trying to excuse the place but she felt protective against an American invader.

'I'm Alex,' the invader said, holding out her hand. 'Alex Zerakowski. I'm in PR.'

'Jackie. Jackie Wainwright. I'm an artist. You can call me Jacks, though. Everyone else does.'

'What'll it be, love?' A barman had appeared and was addressing Jackie.

'Tequila, thanks. Eight of them. With lemon on the side.'

Alex whistled. 'You getting into that stuff so early? You must have staying power.'

Jackie laughed. 'Just felt like ordering something special. I've been on the pinot up to now. Time to live a little more dangerously!'

Antoinette came up and joined them at the bar.

'What's taking so long?' she asked.

'Monday-itis,' Jackie said laughing and introduced herself to Antoinette.

'It's busy, even for a Monday,' Alex said.

'This is where everyone comes, for now. It's like the place to go. Until the clubs. Later on, we'll go on to the Grumpy Mole, or Taylor's, or the Shark Club, depending. Like, around midnight, those places are jumping.'

Alex looked around at the raspberry pink walls covered in portraits of Victorian ladies on one side and delicate prints of roses on the other, meeting incongruously in the middle with a flashing red Coke sign and a wall-mounted TV set tuned to the rugby. The decor seemed most unusual for a trendy pub.

'What'll it be?' A barmaid had appeared and was talking to Alex.

'A pinot noir, please. And a chardonnay for Antoinette.'

'You're new here?' Jackie asked.

'Yes, I arrived two days ago from San Francisco. I'm staying near Hope, with the Darbys and their kids. I've escaped for the night with Antoinette.'

'Oh, you're from Chantal, aren't you. I've heard of your skills. It's a great wine you make there.' She turned back to Alex. 'Don't think I know the Darbys though.'

'They own a vineyard. Hangman's Hill, it's called.'

'That's a great name for a wine label,' Jackie said. 'Haven't they been having some trouble over putting in a landfill?'

'That's them,' Alex replied. She wondered if Jackie had some affiliation with the protesters. It wouldn't have surprised her. Her dress was slightly wacky, but you'd expect that with an arty type. She was wearing two brightly coloured mismatched tops that looked as if they'd been thrown on in a hurry – one was bright orange, the other postbox red with sparkly pearls and sequins around the neck in a clever spiderweb pattern. And a black tea-cosy hat was jammed down over gorgeously mad curls, jet-black streaked with magenta and purple, springing in all directions across her shoulders and down her back. Definitely an arty type.

'You said you're an artist?' she continued, changing the subject. She didn't want to buy an argument. 'Hey, that's interesting. Nelson seems to be a great place if you're creative.'

'Yeah, it is. Especially with the World of WearableArt here. It means we can earn a living as well.'

'You're working on the Wearable Arts?' Alex took a sip and raised her eyes heavenwards in appreciation of whatever brand of heavenly nectar she was drinking. 'Mmmm,' she said appreciatively.

'That's right. The whole team's here tonight.'

'D'you think I could meet them? I've heard so much about it.'

'Well I guess…'

'I just love the buzz of events like that. At home, I used to run events all the time. In the Napa, I started *Opera in the Vines* at one of the vineyards I used to work for. Now it's just huge.'

'You're an events person?'

'Yes, for my sins. My boyfriend used to tell me I got off on ordering people around. But I reckon the biggest thrill was just seeing thousands of people having a good time.'

'Maybe you could give us a hand then? We're always looking for volunteers – especially if they know what they're doing.'

'Hey, I'd love to. What do you think I could do? Publicity?'

'Possibly. I'll talk to our publicity people tomorrow. Come and meet the team when you're ready.'

'Twelve dollars,' the barmaid said.

Alex handed over a twenty-dollar bill, waited for her change then carried the drinks, following Antoinette, who had stopped to talk to an enormous bear of a man over by the wall.

'Alex, this is Wayne. He heads the town's detective force. He knows everyone and everything. Wayne, this is Alex. She's in PR.'

They shook hands. Alex couldn't take her eyes off Wayne's smooth domed head, shaved of all its hair. She reckoned she'd feel safe with him around. He looked like he could beat off an axe-murderer bare handed.

She stood there for a short time, only half listening to their conversation, not knowing who they were talking about, then saw Jackie beckoning her over. She excused herself to Antoinette and Wayne and took her drink over to the large group of people sitting on high stools around three tall, chest-high tables grouped together over by the window.

Jackie introduced her to everyone. When she got to Rick Sorensen, who she introduced as a lawyer about town, Alex experienced that old familiar feeling at the pit of her stomach again. He was very good looking – tall and lean, with dark wavy hair and a noticeable five-o'clock shadow. His carefully casual dress – beautifully cut denim jacket, black polo sweater and loose casual trousers – must have cost him a small fortune. Alex was entranced. She wanted to ask Jackie about him but there was no chance. When Jackie finished the introductions, Rick slipped down off his stool and offered it to her.

'Care for a seat?' he said, standing to mock attention and making a slight bow.

'That's kind of you,' Alex smiled warmly and took the proffered stool. 'D'you come here often?' she said and could have kicked herself immediately. How could she have let such an old line as that slip out?

'Yeah,' he said, apparently not noticing the gaffe. 'It's the place. And these guys from Wearable Arts liven it up at this time of year.'

'Do you have anything to do with the show?'

'Kind of, in an unofficial way. I was one of the models last year, and this year I've offered to give them a hand backstage or with security, or whatever, if they need me. It's one of those things half of the town gets involved with, one way or another.'

Alex was finding it hard to breathe. It was close and warm in the pub, but that wasn't what was upsetting her equilibrium. She could feel herself falling again, for yet another tall, dark and handsome man – just the type Anna said she should avoid. Surely, she thought, if he was a lawyer, he must be reasonably respectable. And he didn't seem vain or up himself like Lucian.

Antoinette came up and joined them, resulting in further introductions, and offered to buy the next round. When she returned, she said, 'I'll have to sit on this one now. I'm driving.'

'Aren't you a lucky girl, then,' Rick said to Alex. 'You can have as many as you like.'

'I don't think I'll be staying out late tonight, much as I'd like to,' Alex said, smiling at Rick. 'I've got heaps of work to do tomorrow.'

'I can't be late either,' Antoinette said. 'I've got to catch the first flight out to Auckland in the morning. I've got to be at the airport at six-thirty.'

'That's an early start,' Alex said. 'I don't envy you there.'

'You'll be in for a bumpy take-off, I'd say,' Rick said. 'There's a big nor-west gale forecast tonight. It'll make for a nasty crosswind.'

'Oh,' Antoinette said, looking glum. 'You fly out of there often?'

'Yeah, a bit,' he said. 'I've got my own plane.' He smiled. 'In fact, I got caught by a nor-wester just a couple of weeks ago. I was coming back from a meeting in Wellington. There was quite a gale blowing and I was struggling to hold her on course approaching the runway. She was dancing around in this terrible crosswind, wanting to go sideways all the time. I was just congratulating myself for bringing her head on and was about to land at full throttle when this bloody great seagull flew into the fucking propeller,' he said.

'Christ,' said Antoinette.

'What did you do?' said Alex.

'You should've seen the mess it made. Fucking feathers and guts all over the windscreen, and then the engine started coughing and playing up, running irregular. Turned out the impact of the bloody thing bent the propeller. It didn't like it at all.'

'Yuk,' Alex said.

'Yeah, it was yuk all right. Bloody disgusting,' Rick said. 'Anyway, I managed to hold her on course for a few more seconds. That's all I needed to land her. But I can tell you it was close. I thought my number was up when it hit. Fucking exploded everywhere. Bang!' he shouted then laughed at his own joke. Alex laughed with him.

'You must be a very experienced pilot, to be able to handle that,' she said admiringly.

'Oh, I've been doing it for a while now. Got my licence on my sixteenth birthday, as soon as it was legal; been flying myself around ever since.'

'What sort of plane is it?'

'A little Cessna 182. Nothing flash. But she's all mine.'

'I suppose it would come in handy for business, if you've got meetings out of town.'

'Sure does. And you don't have to sit around drinking bad coffee and eating up large in all those fancy business club lounges at the airport. Just get in, start the engine, and you're away.'

'It must be a wonderful way to see New Zealand.'

'That's for sure. You can be anywhere you want to be in no time at all. Tell you what,' Rick said looking at her more closely, 'Why don't you and me go for a spin sometime? I could show you a bit of New Zealand.'

Alex couldn't miss the sexy innuendo of that statement. She looked up from her drink intending to thank him for the suggestion and politely decline. But the look in his eyes caught her off guard and before she knew it, the pit of her stomach was telling her what to say.

'Really? That would be wonderful. I'd love that,' she heard herself saying, while her insides turned over with that familiar feeling she had whenever she met someone who inevitably turned out to be all wrong for her. Perhaps Rick would be different, she thought. Perhaps he'd be the Mr Right Anna told her she needed to find. Perhaps his suggestion of taking her flying was a generous gesture to a visitor from a foreign shore.

'Alex, isn't it?'

'Yes, that's right.' At least he'd remembered her name, she thought.

'Right, Alex. What do you say to a trip to… er, let me see… to Queenstown. Do you ski?'

'Not brilliantly. But yes, I can ski.'

'A ski trip to Coronet Peak then. How about next Saturday?'

Alex paused. He was coming on strong all of a sudden, but she wasn't about to look a gift horse in the mouth. Here she was being offered a chance to see a large chunk of New Zealand's most scenic landscape and have a ski day while she was about it, all in the company of this rich, spunky man.

'That'd be terrific. Thank you.' She smiled and hoped the lust she felt inside didn't show on her face.

They agreed to get in touch during the week and make the arrangements. Soon after that, she lost track of him. He'd said he had to go and meet someone at Taylor's nightclub, and Alex opted to stay on at the Vic Rose. He gave her a quick peck on the cheek as he went, but after he'd gone she told herself not to be surprised if that was the last she heard from him.

Antoinette left about the same time, after Skye said she'd give Alex a lift home, since she had to go out towards Hope anyway. 'I stopped drinking ages ago,' Skye said, raising a glass of soda, 'so you don't need to worry.'

It seemed like Antoinette had only just left when a couple of young men came up and introduced themselves to their table, asking about the Wearable Arts.

'Excuse us, but we heard you talking about the Wearable Arts Show,' one of them said in an accent that sounded very much like her own. 'We've seen all these posters everywhere and everyone seems to be talking about it. What is it?'

Jackie spieled off an explanation, making it sound fabulous.

'Wow, we've got to see this, Curtis,' the Californian said. 'Are you all involved with it?'

'Yes,' they all said except Alex, who said, 'No.'

'You're the only one?' the young man said to her.

'No, I'm not involved. But it sounds such fun, I've offered to help out any way I can.'

'Hey, you're from the same part of the world as me,' he said, and stuck out his hand. 'Zhi Kingston. And this is my mate Curtis Williams. We're both from San Franciso.'

Alex looked more closely at them. The one who'd done all the talking wasn't bad looking, but was way too short. He'd be pushing it to be taller than her. He had thick black hair, but short and craggy, and big dark eyes. His mate was taller and sandy-haired.

'Alex Zerakowski,' she said, shaking the proffered hand. 'I'm from San Francisco too. It's kinda nice to hear a familiar accent again.'

'My turn to get the drinks,' Curtis said.

'Mind if we join you?' Zhi asked them all.

'Go ahead,' Jackie said.

'Not at all,' Alex said.

Curtis headed for the bar and Zhi found an empty stool, which he pulled up beside Alex and sat down.

'I know what you mean,' he said. 'When you're so far away from home, it's a relief sometimes to find something or someone familiar.'

'I even felt homesick,' she said. 'I've never felt that before, and I've been away heaps of times.'

'I used to get awful homesick at first, too,' Zhi said. 'I should explain. Curtis and I do the computer stuff on an oil exploration ship. We're stuck in port at the moment after a few problems with the gear. We work for a San Francisco-based company.'

Alex became engrossed in conversation with him and lost all track of time. They swapped college stories, talked about the clubs and bars they liked, restaurants and café bars, movies, music, friends and family. They found some haunts in common and even discovered a relative of Alex's who knew a friend of Zhi's.

'Three degrees of separation,' Zhi said, laughing with pleasure.

By the time Curtis stood and announced they ought to get back to the ship or they'd be in trouble with Franklin, Alex felt she knew more about Zhi than she had about Lucian or any of her past amours. He'd make a really good friend, she thought. There was no spark, no churning in the pit of her stomach. He just seemed easy to get along with, and really interesting to talk to. It would make a nice change, she told herself, to have a platonic friendship with a man her age.

She realised she'd had a bit too much to drink when she couldn't find the bedroom light.

'Oh well,' she excused herself. 'I've only been here a few of days. I can't be expected to know where everything is yet.' She'd given up and staggered to the bathroom, where she'd found the switch, no problem. 'See, I'm all right after all,' she said to her reflection in the mirror, then set to brushing her teeth and getting ready for bed. When that was done, she flicked off the light and headed for the bed, fumbling her way along the side of the duvet in the darkness.

She was just about to pull back the sheets when she thought she heard a loud banging and clattering outside, as if someone were rattling a metal object against the iron rails of the gate. And people were shouting out something. She couldn't hear what it was. Alarmed, she sat up in bed, her heart racing. There shouldn't be anyone outside, she told herself. But then she heard it again. Voices chanting. More than a little scared now, she decided to get up and see who it was.

Growing more accustomed to the darkened room, Alex felt her way around the end of the bed and over to the window, curtains still wide open, where starlight threw the distant Hangman's Hill into a vague silhouette. The noise stopped. There was nobody there.

'You're imagining things,' she told herself. 'Must be all that wine you had.'

She found the bed again, pulled back the duvet and sheets and collapsed into it. The room started to spin.

Almost imperceptibly at first, the chanting started again, growing louder. She tried to work out what they were saying.

'Haw Haw Madras Haw.' Or at least that's what it sounded like. She'd never heard anything so absurd. Funny what your brain did after blinding it with buckets of red wine. She figured the noise would go away as soon as she fell asleep, and boy was she drowsy. She was just drifting off when suddenly, a nerve twitched her awake and with instant clarity she could decipher the chant:

'Whore! Whore! Murderer's whore!'

She sat up in bed wide awake. The lynch mob coming for Carrie could have chanted something like that. So why was she hearing it now, nearly one hundred and forty years later? This was absurd. She flung back the covers and stomped over to the window, which was easily visible now that she was accustomed to the dark. There was still nobody out there. Her imagination was obviously playing tricks on her. Last night's conversation with Gen when she'd learned about the history of the cottage was obviously working in with the pinot and that infinitesimal toke she'd taken on Rick's joint to make her hallucinate.

'This is crazy,' she said to the stars and went back to bed.

23. Tequila Surprise

The music was deafening. Ever since she'd walked into Taylor's with Rick, she'd found it almost impossible to hear anything he was saying. There was an amateur rock band playing half way down the elongated room and somebody had neglected to tell them to keep the decibels at a level that didn't completely block conversation. Alex suspected her eardrums would never be the same again, and her musical senses were also severely damaged. Although opera was her passion, she wasn't averse to rock. But this defied description.

Rick paid for their drinks and they escaped down the other end of the bar, nearer the street and away from the ear-splitting sound.

'Tequila,' he said, passing her a short glass of clear liquor. 'I didn't bother with all that salt and lemon stuff. Let's just shoot it.'

He raised it in a toast then tossed it down in one gulp. She copied him and gasped as it hit her throat. She hadn't done the tequila thing in years – not since Pete – but it tasted just as vile as it had way back then.

'I'll get another drink,' Rick shouted in her ear. 'Want the same again?'

'No,' she shouted back. 'I'll be legless if I have another one. I'd better have a Diet Coke.'

He raised an eyebrow in mock surprise. 'Don't be a wuss. I'll find you something you'll like,' he said and returned to the bar. She figured it probably wouldn't matter now, having another one. She'd had so many drinks already, another one wouldn't make much difference.

She looked around. It was after midnight Thursday – or at least now it would be Friday, Alex realised. The place was packed. There were no tables left, and not a chair to be seen. She was standing beside the stairs, near a few keen people on the dance-floor gyrating in front of a wide-screen video showing silent music videos – the sound drowned by the racket the band was making. Behind her, a group of men and women in bikie leathers were playing pool. In front of her, over by the door, a bunch of skinheads were arguing with each other.

She wasn't sure if she should stay for much longer or go home. This place was outside her comfort zone, but that wasn't necessarily a bad thing. It was good to live on the edge a little sometimes.

She'd agreed to come here with Rick, leaving the others at the Vic Rose where most of the night she'd sat with Zhi, who'd come out with Curtis again. It was the first she'd seen of him since they'd first met three nights ago and she was careful not to drink too much this time. They'd talked of San Francisco again and, like before, the time just seemed to fly. Alex had tried to explain why she was so passionate about opera and Zhi had entertained her with tales of life on the ocean wave.

But when Rick arrived, around eleven, she'd quickly forgotten about Zhi and switched her attentions to the sexy newcomer. He had an incredible pull on her emotions. He seemed to bring with him the scent of excitement, an anticipation of action and thrills to come. Zhi was very sweet, but around the same bar table as Rick, he was bordering on boring. After that, Zhi had seemed to melt away into the crowd.

'For you, my little spin doctor,' Rick had said when bringing her a drink. 'See what sort of spin that gets you in.' He'd brought her a fancy cocktail, creamy yellow and frothy, with a mini paper umbrella and a straw stuck out the side.

'What's this?' she asked.

'A little concoction the barman whipped up specially for you,' he said. 'I told him you were the world's best spin doctor and needed something to help you keep on spinning.' He sat down beside her and played with her hair. She caught his hand and squeezed it.

'You're impossible,' she said. 'You're obsessed with this spin doctor thing. Why?'

'Because I've never met a PR guru before. They're not exactly thick on the ground in Nelson, you know. And because I think it's cool, you being a spin doctor. I should call you Doc.' He laughed and gestured to the others that they should join in on the joke. 'Doc. Do you like that, eh? Doc!'

'Don't be silly, Rick. I'm not a spin doctor. I'm an environmental communication strategist, actually.'

'That's far too fancy for me,' he said, continuing to laugh. 'Spin doctor will do for a small town boy like me. I'm going to call you Doc.'

'Suit yourself,' she'd said. He'd probably get sick of it after a while and think of something else. As indeed it now seemed. He hadn't called her that since they'd arrived in the nightclub.

He returned with a highball glass of vodka and tonic for her and a Mac's for himself. He seemed to be looking for someone he knew. It was impossible to talk over the din, so they stood for a while, sipping, looking around.

'Let's dance,' Rick said suddenly.

'Sure,' she said. He took her drink, put both their glasses down on a nearby table and escorted her to the dance floor. They started jumping around the same way as everyone else but after a while, when the band played something a little slower, he took her in his arms and slow-danced her around the edge of the carpet, pressing her groin close to his. She could feel him hard against her and a shock wave of desire rippled up through her, making her a little breathless.

'You're hot tonight,' Rick said, so close to her ear she could feel his hot breath tickling her.

'So are you,' she replied.

They stayed on the dance floor until the band took a break then retrieved their drinks and stood over by the stairs again.

'Hey, Rick, how'ya doing mate?' One of the skinheads she'd seen earlier – a short fat guy with a number two haircut – had come over and was slapping Rick on the back cordially.

'Hey, Stumpy, how are ya?'

'Who's your hot date tonight, then?'

'None of your business, mate. Whatcha up to?'

'Just cruising, looking for some action. You got any?'

'Now why would I be looking for some action, Stumpy? I've got all I need right here. Can't you see we're busy?'

'Yeah, sure, sure. I just thought you might have seen Jared.'

At the mention of that name, Rick looked around furtively, then pulled Stumpy away from Alex to have a spirited discussion which Alex couldn't fully hear, but gathered that Jared and Rick were into something together that Stumpy seemed to want to be a part of but Rick wasn't interested. Their argument seemed to be dragging on. Alex looked around and realised she was tired and wanted to go home.

'Sorry, Doc,' Rick said, returning to her, looking annoyed. 'He thinks I'm going to hand it to him on a plate.'

Alex wasn't sure what *it* was but was past caring.

'I need to go home now, Rick,' she said. 'I'm buggered and I've had way too much to drink.'

He studied her and apparently concurred with her diagnosis.

'You look like you could do with a lie down. I'd better take you home.'

'No it's okay Rick, you stay here if you want. I'll get myself home. You shouldn't try to drive all that way anyway. You've had a bit to drink too.'

'You're right. I've probably had enough to make it a bit risky. I'll help you get a taxi.'

He escorted her outside and found a cab on the rank.

'Now don't forget. We've got a big date this weekend. I'm flying you to Queenstown. I'll call you at lunchtime and arrange it.'

24. The Eve of Destruction

Alex stood there, swaying gently in the cold night air, until the taxi was just a faint hum in the distance.

'Gotta get inside,' she said to nobody in particular, and turned to face the Darbys' big cream mansion, glowing in the moonlight like a homing beacon. Slowly her brain figured that her cottage was off to the right, behind the big house. Carefully putting one foot in front of the other, she picked her way across the courtyard and around the corner, falling against the smooth plastered wall as she did so.

'Oops,' she said, and smiled at her clumsiness. Her fingers rubbed the smooth cement. 'I'm plastered, too' she said, and collapsed into a fit of the giggles, then spoke sternly to herself, 'Now, Alexandra. Pull yourself together.' She sounded like her father. 'Stop this silly nonsense and get yourself to bed. Anyone would think you'd never been pissed before.'

Putting a steadying hand against the wall, Alex stood and marched herself along the path, carefully avoiding the rose bushes up against the house, her aim set firmly on the gate to the cottage, which she could just make out in the distance.

It proved a devil to open. Somebody must have jammed the latch down hard, because it took ages to get it free. And when it finally clicked up, the gate took off at speed, flinging her at a rakish angle behind it.

'Hey!' she called out to the errant gate as she plummeted after it.

The paving stones on the now familiar path proved an uneven obstacle course, but she managed to make the front porch with only a couple of stumbles. The door key! Where on earth was it? She fumbled in her bag to no avail. No loose jagged piece of metal there. But it had to be in there somewhere. She tipped the contents of her bag out on the verandah and knelt down, scrabbling around in the flotsam to find the wretched keys. Luckily, the three-quarter moon was bright enough to see by – she'd once again forgotten to leave any lights on when she'd left. At last, a flash of silver and she retrieved the key. It took ages to get it into the lock. She'd never realised how tricky it was to open. Once inside, she flicked on the light switch, turned to shut the door and noticed her bag and its contents still on the rough wooden floor outside. She stooped to pick up her wallet and suddenly saw a bunch of stars circling around her head. Oh dear, she thought, bending down wasn't a good idea. She managed to scoop up the wallet and left the rest of the stuff until the morning. Nothing too precious there that she couldn't do without for a few hours.

The door firmly shut, Alex strode purposefully across the lounge to the stairs and, holding tightly onto the banister, pulled herself up to the top.

The sudden darkness at the top of the stairs disoriented her and she stumbled around, arms flailing along the walls, trying to find the light switch. It wasn't the hall light that finally switched on but her bedroom light that practically blinded her, such was the brilliance of the ceiling spots.

'Shhh, not so loud,' she said to the lights and continued on, stumbling on the carpet – there must have been a rise in the floor level, she reasoned, she'd check that out tomorrow – and turned on the overhead neon bathroom light, then rushed back to turn off the bedroom lights. That was better. A nice soft beam from the bathroom illuminated just enough of the bedroom for her to see her way to bed. But first she needed to pee.

The toilet seemed to have moved from where she remembered it being before. Boy, it was a relief to find it, because suddenly she had that awful feeling in the pit of her stomach that warned her she was about to throw up.

That felt better. But now the taps were in the wrong place. She splashed her face with water, as if that might sober her up, but it just felt cold and unpleasant. Towelling herself dry, she let the towel slip to the floor – pick it up tomorrow, she told herself – and returned to the bedroom to undress.

She opened the wardrobe door and draped her jacket over a hanger, then lifted her foot up to rest on the raised wardrobe floor so she could undo the zip at the side of her boots. It slid down three-quarters way to the bottom, then jammed. 'Damned thing,' she shouted at it. 'Why won't you unzip?' She'd have to take it off as it was. But of course, it wouldn't come off. She lifted her leg higher and toppled over, crashing down inside the wardrobe and hitting her head on the far wall. 'Ow!' she cried and put her hand out to save herself falling further. But to her utter dismay, her hand disappeared into the pile of shoes and continued on, straight through the thin plywood floor. 'Owwwuh!' And to make matters worse, half her clothes came crashing down on top of her.

'Shit!' she cried loudly. 'Double shit! What am I going to do now?'

She flailed around under the clothes, trying desperately to extricate her fist through the hole while shoving trousers and skirts off her face. At last, her hand came free and, shaking it impatiently, she crawled across the room to her bed where she finally managed to remove the offending boot, along with the other one, which unzipped effortlessly. She flung the boots and her socks, which she'd also peeled off, across at the gaping wardrobe, which seemed now to be mocking her, its wide open door still swinging on its hinges from its encounter with her, like one hand clapping.

'Stop laughing at me,' she told the wardrobe, then pulled back the covers and clambered up onto the bed, falling asleep almost before she'd lain down.

When she awoke, sunshine was streaming through the windows and the room was a furnace. She'd forgotten to pull the curtains and the bright light was killing her eyes, which were on fire from the sandpaper that seemed to be rubbing on them. Her head was throbbing and her mouth felt like the bottom of a birdcage.

'Oh God!' she said, with only a small croaky part of her voicebox working. 'What have I done to deserve this?' She needed to get up and drink water. But just raising her head slightly from the pillow brought tears to her eyes and made her temples feel as if they were about to implode. She lay there groaning until thirst drove her to stand up and stagger to the bathroom, holding her forehead with one hand and her stomach with the other. She filled her toothbrush mug with water and downed it in seconds, refilling it immediately from the still-running tap. As she looked up to drink the second mug full, she gasped in horror as she saw herself in the mirror. She was still fully dressed, with only her jacket, boots and socks missing. And she looked shocking. She'd not seen herself look back out of a mirror as appallingly as that since the early days of her affair with Lucian, when they seemed to be out drinking almost every night. She needed a shower, badly. Or even a hose down, like at the car wash, with lots of soapsuds and cleansers.

The shower jets were particularly vicious, squirting sharp needles of burning hot water into every pore. She jumped away and adjusted the temperature, managing to douse half of her body with freezing spray before getting it more or less right. It started to feel better. She stood for several minutes with hot water running onto the back of her neck until at least some of the pain went away, then washed herself and her hair thoroughly.

After towelling herself dry and wrapping a towel around her hair, Alex brushed her teeth. Lord only knows what her breath smelt like, she thought, and squirted some breath freshener into her mouth. Then she stepped gingerly across the carpet to find some clean clothes.

That was when she realised, to her mortification, that she'd practically destroyed the lovely old wardrobe. There, under the rubble of clothes and shoes, was a hole in the wardrobe floor, with one of her high heels halfway down it. She went over to it and pulled the shoe out, noticing as she did so a spread of newspaper underneath. Its presence puzzled her, as there wasn't supposed to be anything underneath except the carpet on the floor below. Cautiously, remembering with embarrassment her bull-like behaviour the night before, Alex lowered her hand into the hole, touching the paper and finding a hard surface underneath. The wardrobe must have a false bottom, she realised, because there was a good two inches under its current floor level and then what appeared to be a second floor, which was spread with the newspaper she'd seen. Intrigued, she pulled the remaining shoes out and poked her head into the hole to have a closer look. It was dark. She needed a torch to see properly, but she could make out a black shape in the far corner. It looked like a leather-bound book. She could smell its mustiness – the same mustiness she noticed on her first day. She pushed her hand down the hole and, turning her wrist hard against the second floor, forced it along as far as it would go to reach the book. She found she could just touch it, and with a bit of twisting and wriggling, was able to pull it towards her with her fingertips, until she could reach it easily. The only problem now was that the hole was too small to extract the book through. Oh well, she rationalised, I've made such a mess of it now, I'm going to have to 'fess up to the Darbys anyway, so another couple of inches won't hurt. Selecting one of her sturdy, hard-soled walking boots from the pile on the floor, Alex thumped its heel hard down against the side of the hole several times, until it was big enough for the book to pass through.

Once it was out, she wriggled away from the wardrobe and, sitting on the chair between the wardrobe and the fireplace, held the book up to the light, squinting against the bright sunlight as she did so, acutely conscious once more of her tender head.

It was a plain brown leather-covered book, with no title or author named on the front cover, nor on the spine. Turning it over, she couldn't make out any distinguishing characteristics. Just plain brown leather. She opened the cover. The frontispiece was a mottled, streaky watermark of burgundy and pale pink, with creamy yellow swirls. But still no indication as to what it was. She turned the page to reveal a thick, cream-coloured page covered in dark ink handwriting, a beautiful sloping hand, with neatly shaped letters and occasional flourishes. In the top right-hand corner the page was headed Hokitika, followed on the next line by a date – September 1st, 1866. Today was, she calculated slowly on her fingers starting with the day she'd arrived in Nelson five days ago, August 29th. So this book was almost exactly one hundred and thirty-six years old – it would be that date in three days' time.

The writing was hard to read, but it seemed to be a diary or memoir, with recollections prior to September as well as descriptions of that day's events. She flicked over a few more pages – more dates, more hand-writing – until three folded pieces of thick, yellowed paper fell out into her lap, along with an old sepia photograph. Faded and worn around the edges, it was a picture of a couple at a dance. They were both of roughly the same height. He had a bushy beard and thinning hair on the top of his head, while she had long curly light-coloured hair, the curls escaping from their pins down her back and to one side. She was wearing a tight-waisted ballgown with a high collar and long leg-o'mutton sleeves. By the look on her face, she was ecstatic. Alex turned it over. On the back, she could just make out "Grand Ball, Hokitika, 1866."

She put the picture down and picked up the pieces of paper, placing them carefully on top of the open book. She unfolded one to see what it was. To her amazement, the letter was headed 'Nelson Gaol'.

Thursday, October 4, 1866
My Dearest Carrie
Most willingly I write to you, thanking you for your kind letter and the comforting thoughts and poems you sent me.

In your good and compassionate letter, you have emphatically set out for me the sinner's refuge and trust in Jesus.

You know, more than anyone, Carrie, what an egregious sinner I have been and what a terrible load of guilt I have to account for. But I trust that, through the way to forgiveness that the priest has set forth for me, a merciful and loving Saviour will accept me tomorrow, when I go to the gallows and end my wicked and sinful life. What does the hymn say?

> There is a fountain filled with blood
> Drawn from Emmanuel's veins
> And sinners, plunged beneath that flood
> Lose their guilty stains.

The mail that brought me your sweet letter was the same mail that brought me my death warrant. What an ugly companion accompanied your message of comfort.

Sweet soul, I pray that you will continue to forgive me for the cruel way I have treated you and that our child will never know the shame I have brought on you.

Though my pulse will have ceased to beat in the hand that answers yours, I trust that it will be beating in Heaven. May God ever bless you.

Yours in Christ
Richard Burgess

Part two

25. Another Prodigal Returns

Richard slid down off the big bay and tied the mare up to the rail outside the Hope General Store. He pulled his handkerchief out of his pocket, wiped the dust and sweat from his forehead and eyes and climbed the steps, his knees unsteady after the long ride. It had been more than a month since he'd been in the saddle for such a long time and his backside was already feeling stiff and sore. He'd hired a horse from the stables in Trafalgar Street and had spent the whole morning riding along the road south of Nelson, trying to find trace of Carrie. Hope was the second last town on his list. He was getting desperate. If he didn't find her soon, he'd have to turn around, or he wouldn't get the horse back before nightfall. And that would leave him just one more day to find her. The steamer to America was due to leave on the tide on Wednesday the twentieth of June, and today was already Monday. He was running out of time.

He'd told Tom he wanted to find her to get his greatcoat and other clothing. But he knew in his heart that this was only half the story. He knew he wanted to see Carrie again because he loved her and didn't want to be parted from her. He wasn't sure if this was because she was carrying his child, or if he just simply loved her for herself. Either way, it didn't matter. He was consumed with the single purpose of seeing her again, just one last time, before he had to depart for San Francisco.

'Good afternoon, sir,' a homely looking older woman greeted him from behind a stack of jars and boxes. 'What can I get you?'

'Dick Hill, Ma'am,' Richard said, with a slight nod. 'I've been sent by my employer, a solicitor, to find a young woman for whom I have some good news. I was wondering if you had seen her in these parts. Her name is Carrie O'Neill.'

The woman's eyes brightened with recognition. 'Mrs O'Neill?' she said. 'Why, she was in here this morning ordering her… Well, that is… You've just missed her. My husband arrived home from town less than an hour ago and took her home with her order in the cart.'

'That's wonderful news,' Richard said. 'I've been trying all the villages between here and Nelson and I was just about to give up. I'd be most grateful if you could tell me where I might find her. I have promised to deliver this personally.' He held up an envelope with handwriting on the front and a red wax seal on the back. It contained nothing – he was simply using it as a front – but it looked important.

The woman happily passed on directions to Carrie's new abode, which she described as a commodious farm cottage three miles along the Clover Road followed by a turn into a winding valley road on the side of a hill.

Mounting the bay mare, he headed for the Clover Road turnoff at a trot then spurred her into a gallop along the straight, dusty road until at last he reached the end. It felt good with the wind in his hair and whistling round his ears. About the only good thing to come of his years in prison was appreciation of freedom when he was at large. He revelled in it, calling out Carrie's name at the top of his voice and laughing out loud. "Carrie O'Neill. *Mrs* O'Neill. Married at last, I hear!' He'd been careful not to show any reaction to the woman in the store referring to Carrie as Mrs O'Neill. It stood to reason, after all, for her to pretend to be a married woman, coming into such a foreign place on her own. Especially in her condition. He wondered if she would be showing by now and how she would receive him. No doubt she would put pressure on him again to make an honest woman of her. He would be able to tease her about that, he reckoned, now that she was saying she was married.

He slowed to a trot at the next turnoff and eventually recognised the two-storey farm cottage from the description he'd been given. There was no sign of anyone outside, but he could detect wisps of smoke coming from a chimney on the far side of the house. He hitched the horse to the picket fence and left it to graze at the roadside, opened the iron gate and strode up the dirt path to the front door.

'Hello there,' he called, as he knocked on the door. 'Anybody there?'

Silence. He knocked again.

At last he heard footsteps, tentative, halting. They stopped, but the door remained closed. He was just about to knock again when the door finally opened and his beloved Carrie stood there, one hand pushing self-consciously at the thick red curls of hair that were always escaping from their pins, the other holding an apron that had clearly just been hurriedly removed.

'Carrie! I've found you, my little chick.'

'Richard,' she said hesitantly, scarcely able to believe it was him. 'I was worried I'd never see you again.'

'Why's that, now? You should have known I'd seek you out, wherever you're hiding.'

'But I asked all around Nelson for you. Nobody had heard of you.'

'That's because I've been using another name. You know me.' He smiled what he hoped was disarmingly.

'But I asked for Richard Burgess *and* Dick Hill. I read in the papers about your other name. It was still no use, though.'

'I'm a man of many aliases, my little chick.'

'Didn't you want me to find you, then?'

'No, it wasn't that. Of course I wanted to see you. But I always adopt a different name when I'm new in a town. You never know what might happen.'

'If only…' Carrie was about to say if only he'd trusted her and told her what name he was going to use, but backed away from a row. She knew he hated to talk about how he made his money and why he had to hide things from her. So instead she said, 'But how did you find me?'

'I've been searching for you everywhere. I wanted to see you again.'

'You'd better come in,' she said, opening the door wide and indicating he should enter. 'The Shaw sisters are bound to have their spies out.'

'Then let's give them something to talk about, my little chick,' he said and kissed her on the mouth, gently at first but then more urgently.

'No, Richard. Not here. Come inside, please.'

'Why, Carrie, you've turned into a conservative little thing. Time was, you would have loved to kiss me on the doorstep, just to show the neighbours you didn't give a fig about them.'

'Well, it's a bit different here, so please come inside.' She waited for him to enter, albeit reluctantly, and closed the door firmly behind him. 'I've got to look at how it might be in the long term now, how the people around here will think of me and treat me in the years to come. I'm going to stay here, Richard, and have my baby.'

'But why here, Carrie? You don't know a soul.'

'Exactly. That's exactly why I'm going to stay here. Nobody knows about my past. Nobody knows I've worked in a hotel barroom. Nobody knows I grew up without a father. And nobody knows that I'm not really married. It's perfect, you see. I could be anyone. I could even be *Mrs* O'Neill.'

'Now Carrie, it's not fair to bring that up now. By Heavens, I've only just arrived.'

'You're quite right, Richard, please forgive me. I've been so longing to see you, my words are just tumbling out unformed, without thinking.

I should be making you welcome. You must be exhausted from the road. Let me take your coat and I'll make you a cup of tea.'

'Actually, Carrie, I'd fancy something a bit stronger if you can oblige. It's been a difficult couple of days.'

'I think I've got some brandy in the kitchen. I've only just unpacked everything and it's still a bit of a jumble I'm afraid. Here, let me take your coat, then I'll go see.'

'I should give the horse some water, first. Can you give me a pail and I'll fill it from the well.'

She led him through to the kitchen and out to the back porch, where she handed him a pail, pointed him in the direction of the hand pump then went inside to make tea.

'Good Lord,' she said to herself as she turned up the stove, put the kettle on the hob and fetched two cups and saucers. 'What am I going to do with him?'

She'd felt like crying when he'd stood there at her front door, smiling that wicked, cheeky grin. But she was not going to show her relief or any emotion. Not yet anyway. She could tell there was something troubling him, something much bigger than whether he could find her or where he was going to stay tonight. She stood at the window for a moment, watching him set the pail of water down in front of the big brown horse. He patted its rump, lingering for a moment, before walking up the path and letting himself in the unlocked door. She busied herself with the tea things, found the brandy and fetched the German apple cake from the tin in the cupboard.

'My, Carrie, you've been baking already.'

He'd come up behind her and was holding her gently around the waist. She turned to face him and smiled.

'No Richard, I've hardly had time for that yet. This is a special German cake. You must try it. It's beautifully moist and spicy. Much nicer than any of my feeble efforts.'

'Nonsense. You bake lovely cakes.'

'Oh Richard, if only I could,' she said laughing. 'I burn more than I can rescue.'

'Here, let me.' He took the tray from her and carried it into the parlour. 'Where are we going to sit?'

'Put it down on one of the trunks,' she said. 'There's no furniture yet, but the trunks make do for chairs and a table meantime. And I've a mattress on the floor.'

'So that's what you were ordering down at the store – furniture,'

Richard said. 'The woman there said you'd just been in ordering up something – she didn't say what though. Will it take long to arrive?'

'Most of it should be here within the week.' She poured them both tea, stirred sugar into Richard's cup and handed it to him, along with a piece of apple cake.

'Well, that's good to hear. I want to know you'll be safe and well provided for, Carrie. You're important to me.'

'You've been very generous, sir,' she said, pouring his brandy and handing it to him. 'But from the way you talk, it sounds as though you're going away again.'

'That may well be. I don't know yet, for sure.' He downed most of the brandy in one gulp and held up his glass for more.

'But Richard, you told me to follow you here with your things, and I have done so. I've only just arrived. You can't go away so soon.' She refilled his glass then sat down opposite him on the other trunk.

'I hope not to, no. But I can't make you any promises. I just want to make sure you're safe.'

'It's hard to know, these days. There are so many bad things happening out there.' Carrie took a deep breath before continuing. She was determined to bring this up, to see his reaction and hopefully to allay her growing fears of his involvement. 'When I was in Nelson yesterday, the whole town was talking about those men missing on the Maungatapu Mountain.'

'Yes, I read about that in the paper,' he said with what Carrie suspected was studied casualness. She'd grown to know him quite well in the few short months they'd lived together and she thought she could detect a sudden sharpness in his look, as if his brain had suddenly snapped to attention. 'Dreadful business.'

'It said they were looking for four suspicious-looking men, Richard. You don't have any idea who they might be, do you?' She looked at him closely and he returned her intense gaze. But he didn't flinch. She had to hand it to him – he was cool under pressure.

'I don't think anybody knows. I saw a poster offering a big reward for anyone who finds them.' Richard continued to look at her closely, his eyebrows slightly raised, as if he was daring her to show her hand at a game of cards. But she'd seen enough games in the Golden Age to know how to match him.

'How much is the reward?' she asked.

'Four hundred pounds.'

'Is that right? That's a lot of money for someone looking to pick up some quick cash.'

'It is indeed, Carrie. A lot of money.' His eyes were steely blue. 'It's just as well you're so well provided for.'

She knew, when he said that. She knew that Richard was involved in some way. And he knew she knew. But did he know if she would tell anyone? If she would be tempted by the four hundred pounds? She wasn't so sure herself.

'I am indeed, Richard, and I have you to thank for that,' she said, raising her eyebrows quizzically, like his. 'But there's no point in me hankering after that reward money, is there? Because I wouldn't have the faintest idea who could do such a terrible thing as that. It must be quite something to have on your conscience, the murder of four men.' She looked hard into his eyes to see if there was any reaction, but there was none. He just kept on staring back, his eyes still hard as flint, then broke into a disarming smile.

'Come, Carrie, we're wasting our precious time talking of such things that have nothing to do with us. We should be making the most of our time together. I'd forgotten. I have something for you.' He stood up and dashed out the door to his horse. Carrie could see him through the window picking a box out of his saddle bag.

'Look at this, my little chick,' he said returning though the door and closing it. 'I've been shopping for you.' He handed her the box.

'Thank you, Richard. You shouldn't have…'

'I want you to be happy, Carrie. I hope you like it.'

She undid the string and opened the oblong brown cardboard box. Inside, under a layer of thin white tissue paper was a beautiful dark brown fur shawl. She touched it gingerly. She'd never had a fur before. Slowly, she unfolded the soft, slinky stole and held it up to admire it, before lifting it to her cheek and rubbing it gently against her skin.

'Oh, Richard, it's beautiful. Thank you.'

'It's sable, Carrie. Only the best for you.'

'You spoil me.'

'You deserve to be spoiled, my little chick. I want you to have the best, and have it now.'

'Why's that? Don't you think you'll be around to give me the best tomorrow, or the day after?'

'How can I answer that? You know I can't say.'

'I wish…'

'No point in wishing, Carrie. The best you and I can do is make the most of today; make it count, just in case there's no tomorrow.'

26. Naughty Weekend

Soaring over an ever-changing landscape dotted with green valleys and cobalt lakes in front of the long white spine of the Southern Alps, while listening to the accompaniment of the diva singing Puccini's 'One Fine Day' on the portable CD, Alex felt as if she'd died and gone to heaven. With both ears covered by the aviation headset and one ear plugged in under that to the CD, Alex could hardly hear the drone of the little plane's single engine or the intrusive radio transmitter. It was as if she was flying above the earth, an angel on the wing, serenaded by music so divine it must be coming from the gods. The view was more spectacular than any she had ever seen – more breathtaking than the Rocky Mountains, more enticing than the Greek Islands. On her left, not too far away, was the blue Pacific; on her right, beyond the mountains, the hazy dark green Tasman Sea. And below, alps stretched for mile after mile, glistening with new snow fallen overnight, some peaks so high they pierced the sky. Just moments ago, Rick had pointed out Aoraki, the highest mountain of all, and had named the lakes as they'd flown over. It was a perfect day for flying – not a cloud in the sky.

It was a typical South Island day, Rick had said. A southerly had whipped through, dumping snow and lashing the land with icy winds. Rick had predicted the following day would dawn with clear skies and the land would sparkle afresh under its cover of raindrops and snow crystals. Several times she'd been dazzled as silver ribbons of rivers caught the sun as they flew by.

Below to the right was a big lake and a tiny village on its nearest shore. Suddenly, the plane turned and headed up a valley with mountainous round hills now on both sides.

'This is the Cardrona Valley,' Rick said, his voice coming out the speakers in her headset as if he were miles away. The mountains towered above them. Alex felt very vulnerable in the little plane. She could see its shadow on the bare brown slopes to her right – an infinitesimal dot that looked no bigger than a tussock. 'That's the Pisa Range on the left,' Rick said. 'That's where everyone goes for cross country-skiing.' She looked out her side window at a big flat shelf on top of the high mountain range. Thick with snow, it was as smooth and flat as the top of a wedding cake. 'And there, that's the test-driving range. The big American and European car firms try out their new models up there, where no-one can see how they perform.' Alex could see curvy black road tracks in the middle of the snow, but no cars. 'Over there,' Rick was pointing to the right now, 'that's Cardrona ski area. It's very popular with families.' They were passing a ski road with numerous vehicles on it, snaking their way slowly up the side of a mountain. At the top, getting closer by the second, was a big ski lodge with a tall peaked clock tower and hundreds of figures dotted in the snow. A nearby chairlift was filled with skiers on their way uphill, while dozens more skied down a scattering of trails stretching across the broad, treeless flank of the mountain. It was the first time she'd seen such a big skifield without any trees.

Moments later, they came to the end of the valley and flew over a high snow-covered plateau that suddenly, breathtakingly dropped hundreds of feet down to a wide green valley. The view all around was spectacular – razor-ridged mountains to her left, with another ski road clinging to the steep hillside, an enormous deep blue lake in the distance ahead, and to her right, a big round mountain all by itself. She could just make out several ski lifts running down its middle, and a long thin ski lodge where they ended, about three quarters way up the mountain.

'That's Coronet Peak ski area,' Rick said. 'We'll be up there shortly. And below, that's Arrowtown. It's a historic old gold-mining town. We might be able to squeeze in a visit tomorrow. You'll love it.' Out the front windscreen she could see across a small patchwork plain a smoky haze over a small huddle of houses.

Rick switched on his radio to talk to the control tower. 'This is ZK-TBW, Zulu-Kilo-Tango-Bravo-Whisky, request landing clearance for runway zero-five.'

'Zulu-Kilo-Tango-Bravo-Whisky, you are cleared to land, runway zero-five, numbered one for landing.'

Alex could see the runway in the distance, lining up in the centre of the windshield.

'Zulu-Kilo-Tango-Bravo-Whisky, cleared to land, runway zero-five, numbered one for landing,' Rick repeated into the mike for confirmation.

As the little plane descended into the valley, they were once again dwarfed by snow-covered mountains at eye level on either side. Inexperienced as she was with such squat flying gnats as this one, it appeared to be a very narrow approach with no room for error, but Rick didn't seem at all concerned, not even when they started to bump around a bit. She switched off her CD player and closed her eyes, not liking the look of the fast-approaching runway, which seemed to fill the whole screen in front of her.

There was a slight jolt as the main wheels landed. Alex dared top open her eyes as Rick brought the nose down gently, pulled back the throttle stick and put on the brakes. The radio crackled again and Rick negotiated with the tower where to put his aircraft. The Cessna turned off before the terminal and taxied to a halt in front of a small, basic two-storey building. Rick made another short call to the control tower then cut the engine, pulled out the key, took off his headphones, undid his seatbelt, opened the door, climbed out and held it open for her to follow. After a brief struggle with the complicated seatbelt and stopping to untwist her CD player from the headset cord, Alex clambered out after him, finding Antoinette's borrowed ski suit a little tight for such a wide manoeuvre.

'That was the best flight ever,' she said as she took his proffered hand and jumped down from the wing step, tugging the ski suit back into shape. 'I'll always remember that. I can't thank you enough.' She reached up and kissed him appreciatively, a kiss that he returned with warmth and vigour. She could feel her tummy beginning to flutter with desire.

'You'll have plenty of opportunity to thank me later, Doc,' Rick said with a wink.

'I expect I will,' she said, smiling suggestively.

Rick returned the smile, then patted her on the rump and climbed back up on the wing where he reached inside and hauled out their two overnight bags from behind the seats. She caught them as he tossed them to the ground, then he pulled out his big metal camera case and lifted it carefully down. He'd told Alex earlier he was a keen photographer and was hoping to sell some of his pictures to a tourist magazine.

Once Rick was satisfied his Cessna was secure for the night, he picked up both bags as if they were weightless and told her to follow upstairs to the aero club, where he checked in and completed the formalities. No sooner had they exited downstairs into the car park than a short, shaven-headed man approached Rick with his hand outstretched.

'Mate!' he cried, as he shook Rick's hand.

'Steve! It's good to see you,' Rick said, taking his hand in both of his, as if he were a long-lost relative. 'Did you arrange the hire car for us?'

'No worries, mate. It's just over there,' he pointed to a fat silver Landcruiser parked across the way. 'Here, let me take a bag,' the man said, grabbing Alex's bulging bag. He turned to Alex and shook her hand. 'Steve. Steve Harrison. I promised Rick to get him a car for the weekend. Four-wheel-drives are hard to come by at this time of year.' He laughed and knocked Rick's forearm with his fist. 'Isn't that right, mate?'

Rick laughed too and said to Alex, by way of explanation, 'Steve's an old friend from university days. He runs a courier company down here. He knows everybody and everything about this place. If you want something, Steve'll know how to get it. And he knows all the hot spots around town at night.'

They walked to the chunky Landcruiser; Alex climbed into the front seat and waited while Steve and Rick stood talking at the back of the vehicle. She couldn't make out what they were saying, but she heard the name Warren mentioned more than once and their discussion sounded quite animated. After a few minutes, the back door of the Landcruiser opened and Alex looked behind her to see Rick throw in their bags and Steve thrusting a small brown envelope in side the top of his jacket. She turned back to face the front quickly; she could tell by the surreptitious way Steve was behaving she wasn't supposed to have seen.

Within seconds, Rick was in the truck.

'Steve's going to pick up his business partner in town then he'll be up to join us,' Rick said as they headed out of the carpark and off towards the ski field.

Alex was impressed. Coronet Peak was equal to any of the middle-sized ski areas she had been to in the States and the snow was superb. Even better, there was about half the number of people she would have had to cope with on the slopes, meaning the lift queues were virtually non-existent and the trails were far less busy. Without any trees to get in the way, she could pretty much go anywhere she pleased. Once, while skiing as fast as she could, trying to stick to the fall-line, she found she had the whole run completely to herself. With no-one to hear, she burst into the catchy opening duet from *La Traviata*, singing at the top of her lungs, timing her turns to the music. She'd lost Rick early on – he was much faster than her and totally fearless. He wanted to ski the black diamond trails and take photographs, while she was more confident on the main trails and, although she'd waited at the bottom of the lift to catch up with him, he'd disappeared without trace. But she was having so much fun she wasn't worried. She figured she'd meet up with him in the cafeteria at lunchtime.

'Ooof!' A snowboarder appeared out of nowhere and smacked into her, sending her crashing sideways into the powdery off-piste snow. She came up spluttering. 'You stupid bastard, why don't you look where you're going,' she said, wiping snow off her Oakleys. She couldn't see a thing but she could hear the idiot laughing his head off nearby. She was enraged. 'I should report you and then you'll lose your lift ticket,' she fumed as she cleared the last chunks of snow off her face and caught her first good look at him.

'Steve! You idiot! What did you do that for?'

He stopped his maniacal laughing and his face went hard. She couldn't see his eyes behind his dark goggles. He shook his gloved hand at her, making a fist with the mitten fingers.

'Take it as a warning,' he said. 'If you tell anyone anything you see or hear this weekend, you're dead meat.'

Effortlessly, he pushed himself up, shook the snow off his jacket and, without another word or acknowledgement, slid off down the trail and around the corner, out of sight.

Alex sat there, gobsmacked. She figured he must be referring to the package she'd seen him slide under the carpet in the back of the truck. Unless there was something else she didn't know about yet, something maybe about to happen. And why would she want to tell anyone?

Puzzled, she stood on her skis and reassembled her gear before making a kick turn and skiing slowly down to the base lodge, where she hoped to find Rick. But there was no sign of him on the outdoor terrace. After parking her skis on a rack, she walked back and forth between the rows of tables then tried the cafeteria and restaurants inside. Still no sign. She looked at her watch. It was just after two. She decided to get herself a drink and a late lunch and find a seat in the sunshine where she could wait for Rick.

They hadn't arrived on the mountain until around noon and two hours' skiing was more than enough for the first day. She hadn't skied for over two years and was finding it hard going on her knees and calves; the hired boots and skis hadn't made it any easier. She'd been skiing on fancy new carving skis, which were supposed to make her ski better but they seemed to require more effort and made her feet feel weird. She picked up a panini and a Diet Coke at the counter then found a spare seat.

The sun was going down and it was almost three when she finally caught sight of Rick talking to Steve and a couple of other guys at the bottom of the stairs, near the entrance to the carpark. She stood to go down to them then thought better of it. Something about their demeanour, the closeness of their circle, the furtive way Steve kept looking around, made it clear they didn't want to be interrupted. So she sat down again and waited, watching. She could see that Rick was getting agitated about something. It looked as though he was getting angry. He kept stabbing his finger at the two strangers and started shouting at them. But he was too far away and there were too many people around for Alex to hear what he was saying. The other guys were shrugging, appearing unconcerned at his histrionics. Rick then reached forward and grabbed the shorter one by the front of his jacket and pulled him towards him menacingly, before letting him go, delivering a parting shot, and turning on his heel. He was heading towards her and the stairs.

Alex pretended to be engrossed in watching skiers descending the last part of the trail before queuing for the chairlift. Casually, when she thought Rick should have made it to the top of the stairs, she turned around, as if scanning the crowd for him even though she knew exactly where he would be. As indeed he was. He was standing at the top of the stairs looking around the lunchtime crowd, presumably trying to find her. She wondered if Steve had mentioned their earlier encounter. She doubted it somehow.

Standing up and leaning on the table in front of her, Alex gathered her gloves and hat and waved them above her head in Rick's direction. He didn't see her. She waited until he was looking in her direction and waved again. He spotted her this time, held up his hand in acknowledgement and headed towards her, rocking on his stiff racing boots.

'Hey, Alex, where've you been? I've been looking all over for you!'

'I've been looking for you too. I figured the best way to meet up was for me to stay in the one place for a while and hope you'd walk by. And see, it worked!'

'Clever girl.' He dropped his voice, looking about him to see if anyone was listening. 'We're going to have to go back down the mountain now. Something's come up. I need to get into town and sort it out.'

'Oh, okay.' Alex wondered if it had something to do with the heated exchange she'd witnessed.

'So we need to take our hire gear back and get back to the truck. Sorry to cut your day short, but I have to get into town.'

'It's no problem, Rick, really. I've had a great time. Besides, my knees are knackered. It's ages since I skied. Especially without a break to queue for a lift.' She'd opted to keep her reaction light and seemingly cheerful. She suspected things would be a lot easier if she didn't let on she was getting worried about the turn events seemed to be taking.

The ride down the mountain in the Landcruiser was eerily quiet. They exchanged a few pleasantries about the afternoon's activity before lapsing into silence for the rest of the journey. Not that she minded. She turned the radio dial until she found a classical music station. The music sounded like Vivaldi.

'Is that okay with you?' she asked Rick, who nodded and kept driving.

There was plenty to look at as they wound their way round the hairpins. At one stage, a flash of blue and red and yellow from a tandem paraglider sailed overhead – two people flying through the air on their way down to the valley floor miles below. And then there was the big blue lake, with the sharp-edged snow-capped mountains beyond. She lost herself in the scenery, relating it to the Queenstown guide book she'd picked up in the ski lodge just before, reading up about the ski area she'd just been to and its sister skifield across the other side of the valley, and working out where they were on the map.

When they were almost down the mountain, Rick's cellphone rang.

'Hello,' he said. 'Uh-huh. Nope. Yeah, the photographs are great. I should have them developed for you by the morning. Uh-huh. Sure. Later tonight? No problem.'

He flipped the lid shut and put it back in his top pocket. 'Looks like I'm going to be able to sell those pictures after all. That's good news,' he said, and slapped her on the thigh. 'We're in the money.' He started to laugh. 'We're going to have a great night.'

When they arrived at the hotel, Rick carried their bags in and checked them both in.

'I'm going to have to leave you here for a bit,' he said to her. 'I promised Steve I'd meet him in town. There's some people he wants me to see about the photographs. But I won't be long. They'll look after you and take our bags up to the room. You get the spa bath ready for me and I'll be right along.'

He gave her a quick peck on the cheek and, picking up his camera case, he was gone, not even waiting for her to answer. Feeling slightly peeved, she picked up the room key and both their bags and made her own way to the room, banging the door shut behind her in annoyance.

By the time she'd shucked off her ski gear, poured herself a vodka and tonic from the mini bar and run a hot spa bath filled with the complementary Badedas, she was starting to feel a lot better. She fished out her CD player from her bag, plugged it into her ears, turned it on and set it on the side of the bath then sank slowly into the hot, tingling water, letting the bubbles envelop her.

The Puccini CD was now playing Carreras singing 'Nessun Dorma'. She closed her eyes and let the music sweep away all the unpleasant images and sensations that had unsettled her during the day. Best to do as the awful Steve had suggested and turn a blind eye, she decided. She wasn't going to let his posturing ruin everything. By the time the chorus brought the track to its climax, she found herself thinking of Zhi, wondering if he ever thought of her and how much more pleasant it was in his company. The big problem with Zhi, though, was that she didn't fancy him. She liked being with him. They seemed to spark off each other when they were talking, so that the conversation bounced along, taking exciting turns, covering all sorts of subjects she'd never dreamt of wanting to talk about with anyone other than her closest girlfriends. But there was no chemistry; no feeling in the pit of her stomach; no electrical charge when their hands accidentally touched. That was how she'd always known, in the past, if she fancied someone. She thought back to when she'd met Lucian. The charge had been so great that she'd had to sit down when everyone around her was standing. And it had been much the same with Rick.

'Fat lot of good it's done you,' a little voice inside her said. 'Look at you now. Caught in the middle of something a bit fishy, and all on your own on a Saturday night.'

She pushed it away to the back of her mind again. How could she doubt her instincts like that?

27. Last Supper

Carrie couldn't recall hearing Richard talk like that before. He wanted to make every moment count in case there was no tomorrow, he'd said. That could mean only one thing – he had played some part in the Maungatapu Murders that everyone was talking about and he knew he'd get caught sooner or later if he didn't leave town.

She was surprised he hadn't left already. If he wanted to evade capture, she felt he should get the next boat out of Nelson. But she didn't want him to leave. Now that he'd found her, she didn't want to lose him.

'Oh, Richard, what…' She couldn't finish the sentence. It was more than she could bear to think about a future without Richard to provide for her, to be there for her. She willed herself not to cry. But since she'd been with child, she seemed to burst into tears for almost no reason at all. And now there was a reason, it was proving impossible to hold back. A tear escaped and trickled down her cheek.

'Carrie. My little chick,' he said, and kissed it away. He circled her with his arms and hugged her tightly. 'I'm sorry it's like this.'

'Well, we'd better make it count, in case there's no tomorrow,' Carrie said, repeating his words and attempting a brave smile.

'You're an unpredictable little thing,' he said, lifting one hand to fondle the curls escaping down the side of her face. He brushed his finger down her cheek, stopping under her chin, which he held between his thumb and forefinger, as if studying her for a portrait. 'That's why I love you so much. Come, Carrie. It's time we made it count.' He scooped her up in his arms and carried her through into the bedroom, laughing in surprise at first at the sight of the bedding so low down on the floor, then kneeling carefully, letting her slip down from his arms onto the coverlet and pillows.

He kissed her again, more urgently this time, and pulled her up towards him, gathering her in his arms.

Slowly, they undressed each other, pulling off each garment – and there were many – until Carrie was sitting on the bed, facing him, wearing just her corset and pantaloons. The tightly-laced corset had pushed up her soft white breasts so that they were spilling over the top. Carrie could see that they looked exceedingly tempting and felt a small thrill of anticipation run through her. Richard reached over and caressed the top of each one.

'Let me undo you,' he said and untied the laces on her corset until her breasts fell out from their encasement, soft, pink and slightly swollen from the pregnancy, the areola browner and bigger than before. He took her breasts in his hands, leant down and kissed them while she reached up and pulled at the thick black hairs on his broad chest, tweaking his nipples as he touched hers. He moaned and, quickly removing his breeches, lay beside her, encouraging her excitement with his fingers, bringing her close to the point of ecstasy.

Gauging her readiness, he was on top of her, entering her gently at first then working up a rhythm that matched hers. They climaxed together – Richard crying out to the heavens, shouting her name; Carrie bursting into tears.

'Hush,' my little chick. What is it? Why are you crying? You've never done that before.'

'I'm sorry. I'm sorry,' she snuffled in between sobs. 'I just don't want to lose you.'

He didn't answer. They both knew there was nothing hopeful he could say. Instead, he rolled off her, reached over the side of the mattress and pulled a handkerchief from his trouser pocket. 'Here,' he said, proffering it to her. She took it and held it to her eyes until she could make herself stop, then wiped the tears from her face and blew her nose. Silently, she pulled him towards her and held him in her arms, tightly, as if that would stop him from going.

The sun was going down and a chill was in the air when they awoke.

'Oh, Lord, Richard, it must be after five o'clock!' Carrie said, waking first.

Richard opened his eyes sleepily then sprang up with a start, wide awake. He pulled the expensive silver fob watch – bearing a stranger's initials – from the pocket of his waistcoat on the floor and looked at the time.

'Damn! I said I'd meet Phil back at the Oyster Saloon at five. I'll never make it now. It's ten after five already.' He put his watch down on the floor and looked at Carrie. 'The stables will have to wait for their horse 'til morning,' he said. 'There's nothing for it but to stay the night here with you, my little chick. Can you bear to have me?'

'Of course, of course. I can think of nothing better. I'll make us some dinner. A dinner fit for a king.'

'More like a last supper,' Richard mumbled under his breath.

'What was that?'

'It'll be wonderful,' he said more loudly. 'I'd better go and tend to the horse. I don't suppose there's a stable or somewhere she can shelter for the night? It's going to be cold.'

'There's an empty barn out the back. You can see it from the woodshed.'

It was cold in the kitchen. The coal range was almost out. Carrie revived it with more coal and a good poke, then set about making dinner. She fetched the leg of pork from its hook in the cool outside larder, cut off a chunk big enough for two, placed it in the roasting dish with a slice of fat, rubbed it with salt and pricked it with a few cloves before putting it in the oven, which was starting to heat up to a reasonable cooking temperature. Next, she peeled and cut up some potatoes, swede and parsnip, adding them to the roasting dish and turning the damper down on the fire to prevent the oven getting too hot.

Richard arrived in the back door, removed his boots then stamped his feet to warm them. He placed his boots in before the fire, then stood in front of it, holding his hands out to the heat.

'By heavens, it's cold out there!' he said. 'I've settled the mare down in the barn for the night. She's got some water. And there were a few old oats in a bin there. She turned her nose up at it at first, but now she's realised there's nothing else, she's munching on them.'

'Dinner should be ready in an hour,' Carrie said. 'I'll light the fire in the parlour and we can sit in there while we wait.'

'Oh, I nearly forgot,' Richard said, heading for the back door. He was outside for only a moment before returning with a bottle of champagne held up high in his right hand. 'I brought this for you. I had it in the saddle bag.'

'Champagne! Oh, Richard. I remember the first time you brought me champagne… .'

'Well, this night is just as special.'

He opened it while she fetched two glasses from the cupboard. The cork exploded with a loud pop, making Carrie jump. Richard caught a few drops escaping down the side of the bottle with his fingers and licked them. 'Mmm,' he said appreciatively. 'It's a good vintage.' He poured the bubbling cream-coloured liquid into the glasses and handed one to Carrie.

'To our baby,' he said holding up his glass in a toast.

Carrie gulped. To have Richard acknowledge his child like this was quite unexpected.

'To our baby,' she said, joining in the toast. They both sipped champagne. 'If it's a boy, I shall call him Richard.'

'You don't have to do that,' he said, looking serious now. 'I wouldn't want him to turn out like me.'

'I hope he has your eyes, and your generosity.'

'I hope he's taller than me, though. I wouldn't wish it on my worst enemy, being so short of stature.'

'I like it in a man.'

'So I don't intimidate you, I suppose?'

Carrie smiled, took another sip from her glass and looked across at Richard. 'You do scare me sometimes, though,' she said.

He looked as if he were about to brush it off with a laugh, but changed his mind and his face took on a serious expression. 'I know, Carrie my love. You have every reason to hate me for what I've done. I've made you pregnant, and we both know there's not much chance of me being around to see him grow up. That's why I don't want him to grow up like me. I had every chance when I was a boy to turn out all right. My mother cared for me and made me go to school and get a good education. My blood father was a rich gentleman who was the son of the man my mother served as a housemaid. He gave her plenty of money to see that I was provided for. I only met him once, on one of his rare visits.

'If it hadn't been for that evil interloper she married when I was eleven I probably would've been fine. But I hated him and his children with such a passion it made me do stupid things to spite him. In the end, I suffered, not him. He didn't give tuppence what became of me. In fact, he was glad to see the back of me. It was my life that got mucked up and I really can't blame anyone but myself. It broke my mother's heart the first time the police came knocking on the door and took me away.' He put his glass down on the kitchen bench and took Carrie's hand in both of his, holding it up and kissing her fingers gently, looking deep into her eyes. She could feel his eyes piercing her soul and knew this would be a moment she would always remember, would hold onto when he was gone. 'I want our son – or daughter, if it's a girl – I want them to grow up not knowing about me, not knowing who I am or the damage I've done to people's lives.'

'But…'

'No, Carrie. No buts. I want you to tell them that their father was an honest man who died in a storm at sea, or who fell off his horse and struck his head on a boulder. It's best they don't know the truth. I don't want that hanging over them like a storm-cloud all their lives. Promise me you'll do that, Carrie.' He held her hand in a vice-like grip now and his gaze was so intense she felt as if she were shrivelling under it. 'Promise?'

'I promise,' she said. She had no alternative, she felt. But there was logic in his words. She could see it made sense to keep his true identity a secret.

'Good.' He looked relieved. 'Now let's go through into the parlour and make up for what we're going to be missing for the rest of our lives.'

Carrie lit the fire and they sat opposite each other, perched on the trunks, finishing the champagne, talking of times in Hokitika and the fun they'd had in their short time together. As the wine and firelight warmed them, Richard moved his cushions to the floor and sat at Carrie's feet, his head resting on her lap, his hand in hers, not saying a word. She understood his need for peace and held onto his hand, wishing it could be like this forever. He was staring into the fire and she thought she spied a tear on his cheek, but didn't mention it.

She lost track of the time. Their glasses were empty, the twice-stoked fire was dying again and the room was darkening when Carrie said, 'I think the dinner will be ready now. I'd better rescue it before it burns.'

'And I'll light the lamp and fetch more wood for the fire,' he said.

They came back to the fireplace in the parlour to eat their meal, perching once more on the empty trunks, their plates resting in their laps on Carrie's best embroidered linen napkins.

'This is delicious,' Richard said between mouthfuls. 'Perfect.'

Carrie was pleased with her efforts. She was still far from confident in the kitchen, but this meal of roast pork and vegetables was one of her successes. Even the gravy was tasty.

After they'd eaten she carried the plates into the kitchen and put the kettle on for tea while Richard poured a brandy for himself and lit up a cigar he'd produced from his top jacket pocket. She decided to leave the dishes until the morning, cleaning up the bench and joining Richard back in the parlour by the fire again.

They sat companionably for the rest of the evening – sipping brandy, drinking tea – sharing tales of their past, memories of their moments together, but not once talking about the future. Both knew, in an unspoken agreement, there was no point talking about what might never be. Both knew the future would hold hardship, pain and hurt, and that they would each have to suffer on their own.

When the fire flickered low in the grate one last time they went to bed where they made love passionately, urgently, forcefully, as if angry at themselves for the mess they were in. Later, Richard drew Carrie back to him and they made love again, this time more gently, reverently almost, taking their time. They fell asleep entwined in each other's arms – Richard closed his eyes first. Carrie lay there for some time, watching his even breathing, feeling the rough scars on his back, worrying about what would happen to her and her baby once he was gone.

28. Alone Again

It was early afternoon before Carrie was able to escape the house and walk, alone, along the dusty Clover Road to the general store. Richard had left straight after breakfast. She had cooked him a hearty meal of bacon and eggs, using the bread bought from the store the day before. She'd yet to have time to bake her own. But now, she suspected, she would have plenty of time for that and setting up a house, vegetable garden and paddock capable of making her almost self sufficient. She'd told herself firmly, after the dust from Richard's horse had long settled back on the road, that there was no point moping and feeling sorry for herself. She'd told herself that, for the baby's sake as well as her own sanity, she had to make a go of it here. There was no point in returning to Hokitika, where everyone knew her and would guess who the father of her baby was. But thanks to Richard's generosity, she was well provided for and had plenty of money left, even after the purchase of the cottage, to set herself up for the long term. She planned to buy a cow, some hens, a pig or two, a few sheep, a goat and perhaps, if she could afford it, a horse to get her to town. There was enough space for them all. She smiled.

'Lord, Carrie, look at you,' she said out loud to herself as she walked along the road, kicking stones into the long grass at the roadside. 'Who would have thought that you would end up in a place like this planning on growing vegetables and keeping hens and a cow.'

She'd come a long way since the Golden Age. She'd come even further since the Grey, with her poor mother taking in other people's sewing and mending, trying to earn enough money to put food on the table. Long before her father had died in the accident on the wharf, her mother had worked herself thin trying to earn a few extra pounds to live on, since their father drank most of the money his irregular work brought in. She shuddered at the thought of the man. No matter how hard she tried, she couldn't forget his voice, resonating off the walls of their small kitchen – the only living room in the house – shouting obscenities at her mother before pulling the strap from his belt and threatening to take to the next person – woman or child – who got in his way. Nor could she forget his wandering hands, touching her and her sister under their nightdresses, stroking their half-formed nubile little breasts, touching them down there where they knew it was supposed to be private. Oh well, she thought grimly, that was one thing she wouldn't have to worry about if she had a girl. There would be no father around to interfere with her, no man around to take to her with his belt. Not that she thought Richard would do that, anyway. He'd always been very gentle and considerate with her. It was other people who bore the brunt of his anger at life. She couldn't fathom how he could hold people up at the point of a gun, rob them of their valuables, then leave them with little more than the clothes they stood up in. Even worse, she knew that sometimes he took their lives. And now it looked increasingly likely that he had been involved in the mass murder of a group of men crossing the Maungatapu Saddle from Canvastown. Quickly she put that thought from her mind. She didn't want to believe it possible. Shaking her head as if to get rid of the shame of it all, she looked around her. The fields were bare, the fruit trees almost empty, with just a few over-ripe apples remaining, their sides gaping from holes picked by the birds. The afternoon was sunny and pleasant for this time of year, with a gentle breeze ruffling the branches. This was a beautiful and calming place, she told herself. You should be happy here. But the ache in her heart would not go away. Despite the sunshine, she felt cold and alone.

Mrs McTavish greeted her warmly.

'I hope that nice young man found you all right?' she said when Carrie entered the store, her eyes getting used to the dimmer light inside. 'He said he had a nice surprise for you.'

'He did indeed,' Carrie said, hiding her sadness with a bright smile. 'He found me *and* he had a nice surprise.'

She resisted Mrs McTavish's attempts to pry more information out of her, changing the subject to yesterday's big order and following on with her need to fill up a garden and a barnyard.

'You'll have no trouble getting anything to grow around her, my dear. The soil seems just right for crops and the weather's ideal. You can't go wrong, come the spring.'

She bought some tallow to make soap, some eggs, milk, butter and a few apples and vegetables.

'I'm looking forward to being able to make my own butter and collect my own eggs soon, though,' she said, picking up that morning's *Mail* and adding it to the pile on the counter. She paid Mrs McTavish, swapped a few more pleasantries, then went out into the sunshine, her groceries weighing down her big carpetbag.

Once safely out of sight, she put down her bag, knelt down in the grass at the side of the road and opened the paper. She had a foreboding that there would be further news of the Maungatapu Murders inside. Sure enough, there it was, on page two:

TUESDAY, JUNE 19TH, 1866
ARREST MADE IN MURDER CASE
William Levy, also known as Phil Levy, one of the four men suspected of the murders on Maungatapu Mountain, was arrested last night. A large sum of money was found on him. He was found in the bar of the Wakatu Hotel late on Tuesday, and has been lodging at the Oyster Saloon in Nelson. He is to be brought up before the Magistrate this morning.

The other three men the police are looking for in the case have been named. They are Richard Burgess, alias Hill, 36, 5 feet 5 inches, with brown hair and blue eyes and a gunshot wound on his back; Thomas Kelly, alias Noon, 39, 5 feet 6 inches, brown hair, hazel eyes, face wrinkled, who has tattoos on each arm of a mermaid and sailor; and John Joseph Sullivan, alias McGee, 40, 5 feet 9 inches, stout build, short brown hair, inclined to grey, long face, square forehead, blue eyes, firm mouth, small fair whiskers, no moustache, has the appearance of an old hand.

Carrie put the paper down for a moment to draw breath. The news had confirmed her worst suspicions and although she wasn't surprised, she was shocked nevertheless. After a while, she was able to read on. Further down the column, it went on to describe Richard:

'All but Levy have undergone long periods of penal servitude in Victoria and Burgess has a gunshot wound in his side that was received while he and several others were attempting to escape from the hulk in Hobson's Bay. Burgess was formerly a mate of the notorious Captain Melville; and he has the reputation of being one of the most cool and daring criminals in the Australian colonies.'

She groaned. If only she could stop Richard from returning to Nelson. Just entering the town put him at risk of capture. The police could be lying in wait for him as he returned the horse to the stable, or as he went to his room to collect his belongings. But she had no way of reaching him or getting a message to him. She was powerless. He would have to rely on his own abilities to evade the police – and he had proven himself very good at that in the past.

She stood up, picked up her bag, and continued on towards home, now certain that she would be bringing up her unborn child alone.

29. Crack Shot

'Hey, Doc, wake up. You're supposed to be keeping it warm for me.' Alex sat up with a jolt, sending out shockwaves of bathwater and making the jets suck angrily at their sudden exposure to air. The water was lukewarm, as was her vodka. She looked at her watch.

'Good God, it's almost seven. I must have fallen asleep…'

'My sleeping beauty,' he said laconically and leant down to kiss her. Embarrassed, she tried to cover herself with her hands, but to no avail. He took her chin in his hand and kissed her hard on the mouth. He smelt of beer and cigarette smoke, but she kissed him anyway.

'What say you heat that water up and I join you in the tub for a spell? My legs are like jelly after that race with Steve.'

She pushed the tap with her toe and cold water gushed down her right leg, making her jump and bang her nose on his forehead. She'd intended to add the hot water without interrupting their kiss, but now she'd completely blown it and looked totally uncool.

'Ow, sorry,' she said then jumped again. By now the water had run hot and was burning into her thigh.

'You get yourself and the bath sorted. I'll be back in a minute,' Rick said, standing. He left the bathroom door open and she could hear him pouring a drink and turning on the TV, switching channels until he found Sky Sport. After a few moments he reappeared, wearing the hotel bathrobe, with a glass of champagne in each hand and a small packet tucked under his fingers. He put the packet down on the vanity.

'I hope this is what the Doc ordered,' he smiled, handing her a glass.

She smiled back. She was beginning to like the name now. The way he said it had a very sexy ring to it.

'Thank you,' she said. 'I never could say no to champagne.'

'I hope that's not all you can't say no to,' he said, still smiling, and held his glass up to hers. 'To a great weekend.'

She returned the toast. 'A great weekend,' she said. 'It has been, so far. I'm just blown away by it all.' The bubbles tickled her nose and the yeasty sweet champagne tingled her taste buds, sending a small shiver of pleasure through her. The combination of champagne and a sexy companion was irresistible.

'Well, it's just about to get even better,' he said. 'I've got something that'll blow us both away.'

He ducked out to the bedroom and returned moments later with a chunky hotel guidebook, picked up the plastic packet and knelt down beside her on the tiled floor. Carefully he opened the packet and tapped two lines of coke onto the book's hard flat cover, straightening the lines of powder neatly with the side of the now-empty packet. Holding one nostril, he snorted up one of the lines through a tightly rolled $50 bill then held the other in front of her.

'Your turn, Doc,' he said, waiting for her to inhale it.

She gulped. She'd not touched the stuff in ages. For years, Pete had provided a cocktail of drugs, with cocaine being the most regular aperitif. When she'd finally managed to shake herself free of him, she'd sworn herself off drugs for good. She'd been getting twitchy and paranoiac, finding her concentration slipping at work and her memory lapsing spasmodically. She knew the regular weekend sessions with Pete were largely to blame. Not that the other things she ate and drank in his company would have helped her state of health much. But canning the mind-altering substances had been easy to do once he was off the scene and it didn't seem to take long for her brain to revive and the paranoia to disappear.

She studied the speckled powder in front of her and wrestled with her conscience. At last, she said, 'No, Rick. I can't. I'm sorry. I just can't.'

'No shit!' he said. 'You sure?'

'Yes I'm sure. I can't do it any more.'

'Okay, Doc. It's your life. I'm not going to push you.'

'But that doesn't mean we can't still have a good time together,' she said, hoping this wouldn't mean he'd leave her to it.

'Sure. Sure.' He paused, as if making up his mind then smiled. 'So you better turn those jets up.'

While Alex sipped at her champagne, he quickly scraped the unwanted line of coke back into the packet, shook the few remaining crystals into his champagne glass then took the book back to the bedroom, returning without the bathrobe and stepping quickly into the tub. They rubbed each other's backs with the bath foam and sipped at their champagne until she noticed Rick's tempo moving up a few beats.

His eyes were dark and dilated, his hands gesticulating as he spoke, impatient for action. She could imagine how he would be feeling. She'd felt the rush herself often enough to know he'd be on top of the world right now, raring to go, wanting everything to happen at once. She realised she'd better find a way to give it to him, or risk losing him.

By the time they got out of the tub, Alex felt thoroughly waterlogged but much more relaxed. Even without the heightened sensation the coke would have brought, their sexual romp – in the spa bath and then sliding around on a slippery bathroom floor awash with Badedas foam – was memorable. He'd held back for ages until she'd felt satisfied too, and now she was tingling all over.

She was wearing one of the fluffy white hotel robes and was standing in front of the mirror, blow-drying her hair. She added some product to make it extra spiky. She wanted to look good for Rick tonight. He was taking her to dinner at an expensive restaurant on the Steamer Wharf, which just a few minutes earlier he'd pointed to her out their window as being just a short walk up the road.

'Look,' he'd said. 'That's the *Earnslaw*. She's a famous old steam ship that takes tourists up and down the lake. We've missed the dinner and dance sailing, but I've got something much more special lined up for us than that.'

Once her hair was done, she applied make-up, making her eyelashes extra thick and luscious, outlining her lips to make them bigger then filling them in with bright red lipstick and a smear of gloss. She pursed her lips in the mirror in an air kiss. She had to admit they looked pretty sensuous like that. Then she went back into the bedroom to get the little black dress she'd brought, just in case such an occasion should arise.

Rick turned to look at her, eyes wide, nostrils flaming from a recent snort of coke.

'Hey, Doc, you look stunning. I love your hair like that. It's wild,' he said. He picked up a boutique bag from the bed and brought it over to her. 'A little present for you, to make you even more gorgeous.'

He handed it out to her and she took it, wondering what on earth it could be. A dress? A fur wrap? Diamonds? She laughed at herself. It was far too early in the relationship for such extravagances. She opened the bag and pulled out a parcel wrapped in tissue paper and sealed with a sticker containing a simple black "X". Intrigued, she peeled off the sticker and unwrapped the delicate paper. Several tiny pieces of slinky black lingerie fell out into her hands.

'Good God!' was all she could say. She'd never been a sexy underwear sort of person. Expensive underwear, maybe. But not this black flimsy stuff. She examined it more closely, aware that Rick was watching her closely, a big horny grin all over his face.

Uppermost in her hand was a black suspender belt and a pair of crutchless knickers – something she'd heard about before but never actually encountered. Under that, she found a tightly boned black bustier corset, a pair of black fishnet stockings and a bright red satin garter belt.

'I want you to dress up for me tonight,' Rick said, breathing quickly, panting almost, as he approached her and seized her excitedly.

'All right,' she said. 'Just for you. Seeing you've brought me all this way to this beautiful place. But I wouldn't do it for anyone else.'

30. Private Dancer

I want to watch you get dressed,' he said, still breathing heavily. He switched the hotel radio to a Classic Rock programme and turned up the volume then flung himself on the bed and, hands behind his head, observed her progress.

'You're embarrassing me,' she said.

'No need to feel embarrassed, Doc. I thought you PR people would do this sort of thing all the time.'

She didn't know whether to laugh or be outraged. She'd dressed up in some pretty outrageous outfits with Pete; she still had her collection of wigs and disguises. But this wasn't for laughs. Despite his outwardly carefree appearance, she could see that Rick was serious about this. And what did she have to lose? She reckoned she might as well give it a try. It might be fun. She decided to play along and brazen it out; she would play the part he wanted.

Slipping the bathrobe down to the floor, she stood naked in front of him, slid on the knickers and trailed her finger deliberately in front of them, pretending to be aroused. Then she slowly pulled the suspender belt up over the knickers and slid her fingers out of the elastic, twanging it tantalisingly on her hips.

She perched on the edge of the armchair to get the fishnets on, pulled them out of the packet and fitted them over each toe before fingering them gradually up her long, recently waxed legs, looking up at Rick as she did so, licking her shiny red lips provocatively. Then she slipped on her ultra-high heel black patent Blahniks, glad that she'd brought them after all. He gasped, but didn't say anything. She could sense his increasing excitement and it was starting to reach her too. She was feeling aroused too, now that she was getting into the swing of it and losing her initial shyness.

The corset she wasn't so sure about. Her initial fears that it would not fit were unfounded but, as she wrapped it around her and pulled at the elastic cords in front, she realised it was only going to cover the bottom half of her breasts – the top half resting provocatively on their tight black satin shelf. She turned to study herself in the mirror and had to admit the effect was very sexy indeed. She hardly recognised herself; she didn't know she had it in her to be so alluring.

'See, I knew you'd be terrific. You're stunning, you know.' Rick was getting up from his front row seat on the bed and coming towards her. 'You should do this more often,' he added as he enveloped her in his arms and kissed the nape of her neck. She felt a thrill run down her spine.

'You forgot the garter,' he said in a thick voice, holding it up over his forefinger.

She took it and pinged it at him like a shanghai, then slid it up to the top of her leg, setting it just above her hemline where it could flash alluringly at him when she sat down.

He sank to his knees and kissed it, caressing her thigh gently.

Alex was enjoying herself now. Though she hardly dared admit it, she was actually feeling pretty sexy too.

'Patience now, Big Boy,' she teased. 'You don't want to be late for dinner, do you.'

She gave an alluring shimmy or two in time to the music before whipping her cocktail dress from the wardrobe and dropping it quickly over her head. 'If you behave yourself at the restaurant, I'll let you undress me when we get home.'

'You drive a hard bargain,' he said, standing up and picking up his heavy blue woollen jacket from the back of the chair. Then he held her coat out for her to put on.

After checking his expensive camera gear in its bag into the hotel safe deposit, Rick walked her the short distance to the restaurant, their breath steaming the cold night air. Alex was still feeling aroused. The unfamiliar lace between her legs from the crutchless knickers, the garter gathered around the top of her leg, the bustier so tight she could breathe only shallowly all felt quite exciting. And she could keep up the charade without having to worry about who might be watching. Nobody would know her, she reckoned. She could do whatever she liked and get away with it. So she spent the evening teasing Rick, playing with her garter, dangling her blue pearl necklace in her cleavage, and occasionally talking dirty, to arouse him when they both knew there was nothing he could do about it – yet.

By the time Rick paid the bill and opened the restaurant door for her, she could tell she had him in a frenzy. She deliberately dawdled on the walk home, stopping to admire the quaint *Earnslaw* steamer lit up like a Christmas tree at the wharf now it had completed its evening voyage, and marvelling at the myriad of stars in the sky.

'I don't think I've ever seen so many stars,' she said. 'You must do something special to make them all shine like that here.' She paused to look around the night sky. 'What are those lights up there?'

'That's the gondola. There's a restaurant and movie theatre up there. We might have time to go up in the morning. The view's spectacular,' Rick said, nuzzling into her neck and enveloping her waist tightly with his arm. 'But right now, I want to get you back to our room. We can look at the stars later.'

But she refused to let him hurry her; she knew that for now, she was in control. She deliberately dallied, walking slowly along the street, pausing to comment on the shop window displays. She liked tantalising him.

Back in their hotel room, he could hardly contain himself as he shut and locked the door behind them. The radio was still playing loud classic rock. She could recognise the Stones. Quickly, he extracted the packet of cocaine from inside the hotel guide, lined up the white powder and snorted it up, a nostril at a time. He offered her some but again she refused. Then, eyes shining, he said, 'I kept my part of the bargain. Now you keep yours.'

'What?'

'You promised to strip for me, remember?'

'So I did. It wouldn't be right to go back on a promise like that would it?'

She started with the garter, pulling it down slowly, timing each move to 'I Can't Get No Satisfaction' – an ironic piece of music to be playing given the circumstances, she thought. Rick groaned softly. Next she unzipped her dress and let it slip down, stepping over it and picking it up like a scarf. She teased him with it, wrapping it around her legs provocatively.

'Hey, where did you learn that?' he said appreciatively, with a low whistle. He could hold back no longer; he seized her and threw her on the bed, where they made passionate love, with Rick finally entering her through the crutchless knickers, thrusting again and again, matching her excitement until they came one after the other and collapsed back on the pillows, satiated.

'Hey, not bad!' he said after a while.

'Not bad at all,' she repeated, turning to look at him and returning his satisfied smile.

'Let's go clubbing,' he said.

'What, now?'

'Why not? It's still early. It's only,' he looked at his watch, 'it's only half past ten.'

'Well okay, but I'll have to get changed first.'

'Whatever for? You've never looked better.'

'Not after that little romp. Everything's messed up. Besides, this corset is killing me.'

'It's me it's killing. It's a knockout, Doc. You should come down the road wearing exactly what you're wearing now.'

Alex looked down at herself and smiled. She was attired in nothing but a bustier, a suspender belt, miniscule black knickers with a hole in the middle, fishnet stockings and her spiky high heels, which had somehow stayed on during their love-making session. She looked like a high-class whore from a bondage parlour. And she felt great. Just the same, she wasn't walking down the road like this.

'This show is just for you, lover boy,' she said and leant over to breathe into his ear and nibble the top of it.

'Hey, what are you trying to do to me?'

'Just saying thank you.'

'I knew you'd enjoy it.'

'I bet you say that to all the girls.'

'Who, me?'

'Yes, you.'

'Only the very special ones. Like you. Come on, I'm still buzzing. Let's go out while the night is young.'

When Rick was in the bathroom, she loosened the bustier a little then retrieved her dress from the chair she'd flung it on and slipped it on again. When it was her turn in the bathroom she had a quick wash and fixed her hair and make-up then went out to the bedroom to pick up her coat to go clubbing.

They went to several night clubs, drinking and dancing the night away, teasing each other on the dance floor, keeping very much to themselves – except at one night club, where Rick came back from a trip to the toilet flushed and upset about someone who, he said, had given a hard time in there. But he didn't go into any details and Alex didn't want to know. Why spoil the night? With that one minor exception, it was just as Alex had hoped it would be, the two of them, having a ball together.

It was almost three in the morning when she asked Rick to take her home to their hotel room. But she was too tired to even think about making love again, she just wanted to crash. And Rick, who wasn't ready for bed yet, seemed perfectly happy to go back out to another club by himself. He gave her a good-night kiss and closed the door behind him.

Alex stripped off her dress and sexy underwear and threw herself in the shower, where she let the hot water expunge the naughty night with Rick. She seemed to have a knack of finding men who brought out the wicked side of her. Her sister Kate had once said that she deliberately sought out guys who were signposted 'dangerous' because she had always been attracted to risk and danger. She'd never been able to work out why, but here she was again with a guy living on the edge – the edge of something slightly dangerous, if Steve was to be believed. She hoped they'd be able to get back to Nelson without becoming embroiled in anything unpleasant. She towelled herself dry and went back to the bedroom, where she switched the TV on to the local news and collapsed into bed.

31. The Game is Up

Richard met Joe Sullivan outside the Mitre Hotel mid-morning Tuesday. He'd washed, breakfasted and paid a brief visit to the American Saloon for a shampoo and shave then ventured out into the street in search of his colleagues. He was keen to head for the hills, to hide out until his ship left for America tomorrow. Joe and Tom were planning to catch the *Airedale* up to the North Island and he'd pretended to go along with their plan. But he knew that there was a steamer leaving for the San Francisco goldfields on the same tide and he planned to give them the slip and be on it. He'd talked with the others about spending the next month up in the North Island and then returning to rob the Bank of New Zealand. He'd spent a bit of time there and found its systems so full of holes that it would be easy to rob. But he was now of the opinion that the best course was to get himself to America, find the goldfields and make a killing there. New Zealand was getting too hot for him now. Everybody seemed to be after him.

'Greetings, Dick,' Sullivan said, grabbing him around the shoulder and seizing his right arm as if they'd not met in weeks. 'I've been looking everywhere for you. Have you heard the news?'

'What news, Joe?' Richard said, returning the handshake with some scepticism. He couldn't fathom why Sullivan was acting as if he was overjoyed to meet him. Heavens, the two had spoken not much less than twenty-four hours ago, and there'd been no reason *then* to rush into each other's arms.

'Phil Levy. He's been arrested,' Sullivan said.

'What! When?'

'Last night. He was at the Wakatu Hotel, out on the Richmond Plain. He was brought into the cells and came up before the Resident Magistrate this morning.'

'Good God, Joe. How did they know where to find him? We could be next!'

'I don't think so. We'll be safe now that Jew is taken care of.'

Richard was appalled at this statement, but didn't take Sullivan up on it. He regarded Phil as one of them and had never stopped to consider his Jewishness.

'Have you seen Kelly?'

'Yes, he's taken a horse from Newton's livery stables. He's headed for the hills.'

'I think I'll join him.' Richard felt like a digger sitting on a pile of gold surrounded by vultures. He couldn't wait to be off and out of danger. With Phil caught, he was a fool to be walking the streets any longer.

He and Sullivan picked up a couple of horses from Newton's in Hardy Street – Richard riding on a cream-coloured pony, Sullivan a black one – and headed out of town, Richard throwing down a shilling at the turnpike to pay the toll for both horses.

'Heard any news of the fate of those poor unfortunate men on the Maungatapu?' the young man asked as he picked up the coin.

'The paper said a man was arrested this morning,' Sullivan said.

'So I'd heard. But any word of the missing men?'

'Not a thing,' Richard said and spurred his horse past the toll gate and onto the open road.

After an hour or so they came to the Turf Tavern, where they stopped to wind the horses and slake their thirst with a glass of ale.

'Any news of the missing men?' the landlady, a Mrs Candy, asked.

'I tell you missus, I think it's all moonshine,' Sullivan said. 'I reckon the perpetrators have probably taken some other road and are in the Buller already, or some other place.'

'If such is the case, then they will be overtaken, for a detective and three police are gone by this road today. I hope they are caught and severely punished for upsetting the public mind in this way. D'you know, I've scarcely slept since I heard of this dreadful business.'

Richard made consoling noises and got away as soon as he could. He was sick to death of hearing talk of it. The pair rode on for another hour or so, Richard taking the lead and leaving Sullivan some way behind. Eventually, he reached the Plough Inn at Richmond, where he gave his horse a bucket of oats and a pail of water. While the horse rested, he ordered another pint of ale, this time from a Mrs Ryan, the innkeeper, then took his ale out to the front porch to watch for Sullivan's arrival. He started when he saw the sergeant of the volunteers passing at the gallop on horseback and then noticed Sullivan, still on his horse, lingering at the side of the road for no apparent reason. This puzzled him. He beckoned to him and Sullivan rode over.

'What are you waiting for?'

'I was waiting for the sergeant to pass. I thought I might have to come and rescue you. But he passed on by.'

Richard suspected that if the sergeant had indeed arrested him, Sullivan would have been off like a shot out of a Colt revolver. He wasn't the type to risk his neck to save a colleague. However, he wasn't going to make an issue of it.

'I suppose if the police are going that way, we'd better head back to town?'

'I suppose so,' Sullivan agreed, 'but let me have an ale first.'

He drank quickly, they discharged the bill, mounted their horses and headed back to Nelson, stopping off twice on the way to feed the horses and partake of an ale. On arriving in Nelson, they returned the horses to the stable then departed for their separate lodgings to clean up after the long day in the saddle. They arranged to meet later and spend the night in the hills, staying out of sight until the *Airedale* departed the next day for the North Island.

Both Sullivan and Kelly were waiting by the Collingwood Bridge at the appointed time an hour and a half later.

'Suspicion has fallen upon us, I'm afraid,' Richard said.

'They'll leave no stone unturned until they find us,' Sullivan added.

'I'm going up in the hills until the steamer leaves tomorrow' Richard said.

'Well, I shall remain where I am. I've decidied it's safer to go into the bush than to go North on the boat,' Kelly said.

'I wish you'd come with me,' Richard said. 'I'd never forgive myself if anything happened to you.'

'I'm all right. I'm not moving an inch.'

Richard shook his hand.

'Good-bye, Tom. I must be off.'

'Don't say goodbye. We'll meet in a month at Picton. We'll be together again then.'

Richard knew now this would not be possible, but said nothing. It would take more than a month for this to die down. He planned to be in America by then. But that was his secret.

He told Sullivan and Kelly he was going to pick up his pistol and rifle from their hiding place, then head for the hills.

'I want to pick up those watertight boots I've ordered and my old clothes. I shall doff these and be more comfortable when I face the ranges.'

'I'll follow you shortly,' Sullivan said.

Richard went up Bridge Street to the Oyster Saloon, where he noticed a man pretending to light a pipe. He knew at once he was a policeman. He waited for Sullivan and tapped his foot impatiently at the laggardly pace of the man. At last he came and Richard let him pass. Sullivan crossed the road and stopped on the other side. Richard moved in the same direction and noticed the policeman following him also. Sullivan turned down the street, and Richard continued to follow him towards the Mitre Hotel.

Suddenly there were men running towards him from every side. There was nothing he could do. His revolver and rifle were hidden in the bushes at the side of the road nearly a mile away. He would be overpowered.

He felt sick to his stomach but he knew it was no use to try and fight them. They put their clammy hands on him and he shook them away.

'Get your hands off me,' he shouted, fending them off with his elbows.

'If you'll come quietly then,' the policeman who'd been pretending to light the pipe said. 'The station's just over the road.'

Richard realised the game was up. There were seven or eight of them all around him – police and citizens. He recognised the Italian from the Oyster Saloon, and one of the patrons who'd been in the bar the other day. Once again, he'd been caught. He blanched at the thought of being locked up and clamped in irons. He suspected that this time he might never see freedom again.

'I'll go quietly,' he said.

Less than an hour later, he was joined in the cells by both Sullivan and Kelly. All three were charged with murder – the same charges as Phil Levy the day before. They appeared in court the next morning, a Thursday, and were arraigned until the following Saturday.

TUESDAY, JUNE 26th, 1866.
THE MAUNGATAPU MURDERS.
On Saturday morning last, long before the opening of the Resident Magistrate's Court, the doors were besieged by a crowd of persons anxious to be present at the examination of the men suspected of these fearful murders. When the doors were opened, a great rush took place to gain admission.

We have in custody the gang whose movements have caused such great anxiety on the West Coast but who had, until they reached the climax of crime in Nelson province, managed to elude detection. If the men now in custody are guilty of the Maungatapu

Murders, we have deeply to deplore that an efficient system of police surveillance did not detain them on the West Coast. Not only must the vagrant laws be stretched to the utmost limits, but the number of detective officers must be increased, so that it shall be impossible for wholesale murderers, whose description and history are available, to sail from port to port and roam from province to province, without falling into the fangs of justice, and be prevented from plying their bloody trade.

32. Snow Job

Alex awoke to a hammering on the door. The clock radio by the bed said it was 5.16am. She felt the bed move beside her and saw Rick getting up and groping his way to the door.

'Who is it?' he called out. The hammering stopped.

There was no answer. The hammering continued again.

'Who's there?' he called again.

'Snow,' a stranger's voice said.

'Snow?' Rick sounded puzzled.

'Snow business of yours,' the voice said and started to cackle with laughter.

'Jesus, Steve, you stupid fuck,' Rick said, opening the door. 'Are you trying to get us all arrested?'

Alex could see Steve's silhouette against the hallway lights. He came into the room and Rick flicked the light on, shading his eyes against the sudden brilliance. Alex held her hand over her eyes to block the light too and squinted up at Steve, who was making himself at home in one of the armchairs and was turning on the television.

'Steve, for fuck's sake, can't you see we're trying to sleep,' Rick said.

'Yeah? Well it's all very well for you, isn't it?' Steve stood up and moved over to Rick, threateningly. Rick was only wearing his undies and looked particularly vulnerable next to the stocky courier. 'While you've been snoring yourself silly here, I've been taking a whole lot of shit from Warren that should have been directed at you.'

'It's nothing to do with me, I told you that before,' Rick said, pulling on his trousers and doing up the buckle. 'If they're not prepared to pay what we agreed on, then there's no deal.'

'Yeah, well he thinks you're doing the dirty on him. That you've put the price up since you last spoke to him.'

'You know that's not true, Steve. And you know it's good stuff. You got that sample to try.'

'Yeah, there was nothing wrong with that. It was good. But how do we know it's all going to be that good?'

'You saying you don't trust me? Is that it?'

'It's not me…'

'Oh, so Warren doesn't trust me. I get it. Well, you can both go fuck yourselves.'

'But you need us to… '

'Like hell I do. There's plenty of others would be glad of the opportunity, and you know it.'

'Maybe so. But nobody you've dealt with before. Nobody you know you can trust.'

'Whatever. The fact is I'm not going to give it away. I've got ten ounces for you of eighty-five per cent pure. That's worth at least seventy-K in my book. And I know you'll make a lot more than that on it once you've split it up into grams.

'It's not that simple, mate, and you know it. Warren says it's a lot to offload on a small market like this. He won't be able to let it out on the streets all at once. He says he'll pay two-thirds of your latest price or…'

'Or what, mate?' Rick said, matching the threatening tone in Steve's voice.

'Look, it's not me trying to get the price down. It's him. I'm the meat in the sandwich here.'

'Yeah, well you're off, mate. Your meat is shit.'

There was another knock on the door, just as loud and insistent as the last one.

'Jesus man, can't anyone get a quiet night's sleep around here?' Rick said as he went over to the entrance. 'Who is it?'

'You know who it is,' a deep male voice said on the other side of the door.

'Shit,' Steve said, 'It's Warren.'

'No shit,' Rick said and started to rummage in his bag. After a few seconds, he pulled out a Beretta pistol and tucked it into his back pocket.

'What are you doing Rick? You can't use that thing in here!' exclaimed Alex, horrified. The last time she'd seen a Beretta was when Pete had given her one for her birthday. She'd never quite got over the shock of seeing the cold grey steel as she'd pulled off the ribbon and opened up the case. She'd hoped never to see one again.

'Shut up,' Rick hissed at her, kicking the camera case out of sight behind the bed. Then he crossed to the door.

She slipped out the side of the bed and slid onto the floor, lying flat against the bed, using it as a shield between herself and whoever might come through the door.

The door opened and light from the hallway flooded into the far corner of the room, combining with the blue rays from the TV in the other corner to provide an eerie, other-worldly light. Alex was scared. She'd been in some pretty awful situations before, especially with Pete, but this would be up there with the worst.

'What are you doing here?' Rick asked the silhouette.

'You know what I want,' the deep voice replied. 'I've come to get the deal you promised me.'

'Okay, okay, I'll do your deal,' Rick capitulated, much to Alex's relief. 'But I haven't got it here. I'll meet you up by the gondola base in half an hour. At six. Then we'll talk. Satisfied?'

The silhouette stood there without saying anything for what seemed an eternity to Alex before he grunted some sort of assent and left, closing the door behind him.

'Okay, Steve, you can go now. I'll see you there at six and we'll do the deal. And I'll negotiate the price. Now go. I gotta roll.'

'Thanks, mate. You gotta keep in sweet with Warren. He's like God around here.'

'Yeah, yeah. I know. Now beat it. Until six.'

'Okay, okay. I'm going. Hey, what about later on? Do you want to meet up? I could probably swing you a free bungy jump, or a jetboat ride up the canyon. You interested?'

'No, don't worry about us. We'll be taking it easy in the morning. We'll get ourselves to the airport in the afternoon and leave the truck at the airport rental place. There's no hurry. That okay with you?'

'Okay, fine. I'll be off then,' Steve finished lamely.

'Yeah, see ya.' Rick said dismissively as Steve departed. As soon as he'd closed the door behind him, he said, 'You can pick yourself up from behind the bed now, Doc. We're getting out of here.'

'But…'

'Don't argue with me. Look, I'm sorry you got caught up in this. It wasn't supposed to happen this way. I'd arranged all the meetings away from here. You weren't supposed to be involved. But now that you've got an idea what's going on, I'm trusting you to keep it to yourself, okay?'

'Er… I suppose so… Okay.'

'Promise me? This is really important.'

'I promise,' she said. She could see she had no choice. Now that she knew he was carrying a gun, she figured she was better off going along with whatever he said.

'Good girl,' he said. 'As soon as I've met these guys and done the deal, I'll be heading straight for the airport. Allowing at least half an hour for them to muck around, the timing should be about right. We've got to be up in that plane as soon as the sun's up or there'll be all hell to pay.'

'But why?'

'You don't want to know, believe me. You just get yourself packed and ready to check out when I call you.' Rick turned off the TV, went over to the window and pulled back the curtains a fraction to see out to the main street.

'Can you fly this early?'

'As soon as it's light. That's going to be a few minutes after seven. The wind's come up and there's no frost, so we're lucky,' he said. He paused and looked back and forwards out the window. 'Steve's just pulling away now and there's no sign of Warren. He must have gone. So let's get moving.'

Alex jumped up from her hiding place behind the bed and ran into the bathroom to complete the quickest shower she'd ever had.

'Right, I'm going to check out now and pay the bill,' he said when she came out of the bathroom. 'I'll call you from my mobile when I'm five minutes away. That's your cue to take all the bags downstairs and meet me out on the street. I'll pick you up and we'll go straight to the airport.'

'Sure,' Alex said hoping she sounded confident and unafraid. 'I'll be there. You got my mobile number?' He nodded and pulled a piece of paper out of his front jeans pocket. She checked it was correct. 'That's right. Good. I'll wait to hear from you then.'

He picked up the Beretta off the bedside table, shouldered his camera case and was gone. Alex wondered if the camera case and the expensive camera gear she'd seen was simply a front for the cache of cocaine he appeared to be selling. Presumably he'd hidden it underneath the camera. He'd certainly kept it under lock and key, concealing it in the hotel safe when he wasn't in the room, but she hadn't been surprised – after all, it was an expensive camera.

'Oh well, there's not a lot I can do now,' she said to her reflection in the mirror. She brushed her hair, threw on her clothes, gathered her toiletries and tossed them into her bag along with her borrowed ski suit, her shoes, dress and other detritus. The fancy black underwear she bundled into the empty shopping bag. So much for that little fantasy, she thought, as she stuffed the bag into the bottom of the rubbish bin.

She was ready. But she figured she probably had at least a half-hour to wait. So she made a cup of tea in the cupboard-sized kitchen above the mini-bar and found a muesli bar and a biscuit, which would have to do for breakfast.

She kicked his bag out of the way and sat down in the chair, waiting for the phone to ring. At least she had the security of having his bag, she thought. That must mean he was being straight with her. And if anything went wrong, if he didn't pick her up for example, she supposed she could always take a commercial flight back north.

The cell phone rang. She picked it up.

'It's time,' was all he said.

She put down her cup, picked up the bags and her shoulder bag and walked out the door and down the back stairs, leaving the room keys in the slot, then headed for the hotel doors. As she pushed it open, she was aware that if anyone was a moving target right now, she was. 'You've been watching too many action movies,' she told herself firmly and propelled herself outside into the cold morning air to wait on the street. She needn't have worried – he pulled up as soon as she reached the kerb. She jumped in and they sped off.

What was the hurry, she wondered as they sped through the semi-deserted early-Sunday-morning streets. What could be going on with the deal that made him want to leave town so quickly?

'Sorry we had to cut our trip short, Doc,' he said as if her were reading her mind. 'But there'll be plenty of other opportunities. I might have to go up to the Bay of Islands in a week or so. You'll love it there.'

She doubted it somehow, if this trip was anything to go by. Still, it had certainly been an experience. And she could hear her sister say: 'You want to live dangerously, kiddo. What did you expect?'

All the way to the airport, even at that early hour, there were ski-topped cars filling up with petrol, stopping at early-opening coffee bars, heading for a day on the slopes. When they arrived at the aero club, Rick parked the car outside the main terminal building, which was ablaze with lights, already attracting a few early birds. While Alex got the bags out of the back, he ran in to drop off the rental car keys at the desk then returned to where she'd agreed to wait for him.

'Here, I'll take those,' he said, and picked up the overnight bags. 'You can carry the camera gear.' She wondered if it was any lighter than when she'd picked it up briefly yesterday, but figured ten ounces wouldn't make much difference.

They walked briskly to the aero club building, which was closed and deserted. She waited by the ground floor shed while he pushed the Cessna over to the fuel pump then filled it with gas. He beckoned to her to give him a hand and together they pushed it back onto the tarmac.

'Jump in,' Rick said. He started fussing with the propeller then walked round and checked the wings. She looked at him for guidance. 'You'll have to manage it by yourself. I'm tied up here.'

Gingerly, she stood on the wing and levered herself up along with the bags which, thankfully, were not very heavy. She managed to balance unsupported while she opened the door, tossed the bags in the back then climbed up over the ledge and into the passenger seat. At last he climbed up and sat next to her in the cockpit, closed the door, slotted the key into the ignition and turned it on.

'We're outa here,' he said, carrying out his pre-flight checks on the various instruments and knobs, before revving the engine ready to taxi out to the runway. 'And not a moment too soon. Look!' He pointed back at the aero club where Alex could see the two guys she had seen up on the skifield.

Rick pulled out the throttle and turned the little plane towards the main runway, asking the control tower for clearance to take off. As they slowly picked up speed, Alex looked behind her at the club building and saw one of the men running towards them. But he'd never make it. They were drawing further away from him every second and he slackened his pace, shaking his fist angrily at the departing plane.

'It's time to fly,' Rick said laughing after he'd cleared them for take-off. Alex was so relieved to get away she laughed too, though it came out as a high-pitched nervous squeak.

She doubted she'd be in a hurry to return to Queenstown.

33. Guilty Or Not Guilty?

Six weeks later, on Wednesday, September the twelfth, Richard was brought before the magistrate to enter a plea to the charges and for the trial to begin. He was not alone in the dock. Standing with him were Tom Kelly and Phil Levy. There was no sign of Sullivan. Richard had heard that Sullivan would be giving evidence tomorrow. Richard then realised that Sullivan had been tempted by the big reward and had betrayed them all, turning queen's evidence not much more than a week after their arrest.

Richard stood there, handcuffed, irons around his legs once again, looking around the Courtroom in front of him, feeling sick. The leg irons were hurting like hell, his old wounds having rubbed open again. And his heart was breaking. He would be hanged. He would never see his son or daughter, never touch his dear Carrie again or see her smile. He'd been such a fool, continuing with his wicked ways when she offered him every opportunity to give up his bushranging and settle down with her in comfort. He had plenty of chance to think it through and repent. His bargain with the Lord had been that he would write his confessions and he had done so, at length, in prison. His guilt was now beyond doubt. It was all there in black and white. And the price for his foolishness would almost certainly be his life.

The high, wood-panelled walls and narrow, arched, latticed windows rose over the biggest crowd he'd even seen at a hearing and they all seemed to be baying for his blood. He searched through them for Carrie's familiar face, wondering if she would come to see him thus humiliated. Much as he longed to, he was relieved he could not see her.

His search was interrupted by a prod in the ribs from the sergeant behind him.

'Guilty, or not guilty?' he heard the judge ask, and realized he was talking to him.

He coughed and waited a moment before he replied. He had

rehearsed over and over what he was going to say and he wanted to get it right.

The whole world knew by now that he had confessed to the charges of murder a month previously, in this very courtroom. He'd read out before the court his statement, 'written in my dungeon drear this 7th of August, 1866,' he'd said. It had taken him two full days to write and nearly five hours to read. When he had finished, the clerk who had painstakingly recorded everything in shorthand, read it back to him and he'd signed it. He knew very well it meant he was signing his own death warrant.

'I have already acknowledged before God and the public that I am guilty of these awful murders,' he said at last in a strong, clear voice, facing the Judge directly, 'and I do not mean to depart from that now, but for the sake of form I shall plead not guilty!'

There was a commotion in the courtroom until the Judge banged his gavel on the bench.

'Silence! Silence in Court!' he cried until the racket died down and all was quiet again.

Both Levy and Kelly also pleaded not guilty and the trial began. To Richard's relief, the three prisoners were allowed to sit down.

For the first hour or so, the Judge delivered a lengthy peroration about the case, about Sullivan's confession under oath and Burgess's confession made as a judicial statement before the Magistrate, implying that perhaps the latter's might not be fully believed. Richard found it hard to sit still under such circumstances, wanting to jump up and cry out the truth of the matter – that Sullivan was a thieving liar who had perjured himself just to nail him. It wasn't quite so bad, though, when the judge was saying that Sullivan's evidence had to be taken with a grain of salt because he was clearly only making a confession to the murders in order to receive a Queen's pardon. And it was downright delightful when the Judge said that Sullivan would still be tried for the murder of James Battle – the poor old sod who'd been travelling in front of the four they'd murdered and who'd had to be dispensed with too. Richard was overjoyed at this news. It meant the traitorous Sullivan wouldn't get off after all, but would have to stand trial for the additional murder once this trial was over. There was some justice in the world, he thought.

Richard looked around him again as the Judge droned on. And then he saw her – Carrie – in her bonnet and shawl, sitting down the back of the Courtroom, almost hidden behind a large burly man with a moustache. She was looking right at him. He tried to smile at her, but it was impossible, with all those people watching, not to give her away. He knew he'd caught her eye, though. He felt ashamed and looked down at the floor. He wondered if she'd got the letter he'd written her more than a week ago now. It had been tremendously difficult to write. Harder even than his autobiography, *The Confessions of Richard Burgess*. He'd taken a long time to write that, and his uneven script had been edited by the local *Colonist* newspaper editor, Alfred Hibble, a thoroughly decent man. Once he'd got started, the autobiography more or less flowed out of him. But writing the apology to Carrie was one of the hardest things he'd ever done. He'd written it himself, in his best handwriting, asking her forgiveness before God, and confessing many of his past misdeeds while living with her in Hokitika. Knowing that she would bear his child before Christmas, while he could well have gone to the gallows by then, made him feel sick with grief. And he had nobody to blame but himself. He put his head in his hands in despair.

By the sixth and last day of the trial Carrie was exhausted. She'd taken a room the night before in a small hotel not far from the Courthouse, to save her the long trip home. The evenings were still short and the nights cold, and now that her advancing condition was making her feel tired, she couldn't face the carriage ride followed by the walk up the Clover Road in the dark, as she'd done last week. She had arranged for Annie Kempthorne to milk the cow and feed the hens, putting up an excuse that she had to visit her lawyer and then the doctor in town. But despite spending a comparatively comfortable night in the Mitre Hotel, the stress and pain of the last few days was taking its toll.

For a time, it had looked yesterday as if the trial might conclude before nightfall, but by the time the Crown prosecutor, Mr Hart, had finished his address to the jury, night was closing in and the Judge said he'd leave his summing up until the morning.

She'd been almost proud of Richard and the way he'd conducted himself during the trial. He'd managed good cross examination of other witnesses and had made an excellent closing statement at the end of his defence – if you could call it a defence, after confessing publicly that he was guilty. The Judge had picked him up on this.

'Gentlemen of the jury,' Richard had said, 'you are already in possession of my guilty confession, which I have no doubt you have seen in the press, and therefore you know of my blood-guiltiness in killing these men. I shall now unfold fully.'

The judge had looked down his gold-rimmed spectacles at the

prosecutor, then peered up at Richard, his face screwed up in extreme distaste.

'I think it a most extraordinary proceeding,' the judge had said, 'for a man to plead not guilty and then tell the court and the jury that he is guilty.'

But she thought Richard had gone too far in admitting his guilt. He'd gone into far too much detail about each murder, shocking the people in the court. Heaven only knew what effect it had on the jury. The crowd had become so angry that they'd stood and surged forward, as if they would kill Richard themselves. She'd wanted to cry out to him to stop. But she couldn't say a word. If any of these people knew of her relationship with Richard, they'd undoubtedly take their rage out on her instead. As it was, the policemen on duty had moved to protect Richard from the crowd and the judge had banged his gavel, threatening to clear the court if they couldn't restrain their feelings.

Richard had then spent an inordinate amount of time trying to show that Kelly and Levy had nothing to do with the murders, while he and Sullivan were the guilty ones. But she could tell the judge and jury wouldn't fall for that. Sullivan's evidence the previous week had been so convincing and consistent – even after eight hours in the witness box – that everybody believed him. She wished Richard wouldn't try to be so heroic. He couldn't possibly save his two colleagues; at the very least he could paint a less evil picture of himself. He finished his address gallantly, the innocence of his two friends. 'And now, gentlemen,' he concluded, 'I leave the case to your superior judgment.'

Kelly, on the other hand, had sickened her with his groveling address to the jury and his claims of innocence. He'd made some very good points about Sullivan's guilt and the lies he'd told during the trial.

'I have been in Sullivan's company for seven weeks since I met him thirty years ago. I knew him and his two brothers in London and, as he denies this, you must not come to any conclusion except that he would swear anything about me that is not true.' He'd gone on to point out the unfairness of not having legal representation and having to conduct his own case, then concluded:

'You, gentlemen of the jury, will be my counsel. I throw my life into your hands. Do your duty and give me a verdict of acquittal. I declare my innocence. Although I am a marked man, I have not killed any of these men.' Then he'd broken down into sobs.

And now it was the final day, the day the verdict would be given. The courtroom was so crowded, the police had allowed women spectators inside the bar. Because her condition was now obvious, they'd made a point of finding a chair for her, and she now found herself closer to the dock than she would have liked. However, it would appear suspicious if she'd turned down such a favoured position, so she kept her head down and hoped that Richard wouldn't see her.

Judge Johnstone had taken his seat punctually at nine o'clock and settled down to a summing up that had gone on for over six hours, with only a break for morning tea and luncheon. Carrie was thankful she had a chair, but was beginning to wish she'd gone back home instead of waiting for such lengthy philosophising. They were now waiting for the jury to return. She knew perfectly well that there was no judgement possible for Richard other than guilty. But she wanted to hear it herself. There remained within her, despite all the evidence, a faint glimmer of hope that some miracle might save him. She heard a rustling and raised murmurings all around her and looked up to see the jury returning, followed by the judge. The clock on the wall showed it was just before five thirty.

'Silence in the court!' shouted the usher. But the court was already deathly quiet.

'Gentlemen of the jury, have you agreed on your verdict?' asked the registrar.

'We have,' answered the foreman.

'How say you gentlemen, with respect to the prisoner Burgess. Is he guilty or not guilty?'

'Guilty.'

Carrie willed herself not to cry out or show any signs of distress. She felt like fainting. She focused on Richard's face, feeling as if her baby was being torn from her womb as she saw his look of proud defiance.

'Richard Burgess,' asked the registrar, 'have you anything to say why the sentence of death should not be pronounced against you?'

'May I address the court, your Honour?' Richard said.

'Only on a point of law,' the judge said.

'Then I have nothing to say.' He looked down at the floor and Carrie knew that she had lost him.

The judge then went on to ask the verdict for the other two prisoners and gave them the chance to speak. Both went on for an eternity proclaiming their innocence. Carrie did not believe them. And neither, it seemed, did anyone else. In the end, the judge cut them short.

'Richard Burgess, Thomas Kelly and Philip Levy,' the judge said, 'you have been convicted by a jury of your countrymen of the crime of murder. I shall now speak to you severally and individually.

'You, Richard Burgess, have put yourself in a position which, according to my experience, is unparalleled in the history of British trials. You come to the bar of this court and say you plead not guilty, although you are guilty, and freely acknowledge your guilt.

'I hope that those of you who have heard you make your unparalleled statement, with its flippant and daring impiety, will be taught that your pretence in favour of religion and justice is only such as might be expected from a man who has shown some of the cunning of the fox and a little more than the blood-thirstiness of the wolf.

'Richard Burgess, by your own admission, you are the murderer of several men. You have been convicted after a patient trial, of the murder of these men and I now proceed to pass on you the sentence of the law, and that is: that you be removed to the place from whence you came and that there in the due course of law you be hanged by the neck until your body is dead. May Almighty God, in His infinite mercy, have mercy on your soul.'

Carrie saw tears trickle down Richard's face and could not stop hers from flowing too. She hoped the sides of her bonnet would hide them from the women all around her. But she need not have worried. All eyes were on the prisoner who had composed himself and said,

'Your Honour, I have deserved my sentence and I receive it with humility.'

He was then escorted from the dock by a policeman and left the room. Carrie watched him go, the tears still streaming down her face. She'd known this outcome was inevitable from the day she'd read in the paper that he'd confessed. She'd known he'd been writing his confessions in prison and that he had effectively, as he'd said in court, signed his own death warrant. But hearing it, and seeing him led away like that, was proof to her that it was final.

She couldn't bear to listen to the rest of the proceedings. She wanted to escape, to wipe her eyes and go home, to be as far from this stuffy, crowded, hateful courtroom as possible. But she had to wait until everything was over; people might wonder if she left now. As she sat quietly, surreptitiously brushing the tears from her eyes, she resolved that she would write to Richard and would attend his hanging, whenever that might be. She needed, somehow, to say goodbye.

34. Rehearsal

The sun was just going down as Alex was driving Gen's Saab convertible to the Wearables rehearsal room on the far side of Nelson. She hadn't heard from Rick since he'd dropped her home on Sunday morning, and she wasn't at all bothered about it. In fact, she was hoping not to hear from him or run into him for a long time. She'd reckoned she'd had quite enough excitement to last until Christmas and had no inclination to get herself further involved with someone who was clearly dealing in drugs worth a lot of money.

She had no idea where he'd got them from, but she had her suspicions. She remembered Rick talking about a friend from Australia he'd bumped into last week. He was visiting Nelson on a yacht and had gone by the weekend. It wouldn't have been too difficult for him to bring something in, she supposed. She'd heard of drugs being hidden away inside hollow safety rails on yachts, in the rigging, even in the keel. And Rick's little plane was the perfect courier vehicle to deliver them quickly and privately anywhere around New Zealand.

All Sunday, she'd been going over it in her mind. She'd helped Ollie in the vineyard in the afternoon and joined him and Gen and the kids for a Sunday roast dinner around the log fire early in the evening. It had been a calm and cosy occasion after the wild events of the previous twenty-four hours, but while she was easy-going and relaxed on the outside, her mind was in turmoil. She kept reliving the moment when Rick had pulled the pistol from the side of his camera bag and tucked it in his back pocket. And she kept going over and over the conversation that had ensued.

This morning she'd had a meeting with Gen and Ollie and one of the scientists from the landfill company, going through her plan and working out the timing of her various recommendations. They all said they liked her ideas and wanted to get started as soon as she could, so the rest of the meeting had been devoted to putting together a day-by-day action plan and working out how much it would cost and who would need to be involved.

Around lunchtime, Jackie had phoned and asked her if she'd like to come to the rehearsal and help out.

'There's always something needs doing,' Jacks had said. 'You'll find yourself in demand. Just be careful you don't take too much on.'

Alex was quite excited at the prospect of being involved, partly because Gen had told her was the highlight of Nelson's year, but also because she'd missed the buzz of the events scene. Gen had shown her some pictures of previous *WearableArt* award-winning garments and she'd been amazed at the combination of creative genius and intricate needlework that had gone into each one. 'You can see how they take hundreds and hundreds of hours to make,' Gen had said in response to Alex's exclamations.

She parked the car and found the side entrance to the school hall where the rehearsal was being held.

'Hey Alex, over here!' Jackie was calling her, gesturing for her to come over. She was standing amid a swathe of plain white fabric, which stretched out almost the entire length of the hall. 'Come and hold this for me. I need to see how far it'll go.'

As Alex walked across the polished wooden floor, everyone she passed called out a friendly greeting as they looked up from whatever they were doing. Most of them – men and women – were grouped together around an arty-looking woman wearing what appeared to be a flower-petalled bathing cap.

'This is going to be the stage,' Jackie said when she reached her, waving her arms out to each side. Alex looked up and down the big hall and could see two broad white chalk-marks on the floor about ten feet apart, running the length of the room. 'Now I need you to stand here.'

The time flew. Alex was at Jackie's beck and call, running errands, fetching and carrying, and helping to make sure the models came on stage at exactly the right time.

'Can you come again tomorrow?' Jackie asked as they were wrapping up and Alex was getting ready to go.

'Sure, no problem,' Alex said.

'I hope it hasn't been too tedious for you, all that running around.'

'I wouldn't have missed it for the world. I love this sort of thing.'

'It's been great to have an extra pair of hands. D'you want to join us for a drink?'

'Not tonight, thanks Jacks. I'm bushed. Maybe later in the week.'

'So how was the weekend with lover boy, then?'

'Weird, I guess would be the best way to describe it.'

'Weird?'

'Not at all what I expected. The skiing was great, and we saw plenty of the nightlife…'

Jackie laughed. 'That would figure. Rick likes his clubbing. The town'll be quiet this week without him.'

'Why's that?'

'Apparently he's away up north all week. Hadn't you heard?'

'No, I haven't heard from him since Sunday. Not that I expected to,' Alex said. Then, to change the subject, 'How was your weekend?'

'Oh pretty quiet in the end. I was just glad of a break. I ended up sleeping most of Sunday.'

'What! You didn't go out at all?'

'Only for an hour or two on Saturday. I ran into Zhi in the Vic Rose. He asked after you.'

'Did he?' Alex tried not to show that she was pleased.

'He said he hoped to catch up with you before his ship had to go back to sea,'

'Did he say when?'

'No. I think he's got still another week though. You'll have to come along with us and find out for yourself.'

Alex could see Jacks was playing with her.

Half way through the next night's rehearsal, Alex was called over to stand in for one of the models who'd failed to show.

'You're about the same height and size as her,' said Chloe, the woman with the mad hat. 'Would you be able to take her place, love, just for tonight? I'm sure she'll be back on deck tomorrow.'

'Sure,' Alex said, delighted with her elevation to the models' ranks. She joined them, rehearsing their timing and the pace of their walks.

'Costumes next week,' Chloe said.

'That'll slow us down some,' one of the models said to Alex.

'Yeah, but it makes it more exciting,' said another. 'That's when you get to see what all this parading up and down is all about.'

The next two days were make-or-break for getting the message across to the neighbours about the landfill and the benefits of the recycling centre. Alex and Ollie spent the whole day personally visiting all their neighbours – including people living along the roads the trucks would be coming down each day. It was the second time Alex had been to see them, but this time was different – this time she had to persuade them to accept it and call off the protesters. They had their spiel carefully rehearsed so that they could get all the key points across in the first few moments, hopefully persuading people to give them a fair hearing. Then they went into the longer explanation, showing maps and pictures of other landfills and how they fitted in with their local communities, and leaving a simple information leaflet behind with each family. They were aware everyone would be phoning the others, warning them of their approaching mission, but they were prepared for that at each door-knock and still managed to talk their way into the kitchen or living room where they could sit down and discuss it more thoroughly. One or two were almost welcoming, most were hostile, and one even refused to talk to them. But apart from them, they were all much less angry about the landfill once they'd talked it through and answered their questions.

'It's amazing what a difference it can make, just sitting down quietly and talking it through, being prepared to answer all their questions and explain it properly,' Ollie had said as they walked down the drive from their ninth visit. 'It's simple common sense, yet we'd never thought to do it.' They were walking from door to door rather than driving. Alex had said she thought it would be less threatening than having a big truck coming up their drives. And it made them appear more vulnerable and open. And when they were finished, she could call Gen on the cell phone and ask her to come and pick them up.

'The exercise'll do us good,' she'd added, prodding Ollie's small paunch.

On the evening of the second day, the three of them were in the family room – Gen fixing dinner for Claudia and the baby, Alex and Ollie perched at the breakfast bar. They were discussing the day's events over a glass of wine when the phone rang for Alex.

'Hi there,' said a familiar West Coast accent.

'Zhi! How are you?' Alex was both surprised and delighted to hear from him.

'Fine, thanks. How are *you*?' Zhi asked.

'Oh, I'm fine too. Busy, you know how it is.'

'Alex, I was wondering if you'd like to meet me for a drink at the weekend. Say tomorrow night, or Saturday?'

Alex was taken aback.

'Er… yes. I guess so. Saturday would be better.'

'That's great. How about I pick you up at seven? I've hired a car for a few days. I thought we could go somewhere out your way, around

Hope or Richmond. It'd make a change to get out of the city.'

'Sure, why don't you pick me up around seven, and we'll decide then where to go.'

'Another date? My, you're Miss Popularity around here,' Gen said as soon as she'd hung up.

'Who is it this time? Who could beat a rich lawyer with his own private plane, I wonder?' Ollie said.

'Stop it, you two,' Alex said blushing. 'It's a guy I met in town a couple of weeks ago. He's something to do with oil exploration. He's very nice.'

'An oil baron, eh?' Ollie said, laughing. 'You sure know how to pick 'em.'

'No, not an oil baron. Far from it,' Alex said. 'He's a computer geek. The money's good, but he certainly doesn't own the show.'

'Well I hope he's got a better rep than that lawyer fellow,' Gen said. 'I've heard he's got a few too many contacts in the underworld.'

'Yeah, they say he gets a bit close to some of his clients,' Ollie added.

'Really?' Alex said. She was tempted to tell all. She was dying to share it with someone and ask what she should do. But she couldn't bring herself to talk about it because she'd end up having to tell the police and that was the last thing she wanted. She'd had enough of that with Lucian. She sighed. 'I don't seem to have very good taste in men,' she said in the end. 'It wouldn't surprise me at all if he was a bit of a bad boy. I seem to attract them.'

Gen stopped spooning pureed vegetables into Georgia's mouth and turned to Alex, smiling sympathetically. 'I used to live a little on the wild side, when I was overseas,' she said. 'Before Ollie came and saved me. I know what it's like to want a bit more action than your dull old life is giving you.'

'You did? I can't believe it.'

'I did.' She turned back to Georgia, who was demanding more. 'I'll tell you about it one day. If I hadn't met Ollie at the winery, I'd probably still be running around looking for trouble.'

'Yeah, the knight in shining armour. That's me,' Ollie said, smiling broadly.

'We need to find you one of them. Alex. What about the one who's just asked you out? Could he be the one, do you think?'

'Or is he another wild boy?' Ollie added.

'Hey, give me a break,' Alex laughed. 'You two are just as bad as the Rossinis. They were always trying to fix me up with a nice boy. They gave up in the end. I'm an impossible case, I'm afraid.'

'Nonsense, I don't believe it,' Gen said, giving up with the spooning and wiping the splatters off Georgia's high chair. 'I'm going to treat you as my special personal project from now on. If you can't find a nice boy in this paradise, there's something wrong.'

'Perhaps one of the protesters?' Alex teased. 'I've a real fondness for dreads.'

'Now there's a thought,' Ollie said. 'I could fix you up with that chap I saw wearing socks under his sandals. He'd be just the ticket.'

'I can just see you eating mung beans and tofu for breakfast.'

'And spinning your own wool.'

Alex pulled a face.

'Sorry,' Gen said. 'We're getting carried away. It's none of our business, I know. We just want you to be happy while you're here.'

'And if you meet a handsome prince who has a few oil wells tucked up his sleeve…'

'Stop it, Ollie. Give her a break.'

'Sorry, Alex,' Ollie said.

'You up to anything tonight?' Gen asked.

'Another rehearsal in an hour. So I'd better whip up something to eat and get moving.'

'You want to eat with us? You're welcome to.'

'No thanks, Gen. I've got a nice bit of tofu in the fridge…'

They all laughed.

'No, seriously, I've got tuna steak for tonight and salad. It'll only take a few minutes to cook. I must get going.'

Later, when she was just about to crawl into bed, exhausted from the exacting rehearsal, she caught sight of the old leather diary sitting on the desk, poking out from under some papers. The sight of it made her feel guilty. She'd meant to show it to Gen and Ollie before she went to Queenstown but had got so caught up in events that it had completely slipped her mind. Until now. She resolved to show it to Gen in the morning.

Plucking the old leather volume out from under the pile of papers, she took it to bed with her, opening it up at random.

It is the evening of the fateful day upon which the father of my unborn child has been found guilty of the murder of four innocent men and condemned to die for his sins against humanity. The whole province is in uproar. The papers are full of his treachery.

If anybody discovered my secret, I would surely be lynched.

I write this at home where I have thankfully returned after spending a fitful night in a Nelson hotel, awaiting the last day of the trial and the jury's verdict. I sit here alone by the light of a single lamp, feeling my solitude weighing heavily on me. As Richard is condemned, so am I. I shall never see him again. My tears have wet this page so that I cannot write further.

35. Last Rites

Richard was preparing to meet his maker. It was October the fourth, a Thursday, and tomorrow morning at dawn he had an appointment with the executioner. The piety and religious sentiments he'd expressed in his autobiography and in letters these past two months had seemed genuine at the time, but looking back now – with the gallows just hours away – the sweeping statements he'd made about merciful God finding it possible to forgive him seemed shallow and hypocritical. If it hadn't been for the succession of priests coming to visit him, each one offering their own road to salvation, he would not have known what to say, how to phrase it.

But now the need to repent and to be forgiven was indeed genuine. He feared the fires of hell and eternal damnation that he knew were awaiting him; his only chance of salvation was to throw himself at the mercy of the Lord.

One of the vicars – his favourite, the Reverend John Daniel – was due within the hour. He planned to spend the intervening minutes in pious contemplation.

He looked up through the narrow slit of a window at the darkening sky outside. It was his last evening on this earth and here he was locked in a tiny, bare wooden cell, his leg in irons, his clothes the raw, rough cotton of a prisoner's uniform. It was appropriate somehow that his last hours on earth should be like this. After all, he'd spent much of his lifetime in such a situation. If he'd counted the days he'd been alive, he knew he would have spent many more behind bars than free. And he had nobody to blame but himself. He cursed his stupidity for wasting what should have been a good and humble life. His mother had given him every chance to do well – an education, clothes on his back, a decent roof over his head in Hatton Gardens, and enough food to satisfy his belly. But he'd wanted so much to show her how much he hated her new man and his mean children that he'd fallen in with a street gang and ultimately broken her heart.

Everything else that had happened to him in his rotten life seemed to have led on from there, with the inevitability of crime and punishment. Being transported to the colonies, he'd returned to petty crime on his release, only to be sentenced to ten years for a robbery he had never committed. He would never forget the hellhole of the Melbourne Gaol and the prison hulks in Hudsons Bay, floating hells of misery. He'd escaped twice, only to be brought back and flogged. No sooner was he released, than he was arrested for another crime and was in prison again.

You'd think you'd have learned your lesson by then, he told himself.

Released again, he'd sailed for the Otago goldfields, where he'd met up with Kelly, and the pair of them had made easy pickings from the diggers there until they were arrested again, escaped, and then faced a series of trumped up charges and a three-year prison sentence, which even the diggers they'd stolen from thought was unfair. He'd vowed from that day on to devote himself to taking his revenge on society and on the sergeant who'd lied to convict him, and now he was paying the price. He'd had his revenge all right, robbing and murdering innocent, hard-working diggers and bank clerks.

He could see it clearly now, now that it was too late: he'd spent his life trying to settle scores, taking revenge for problems that were largely of his own making. He'd sought revenge on his mother for taking up with that vile man who became his hated stepfather; and he'd sought revenge on society for putting him in prison.

But the tables were turned and society was about to exact its revenge on him. He understood at last that the death sentence was more than deserved – for the murders on that wretched mountain and for all the previous murders he'd committed – and he was genuinely remorseful and repentant. He had taken the lives of dozens of innocent men and those he'd spared, he'd robbed of their livelihood. He was a guilty wretch and the world would be a better place without him. He prayed, over and over, that God would be merciful and forgive him.

He turned from the window and crossed the narrow patch of floor to the small wooden table and chair in the corner by the cell door. There lay his autobiography – neatly tied with string and ready for Alfred to pick up later that evening. Alfred Hibble, the editor of the *Nelson Colonist* newspaper, had edited his handwritten manuscript, correcting the spelling and grammar, which was none the best thanks to the infinitesimal amount of attention he'd paid in school. It was appropriate that Alfred should take the manuscript and do with it as he saw fit. Alfred had said he'd like to publish it, one day. 'But I think we'll have to wait for all the fuss to die down first,' he'd said. 'If the people out there knew that this existed, there's some would try to tear it to shreds.'

] Footnote: Hibble is thought to have passed the manuscript on to the *Lyttelton Times* (the forerunner to *The Press*) and later in 1866 the *Times* published it as a 47-page booklet entitled "Life of Richard Burgess, the Notorious Highwayman and Murderer, written by himself while in prison shortly before his execution, which took place in Nelson NZ on the 5th day of October, 1866."

On the table beside his confessions was a letter from Carrie. It had arrived at the same time and in the same mail as his death warrant. He picked it up and pressed it to his cheek, as if it were her hand, and breathed in deeply, trying to detect any faint aroma that might remind him of her. But there was none. The thick cream deckle-edged paper he hadn't seen before. Only her handwriting was familiar. The message was short and poignant:

Monday, October 1st, 1866
My dearest Richard
It grieves me more than words can express to know that in a few days time I will lose you forever. Even at the trial, I held out some hope that your life might be spared. I visited the courtroom daily so that I could see your face, praying that it would not be for the last time.

I will keep my promise not to tell our child about you. You are right – it is best that he or she does not know the seed from whence they came. But I will tell them that your name was Richard and that you were a brave and strong man, who was always kind to me and generous. I will tell them you left me well provided for and maybe one day, when this episode does not burn so in the minds of the people in this province, I will show our child the photograph I have of you that I treasure so much – the photograph taken of you and me at the Grand Ball in happier days.

May God protect you and bless you and welcome you into the kingdom of Heaven where I hope that you will receive more mercy and kindness than you received here on earth.
I remain
Your loving
Carrie.

36. Power of the Press

As promised, Alex took Carrie's diary over to the house the following morning, wrapping it carefully in a plastic bag to protect it from the rain. It was pelting down. From her bedroom window, she'd seen it driving against the awakening vines. And as she ran across to the Darbys', great sheets of water were running down the side of the house and collecting in puddles in the yard. Not an auspicious start to a day that would have benefited from sunshine. Today was the day Nick Thompson, the big boss from GreenWaste International was coming down to meet her and she planned to introduce him to the Davenports and some of the other upset neighbours. She didn't fancy getting drenched.

Gen was in the kitchen, tidying up after the girls' breakfast.

'Like a coffee?' she asked Alex as she came in the door, shaking raindrops off her coat.

'Love one. Yes please,' she said as she hung it up on the peg. 'I've got something to show you.'

Gen poured them both a coffee and set the mugs down on the kitchen table.

'Isobel's gone with Ollie to pick up Nick Thompson. They'll be another twenty minutes yet. And Claudia has gone back to sleep. So for once I've got a few minutes' peace,' Gen said, collapsing into a chair, propping her elbows on the table and resting her chin in her hands. She looked exhausted. She caught Alex looking at her with amazement and laughed. 'I know, I know. It's only half past eight on a Thursday morning and already I'm bushed. It's enough to put you off having children for a long time.'

Alex sat at the table too and pushed the plastic bag across to Gen.

'I'm glad we've got a moment or two to ourselves,' she said. 'There's something in here that I think you'll want to spend a bit of time over.'

Gen picked up the package and, intrigued, slowly unwrapped the supermarket bag from around the book.

'Good God!' Gen said as the old leather diary emerged. 'What's this?'

Alex didn't say anything. She thought it best for Gen to discover it herself.

Gen turned the book over, looking for signs of what might lie within, but there was no lettering or title to be seen. She opened the worn brown leather cover, turned the next page and let out a cry of excitement.

'It's Carrie's diary!' she exclaimed and turned two more pages over, closely inspecting each one. 'Look, there's the date, 1866, and she's talking about how she met Richard Burgess. This is amazing. Where did you find it?'

Looking rather shamefaced, Alex described the drunken incident when she'd managed to put her fist through the floor of the wardrobe and had discovered the diary under the floorboard.

'I'm really sorry, Gen. I meant to bring it over before I left for Queenstown, but events got in the way and I only remembered it again when I saw it last night.'

But Gen wasn't taking much notice. She was poring over the diary, her coffee sitting untouched on the table, going cold. Alex felt superfluous, so went over to the bench to pick up that morning's newspaper, still rolled up and unread. 'Mind if I...?' She asked Gen, but she was oblivious to the outside world, engrossed in the diary. Alex unfurled the paper and opened it up, taking a sip of her coffee as she did so.

But when she saw the front page headline she nearly choked on it.

'HAZARDOUS WASTE
IN LANDFILL WILL
RUIN WINERY SALES' shouted the headline.

The story underneath was appalling. It quoted Water Protection, one of the organisations against the site, saying they'd found out that hazardous waste was going to be dumped in the landfill from two of the processing plants in the region and claiming that it would leach out into the water supply and ruin the entire wine-growing region around Richmond and Hope.

'Bugger!' she said. There was always something like that from left field, when you were least expecting it. And just as she thought they were starting to get things under control. 'Bugger!' she said again.

Gen still didn't take any notice. Alex closed the paper so Gen wouldn't see it. No point in ruining her morning when she'd just had such an exciting windfall.

'Gen,' she said, touching her arm to get her attention. 'Gen, I'm going to wait for Ollie in the lounge. He said we'd meet in there.'

'Oh, no problem,' Gen said, looking vague. 'The gas fire's on in there, so it should be warm. Make yourself at home.' She returned to the pages of Carrie's diary.

Alex went and stood by the window, watching the approach to the driveway. She thought she could see a few dots of figures down the end of the long approach then she saw, coming slowly through them, Ollie's Range Rover. That'll be a timely reminder to the boss, seeing the protesters in the flesh, she thought. She hoped, rather wickedly, that he would be subjected to the same drubbing on the car door that she had, just to show him what they were up against. The protesters had drifted away in the last couple of days, since she and Ollie had been to visit the neighbours. But this morning's headlines would start them all up again, she realised.

'You must be Alex Zerakowski,' the MD for Asia said as he came through the front door. He held out a black-leather gloved hand for her to shake. 'Nick Thompson.'

'Yes, I'm Alex,' she said, shaking the gloved hand in return. 'It's good to have you here.'

Nick Thompson was the typical Alex turn-on. Tall, dark and handsome, he was, however, slightly menacing. He was grim-faced, his thin lips slit shut like a post-box. And he was wearing a long dark woollen coat, which gave him the appearance of Darth Vader. As he pulled off his gloves, Alex half expected him to have a steel claw in place of one hand. 'Don't be so ridiculous,' she told herself. 'He's on your side!' She reckoned she'd have to dissuade him from wearing that coat and the gloves if she took him to visit the Davenports, or he'd be regarded as a pariah as soon as they looked at him.

'Come on, come on, don't stand in the doorway. It's freezing out here,' Ollie said, ushering them inside the small lobby, where he took Nick's coat and hung it in the closet. 'Come on through,' he added, opening the door into the lounge.'

Nick stood in front of the fire, rubbing his hands, then turned to face Alex. He looked angry.

'I take it you've seen this morning's paper?' he asked accusingly.

'I've just been reading it now,' she said, looking at Ollie. She could tell by the look on his face he'd heard all about it from Nick and that their boss wasn't happy about it. 'It's amazing how these things can shoot up from nowhere. We had no idea they'd come out with something like that.'

Nick gave her a withering look. She realised she'd have to pull a few rabbits out of the hat to satisfy him now.

'Especially as it's all lies,' Ollie said crossly.

'Indeed,' Nick said coolly.

'We'll have to set he record straight, I'm afraid,' Alex said. 'It's difficult when a story blows like that. The more you deny it, the bigger it gets. But we simply can't let that go uncorrected.'

Nick agreed and, relieved to be able to get away from the tense atmosphere, she fled back to her cottage to sort out the story. She'd have to talk to all the media, she reflected as she dodged the puddles across the yard. Even TV. Nelson often escaped the evil eye of the TV news. But if something big were happening, they'd hire a stringer or fly a crew over the strait from Wellington. It was only a short half hour ride, as she knew from her own journey less than a month ago. If they were coming, they could be on the doorstep any minute.

Back in the little upstairs office, Alex flicked on the radio to listen to the next bulletin then got her media list out and started phoning. She began with the two main radio news networks. She figured they would probably have been running it for most of the morning and she needed to kill it quickly. She kicked herself for not listening to the news this morning. She'd been so preoccupied with the diary and Nick Thomspon's impending visit, and so comforted by the neighbours' responses over the past couple of days, that she'd never thought there'd be any trouble.

She had a very productive talk with one of the reporters, but the one from the rival station proved more difficult. She emailed him GreenWaste's proposal to the local council about the waste stream and what would be in it, as well as a copy of the plans for the recycling plant then phoned him back to talk it through further. He seemed more convinced this time and, like the first radio reporter she'd spoken to, agreed to interview Nick and the geologist over the phone later on.

Then she phoned the *Mail* and politely repeated herself – until they accepted her invitation to talk to the waste manager at the council and then come out later and interview Nick and the scientist about what was really going into the landfill.

It turned out the council had already been on the phone to them, complaining mightily. To help make amends – although of course they never said as much – they also promised to do a feature about the recycling plant that would be such an integral part of the site. She phoned Simon, the geologist, and went over with him several times what they would ask, guiding him through his responses. Then she contacted the Wellington newsrooms of the two main TV stations. Sure enough, one of them was on their way, hot on the trail of an environmental scandal, as they put it.

Alex laughed and gently put forward the recycling story, scotching the claims of hazardous waste.

'That's incorrect,' she said. 'They're making it up. I think if you check the facts you'll find the *Mail* has been taken for a ride.'

The news director sounded sceptical so she quickly emailed her the evidence – the same documents from the council and GreenWaste that she'd send to radio and the *Mail* – as well as the proposal for the recycling centre and evidence of how beneficial it would be in such a fast-expanding grape-growing area.

She made a few more calls then stuffed all her files into her satchel and scooted back to the house to update Ollie and Nick. She hoped that Nick would be a little more receptive this time. She needed to prepare him and Ollie for the media grilling they were about to get and she'd need all the cooperation she could muster.

She needn't have worried. The boss had been humoured by Ollie's bonhomie and she found them both sitting at the kitchen table, sampling Ollie's chardonnay and picking at a platter of cheeses, smoked chicken, olives, sun-dried tomatoes and pickles.

'Come and join us, Alex. Here I'll get you a glass,' Ollie said, standing to get her one. 'What's the story?'

'No, thank you. I'd better not,' she said. 'There's a lot happening this afternoon and I need to stay on top of it. And you two had better go easy on it too. *One News* will be here in an hour or two to interview you both, as well as Simon.'

That had put a damper on proceedings. But she figured the wine and food had done the trick and softened Nick up after his terse arrival, so it wouldn't hurt for them both to stop now. Ollie had swept the bottle off the table, teasing Alex for being such a killjoy but agreeing with her that it was the right thing to do. Then they'd settled down to working through the media interviews ahead, going over and over what they'd be asked until they were happy with their answers. When Simon, the geologist, arrived, she put him through his paces too. For a scientist, he wasn't too bad at explaining things, Alex thought, and he sounded terribly authoritative and convincing.

Just before six that night, Alex switched her video on to record *One News*, then ducked over to the house to watch the news with Gen, Ollie and Nick, who had decided to stay on another day. He still had to make the visit to the Davenports and talk to several people from the local residents' association, who wanted to hand him a letter and talk to him. She'd already seen the TV news promos, and there hadn't been a mention of the landfill, so she was keeping her fingers crossed that it would be too lukewarm to make it into the bulletin. She couldn't afford to have anything further blow up tonight – she had to be at rehearsal at seven.

Luck was not with her, however. The landfill story was fourth in the news hour, starting with footage of wine bottles in a Nelson supermarket that had been plastered with fluorescent orange stickers.

'PRODUCT OF HAZARDOUS WASTE,' the stickers said.

'The bastards,' Ollie said, jumping out of his chair and shaking his fist at the television.

'Oh no, that's Chantal's wine,' Gen said. 'They'll be furious.'

Nick was tight-lipped.

'Bottles of wine from award-winning Chantal winery have been the target of protesters trying to stop a proposed landfill development just outside Nelson. They claim the wine contains grapes from the vineyard that plans to accommodate a landfill site in the middle of this popular grape-growing area,' the newsreader was saying as the camera panned across the beautiful Hope countryside, showing the bare vines. Then the reporter came on camera, saying how Water Protection believed hazardous waste was going to be dumped at the site. There were a few frantic seconds when an earnest young woman from WP waved her arms around and claimed she had evidence that hazardous waste would be trucked past the wineries and dumped in the Hidden Valley. There was, of course, no evidence.

'And then it will get into the water supply and kill us all!' she finished.

'That's an utter lie!' Ollie shouted at her image.

'I don't believe they can get away with saying that,' Gen said.

Nick looked as though he'd eaten a lemon.

Alex was appalled.

But then it got a little better – if such a thing were possible.

Nick's face came on screen and, to Alex's surprise, he came across as a warm and caring businessman who wanted to do the right thing. He produced the evidence scotching the Water Protection woman's claims, which came up on the screen in quotation marks. Then someone from the council came on, backing him up. Ollie was up last, enthusing about the recycling plant and how good it would be for all the wineries in the area.

'This will be a first for New Zealand,' he was saying. 'We'll be showing the rest of Australasia the way forward. It's been a godsend to the wineries in the Napa Valley. And we know we can make it work here.'

By the time the item was over, the overriding impression was of a protest without substance. But it still rankled with all of them that the accusations had been broadcast at all. Radio had stopped running the story after its midday bulletins and now that TV had its story, maybe the trumped-up allegations would die down again.

Ollie turned off the TV and his recorder. Gen had to return to the kitchen with Claudia and Isobel, who'd both been amazingly quiet during the news item – as if they understood its significance, Alex thought.

'Will tonight's *Mail* have arrived yet?' she asked Ollie. "We ought to see what they've come up with.'

'I'll go and get it. It takes a while to get out this far, but it'll be here by now.'

He took off and in seconds Alex could hear the Range Rover roaring off down the drive. He was back in no time with the paper, which he unrolled and spread on the coffee table in front of her and Nick.

'LANDFILL PROTESTERS
PLASTER WINE BOTTLES' the heading said.

It was next to a photograph of rows of wine bottles covered with the 'Hazardous Waste' stickers.

The story went on to quote the owners of the Chantal winery saying how upset they were that their bottles had been defaced. 'We put a lot of time and passion into making that wine and we think it's despicable for someone to come along and do something like this. They obviously don't appreciate good wine,' they said. The story went on to refute the claims of hazardous waste making its way into the landfill, with a lot of space devoted to the man from the council and to Nick and Simon. This time there was plenty of evidence against WP's allegations.

'That's more like it,' Ollie said over her shoulder as he finished reading. 'Anyone reading that could see for themselves that the Water Protection people have been making it up.'

'You'd have to be pretty thick not to see it was a complete fabrication,' Alex agreed.

'You've done well,' Nick said, smiling slightly.

Alex was enormously relieved at that, although she didn't show it she had a suspicion that Nick was not a man to get carried away with praise.

The phone started to ring again. It had rung on and off out in the kitchen through the news item, but Ollie had let it ring. This time, Gen answered it and moments later put her head round the door.

'That was Antoinette. She's furious with the Water Protection people. Chantal is going to lay a complaint to the police. I said I'd call her back later when the girls are in bed.' She returned to the family room, where Alex could hear Isobel wailing. Thankfully, the noise faded into the background when Gen closed the door behind her.

'You might as well go, Alex. You've got a rehearsal to get to and there's nothing more we can do now.'

'I'll phone the radio newsrooms first,' Alex said. 'I'd like to know what they're planning to do on *Morning Report*, if anything. And I think I might plant a few seeds of discomfort with them. Make them think about the ethics of an organisation that would make up something as upsetting to the public as hazardous waste.'

'How will you do that?'

'I found out some interesting information the other day about the past of that woman from WP on the TV before. Someone was telling me about the organisation and saying we should watch out for her. She's very unusual, is all I'll venture to say now. Any reporter worth their salt should have been able to find that out straight away. It's all publicly available. But of course they don't bother to do that any more. They accept most things protesters say at face value.'

'We'll leave you to it,' Ollie said. 'You seem to have it all under control.'

'I don't need to go to rehearsal, tonight. I can stay if you need me.' She really didn't want to miss rehearsal. If you missed too many they threw you out of the show. But she didn't want Nick to think she wasn't committed.

'I don't think there's much point in waiting around,' Nick said. 'You seem to have everything covered.'

'You'll have your mobile?' Ollie asked.

'Of course,' Alex said.

'Then we can get you if we need you.'

'Okay, thanks.'

'Oh, and Gen showed me the diary,' Ollie said. 'She's over the moon to have it. You've been a godsend coming here. It was meant to be.'

Alex laughed. 'I don't know about that. We're not out of the woods yet with this hazardous waste thing, although it looks as though the worst is over. Has she read it yet?'

'You bet. From cover to cover. Isobel has been running riot all day and the baby has been toddling around after her. You should see the family room. It looks like a bomb hit it. She took it over to her mother's just before and left it with her to read. It's caused great excitement in the family. I know she'll want to talk to you about it when you've a moment…'

'I'll catch her on the way through,' Alex said.

Gen was in the kitchen making a start on cleaning up the chaos, Claudia in one arm, Isobel following behind, dropping more toys in the Gen's cleared wake.

'I let it get away on me today, I'm afraid,' she said as Alex nearly fell over trying to avoid tripping over an assortment of dolls, prams, books, Lego, and chunky toddler toys and blocks scattered across the floor. 'I haven't been able to do anything else today except read the diary and think about what was in it. I can't get over it. It's such a wonderful surprise.'

'Did you know it existed?'

'Mum says she can remember her grandma talking about it once, but nothing was ever made of it. I don't think she ever really believed there was one. Certainly not enough to hunt for it.'

'I couldn't believe it when I found it. It had lain there undisturbed all these years.'

'You'd think someone would have noticed when they'd painted the wardrobe, when we did up the cottage,' Gen said.

'It was quite a shallow floor,' Alex said. 'I suppose they never noticed the difference on the outside.'

'Mum's just ecstatic,' Gen said. 'She's reading it right now. Every now and then she rings me up to read bits out to me.'

'That's great Gen. I'm glad I found it. I'll come and see you later tomorrow, when all this fuss has died down, and you can tell me all about it. I haven't read much of it yet. But I'd better fly. I've got to be at rehearsal in ten minutes. I'll never make it. They hate it when you're late.'

'You'd better get moving then,' Gen said. 'You can take my car again. I won't be going anywhere tonight.'

37. Moonlight Serenade

On Saturday, at seven on the dot, Zhi parked the blue S-type on the drive, found Alex's cottage behind the main house, more or less as she'd described it, and knocked on the door. He waited, listening to the sound of feet scurrying backwards and forwards behind the door, until Alex finally appeared. The dim porch light made it difficult to see her. Behind her, the bright lights of the lounge appeared almost like a halo.

'Come in,' she said, looking a little distracted. 'I'll be ready in a minute. I just can't find my bag. I know it's here somewhere.'

He stepped inside and got his first good look at her in some time. Black trousers hugged her hips, emphasising her slim figure and covered black stack-heeled shoes, making her legs appear even longer. Under a long denim jacket she was wearing a simple white top, and draped around her neck was a long woollen hot-pink scarf. Her hair still had that familiar spiky shagginess that he'd been so attracted to when he'd first caught sight of her in the Vic Rose. It reminded him of Meg Ryan on a really bad hair day, and he loved it.

'You look great, Alex,' he said.

'Not too casual, am I? I wasn't sure what sort of pub we're going to.'

'Perfect. It's just right,' he said, feeling a fool for not being able to think of anything better to say. Why did he always have to behave like such a klutz when confronted with a woman he fancied?

Alex was still scooting around the house, darting into the kitchen and out again. Then flinging back the cushions on the couch she discovered the missing bag and held it up triumphantly. 'There!' she cried. 'Sorry about that. Right, I'm ready.'

He escorted her out to the car, glad that he'd upgraded to the rental company's special luxury model. Hang the expense, he thought. He could easily afford it.

'Wow, a new Jag,' she said, clearly impressed.

'I felt like treating myself to something special,' he said. 'Especially when I knew you were coming out with me tonight.'

She sank down into the squishy passenger seat and he shut the door behind her, catching a whiff of the new leather.

'It's beautiful,' she said as they swept away into the night.

'Thought you'd like it,' he said. 'I'm going to take it for a bit of a spin. I heard about a great band playing at Hot Mama's tonight, so I thought we could go there.'

'Hot Mama's?' Alex said.

'Yeah, apparently it's in Motueka. About half an hour from here, round by the waterfront. It's a nice drive, they tell me.'

He turned up *Boheme* on the CD player.

'How did you know that's one of my favourites?' Alex asked.

'I listen to you when you talk, that's how,' he said smiling.

She didn't say anything. Maybe, he hoped, she'd give that some thought. He suspected most of the guys she went out with were not the listening kind. Certainly that shady-looking character she'd been so besotted with in the Vic Rose that night had certainly not shown much interest in what she had to say. He was too full of his own importance to pay much attention to Alex. Zhi had felt like going over and giving the guy a good shake, telling him that he shouldn't be so rude to Alex. But he'd resisted the urge. Better to let him show his true colours and then, if Alex was half the woman he thought, she'd realise what a jumped-up prick he was and ditch him.

He concentrated on driving. The car purred along the narrow country roads, hugging the corners as if glued to the road, taking them so smoothly you could hardly notice any movement.

Hot Mama's was a small café-bar in the middle of a small one-street town. It was filled with young people. The band wasn't due for another hour at least; in the meantime the sound system was playing reggae. Zhi ordered drinks, a Mac's for him, a pinot for her, and they found two empty seats at a table of youngsters who looked to Zhi as if they were still at school. Alex caught his look of surprise and smiled.

'They're talking about lowering the drinking age even further,' she said sotto voce in his ear.

He raised an eyebrow. 'Seems low enough to me already,' he whispered back.

As they talked, the time seemed to fly. They started by talking about opera.

'I loved listening to *Boheme* on the way here,' Alex said. 'It was so sweet of you to think of me like that.'

'I like to please,' said Zhi, smiling. 'Besides, I like it myself. I've seen it heaps of times, and your other favourite, *Traviata*. I like them both too. In my travels around the world, following oil, I've made a point of getting to the opera whenever I can.'

'That's funny, I do that too,' Alex said.

They found they'd been to some of the same opera houses, even the same opera at one theatre in Florence, though on different nights. He told her how he'd also seen *Traviata* performed in Tokyo, Moscow and Oslo, which was more than Alex could lay claim to. He confessed to having a love-hate relationship with his job. Travelling the world, seeing new places, meeting new people, being constantly on the move – he loved and hated it in equal measure. He admitted he blamed his job on his inability to settle down and have a family. He'd even bought an apartment in San Francisco, but he'd been home so rarely he'd eventually rented it out.

'I don't seem to be able put down roots. I've just never found the right person to settle down with,' he said, looking across the table at her, captivated by her fair skin and freckles, trying not to drown in her deep blue eyes. He dragged his gaze away and took another swig of his beer. He realised he'd sounded far too serious and kicked himself for bring up such a heavy suject at such an early stage. So he deliberately made light of it by telling her about his mother and her constant demand that she be given a grandchild before she died. He made it sound hilarious, especially when he mimicked his sister Xanthia.

'That's an unusual name, like yours,' Alex said. 'I've been waiting to find out where Zhi comes from, hoping you might tell me. But I can see I'm going to have to ask. How did you and Xanthia get such exotic names?'

'I think it's my mother's Spanish blood,' Zhi said smiling. 'You're right, people are always commenting on it. But at least it's memorable. They hardly ever forget it. Mom used to tell us that they were ancient names handed down over generations. But Zannie and I reckoned that was hogwash. We could never find any names like that in our family tree. We reckoned Mum was trying to use up the last letters of the alphabet, just to be different from everyone else.'

She told him about her mother and the pain of losing her and the terrible effect it had on her father. Then, as if she were also aware she was getting too serious, she regaled him with tales of the mischief she and Kate used to get up to on summer camp.

He asked her how she was getting on at the vineyard. He'd seen the TV news, he said, and wondered how she was coping. She described how she'd worked her butt off to fix it up and how the media were being much more positive about the whole thing now. Pushing the recycling aspect had turned the tide, she said.

'Until the next catastrophe, of course,' she said, laughing. 'They have a way of hitting you when you least expect it.'

She told him about the Wearables rehearsals and how she was a model now, elevated in the ranks from a backstage helper. He was impressed. He'd love to be able to do something like that, but he was never around in one place long enough to get involved in local activities. As it was, his ship was leaving on the morning tide and he'd be gone again. He hadn't let on to Alex yet. He didn't want to spoil the evening. But he was also being a coward and he knew it. He was dreading having to tell her.

'But you've hardly told me anything about your job,' she said. 'How do you find oil?'

He described his day, pointing out it was a fairly laborious process staring at computer screens day after day searching for changing patterns in seismic waves. Just the same, he said, there was nothing as exciting as experiencing the thrill of finding oil after months, sometimes years, of hard work.

They ordered a meal – Alex chose the chicken burger with chunky wedges and a funky salad and another pinot. Zhi said he'd better have a ginger beer, since he was driving.

'Goodness, look at that,' she said. 'I've been so engrossed in conversation, I've sat on the same drink for nearly an hour.'

'You sound as if that's quite something?'

'I guess it is for me. Usually when I'm out with someone I drink like a fish.'

A band called the Coalrangers came on some time after eight o'clock and played a mix of country rock music that made him want to get up on the dancefloor.

'Let's dance,' he suggested and she nodded agreement. They found a space by the door where a few others had taken to the floor. They danced until Zhi had to call for a break.

'I'm not as fit as I used to be. Let's get something to drink.'

He ordered coffees and a large glass of water each.

'Heavens, look at the time!' Alex said when sipping her latte. 'It's nearly eleven o'clock. I've got to be up early helping Ollie. I ought to be going home soon.'

They had one last dance then Zhi drove them back towards Hope. Just past Mapua, he saw a sign marked 'Wharf' and, guessing that it might be a quiet romantic spot, turned off the main road and eased to a halt at the entrance to a jetty stretching out into the bay.

'Let's admire the view,' he said. He got out of the car and came round to her side, opening the door for her. The strains of *Boheme*'s 'Quando m'en vo' on the S-type's magnificent CD-player washed out of the car door and across the moonlit harbour.

'That's the song out of the movie *Moonstruck*,' Zhi said smiling. 'It's just the thing for a moonlit night.'

She smiled back at him.

'You've a lovely smile,' he said. 'I think I'm moonstruck!'

He took her hand and walked her the length of the wharf then sat down at the top of some steps, putting his arm around her shoulder.

She snuggled into him, repressing her critical faculties. So what if he was short? So what if he didn't make her knees turn to jelly? If this had been Rick or Lucian, she thought, she'd be feeling a faint flutter about now. But there was nothing. No chemistry. No spark. Yet Zhi was, as Gen would have said, such a nice boy.

Besides, she told herself, Zhi is interested in me. He listens and responds. Rick and Lucian never took the slightest bit of notice of anything I had to say. She could see now that she'd subjugated herself to them and had almost lost her own personality, adapting herself to follow their passions rather than hers. She shuddered as she thought of herself dressed up in Pete's bike leathers and Rick's sexy underwear. Her sister Kate would have put her right if she'd seen her and told her she looked like something out of a bordello. And she'd have been right.

The moon lit up the tiny harbour, reflecting in the water, which had hardly a ripple on its surface. The few clouds on the horizon shone silvery white and the trees and buildings around the sea's edge were bathed in an eerie light.

'It's beautiful,' Alex said softly. 'I'm glad we stopped here.'

'Me too,' Zhi said, then turned and kissed her – a long, gentle kiss that made her feel warm inside. But she still didn't feel the spark she was hoping for. She felt annoyed with herself. She tried kissing Zhi back to see if that would arouse her passion. But nothing happened. At least, not to her. Zhi, she could tell, was getting stirred up.

He cleared his throat and pulled away from her. He realised he couldn't let himself get aroused tonight. He'd be gone in the morning and, much as he'd like to sweep Alex off to the back seat of the S-type and make love to her, he had to keep his cool. It wouldn't be right to get involved to that extent on the eve of his departure.

'We'd better be going,' he said. 'You're getting cold and you need to be up in the morning.'

They held hands for much of the way after that, the Jaguar almost doing the driving for him. Pulling up outside her cottage, he leaned over to kiss her goodnight.

'Why don't you come in for a nightcap?' she asked.

'I'd like that,' he said.

She poured him a glass of wine while the jug boiled and he sat at the kitchen table while she made tea.

'What a quaint old cottage,' he said. 'It's been beautifully done up. But it must be easily a hundred years old.'

'It's got an amazing past. The Darbys told me all about it.' She sat beside him and they sipped their wine while she told him Carrie's story and the reason for the name Hangman's Hill.

'Wow,' he said when she'd finished. 'It's a wonder you can sleep at night. It's a wonder it doesn't have ghosts, with such a turbulent past.'

'Well it does, in a way,' Alex said. 'I've heard noises a couple of times, and imagined I saw someone once. Which is daft really. I'm not the sort of person who believes in that sort of thing. Then there's the diary I found…'

'Diary? You found a diary?'

'Yes. Hidden at the bottom of the wardrobe. Just after I arrived. I haven't got the original any more, but Gen drove into town yesterday and made a copy for me, and another for her mom. I'll show you.'

She ran up stairs, fetched it off the bedside table where she'd left it and ran downstairs again.

'There it is,' she said as she placed it gently on the table in front of Zhi.

'It's come out in the copier okay,' Zhi said. 'But you can see how old it must have been. The pages are all crinkly and chewed at the edges.' He flicked over to an inside page. '1866. Goodness. What a find.' He started to read from the first page that fell open:

October the fourth, 1866.

Tomorrow, Richard faces the executioner's noose. Tonight, I have wept myself dry of tears.

I know that justice must be done and that he has deserved such a fate. But in losing him, I am losing the kindest man I ever met.

I wanted to shout out to the jury that he was not as evil as the witnesses made him out to be.

I wanted to write to the newspapers and tell the world that there was a good side to Richard Burgess, a side that nobody else knew.

But of course I did not utter a word. I did not put pen to paper. I am too afraid to stand up for him because I know that will be my downfall.

My only recourse is to fill these pages with my pain.

My only hope for the future is the new life that awaits within me. I pray that Richard's baby will bring me the solace and comfort that he will never again be able to deliver.

'Hey, this is incredible. What did the Darbys say?'

'Gen and her mom are ecstatic. I had a long talk to Gen yesterday afternoon and she told me all about it – about Carrie and how little her family knew. They'd sort of hushed it up over the years. She told me what it was like, to belong to the family of the woman who once was so notorious they hounded her out of town. Gen and her mom are descended from the red-haired Christina, although the family history is a bit vague about who she married and where she lived. But at least now they've got the diary they know a bit more about what it was like for her, and Gen and mom have decided to take it on as a project. They're going to trace back the family tree and find out just what did happen to her.'

Zhi turned back to the photocopied pages, picked out another page and started to read.

She put their mugs of tea on the table and found some homemade apple shortbread Gen had given her in a tin.

'Delicious,' he said after his first taste.

'Not my baking, I'm afraid. Gen made it.'

'Well, she's a good cook.'

'I'm afraid I'm not much of a baker. But I'm great on intimate dinners for two.' She gave Zhi an inviting look.

'I can't wait to find out if that's true,' he said, putting the book down and leaning over to kiss her. 'But we'll have to take a raincheck on it for now, I'm afraid. The ship's sailing tomorrow. They told us this morning they're leaving tomorrow on the morning tide.'

'Oh,' she said, disappointed.

'It's a real pain, I know. Especially after tonight. I was hoping to see a lot more of you over the next couple of weeks,' he said suggestively.

'Why do you have to go back so soon?'

'They've been having problems ever since the ship's systems crashed with a computer bomb about a month ago now. That's why we've been tied up at the Port of Nelson for the past two weeks. We managed to get everything up and running again, but we're still having a few problems. They want to get to sea and conduct some trials to find out what's still going wrong.'

'Did you say computer bomb?'

'Yes. A computer time bomb really. Some wanker planted a worm in the operational system at head office. And when he wasn't there any more to disable it, it went off, wiping out the mainframe and crashing all the systems running off it. Including the one on our ship.'

'Good God!' Alex said.

'It was incredible how quickly it happened. We lost everything. It even did something to the ship's operating system. We lost power for a bit. Things got really hairy. As luck would have it, we were caught in a storm and without power, the ship was tossed around like a cork. It seemed like forever before we got way on again.'

'Just on a month ago?' Alex said.

'Yes. August the twelfth, to be exact. A day that will forever be imprinted on my memory.'

'I can imagine. It's imprinted in my memory too.' Alex had just realised that this was the very time bomb that Lucian was now serving time for in San Francisco; the one that he'd planted and that had gone off after he'd been fired. There could only be one fleet of exploration ships in the world affected by his actions. And here she was becoming involved with someone who had been directly affected by it.

'You're not going to believe this,' she said, pausing to find the words, 'but I know the rotten sod that planted the time bomb back in San Francisco. He was the reason I ran away to New Zealand.'

She poured out the whole story to an incredulous Zhi, concluding with the observation that she seemed to have a knack for getting herself into trouble and she was determined to play it safe from now on.

'Amen to that,' Zhi agreed. 'I shall regard it as my personal challenge to make sure you stay out of trouble from now on. While I'm away, I want you to email me every day and let me know what you're up to. And if I don't hear from you, I'll phone.'

They swapped email addresses and he stood to go.

'I'd love to stay with you tonight, but it wouldn't be right,' he said, as if he could read her mind. 'I'm going away tomorrow. But I hope to be back in time for the *WearableArt Awards*. Your friend Jackie gave me a ticket and a backstage pass. I think she's keen for you and me to get together. I've heard so much about it, I wouldn't miss it for the world. Besides, I've got an even bigger reason to come back now – I want to be with you.' He bent down to kiss her.

'You're such a romantic,' Alex said between kisses. 'I'm not used to this. I don't know what to say.'

'No need to say anything. Just wait for me.' He kissed her once more and was gone, the S-type purring away into the night.

By the following week, when the costumes arrived, Alex was still substituting for the hapless model, who'd come down with glandular fever and been forbidden by her doctor to take part.

'Sorry, love, but it looks like you're it now. Can you help us out and stay with us?' Chloe asked.

'Sure. Be happy to,' Alex said. She was delighted. She hadn't had so much fun in ages. And what with the landfill work and this, she'd been too bushed to go to the pub with the others after rehearsals. Which meant that there'd been no likelihood of running into Rick. She imagined that he'd be back from the North Island by now, and she wanted to avoid him.

Rehearsing with the costumes – or at least with most of them – certainly added another dimension to trying to move.

Alex was modelling four costumes. The first was an award entry – an elegant-looking silver wedding dress made almost entirely from white venetian blinds intricately woven to make a stiff empire-line dress with long medieval sleeves. It was topped with a flimsy silver train and veil and required silver high-heeled medieval-looking tasselled shoes.

Later in the first half she was a glamorously weird mermaid, sitting atop a high plinth, waving her sceptre at her watery, fishy subjects below. This was one of the special themed pieces – as a lead-up to another round of award entry costumes – and this year they'd chosen an underwater theme. There were men dressed as deep-sea divers, complete with wetsuits, goggles and snorkels, who flew across a wire above the stage to give the impression that they and the dancing fish, fronds of seaweed and other creatures below were actually under water.

Like all the other models, she had to learn how to complete speedy costume and make-up changes in the basic dressing rooms back-stage, as well as the steps and moves to the music while in front of the audience. When she'd first heard that they rehearsed every weeknight for a month, she'd wondered what on earth they did all that time. Now she knew – and there wasn't a moment to spare. It was full on, all night long.

38. Time's Nearly Up

The warm flank of the cow was like a comfort blanket on a cold and lonely night. Carrie pressed her cheek hard against the jersey's solid rump, inhaling the animal smell, welcoming the touch of the smooth brown and white hair against her skin. The milk was flowing in even squirts, slowly starting to fill the pail, its heady aroma penetrating her loneliness and jolting her out of the living nightmare that had made sleep impossible last night.

One-two. One-two, she counted as her hands moved up and down. It had taken two days to get the rhythm right. At first, her hands had wrung poor Daisy's teats until her fingers were red and raw from rubbing and the cow shied away in annoyance, kicking her spitefully on the arm. And all the while, hardly a drop had fallen into the bucket. But now she was an old hand and Daisy submitted contentedly to her ministrations.

Carrie kept up the rhythm with her hands, trying desperately to block out from her mind the events that were about to unfold this morning. In an hour and a half, Richard would be dead. The papers said that the hanging was due to take place at eight o'clock on Friday, October the fifth. She would not be there.

The editorial in the newspaper had been so damning of Richard and so rigorous in its justification of the death penalty that she'd burst into tears and had taken a long time to calm down again. She seemed to be crying a lot these days, though whether this was due to her condition or the imminent loss of Richard she did not know. Her propensity to cry at even the smallest upset led her to the conclusion that it would be exceedingly foolish to risk discovery or comment at the execution, where she would be sure to weep copiously.

Instead, she felt the calming influence of milking her cow and collecting the eggs from her six glossy-feathered brown hens, would be much better for her and the baby.

The milking over, she stood, patted Daisy on the rump to send her back to her paddock and carried the pail inside where she would put some in the larder after separating the cream off to perfect her new-found skills at churning butter. Returning to the barn, she opened the gate to let the cow back into her pasture, closed it behind her then entered the barn to collect the morning's eggs. She picked a handful of grain from the covered hinged-lidded box inside the door and scattered it on the barn floor for the hens to scratch for, then roamed around looking for the eggs, which were usually to be found in the straw at the back of the small wooden building. She managed to find seven big brown eggs – one she hadn't found yesterday adding to the day's usual total.

As she was bending to pick up the last one, the baby delivered an almighty kick under her rib cage, making her cry out with surprise. She put her hand to her swollen belly and could feel more bumps under her skirts and petticoats.

'Oh, little one, what will happen to us now?' she said. Her time was nearly up; the baby was due in two months, in December. The months had flown since the unexpected conception in those happy late-summer days with Richard in Hokitika. At first, she'd found it hard to believe she could have fallen with child so quickly. She'd put off telling him until the night of the ball and just a couple of weeks later, he was gone. That was in May, when she'd been carrying the baby for two months. But now she was seven months gone and the days were getting warmer, she was getting tired easily and she would be glad when the pregnancy was over. On the other hand, she wasn't looking forward to looking after a baby on her own. The delivery was well planned, with a doctor close by if needed and a midwife not far from Hope. The accoucheuse in Nelson had looked after her well and given her good advice and she'd made friends with Jane Reichman, a young woman not long out from England, who lived just half a mile down the road. She had recently married her German-born husband, Eberhard, who was often away in Nelson on business, so Jane was as glad of Carrie's company as Carrie was of hers. A couple of weeks ago, when it was plain that Richard would never be returning to Hope, she'd told Jane that her husband had been drowned in an accident on the West Coast. That had doubled Jane's kindness towards her and she had promised to come and help with the birth. No, it wasn't the birth Carrie was dreading, but the months afterwards.

The kicking stopped and she continued on her way back to the house, where she would separate the milk, churn the butter and have another attempt at baking bread in the coal range. She had yet to get it quite right; unlike making soap, at which she had become adept. Two weeks ago, when everyone said the frosts should have passed, she'd sown lavender and herbs alongside the vegetable garden she'd planted and planned to experiment with scented soaps, which she could sell at the general store.

Deliberately refusing to enter the parlour, where the mantelpiece clock would remind her of what was about to happen, she set about her daily chores, looking forward to the evening, when she could sit down at her writing desk while her dinner was cooking and add to her diary. There would be plenty time then to reflect on the significance of this day.

39. Die Like a Man

The night had passed slowly and fitfully at first for Richard, with the sound of the workmen constructing the gallows until the early hours of the morning. The man who brought his meals said they were sorry about the constant hammering, but the arrival of the execution order had caught them unawares and they had to work through the night by lantern-light so the job could be finished in time for the morning. The gaoler had looked sheepish when he'd said that and quietly left the cell, leaving Richard's dinner on the table.

Sleep while that racket was going on was impossible. It seemed grossly unfair that they should do this to him. Each nail driven home was like a nail in his coffin.

At times, Richard had felt his head would burst with all the things he still needed to say. But in the chill hours of the early morning, when he was quite alone and the hammers were quiet at last, he prayed to the Lord for forgiveness – again and again.

At twenty minutes to eight, after a light breakfast he'd found hard to swallow, the gaoler entered his cell, followed by the executioner – a tall man, whose face was hidden behind a mask of black crepe.

'We have come to take you to your execution,' the hangman said in a voice that Richard thought sounded far too small and scared for someone in his position. Perhaps he'd not done this before, he wondered. The man then removed his leg-irons and pinioned his arms behind his head before marching him out of the cell and into the soft light of a late spring morning. The leaves on the trees were bright new green, the sky was blue with white fluffy clouds racing across the sun. He noticed everything around him as if for the first time, because it was the last time he would see them. Things he'd taken for granted were now suddenly significant.

There was a small crowd in the prison courtyard – mostly officials and newspaper reporters he'd been told. The public had been kept outside. He wondered if Carrie would be there, trying to catch one last glimpse of him. He couldn't see beyond the prison walls.

Turning a corner, he was confronted by a high wooden platform with roughly made steps leading up the back of it. Reluctantly, he raised his eyes to see three nooses hanging from three separate gallows. He was still staring transfixed at the awful sight when he heard a noise behind and turned to see Tom and then Phil being led out to join him. He shook their hands. Phil looked a quivering wreck; Tom had tears in his eyes. Then they were led up to the base of the platform.

Richard made his final speech:

'I wish it to be understood that I make this asservation in the most solemn manner, as I am incapable of calling upon the Almighty to witness a lie when I am so soon to be ushered into His presence.' He shook hands with the officials and congratulated two of them on their handling of the case. He shook hands with the Rev Daniel, calling him his 'friend of friends,' then addressed the crowd:

'I have no more fear of death than I have of going to a wedding. Indeed, although this is the morning of my death, I consider it the morning of my wedding!'

He looked over at the reporters and notice with some jubilation that they were scribbling furiously. He hoped Carrie would hear his words. They were meant for her. His refusal to grant her the one thing she had wanted from him – to make an honest woman of her – now seemed petty and cruel. If only he hadn't been so intransigent. Swiftly, he cut off further thought of her. He could feel himself on the brink of tears and he was determined to die like a man, with his head held high.

'Now, Mr Sheriff,' he said, 'I am ready.'

It was Kelly's turn next to have his say but unfortunately he was well primed with brandy and he got carried away with the sound of his voice, as if by talking longer he could stay the execution.

Phil and Tom continued to whitter on, holding things up terribly. The sheriff was becoming extremely agitated. At last, the gaoler began to form the procession for them all to ascend the scaffold.

'I'm innocent,' Kelly shouted. 'Don't be in such a hurry!'

Richard was appalled. 'Shut up, Kelly,' he hissed. 'Die like a man.' Then he ran up the steps, walked over to the centre noose and kissed it, saying dramatically, 'I greet you as a prelude to Heaven!'

Those were his last words. He knelt while the executioner strapped his wrists and ankles tightly. Then, with the help of the hangman, he stood and felt the noose slipped over his head to rest on his shoulders.

He could hear Levy and Kelly ranting on still on either side of him, wishing the executioner would get it over with. He heard someone say it was twenty-seven minutes past eight and it was long past time. Then he heard the Rev Johnston intone the opening words of the burial service:

'I am the resurrection and the life, saith the Lord, he that believeth in me, though he were dead, yet shall he live…'

'Amen,' Richard whispered to himself and looked up across the prison walls to the yard beyond. He could see outside the gaol quite clearly now – could see the crowd gathered there. He searched for a sign of Carrie, and thought he'd found her when…

There was a clanging sound as the hangman pulled the lever.

40. Christmas Visitors

It was ten weeks after Richard's execution when the lynch mob came for Carrie.

Alarmed at what she'd seen outside, she hurried down the stairs, clutching Christina in her arms, and crossed the parlour to the front door. Through the stained glass at the side of the door she could see the torch flames flickering. Terrified, she opened the door. To her astonishment, Eberhard was standing there, his face contorted with a strange mixture of fury and embarrassment.

'Why, Eberhard...'

'You should leave! You should leave now! I've been sent to warn you,' he turned round to the others behind him, as if for a helping hand.

'Warn me about what?' Carrie said.

'Look Mrs O'Neill, these people mean to take revenge. Heaven knows what they will do in their anger.'

'But why, Eberhard? What have I done to them?'

Eberhard's eyes narrowed into slits of contempt.

'You *know* what the trouble is. You were the mistress of that savage murderer Richard Burgess,' he spat, with spittle from each aspirate landing on Carrie's face. 'And that... that... child is his bastard baby.'

Carrie blanched, but managed to keep herself from uttering any exclamation. She pulled Christina towards her protectively.

'How on earth did you get that idea? Christina's father is buried on the West Coast after drowning in a river crossing. You know that, Eberhard. I told you and Jane that even before she was born.'

Eberhard looked down at the ground, his embarrassment showing in the nervous shrug of his shoulders and repeated stubbing of his toe on the porch.

'I know you did. But you see, the trouble is, Mrs Murray, the postmistress, she found out that wasn't the truth. She found out that your mail from town contained a letter from Burgess himself acknowledging that you were having his baby.'

Carrie couldn't help herself. She gasped out loud, putting her free hand up to cover her mouth as if to erase the sound. That nosey old busybody must have opened the big envelope from Mr Hardacre, her lawyer, and found the letter that Richard had written on the night before his execution. It had taken nearly two months to reach her, and finally arrived with an explanation from Mr Hardacre that the gaoler had held up its delivery because he had not known how to find her. She thought back to the day she had picked up the packet at the post office, just over a week ago. Mr Hardacre's letter was dated December the fourth. How long, then, had Mrs Murray held onto it, carefully lifting the seal and reading every word, before passing it on to her? And all the while, the hateful woman would have been stirring up the local community.

She was startled by the sound of glass shattering in the window next to her, followed by a loud thud of a rock landing on the wooden floor amidst the broken shards.

'What's taking you so long?' a familiar voice called out. Carrie recognised it as Arthur Kempthorne's, her close neighbour. She looked up to see where he was and was shocked to see all her neighbours there – at least all the menfolk. There were a few women in the group. She could see the Shaw sisters and several others she knew. The flickering torchlight lit up their faces, many of them filled with hate.

'Tell her we don't want her here any more. We don't want murderer's whores in this neighbourhood,' another voice shouted.

'Yeah. Tell her she'll be gone by morning if she knows what's good for her,' called another.

'I'm sorry, Mrs O'Neill. I know you don't mean anyone here any harm,' Eberhard said quietly. She could just hear him over the mounting noise from the crowd. 'But you must leave tonight. Otherwise I can't be responsible for what will happen to you.'

He turned and strode back up the path to the others, talked to several of the men and seemed to be encouraging them to leave, pointing in the direction they'd come from. Then they turned as one towards Carrie, waving their torches and sticks and calling out angry threats.

'Begone, murderer's whore. Begone,' someone shouted.

Another windowpane shattered beside her and several stones clattered against the weatherboards, one landing on the porch not far from where she stood. Christina started to wail again.

'And take the murderer's bastard with you,' screamed a female voice.

Carrie stood there stunned, staring blankly at these people who had once been her friends and neighbours. She couldn't bear to listen anymore. Closing her ears to the curses and savage accusations, she turned and went inside, shutting the door behind her. Clutching Christina tightly as if her life depended on it, she crumpled back on the solid wood, her knees shaking with terror, her heart beating erratically. After what seemed an eternity, the noise outside faded. She presumed the crowd was returning to Clover Road. Christina was now crying loudly. Carrie let down her guard for a moment and cried with her, softly at first. But as she began to realize the enormity of her situation, great choking sobs of despair escaped from her. She stumbled over to the chair by the fire and collapsed onto it, weeping uncontrollably. Christina's wails crescendoed, to match her own until at last she managed to pull herself together and calm down. She found a handkerchief in the pocket of her skirts, wiped her eyes and blew her nose.

'Shhh, little one. Hush,' she said over and over, trying to soothe the baby. While she rocked Christina gently in her arms, she ran to the window – now open to the night air – and, crunching her way across the broken glass, pulled the heavy drapes across to shelter her from the blustery wind whistling through the shattered panes. She went into the kitchen and pulled the curtains across there too. She was frightened of being seen or of being the target for further stones and missiles. Then she sat at the kitchen table and stared emptily ahead at the blank space on the wall where Richard's picture had been. She'd taken it down, of course, after his arrest, and hidden it upstairs. She wondered what she should do. Her neighbours were adamant she should leave, that much was clear. But where could she go? And how would she look after Christina? She still had a tidy sum of money lodged with her solicitor in Nelson which she could access. But it would be foolish to stay anywhere near this place now that her secret was out. These people would spread the news quickly enough and she wouldn't be safe from their rage until she put at least a hundred miles between them. She couldn't go back to Hokitika. They would know there too, or at least would work it out soon enough. She needed to go somewhere where the Maungatapu Murders hadn't been splashed across the newspapers every day. That would mean Australia, or perhaps somewhere in the North Island that knew little and cared less about Richard Burgess.

'That's what we'll do,' she said to Christina. 'We'll pack as much as I can fit in a big carry bag, then we'll flee to Nelson and catch the next steamer north.'

Then she realised that she'd never see the lavender and herbs she'd sown or the vegetables she'd planted. She would never get to use the soap and butter she'd made. And Daisy and the hens – what would become of them? Unless the neighbours looked after them, they would die. She started to cry again, but willed herself to stop. She had to be strong – for Christina's sake. She stood and carried the now-sleeping baby to her cradle and placed her, tightly swaddled, under the covers, tucking her in and kissing her tenderly on the cheek.

'Good night, Chrissie. You sleep well now so that your mother can pack up our things.'

A few moment later, back downstairs in the kitchen, when she had just started to pick out a few things she needed to take with her, she heard strange sounds outside – sounds of crackling and roaring, and of splintering wood – coming from the back of the house. Puzzled, she opened the back door to see where the noise was coming from. To her horror, the barn was ablaze, flames leaping from the roof and out the barn door, fanned by the strong wind.

'My God,' she cried out and ran towards the inferno, stopping only when the intense heat drove her back.

'Daisy!' she screamed in desperation. 'Daisy! I can't get to you!'

Then she remembered the hens, also trapped inside. There was no hope for them, that was obvious, nor for her precious Jersey cow. She'd come to think of Daisy as a friend by now, talking to her at milking and, when she was feeling happy, singing even. Daisy didn't deserve to be burned alive, and neither did the hens with their thick, gleaming brown feathers and imperious pecking ways.

She screamed again, in frustration, in anger and in despair.

As she stood there, watching the barn explode in a fireball of flames, she could feel the heat burn through her limbs, inflame her face and ignite a desire for revenge. How dare these people burn defenceless animals alive in some warped display of retribution!

Sobbing, she crumpled in a heap on the yard. There was nothing she could do now to save her precious animals. She stayed there for at least an hour watching the small barn burn to the ground, the flames flickering around where the door had been, the roof beams sticking up at rakish angles, blackened monuments to her departed friends. There was not a trace of Daisy or the busy hens.

She couldn't bear to watch it any longer. Heaving herself sorrowfully to her feet, she went back into the kitchen and collapsed in a chair at the kitchen table, her elbows in the table, head in her hands. That's when she noticed a small piece of paper at the end of the table with a kitchen knife sticking out of the middle, pinioning the paper to the wood. Reaching across, she pulled out the knife and dragged the paper across the table until it was close enough to read.

TAKE THIS AS A WARNING, it said in irregularly shaped capital letters.

BE GONE BY MORNING OR
YOUR HOUSE WILL BE NEXT.

Carrie crumpled the piece of paper in her hand and left it on the table. Wearily, the fight gone from her, she stood and crossed over to the larder cupboard to pick out all the perishables and throw them away. The heart-breaking task of packing up the house for a long absence had begun.

Just before dawn, as the first glimmer of the sun's rays washed the eastern sky with a pale grey light, Carrie awoke Christina, changed her napkin and fed her. She then returned the baby to her cradle where she gurgled happily on her back while Carrie put on her warm coat, her sable wrap, her bonnet and the beautiful cashmere shawl Richard had given her in Hokitika. Picking up Christina again, she wrapped her tightly in her white knitted jacket and her warm woollen shawl then, holding the baby against her shoulder, she carried her down the stairs where she collected her carefully packed, large carpetbag from beside the parlour table. Slinging it over her other shoulder, Carrie walked over to the front door.

Resting her palm on the cold, round knob, she paused briefly and took in the cottage she'd grown so fond of – the parlour furnished now with chairs, tables, an ottoman and pictures on the walls, the German Christmas tree in the corner with its little gifts remaining for her friends and neighbours, the kitchen with its comforting coal range and all her crockery and china arranged neatly on the shelves. She'd been up all night, not even trying to sleep, knowing it would be futile, wanting to make the most of her last few hours in this place she had hoped would be home. In her bag she'd packed a change of clothes, a few under-garments, Christina's gowns and necessities, the photograph of her and Richard at the ball, her diary containing Richard's letters, and the velvet case containing the pearls he'd bought in Hokitika.

Closing her eyes, trying to capture the scene forever in her mind, Carrie opened the door, let herself out into the cold dawn air, and closed it behind her, turning the lock and dropping the key into the bottom of her bag. She turned at the gate for a final farewell view of the cottage and, closing the gate behind her, walked purposefully down the middle of the empty road on her way she knew not where.

41. Backstage Pass

After a week of rehearsals in the Trafalgar Centre, where the show was to be held, the atmosphere backstage was electric. It was the final dress rehearsal – or at least it was called a dress rehearsal. But in reality it was their first performance, since every seat in the house had been sold. So popular were the *WearableArt Awards* that seats to every show were sold out months in advance. The dress rehearsal had turned into an extra performance.

The big night, however, was tomorrow, Friday, when the Prime Minister and all the big shots in the country would attend the awards show and make the announcement of which creation had won its section, and which one would carry away the prize for the Supreme award for the best of them all.

Alex was made up and waiting in the wings, wearing her venetian blind costume, when she was surprised to see Rick edging towards her past the other models.

'How did you get in here?' she hissed when he was close enough to hear. 'You're not supposed to be backstage.'

'I wangled a pass,' he said. 'You know me. I've got friends in all sorts of high places.'

'What are you doing here? You'll get in the way.'

'Just wanted to make sure you're all right, Doc. I've just got back from up north and couldn't wait to see you.'

'Of course I'm all right. I've been all right – not that you'd know – for the whole three weeks since we were in Queenstown. Despite the fright you gave me.'

'Yes, well, I'm sorry about that Doc. I told you, it wasn't supposed to happen that way. Things have been a bit difficult since then. I would've contacted you, but I've been on the go all that time.'

On the run, more like, Alex thought, but didn't say so.

'You're on next,' the call-boy told her.

'You'll have to go, Rick. You can't stay here.' She moved towards the backstage curtain that led onto the long catwalk, practising the gliding movement she'd rehearsed again and again. The stiff, full-length costume wasn't made for ease of movement, but she'd almost perfected it. Her feet, encased in tight, tasselled medieval heeled slippers, made quick neat movements while the rest of her sailed along above, hardly moving any of her upper muscles. The overall effect was of serenity and calm – far from what she was feeling underneath. Everyone was nervous, though, she told herself. She breathed as deeply as she dared, waiting her turn.

'You're on,' someone said at her elbow, and she was out in the glare of the spotlights, reflecting a thousand upturned faces, with cameras flashing and the theme music blaring. She could feel the excitement all around her as she tripped slowly along, careful to keep her pace steady and her upper limbs virtually immobile except for a slow rotation of her head, from side to side, with a slight nod at each turn, a bit like a marionette. She ignored the other models around her in their weird and wonderful outfits and focused on her goal – the end of the catwalk, which had seemed a mile away when she first stepped out but was now inching closer. In a way, she didn't want to get there; she was starting to enjoy her moment in the limelight. When she finally made it, she circled around to the other side, and began her slow but steady progress back to where she'd begun. Another sea of faces; another bank of flashlights; another round of appreciative oohs and aahs; this was magic! The attention combined with the pulsating rhythm of the techno music swept her away, almost to another dimension. She felt as if she were floating on air; the weight of the costume was lifted from her; the awkward headdress was a feathery crown; the tight high heels were wings on her feet.

She came quickly down to earth with a crash when she wafted through the backstage curtain and was set upon by her dresser.

'Come on, Alex. You're needed in make-up.'

She was escorted back to the dressing room – a large marquee set up at the back of the big sports stadium – and undressed carefully so as not to damage the costume. She threw on her shirt and Levis, slipped on her comfortable sneakers and dashed off to make up, leaving the dresser to wrestle with the costume and put it back on its stand, ready for tomorrow night.

The make-up session took longer than the first one because her face and hands had to be turned into a sea-watery blue-green, and on top of that she had to resemble an exotic, siren-like mermaid. After the make-up, a wig was fitted over her short hair, with long, curly silvery-gold tresses falling down her shoulders. When the transformation was complete, she hardly recognised herself – thick dark-green false lashes batted up and down every time she blinked her eyes, streaks of mauve and green ran from her eyes up to her temples and more swirled down her cheeks. Added to this was the unaccustomed long, curly hair – it all looked bizarre atop her plain white shirt and jeans.

But it started to come together back in the dressing room where, with the help of her dresser, she donned the mermaid's gold and green scales.

'Quick, over to your seat,' the dresser said. 'You're on in five minutes.'

She was helped up onto her painted rock and into her mermaid tail, where she was to sit for the next fifteen minutes, playing the part of the queen of the underwater-world. A gold-painted crown was placed on her long-flowing curls, an orb and sceptre produced for her to hold in each hand. Then, without a moment to spare, she was wheeled out into the middle of the catwalk, holding her head high and affecting a queenly bearing, just as she'd done in rehearsal.

Although she'd seen them in their costumes many times before, she was still fascinated by the dancers and models passing by, many glowing in bright fluorescents under the ultra-violet light on the semi-dark stage. The music was especially weird for the underwater section and the combined effect almost disoriented her. She was just getting used to it all when she was wheeled out again, back through the curtains and off to a side bay, where someone was climbing up to help her down.

'Rick! What are you doing? This isn't your job!' She was incredulous that he was still around, let alone offering to help out.

'Shhh, don't let on,' he hissed. 'I just want to help you, that's all. You look so sexy like that. I just can't keep my hands off you.' He was holding onto her waist, lifting her out of the fishtail. As soon as she was standing, he pulled her to him and started to fondle her through her costume.

'Rick, stop that! I've got to wear this tomorrow, and the night after that. Leave me alone.'

'But you look terrific. That make-up is so-ooo sexy. I could ravish you right now.'

'Well you can't, Rick, that's all there is to it. I've got to get this off and get ready for the next costume after the interval.'

'You're such a spoilsport. I'll have to content myself with ravishing your fishtail instead.'

He started to stroke the empty tailpiece she'd just climbed out of, fingering each of the two tail-ends as if feeling for something inside.

'Leave it, Rick, it's very precious. You're not supposed to touch it.'

'I'd rather be touching you.'

'Well you can't. Look, I've got to go.'

'He giving you some trouble?' asked a voice.

'Zhi! You made it!' Alex said.

'Yup. And just in time, by the sound of it. Do you want me to get the security guard?'

'Hey, no need to get hostile, mate. I'm just leaving.' Rick jumped down off the plinth and wandered off along towards the back of the side bay.

'Thanks, Zhi. He was being a pain.'

'No problem. Glad to be able to earn my backstage pass.' He stood back and looked at her properly. 'Wow! You look amazing with all that stuff on. I bet it feels really weird though.'

'It sure does, and I've got to go and get it taken off and another lot put on. I'd better run. Where can I find you later?'

'I'll meet you when the show's over,' he said.

'We've all got to meet with the choreographer and producer when it's over. It could go on for a while.'

'How about tomorrow then?'

'Sure. The Darbys have given me the day off. So why don't you come on out to the vineyard? I'll make us a special brunch for two.'

'I can't wait,' he said, giving her a light kiss on the neck before departing.

It was after midnight by the time she got back home and was ready for bed. The post-show meeting had taken longer than she'd expected and although there had been food and drinks available, she'd been too tired to want anything. She made herself a hot chocolate, picking up the chunky photocopy of Carrie's diary as she did so. She sipped at her drink, slipping back in time to Carrie's unhappy predicament.

I write this in haste as I prepare to pack up my house and leave on the morrow with Christina and as many of my belongings as I can carry. Not long ago, an angry crowd came to my door and told me I must leave. I could not believe it at first. I opened the door to find my neighbour, Eberhard, standing on the porch, speaking for all of them. Eberhard, who has always been kind to me, had a look of such anger on his face I could hardly recognise him. Many neighbours who I had counted as friends were there, brandishing torches and pikes and shouting.

The noise awoke Christina, who cried loudly. After they left, I managed to settle her down and put her into her cradle. Moments later, upon hearing a strange noise outside, I opened the back door to find the barn ablaze and my poor Daisy and the hens trapped inside. I do not have the heart to write more. My spirit is gone. There is nothing here for me now. I would be foolish to stay.

Christina is all I have in the world; she is all I have to live for.

Alex couldn't help shedding a tear at that point. Carrie and her tiny baby had been so alone, with nobody to protect them from the hatred that had festered away in the community until it reached boiling point. She carried the photocopied diary upstairs and put it on the bedside table.

She didn't need to cleanse her face as the make-up ladies had done that for her and covered it with moisturiser, so all she needed was a quick shower before she collapsed into bed, expecting to fall asleep straight away, she was so exhausted.

But sleep wouldn't come. She watched the bright red digital display on the clock radio click over past one then two in the morning and still she couldn't get to sleep. Her mind wouldn't stop racing. It was obviously in turmoil about the events in Queenstown and now, added to that, were the strange goings on tonight, with both Rick and Zhi turning up unexpectedly, Rick behaving most peculiarly. Also flashing in and out of her mind was the landfill project. Despite the ruckus over the hazardous waste fabrication two weeks ago, she and Ollie had continued to make slow but steady progress with the neighbours. But after the hazardous waste fiasco, she kept worrying that something else like that would crop up unexpectedly.

Last week, she and Ollie had organised a neighbourhood meeting, to give everyone the opportunity to have their say and ask questions. Nick had come down from Auckland and had managed to appear friendly and open. She'd risked it and told him to abandon the heavy coat and gloves and came up with some more informal clothing suggestions that would help him lighten up his appearance. She'd nearly fallen over when she saw the Lowes, the couple who had refused to let her and Ollie in the door last time they'd visited, shaking Nick's hand and chatting to him over a cup of tea after the presentation. Afterwards, Nick told her – looking immensely pleased with himself – that Mrs Lowe had been tremendously taken with the plans for the recycling plant and wanted to know about the grapeseed oil and what sort of things you could do with it. She'd been most impressed with Ollie's talk about its health properties – high in linoleic acid and the cholesterol-lowering polyunsaturated fat, it was an supposed to reduce the risk of heart disease and act as an anti-oxidant – and how good it was to cook with. Alex had gone over to her and told her the oil was favoured not only for its health properties but chefs loved it because it could be heated to high temperature with less smoke and less danger of burning than other oils. Alex had promised to drop by and give Mrs Lowe the recipes she'd seen for tarragon vinaigrette and banana nut bread which, she'd heard, owed their special flavour to the light, nutty taste of grapeseed oil.

'Wouldn't it be wonderful if we could start something like that here,' Mrs Lowe had said. 'I can see how good something like that would be for around here. I always thought it was a terrible waste to get rid of all that grape marc and stuff.'

With the Lowes looking like coming on-side, it seemed as if the tide were turning. But it was too early yet to pat herself on the back for a job well done. She knew from past experience it was never a good idea to count your successes until the job was complete and the cheque was in the bank. And she knew she was a long way off that.

In desperation, she turned over on her left side for what seemed like the umpteenth time and found herself staring at the old wardrobe, its mirror reflecting a ghostly white glow from the moonlight shining through the gap in the curtains. Her own problems, she realised, paled into insignificance when compared with the lynch mob Carrie had been confronted with. As she was thinking of her, the figure of a woman manifested itself in front of the mirror, ethereal, hovering, not touching the ground. She was wearing a long, dark-coloured dress with a full, wide skirt and pinched waist and had a white shawl draped across one shoulder. She turned towards Alex and the shawl filled out and took on the shape of a baby, tightly wrapped, being rocked in its mother's arms. Then from outside her window, she could hear it again, the chanting she'd heard the other night:

'Whore! Whore! Murderer's whore!'

She wanted to reach out and offer to help Carrie. She was so vulnerable.

You fool, your mind's playing tricks on you, her subconscious told her.

But still the vision lingered, undeniably there. Even if just in her subconscious, Carrie was in the room. Her face was pale, almost translucent in the reflected moonlight and all around her head was a sort of ghostly halo, like a ring around the moon.

That's ironic, Alex thought, closing her eyes to see if that would get rid of the apparition. Carrie was no angel. She didn't suit a halo. A barmaid, she'd got herself pregnant to a man who turned out to be a cold-blooded murderer. But then she, Alex, was in no position to cast the first stone. She was no angel either. Her own record was hardly blemish-free. She'd only recently been consorting with a drug dealer – in fact had been present when the deal was being made – and prior to that had been on the spot when her previous lover had been arrested by the FBI. She and Carrie made a good pair, she reckoned. They would probably have been good friends. They might even have been able, between them, to work out how to rid themselves of such devilish men.

Alex opened her eyes again and Carrie had gone. The wardrobe mirror was glowing in the moonlight, as before, but there was no ghostly figure in front of it.

42. Knife Edge

The warm blustery wind of the night before had died and it was now calm. It was still dark, although there was a glimmer of pale light behind the hills. Holding tightly onto Christina, Carrie started the long trudge down Clover Road towards Hope. Suddenly, as she was passing a clump of trees and bushes by the side of the road, a man sprang out of the bushes and ran at her, crying out something she couldn't distinguish. He stood in front of her, threateningly, blocking her way. In the dim light, she could see he was wearing a triangle of cloth over the bottom half of his face and a large, wide-brimmed hat. She could not determine who it was.

'Who are you? What do you want?' she cried, clutching Christina more tightly to her, fearful her baby might be harmed.

'Don't you worry who *I* am,' he said in a thick, rough voice she didn't recognise. 'It's who *you* are that matters.' He raised his right hand above his head as if to strike her and she flinched. That's when she noticed the blade of a knife glinting in the dawn's rays. She gasped in terror.

'I don't know what you mean. I haven't done any harm.'

'Hah! That's a lie for a start,' he exclaimed, brandishing the knife in her face. It was so close she could have read the inscription on the blade if he'd kept his hand still. 'You brought shame on our village and on the good people here,' he said, sweeping his other hand in the direction of the countryside. 'You're the whore of that evil murderer Burgess. You brought him here, among these God-fearing people, and put all our lives at risk.'

'It's not true. I didn't…' Carrie protested.

'Oh, it's true all right,' he said menacingly, twisting the knife in front of her face. 'The Shaw sisters saw him.'

'But they can't have, he wasn't…'

'Don't lie to me,' he growled. 'I'm not taken in by your lies.'

'But I'm not…'

'Your type isn't welcome here. This is a place for honest Christian people.'

'But I'm leaving. Can't you see…'

'I want to make sure that you never come back,' he spat in her face. He drew the blade under her throat so that she could feel the flat cold steel resting under her chin. She didn't dare move.

'Please don't hurt me. Please. I'll never come back if you just let me and my baby go.'

'That bastard baby doesn't deserve to live,' he hissed. 'Like its father didn't.' He turned his attention to Christina, waving the knife around at the back of her head. Carrie was petrified.

'Please don't touch her. It's not her fault. She's just a helpless little baby.'

The man pulled the knife up above his head and moved to plunge it into Christina's back. Instinctively, Carrie pulled away and covered her baby with her hand and forearm. She saw the knife flashing down on her, then felt a tingling on her cheek and a searing pain in her hand, watching horrified as the knife tore into her flesh and out again. Blood started spurting out of the back of her hand, covering Christina's clean white shawl with a growing red stain. She screamed in horror.

'Oh, my God! What have you done?' she cried out to her attacker, who was starting to flee, bloody knife still in his hand. For a second, he turned. The cloth covering his face had slipped with his assault on her, because she could now see enough of his face to recognise Diedrich, son of the pastor from the Lutheran church on the other side of Hope. Then he turned away again and was gone, running in the direction of Clover Road and Hope beyond.

'Oh, Christina. What am I going to do?' It seemed she was caught up in some nightmare. In less than a day, her life had been completely turned around from comparative calm and contentment to absolute mayhem and terror. She'd thought last night's lynch mob was bad enough, but this was even worse.

She sat down in the long grass at the side of the road, slipping her heavy bag off her shoulders and laying the now sleeping Christina down in a patch of soft short grass.

Her left hand hurt immensely, and she could tell by a deepening mark on the front of her coat that her cheek must have been cut open as well. She put her uninjured hand up to feel it – yes, there was a gash about two inches long across her cheek and it was bleeding profusely.

Fighting back the tears, she took off her bonnet, opened her bag and pulled out the only petticoat she'd packed, ripped it into strips and tied it tightly around her cut hand, pushing the skin together over the wound to try to stem some of the bleeding. Then she tore more strips of material and wound them around her head, covering her cheek and anchoring them under her chin before replacing her bonnet, tying the ribbons on top of the makeshift bandage, coving it as much as she could.

By now, the sky was shot with red and pink streaks as the clouds picked up the warmth of the rising sun. Soon it would be fully daylight and she would be easily visible by all and sundry. It was imperative, she realized, that she make her way down Clover Road to the main road as soon as possible before anyone else caught sight of her and had another go at her. She sat for a moment more, gathering strength, mustering the will to keep going. If it weren't for Christina, she thought she'd probably just lie down at the side of the road and wait for the next knife-wielding assassin to come along and finish her off. If it weren't for Christina, there would be no point in carrying on.

Slowly, she rolled onto her knees then stood, teetering with dizziness. She breathed deeply, waiting for her head to clear and her vision to return. Then she slung her carpet bag back over her left shoulder, picked Christina up and cradled her in her right arm, leaving her injured hand free, and started off down the dusty road towards the main road to Nelson.

The miles seemed to take longer than ever to cover and she wished dearly for a flask of water. Richard would have prescribed brandy, she thought wryly. But at last she made the highway, crossed to the other side and settled down with Christina to await the first passing dray.

With luck, an old man from Brightwater stopped for her after about ten minutes. He was on his way to market with a load of potatoes and onions and she gladly climbed up, baby in her arms, onto the bare wooden seat in front of the wagon after depositing her bag inside the cart. She deliberately kept the right side of her face turned away from the driver so that he wouldn't see the bandage around it. The brim of her bonnet assisted the deception, shading her face even further and her shawl which, being down her back, had escaped most of the blood from her face, was drawn around her neck to hide the bloodied bandage and coat underneath. She passed off the ties round her hand as a cut she'd received on a scythe the day before, explaining she was going into Nelson to have it attended to. The farmer seemed content with that.

By the look of the sun now, she calculated it would be somewhere between seven and eight o'clock in the morning. She should be in Nelson in a couple of hours, taking into account the pace of the dray. First off, she would visit a doctor and then would, she hoped be able to see Mr Hardacre before the day was over. Meanwhile, she could look up the shipping departures in the paper and inquire about booking a passage on the first steamer north.

43. Blossom Festival

In the morning, after her run and shower, Alex made herself a strong black coffee and filled a bowl with Fruitful Flakes and trim milk. As a treat, she went back to bed to finish reading Carrie's photocopied diary. It was a Friday, but she was taking the day off in between the first two *World of WearableArt* shows. She was expecting Zhi around midday, so there was plenty of time to get through the remaining quarter inch of pages before showering and getting ready. She planned to cook a frittata and serve it with some crusty French bread she'd borrow from Gen, a salad and some of Ollie's wine. She propped the diary up on the bedcover.

This will be my last entry in this sorry collection of pages that account for my life these past six months. I started to write this diary the day I found out that my beloved was the most hated man in the country. Tomorrow Christina and I will be aboard the Airedale, on our way to the North Island and a new life away from the suffering I have known here.

I have visited my lawyer, Mr Hardacre, informed him of my situation and settled my affairs. I will not be selling the house at this stage. Mr Hardacre pointed out, quite sensibly, that nobody would buy it. But I am fortunate that Richard has left me well provided for, and there is more than enough for Christina and me to live comfortably until such time as I can find a way of earning some money.

I have also visited a private surgeon. This was my most urgent need upon arriving in Nelson, as my cheek wound was seeping blood into its bandage and not only causing pain to myself, but attracting the attention of others.

I feel that after all my pain and suffering these past hours, nay months, I have more than atoned for any sins I have committed in loving the man who led the Burgess gang into such treachery.

I shall never be able to understand how he could be so heartless to his fellow men, yet so loving and kind to me. The papers say that his confessions are to be published soon. Perhaps that will explain him to me.

If I could speak to him now, I would want him to know that he will always hold a place in my heart, no matter what may be.

'Did you know Carrie was attacked?' she asked Gen when she went over to the house just before midday. She'd stayed in bed all morning until she'd finished reading the diary and now wanted to talk about it to Gen, who was picking Lego up off the family room floor. Isobel was engrossed making a bed for her short-haired Barbie doll and Claudia was asleep. 'Did you know what that man did to her?'

'Yes,' Gen replied, dropping a handful of Lego into a big box with a loud clatter. 'It became an enduring legend of Hope. Eventually, everyone felt ashamed of the way they'd treated her. It took a long time, but in the end their Christianity prevailed. I think her acceptance back into the community was largely fuelled by guilt.'

'It was so awful,' Alex said. 'I only read that last bit this morning and I couldn't believe it at first. I had to stop and get up and make another coffee. I was so shocked, I couldn't go on.'

'People were fairly barbaric in those days, especially where religion was concerned. I suppose we're lucky we haven't had a lynch mob come to visit us!'

'You have in a way,' Alex said. 'You've had more than your fair share of protesters.'

'It seems they've gone now, thanks to you. We haven't seen them since you and Ollie made all those visits. That must be what did the trick.'

'That and the fairer coverage we've been getting in the *Mail*. Taking Ollie in to talk sense to the editor and the council reporter when that hazardous waste story had died down was a good move. It was amazing how prejudiced they'd become after being visited so often by the protesters.'

'Do you think it's over then? Do you think they'll accept it now?'

'I wouldn't count my chickens yet, Gen. Especially the Davenports. I think they're still a bit worried about how it'll affect them.'

'I thought you and Ollie had resolved all their issues with it.'

'Yes, sort of. But I left with the impression that they didn't totally believe us. We should go back and see them again before too long.'

A car pulled up and there was a knock at the door.

'That might be Zhi,' Alex said as Gen went to answer it, with Isobel trailing close behind.

It was Zhi. She introduced him to Gen and Isobel then took him over to the cottage to cook lunch.

'What do you think of that?' she asked Zhi as she produced a bottle of pinot noir carrying the stark Hangman's Hill label. 'Unusual, eh?'

'After what you told me the other night, I think it's brilliant,' he said. 'You got a name like that, you might as well make the most of it.'

Alex poured two glasses of the velvety red wine and handed one to Zhi.

'Ollie's afraid it would bomb on the open market though. He just makes enough wine for himself under that label and sells the rest of his grapes to the highest bidder.'

'Well I think it's a great name.' He held the glass up to his nose. 'Mmmmm. Nice.' He tasted it. 'Not bad, is it? I'd say your Ollie knows what he's doing.'

'He's a perfectionist, I think. He seems to know everything about growing grapes and making wine. Gen's good too, but she's dropped out of it a bit since having the girls.'

After lunch, they went out the back to the orchard and scooped up some of the fallen blossom off the grass, throwing it at each other like children.

'You're the cherry blossom fairy,' Zhi said as he scattered a handful of pink petals onto her hair. 'You're my queen of the May.' He fell onto the ground, laughing, and pulled her slowly down beside him so that she lay half on top of him, with petals falling from her hair onto his face. He caught one and put it to his lips, licking it then swallowing it. 'Mmmm, tastes good.' Next thing she knew they were rolling in the grass, enveloped in each other's arms. When they were still, he kissed her. 'Mmmm, tastes good,' he repeated, and kissed her again.

With the flowers falling on them intermittently, they made love under the shelter of the blossom tree, hidden from the front gate and pathway by the lavender, rose bushes and other spring blooms bursting into new life. It was a gentle and tender love-making, touching and exploring each other, with none of the vigorous thrusting or passionate posturing she'd become used to in recent years. Instead, Zhi seemed to have a knack for dilating her desire, bringing her to a climax that was somehow more fulfilling than she'd experienced before.

The spark that Alex was waiting for was still elusive. But instead, she found herself feeling more satisfied and complete than ever she had with Rick or Lucian or Pete. She had no idea what this meant, or if it meant anything at all, but in the afterglow, as she lay on the grass looking up at the bluest-blue sky through the fluffy pink blossoms, she decided it didn't matter. Maybe the chemistry she thought she'd felt for the others was no more than unbridled lust. Or maybe it was simply akin to the thrill of devouring forbidden fruit.

She turned to Zhi as they lay side-by-side and said, 'You're really something, you know that? You've swept me off my feet just when I was telling myself you're not my type at all.'

'Not your type? What is your type then?'

'You don't want to know. And neither do I any more. I'm turning over a new leaf.'

'Well, when you finished turning,' he said, picking up a leaf and tickling her under the nose with it, 'I hope I'm around to see what you've decided to become.'

'I hope so too,' she said.

The phone starting to ring inside the cottage.

'Damn,' she said. 'I'd better answer it.' She grabbed her discarded clothes and ran inside through the back door, picking the phone up off the kitchen wall. 'Alex speaking.'

'It's Ollie,' a breathless voice said at the other end. 'I need you over at the house right now. Something's come up.'

'What? What is it?'

'I'll tell you when you get here,' he said, lowering his voice. 'But please hurry.'

She thrust on her beige trousers, hoping there were no grass stains showing, and ran back out to Zhi.

'Something's going on over at the house. I have to go,' she said.

'That's bad timing. Anything I can do to help?'

'I don't know. I don't think so. But Ollie wouldn't say what it was. It's probably best that you go. How about lunch again tomorrow?' She gave him an inviting look.

'How could I refuse,' he said, standing up and brushing blossoms out of his hair. 'Til tomorrow then.'

'Tomorrow,' Alex said, running over to give him a farewell kiss.

'You'd better check yourself in the mirror before you go anywhere,' Zhi added as she was departing again. 'You're covered in pink petals.'

'No time,' she said, brushing her hand through her hair and down her clothes as she went. 'See you tomorrow.'

She entered through the back door, approaching the kitchen from the hall. She stopped when she heard voices raised in argument. Peeking round the door, she could see Ivan Davenport sitting at the dining table opposite Ollie.

'I don't see how that can be true,' he was saying, thumping the table. 'It's going to ruin any chance we've got of having a high-class restaurant anywhere near this roadway. You can talk recycling 'til you're blue in the face, but it won't change a thing for us.'

'Ivan, believe me, it's not just the recycling…'

'It's the whole package,' Alex said, coming through the door and greeting Mr Davenport as warmly as he would allow. 'The landfill company will have to upgrade all the roads around here to get access for their trucks, so for a start you'll get a proper paved road right to your door.'

'Oh, I see.' Ivan Davenport sounded slightly mollified. 'But all that won't keep away the noise and dust from the trucks passing by every twenty minutes or so, will it?'

'There won't be any dust, Ivan. The roads will all be widened and sealed. And of course, they'll have to give you a new sign to make up for the road widening.'

'And the noise will be minimal behind the lovely Mediterranean-looking plastered wall they'll have to build for you,' Alex added. 'Besides, you saw a picture of the landfill trucks. They're no different from a container truck.'

'And don't forget there'll be a strict speed limit on the road.'

'With penalties so harsh, they won't be breaking the limit in a hurry.'

'Stop, stop, you're overwhelming me,' he said. 'I'm not sure I believe all of that. It sounds too good to be true to me. But you and I are neighbours, Ollie. And I guess if we're going to be neighbours for a long time, I'll have to trust you that it'll be all right in the long run.'

'I'll make damn sure it is,' Ollie said.

'I'll have it all in writing just the same,' his neighbour said gruffly, standing to go.

'I'll see to it this afternoon,' Ollie said, standing and holding out his hand.

After a moment's hesitation, Ivan Davenport took his hand and shook it.

'I hope you're doing the right thing,' he said, heading for the back door where he picked up his hat and let himself out.

'Whew, that was close,' Ollie said when he'd gone. He turned to look at Alex. 'What have you been doing? You're covered in blossoms and grass stains!'

'Am I?' Alex tried to say nonchalantly, but could feel an embarrassed blush creeping up her cheeks.

'Oooh, wait 'til I tell Gen about this,' Ollie said, rubbing his hands with glee. 'She'll be delighted if you've found yourself a nice boy at last.'

'I don't know that he'd qualify for one of her knights in shining armour,' Alex said then made her escape out the back door, saying, 'I'd better go and clean up.'

44. The Weird, Wacky, Wonderful World of WearableArt

Backstage that night, the Trafalgar Centre was abuzz with anticipation. Everything was in its place; everything had to be done in the same order and the same way as the night before. But tonight was the biggie. The Prime Minister was in the audience and so, it was rumoured, was the famous actor Sam Neill, accompanied by *Lantana* actress Rachael Blake. The two had just finished filming *Perfect Strangers* on the rainy, windswept West Coast and were supposed to be in Nelson catching up on sunshine and culture. The marketing manager had offered them tickets. Other famous names were being bandied around.

'Holmes is here,' one of the models was saying. 'I saw him at the cocktail party,'

'And I'm sure that was Matthew Ridge.'

'I saw Nicky Watson and her man. She had the most stunning outfit on.'

'It's a regular *Woman's Weekly* cover contest out there,' Jackie said coming into the dressing room, her hands full of props, a feather boa trailing out one end.

'It looks as though half of Parliament has decamped into the front row of the auditorium,' one of the dancers said.

'Hey, we could run the country from here,' another joked.

Alex didn't know many of the names they were bandying about but picked up on the excitement. Everyone was preparing to put on the best show ever. She hoped that Rick wouldn't reappear. His behaviour last time had made her realise that her attraction for him had vanished. And although Zhi had a backstage pass, she didn't think he'd be here. There was no reason for him to come – he knew he was seeing her for lunch again tomorrow.

Everything about the big night went off without a hitch until she was being helped into her mermaid's fishtail. It felt different somehow.

She wiggled her toes and ankles as much as she could, but there was nothing there. It all happened in such a hurry she had no more time to investigate before she was whisked out onto the stage for the underwater scene. She noticed a slight heaviness in her fishtail each time she had to flick it up and thought she could detect something sharp at one stage with her big toe. But it was gone as soon as she noticed it and she thought no more of it under the glare of lights and blare of the trance music.

Backstage again afterwards, she was rolled on her plinth to the back of the side bay, but the stagehand took off before she could ask him to help her down. There was no sign of her dresser.

'Damn,' she said out loud. There was nothing for it but to struggle out of the fishtail herself. She was looking round for somewhere to put down her orb and sceptre when she was grabbed from behind by strong, male hands.

'What…?' she cried out before a hand clamped over her mouth. Her props clattered to the ground. 'Not another word,' a familiar voice behind her said. 'You'll come to no harm if you just do what we say.'

She recognised him – it was that deep-voiced man that had come to the hotel room in Queenstown. Warren, that was his name. She tried to turn round to see his face, but his hold on her was too tight. She couldn't move.

'We have reason to believe that you're in possession of something that is rightly ours,' another voice said out of the darkness to her right. She looked at where it came from and could just make out a dark figure wearing a black beanie pulled down almost to his eyes. It sounded very much like Steve.

A shiver of fear went through her. If these two were here in Nelson, they must be after Rick, or at least after something that belonged to him. That could only mean one of two things – drugs or money. But why they should be attacking her, and at this particular time, was more than she could fathom.

'You're going to have to get out of your tail,' Warren said. He was lifting her, jerking her roughly upwards, holding her so tight she cried out in pain. 'Quietly, or I'll have to make you quiet,' he said.

She didn't doubt that he would carry out his threat, so bit her lip while he tossed her off the side of the plinth like a rag doll. She landed awkwardly, scraping her legs against the sharp painted shells attached to her throne.

'Not a word,' she heard Steve's voice again. He grabbed her this time, coming out from the darkness and holding her in a vice-like grip. Above her, Warren had moved down to the now-empty fishtail and was detaching it from the plinth.

'You can't do that!' she couldn't help herself from crying out. 'That's part of my costume. We've still got another night…'

'For Chrissake shut up,' Steve hissed, grabbing her mouth and holding it shut. She resisted the urge to bite him. She'd seen it done in the movies, but she suspected that it wouldn't help her get away from these two.

'Why don't you tip the stuff out on the floor and leave that stupid thing behind?' Steve asked his mate.

'No time to stuff around,' Warren answered between grunts as he wrestled with the fishtail. It was more securely attached than he'd expected. 'Besides, it's easier to carry in this. If I can get it off that is… Shit!' The green and gold scales quivered in his hand, free from their anchor. 'Got it. Come on, we're outa here.'

'What about her? She's seen us. She knows who we are.'

'What do you expect me to do? Tie her up? Take her with us?'

'We can't take her with us looking like that,' Steve said. 'She'd stick out like a sore thumb with that getup on.'

'I dunno, looks kinda kinky to me,' Warren said. 'Maybe we could…'

'Don't even think about it, mate. You're forgetting what we came for.'

'You're right. But it is tempting. I've always fancied me a mermaid. Especially one of Rick's mermaids.'

'Priorities, Warren. Priorities. You got your revenge on the stupid prick anyway.'

'Yeah, he should be wishing he was dead by now.'

'You hear that, fishwoman? Your boyfriend's going to be swimming at the bottom of the ocean soon.'

'Or at least he will be when the tide comes in.' They both laughed coldly.

'Come on, we gotta go. Before someone comes.'

Warren stuffed the fishtail under his jacket and tried to pull it shut across his chest as far as he could. But the zip wouldn't do up. Alex could see the shiny scales catching the dim backstage lights as the pair made their escape. Surely, she thought, someone will notice. She waited until they'd gone before running to the main backstage area. She knew just where to find the security guard.

'I know this sounds ridiculous,' she gasped, 'but a couple of guys have just stolen my fishtail. One of them's got it under his jacket.'

'You're right, it sounds totally crazy. But on this show, crazy is normal. Which way did they go?'

'I… uh… I don't know.'

The security guard was talking into his two-way radio. After a moment or two, he turned back to Alex.

'There, I've alerted them at all the entrances. They should be able to stop them. And we've several men outside in the carparks and behind the building. Someone'll catch them, for sure. Fishtail, you say? Boy, I've heard everything now.' He raised his eyes to the ceiling then looked back down at Alex. 'I'd better take your details. Here,' he thrust a small notebook, 'pop your name down there. We'll have to alert the police, so you should expect to see them at the end of the show and tell them what exactly went on.'

She scribbled her name and cellphone number on the piece of paper and handed it back to him, trying to wipe the mention of police from her mind.

'Can I go now? I've got to get ready for the next outfit.'

It was only when she got back to the dressing room after getting her make-up redone that she started to shake. She didn't like to tell the others. She felt it was all her fault somehow. If she hadn't taken that flight with Rick to Queenstown she'd never have got enmeshed in the whole messy business, and now they'd run off with a piece of her costume. She felt like crying. She'd been so thrilled to be a part of the show, and now she'd stuffed it all up.

All around her, models and dancers were getting ready for the next scene. Tension was mounting as awards time drew even closer. But Alex found it hard to feel a part of it now.

'What's the matter, Alex?' Jackie had stopped as she was passing.

'Oh, Jacks. I don't know how to tell you,' she stammered and burst into tears.

'Hey, careful sweetie. You'll ruin your make-up.' Jackie handed her a box of tissues from a nearby table and put a comforting arm around her, making Alex sob even harder. 'What's the matter? What's happened?'

Alex took a deep breath and willed herself to stop crying. She blew her nose, dabbed under her eyes and looked up at Jackie, trying desperately to get a grip. She couldn't talk about Rick and the drug deal. But she knew she had to tell Jackie about the fishtail.

'You told security?' Jackie asked when she finished.

'Yes, but…'

'Don't worry, they'll sort it. I bet you the tail is back on you watery throne before morning.'

'Oh Jacks, I hope so. I feel so responsible…'

'Nobody's blaming you, sweetie. You'll see, it'll be fine. Besides, if the worst happens, we can make another one without too much trouble. It's only a quick job on the Bernina and a few licks of paint. Now,' she sounded authoritative, 'hadn't you better get ready for your next appearance? Where's your dresser?'

'It's not my turn yet, I don't think,' Alex sniffled. 'She'll be along any minute.'

'I suggest you have yourself a strong cup of coffee with plenty of sugar in it then, while you wait. Or find something sweet to eat. You could do with something to perk you up. And you'd better get the nurse to patch up your leg. It's been bleeding.'

'Thanks Jacks, you're a gem.'

Jackie picked up all the stuff she'd been carrying and had jettisoned to comfort Alex.

'No problem. Goes with the territory,' she said as she disappeared down the aisle.

Alex was relieved in a way that none of the outfits she'd modelled won one of the big prizes. She'd grown fond of her costumes; although they were difficult to wear, they'd become a part of her life these past few weeks. But she didn't think she could face any more limelight. It was enough going on stage wearing the creation she'd modelled in the last section and joining in the final number with all the others.

When it was all over and she'd removed the last shred of make-up, she collapsed back in her chair, wishing she could crawl under the trestle table and die.

'Someone to see you outside, Alex,' Jackie called.

She pulled herself together and walked to the door. It was Zhi.

'Boy am I glad to see you,' she said, falling into his arms. 'Let's go somewhere quiet. I need to talk to you.'

She found an empty corner of the canteen, grabbed a Diet Coke out of the coin-machine and offered another to Zhi then collapsed onto a chair and spilled the whole story out to him, from go to whoa. The cocaine, the packets in the camera case, the deal that had somehow gone wrong, the hasty exit at the airport as they escaped their pursuers, right through to the theft of the fishtail. The only bit she left out was Rick's sexy underwear. Zhi didn't need to know about that.

'It all sounds a bit fishy to me, if you'll pardon the expression,' Zhi said, smiling laconically.

'I reckon Rick had put his stash in the bottom of the fishtail. He wanted to put it somewhere he thought no-one would ever find it.'

As she said it, the words of the two hoods about Rick wishing he was dead flashed into her mind. What was it they'd said?

'Oh my God, Zhi. I've just remembered something else. Those two guys said something about Rick being at the bottom of the ocean soon. As soon as the tide comes in, they said. Much as I detest him, I wouldn't want his drowning on my conscience.'

'Miss Zerakowksi?' a woman's voice called out.

She turned round to see a policewoman approaching along the space between the tables and chairs. Behind her was a policeman.

'Oh no,' she groaned. She'd forgotten the security guard's warning that this would happen.

'Linda Moore,' she introduced herself. 'And my partner is Ryan Simmonds. I believe you have some information for us?'

Alex looked at Zhi.

'You've got to tell them everything,' Zhi confirmed what she knew she must do. So she told her story again, rushing through it so she could get to the bit about Rick being at the bottom of the ocean soon.

'So he must be in danger somewhere,' she finished.

'By the sound of it, they've beaten him up and left him somewhere below the high tide line,' PC Moore said. 'What do you think Ryan?'

'I think we'd better radio back to headquarters,' he said. 'And we'll need to put everything Miss Zerakowski has said down in writing and get her to sign it.'

'Oh no,' Alex protested. Not again, she thought to herself.

She didn't get home until two in the morning. By the time she'd gone down to the police station in the middle of town and made a sworn statement, then repeated her story to the local detective, Wayne – the same man she'd met briefly in the pub that night with Antoinette – then answered all their questions and endured a telling off about her complicity in the drug deal, it was very late at night and she was worn out. But still she could not sleep. She went over and over the events of the past night in her mind, tossing and turning, wishing she'd never come to New Zealand, wishing she was at home in San Francisco or, even better, safe in the bosom of the Rossini family.

'Why me?' she shouted angrily into her pillow, pummelling it hard with her fist as she turned over yet again. But she knew the answer to that as soon as she'd said it. Because you've always gone and looked for trouble, she told herself. Ever since your mother died, ever since you were in ninth grade, you've deliberately sought out friends – of both sexes – who would push you over the limit and bring out the worst in you.

45. Hope

The front door wouldn't budge. Carrie had unlocked it with the key she'd kept these past two years and given it the same sort of shove she'd had to give to open it then. But it wouldn't move.

'Here, let me try,' Heinrich said.

Her husband now for just over a year, Heinrich Weiss was a huge bear of a man, tall, sturdy, blond, dependable; her rock in what had been very uncertain times. She'd met him in Auckland where she'd fled from Nelson, taking up lodgings above a milliner's shop not far from the waterfront and earning a small income from making glycerine and scented soaps in her tiny kitchen.

Heinrich had asked her for directions when she was on her way to the draper's to buy some pretty fabrics to make dresses for Christina, who had just turned one. Carrie had learned to smock them herself and took pride in dressing her beautiful daughter with her long red curls and pale, soft face. Heinrich's English was none too good, but she managed to work out that he'd arrived just that day off a steamer from Europe full of eager immigrants like himself, ready to start anew in the promised land. He was a builder, he told her in halting English and needed to find Symonds Street, where there was work waiting for him. It took such a long time for each of them to fathom what the other was saying that, by the time she'd directed him to his destination, they'd struck up quite a rapport. Heinrich had fussed over Christina who sat up in her perambulator and smiled at him. Carrie had secretly admired Heinrich's powerful build, his strong square chin, dimpled face and wide, sensuous mouth. She'd surprised herself. She'd not so much as looked at a man that way since Richard. She'd surprised herself even further by suggesting they go to the little tea shop over the road and share a sandwich and a pot of tea together.

From there, courtship and marriage had been a whirlwind, with Heinrich learning the language very quickly in her frequent company.

His carpentry was well paid, but he was impatient to have his own home to house Christina and the new baby on the way, so Carrie had told him about the cottage near Hope, and the whole sorry saga of having to leave. She'd already told him about Christina's father, passing it off as an aberration in her past, a fatal attraction for a man who made a point of being irresistible to women. And she'd sworn him to never tell Christina who her father was.

At first, Heinrich had refused to move south, claiming – quite logically, Carrie had to admit – that the locals of Hope were unlikely to have forgiven and forgotten so soon. But as time went by, the idea had grown on him and eventually he'd capitulated and agreed to give it a try.

'If they are still hostile to you, we can go to Christchurch,' he'd said. 'There is plenty of building work there. That is what Karl says, anyway.'

So here they were, about to enter the little cottage that had been her home so briefly two years previously and that had seen more than its share of heartache and grief. It was a typically hot, sunny summer's day. The sun was high in the deep blue sky, with the clouds banished as usual to the western hills, far away across the plain. The fruit trees on the farms all around were bursting with ripening apples and pears; the hops were climbing up their wires and the tobacco was already two feet high. If only she could open the door to the cottage!

Heinrich applied his broad muscled shoulder to the door and gave it an almighty shove. It burst open, banging against the wall behind it and nearly catapulting Heinrich onto the floor.

'Mein Gott!' he cried as he struggled to stay upright.

'Oh, well done!' Carrie said laughing nervously. She'd managed to work herself up into a state of anxiety and dread over this homecoming and was not looking forward to what she might find. Already, the sight of the broken windows – untouched since that awful night – brought back horrific memories. The roses she'd planted along the pathway were bushy and tangled, their thorns catching her wrap as she'd passed by. The lavender underneath the roses was thick and woody; perhaps her herb garden had thrived too, she surmised. The lawn had sprouted long waving fronds, browning in the summer sun; the cream paint was peeling. She hadn't dared look beyond the house to where the barn once stood. She refused to let herself get upset about it all again. She'd wept enough tears for Daisy and the poor defenceless hens in the lonely nights after she'd fled Hope, without revisiting it now.

But she felt like weeping when she crossed the doorstep and beheld the destruction within. Her beautiful chairs and tables, the ottoman, all were upturned and mangled, their stuffing protruding where they'd been cut open, their fabric hanging in shreds. The pictures on the walls were slashed and at rakish angles or on the floor, amid a pile of shattered glass, twisted picture frames, books and broken china.

Letting go of Christina's hand, she ran to the kitchen where the sight was much the same – her beautiful dinner set in smithereens on the floor; her pots and pans strewn around the kitchen; her crockery smashed; her soaps slashed to pieces. Everything was covered in dirt and dust and old autumn leaves. The broken windows had left everything open to the elements, seemingly for the whole two years she'd been away.

'It will be all right, Carrie,' Heinrich said quietly, coming in behind her with Christina clutching his hand. He enfolded her gently in his great big arms. 'We can fix all this up in a week or two. We have enough money to buy everything new. We'll be fine.'

Carrie relaxed for a moment against his chest; she could feel his muscles tight and tense, as if he was trying to protect her from harm. She reached out and found Christina's hand and held it too. She had a family now. It felt safe and secure.

Unpacking the next day took no time at all. They'd brought very little with them, expecting most of the original furniture still to be usable; it was much cheaper to sell their things than transport them so far south. Carrie hung the clothes from her trunk in the wardrobe, which had remained intact, as had the bed and most of the furniture in the upper floor. The only item to suffer was the mattress, which had been slashed from top to bottom, feathers spilling all over the floor. She'd patched it up last night, hastily sewing a scrap of material over the gap before covering it with the new linen she'd bought before leaving Auckland – special linen from Ireland that the shopgirl had told her would feel warmer and softer than anything she'd slept on before. And in spite of the mended mattress, her advanced pregnancy, and the insecurity of her situation, she had indeed found the bed remarkably comfortable, sleeping soundly all night.

The warm mid-February weather was much easier to bear in the southern latitudes of Nelson. The humidity of Auckland had caused her many a restless night in her advanced stage of pregnancy. She was due to have Heinrich's baby at Easter and hoped to reacquaint herself with the midwife and doctor before her time was up. She was also hoping against hope – ironically, she thought, given the name of the township – that the locals would accept her and Heinrich and not try to run her out of town again.

As she emptied the trunk of all their clothes and accessories, she found the old leather-bound diary she'd written around the time of Richard's arrest, trial and execution. She looked at it with distaste mingled with a trace still of fondness. She had yet to resolve her feelings for Richard, to understand how she had become embroiled in such an appalling crime and what fatal flaw existed within her that led her – at least in those days – to be attracted to a man who, beneath his generous and entertaining exterior, was evil, ruthless and dangerously bad for her.

She held it up to the light of day, caressed its smooth hide and inhaled the rich smell of leather and musty paper. Quickly, only half looking, she flicked through the pages, which stayed open briefly at the letters from Richard she'd tucked in the middle somewhere. She could see them clearly, without needing to open the folded pages – two letters from Nelson Gaol and one from the Hokitika solicitor advising her of Richard's windfall. And behind the letters, the old photograph, slightly battered now that it had been removed from its frame. She pulled it out. There she was, wearing that wonderful expensive ballgown Richard had bought her, smiling rapturously, Richard at her side standing stiff and formal, as if afraid of being captured on film. It seemed like a world away, like a dream that had happened to someone else. That happy smiling woman could not be her.

Out of nowhere, she felt a pain inside, a wrenching deep in her stomach. She winced. Even after everything that had happened, even now that she was happy with Heinrich and would soon be giving birth to his child, it seemed the passion she once felt for Richard was still there. All it took to be released was the sight of him in a faded photograph. If that was the case, she reasoned, she would have to bury it somewhere she would never see it again.

She turned around to find a place to put it. She had kept the diary and its contents from Heinrich all this time – more to save his feelings than anything. Heinrich knew the basic facts about her relationship with Richard; but the diary's detailed descriptions of her emotional passage would only upset him unnecessarily.

Besides, there was no point in having this incontrovertible evidence against her and Christina out in the open for anyone to read. She never wanted Christina to see it. But she didn't want to destroy it; there was too much of her own pain and recovery in there to throw it into the fire and let it burn.

Apart from the bed, the wardrobe and the dresser were the only pieces of furniture in the room. The wardrobe, she thought, would be the last place Heinrich or anyone would look for a diary. She decided she would leave it there, hiding it permanently from prying eyes with a false floor that she would get Heinrich to make under the pretext of leaving her most precious things there – things like her land title deed, her sable fur and, although she would never mention it, her diary of troubled times.

There was a knock at the door. Carrie hurried downstairs, half afraid who it might be and whether they would want to her to leave again.

Even before she opened the door she could tell it was the Shaw sisters. She could hear them bickering about whether to knock again.

'Good day, Mrs O'Neill... er... Mrs Weiss...' Kittie was smiling nervously, her hand extended. Mary Anne was just a few inches behind her, a large baking dish covered with a cloth was clutched in both hands.

'Oh you silly goose,' Marry Anne interrupted. 'Can't you get it right for once?'

'We heard last week that you were coming back and we just wanted to make sure you were...' Kittie added.

'Oh you don't know how pleased I am you're both here,' Carrie said, grinning. 'Do come in. I'll make a cup of tea.'

Mary Anne and Kittie then started whittering, just as they used to before she'd had to leave. She felt like hugging their silly, gossipy selves with joy. Instead, though, she took Kittie's proffered hand and shook it gladly before moving forward and grasping her in a cautious, hesitant, yet warm embrace.

'Please come inside,' Carrie said.

Mary Anne handed over the baking dish and Carrie took it inside to the kitchen, indicating to the sisters that they should follow her.

'It's such a relief to see you're... well, you're all right,' Kittie said as they reached the warm kitchen.

'That you *look* all right,' Mary Anne added.

'You mean that my face isn't too scarred?' Carrie said bluntly.

'Well, yes,' Kittie said hesitantly. 'We thought...'

'We've been worried sick ever since you went away...'

'Worried that you'd be maimed for life...'

'That you might be incapacitated permanently...'

'Well, as you can see, you worried needlessly,' Carrie said. 'I'm fine. The scar across my cheek,' she pointed to it, its redness now faded significantly, 'is a neat thin line, thanks to the skill of the Nelson surgeon.'

'That was a dreadful night, Mrs... er Mrs Weiss,' Mary Anne said. 'Everyone was so fired up about that Burgess man. They took it out on you, I'm afraid.'

'We've been ashamed of ourselves ever since.'

'We shouldn't have got involved.'

'It was the heat of the moment…'

'We'd like to apologise…'

'On behalf of everyone, really. There was just no excuse for it.'

'There's no need,' Carrie said, repressing the urge to laugh. The sisters were quite overwhelming as a double act.

'No, it's important that we make it up to you,' Kittie said,

'We all over-reacted.'

'Especially that Diedrich.'

'He always was a bit of a fanatic.'

'How did you know…?'

'He confessed to his father. He thought the parson would be pleased.'

'But he was furious. He preached a sermon on it the following week.'

'About forgivenness and tolerance.'

'And not taking the law into our own hands.'

'There was absolutely no excuse for what he did. It was simply scandalous…'

'His father made him leave the district…'

'He left that very day…'

'The police were never called…'

'But he's served his time, as he should.'

'He's been gone these past two years and his father doesn't speak of him.'

'Some people thought of him as a hero for a while…'

'Tush, Mary Anne, that's not really the truth. Some people were glad that you left town, Mrs… er… Mrs Weiss. There was a lot of feeling that you and your baby had brought shame on the district.'

'Yes, and you'll find there's still *some*,' Kittie gave her sister a knowing look, 'who'll make life a bit difficult for you for a while.'

'That's for sure. But there's plenty more genuine Christian folk who will make up for them.'

'Jane Reichman said to pass on her regards. And so did Annie Kempthorne. She'll be over as soon as she can, she said.'

Carrie smiled. Word certainly got around quickly in these parts. She and Heinrich had only just arrived and the greetings were already coming in. But at least they sounded friendly.

'Would you believe, she's had two more babies since you left? Poor woman.' Mary Anne clicked her tongue disapprovingly.

'I can see you'll be having a little one soon too,' Kittie said. 'That should help take the heat off your little girl.'

'We've told everyone, we'll keep an eye on you; we'll make sure you're all right.'

'By the look of that husband of yours, though, you'll be well protected anyway.'

Carrie smiled. 'He is a big man, isn't he,' she said proudly. 'He won't put up with any trouble against us.'

'We hope he won't have to,' Mary Anne said, smiling also. 'We won't let it get out of hand again like it did last time.' She pattied Carrie's hand reassuringly.

Carrie was overwhelmed by the verbal barrage but at the same time relieved at their message of acceptance.

'Everybody was horrified about the barn,' Kittie said. 'That was a long way outside the bounds of sanity.'

'That lovely Jersey cow and those poor hens…'

'How anyone could have done that…'

'We still don't know who did it.'

'It could have been Diedrich, of course.'

'But he never owned up. Nobody did.'

'Nobody in these parts condoned it.'

'Nobody this side of Hope, anyways,' Mary Anne added. 'There's some fanatics on the other side would stop at nothing to see their brand of religion is adhered to. We make no apology for them.'

'Besides,' Kittie said, looking conspiratorial, 'there's a lot of folk round here have yet to make their hatches and matches legal.'

'That's right.' Mary Anne looked sanctimonious. 'That Reverend Graham, remember him? He's the one I told you about, who forgot to register all the baptisms and marriages.'

'Oh, yes,' Carrie said.

'Well some people said it wasn't fair to go pointing the finger at your wee baby, saying she was born out of wedlock and all, when half the children around here are in the same boat.'

'Yes, that put the willies up some of those nasty gossips.'

'Let him cast the first stone…'

'Left them without a leg to stand on.'

'Pity they didn't think of that before someone *did* cast the first stone.'

'But we want you to know, are genuinely sorry for our unchristian behaviour that Christmas eve.'

'And we'd like to make amends.'

'So we're giving you six of our best-laying hens – lovely brown ones like…' Mary Ann trailed off. 'And the Kempthornes are bringing you two lovely jersey cows. Annie says you'll be needing more than one cow now you've got a family.'

'And the pastor from Hope has rallied his parishioners into collecting enough timber and materials to build you a new barn. He says he's so ashamed of his son…'

Carrie took both their hands in hers. 'You don't know how happy I am to hear this,' she said. 'I've been hoping against hope that you would accept me back.'

'Everybody we know wants to make amends,' Kittie said.

'And so do we.'

'Oh, Mary Anne and Kittie. Just by being here and being so kind, you *have* made amends. You wouldn't believe how scared I've been of coming back here and what reception I'd get. I know it won't be plain sailing. There are bound to be some people who will find it hard having me back. But to know that you'll accept me again as a neighbour is more than I'd hoped. Your words have opened up my heart again. Maybe everything will be all right from now on.'

46. Christmas Bells

When Zhi arrived for lunch the next day Alex was still in turmoil. The police had been out to visit her and ask more questions at some ungodly hour when she'd just got back from her run, looking like she'd been dragged through a bamboo grove backwards.

She apologised profusely for not having had a shower yet.

'You'd better come in,' she said ushering them into the kitchen and offering them tea. It was the same policeman and woman she'd seen last night. They declined the tea and took the seats she'd indicated for them at the table.

'We found your friend, Rick Sorensen,' PC Simmonds said.

'Oh, was he…?'

'He was alive, just,' he continued. He'd been badly beaten up, and his arm had been broken. But he'll live.'

'He'll be fine in time to give evidence in court,' PC Moore added.

'Was he…?'

'We found him along the seafront, under an old disused jetty. The tide hadn't reached him, but it wasn't far off.'

'It was just as well you alerted us to that, or he might indeed be at the bottom of the ocean by now.'

Alex didn't know if she'd done Rick a favour or not. She supposed it was better for him to be alive, but he must be in a lot of pain and now he would have to stand trial for drug dealing. If convicted, he'd be up for several years in prison.

'Did you catch the other two?'

'Yes, we picked them up in a roadblock south of here. They'd managed to slip through the cordon the security guards put around the Trafalgar Centre and had driven as far as Wakefield before we caught them.'

'What about my costume?'

'It's safe and sound. The DI is keeping it for now to conduct some tests on it. But he's promised your boss she can have it back in time for the last show tonight.'

'You don't know how relieved I am to hear that,' Alex said.

They asked her a lot more questions about what had happened in Queenstown and why she hadn't reported it to the police immediately. She hoped she convinced them that she was scared to do so, that she feared for her life once she realised Rick had a gun. That had led to more questions about what type of gun and whether any of the others had weapons too. She'd known it was a Beretta, she said, because she'd seen one before back home. They seemed very interested in this and radioed back to headquarters to look out for one.

'They will have searched his house and plane by now,' PC Moore said. 'But it's best to pass it on, just in case it wasn't found.'

The police had only just gone when Zhi knocked on the door.

'I'm sorry Zhi, I haven't got any lunch for you today,' she said when he followed her into the kitchen. 'It's been kinda busy here.'

'No problem. I've been shopping in Richmond,' he said and produced a shopping bag filled with bagels, salads, sliced ham and cherry tomatoes.

'Zhi, you're an angel,' she said and fetched a couple of plates from the cupboard.

'No, let me,' he said, taking the plates off her and pulling out a kitchen chair for her to sit on. 'My turn to get lunch today. You've had enough on your mind.'

'You can say that again,' Alex said and sighed as she sat down.

'It's not that bad, surely?'

'It feels it. I don't know what to do. I think it might be a message to me that it's time to go home.'

'What, to San Francisco?'

'Yes, home to Frisco. I think I've done my dash here. Well and truly.'

'What about your work?'

'That's pretty much done too now. I wouldn't swear it was all sorted, not completely. But I've done as much as can be done for now and the Darbys and the landfill company have got a very detailed plan to keep following after I'm gone.'

'Oh,' Zhi said.

'There's just one problem remaining.'

'What's that?'

'You,' she said, smiling up at him.

'Why am I a problem?' He deposited a plate with two filled bagels on the table and sat down opposite, fixing his eyes on hers.

'Because I don't want to leave you. I've become quite fond of you.'

'Fond of me?'

'Yes, you fool. Fond of you.'

She stopped there, not sure how to go on or how he felt.

'Well, I've become quite fond of you, too. Very fond, in fact.'

He leaned across the table and took her hand.

'Fond enough to follow you back to San Francisco before Christmas.'

'Really? That's pretty fond.'

'Above and beyond fond, in fact,' he smiled, his eyes twinkling with laughter.

'You're having me on,' she reproved.

'Now, would I do a thing like that? Seriously though, I am going to be back home in time for Christmas. This particular project finishes in six weeks time, so they'll fly me back to base in Frisco and I'll be able to see my Mom for the first time in nearly a year. And even better,' he squeezed her hand, 'I'll be able to see you.'

'Christmas bells, those Christmas bells,' Alex sang the line from the famous Snoopy song.

'Enough! Enough!' Zhi cried. 'That's a terrible song.'

'Ringing through the land,' Alex continued, teasing.

'Right, you asked for it!' he said, pushing his chair back and darting round to Alex's side of the table, where he silenced her with a long, tender kiss.

47. Counting Blessings

Alex watched in awe as the ancient priest stepped up to the side of the big wooden holding bin full of freshly picked grapes – the last of the season, apart from the two rows saved for late-pick November botrytising. The warm fall afternoon combined with the heady aroma of grape juice to lull her into a pleasant haze. The later afternoon sun was shining across the doorway of the barn, revealing a myriad midges and dust particles hanging in the air.

The old man looked so stooped and frail she wondered if he'd be able to reach up high enough to see over the top. David stepped forward to give him a hand up the small steps he'd placed in front of the mountain of dark purple grapes and the priest raised himself slowly upwards until he was standing facing them. Holding the side of the bin, Father Piumelli turned round to look at the thirty or so family and friends of the Rossinis gathered in the big high-ceilinged shed and smiled.

'We are gathered here today,' the old man said in a surprisingly strong voice for his frail frame, 'to bless this harvest.'

He said a few words about this year's crop, asked for the Lord's blessing on it, and said a prayer specially for the harvest.

'Jesus said, "I am the vine. You are the branches. If your friendship with me is real friendship, it will reap great harvest",' he concluded. Then he led them all in a hymn: 'Now thank we all our God,' he started, in a strong tenor voice. Everyone joined in.

Making the sign of the cross over the grapes, he sprinkled some holy water over them, said another prayer, and asked everyone to join him in the response. Then he opened his Bible and read from Revelations, Chapter 14: 'I looked and there was a white cloud, and sitting on the cloud one who looked like the son of man, with a gold crown on his head and a sharp sickle in his hand. Another angel came out of the temple, crying out in a loud voice to the one sitting on the cloud, "Use your sickle and reap the harvest, for the time to reap has come, because the earth's harvest is fully ripe." So the one who was sitting on the cloud swung his sickle over the earth and the earth was harvested.'

Father Piumelli then led them in a short hymn to the harvest, which Alex joined in with gusto. She'd heard it several times before, at previous harvests at Rossinis and at other wineries she'd been invited to with them.

'All God's gifts around us

'Are sent from heaven above,

'Then thank the Lord, Oh thank the Lord,

'For a-a-all His love,' she sang.

When it was done, Father Piumelli stood down and indicated to Pietro that it was his turn.

'Pietro has offered to serenade us with a song that celebrates wine and the good things it can bring,' David said by way of introduction.

Pietro moved forward and stood right beside the steps, the glistening grapes providing a fitting halo above his head.

'*Libiamo ne'lieti calici,*' Pietro started to sing in his fine tenor voice. Alex recognised 'Brindisi', the famous drinking song from *La Traviata*.

At the end of the first verse, he gesticulated towards her. 'Come, join me, *caro*,' he called to her. I know you can sing it. I've heard you often enough in the vineyard.'

Alex blushed. But she didn't like to hold up proceedings, so she did as he asked and sang Violetta's verse. Then they both sang the chorus together, encouraging the others to join them. Many did, and they concluded by singing it again. When they finished, Pietro took her hand and made a sweeping bow, indicating she should do the same. Everyone applauded enthusiastically, calling for an encore.

'Once is more than enough,' Pietro said.

'You're right there,' Madelena called out. 'No more.'

'Thank you for indulging me,' Pietro said, ignoring her. 'And thank you, Alex, for partnering me in such a delightful duet.'

Alex blushed again and retreated to the back of the room.

'And now, let's celebrate!' David cried, waving a bottle of last year's *Don Giovanni* chardonnay. 'Luckily, I managed to save a few bottles for today,' he added. 'There was such a rush on all our wine after the publicity CBS News gave Rossinis, we were lucky we had to recall it. It's the only wine from 2001 that we have left.'

'And not one of these bottles has been tampered with,' Pietro said. 'I can give you my personal guarantee.'

'Yes, he personally tested every one,' David said, affectionately cuffing his father on the arm. The guests laughed as David poured the first bottle and handed glasses around. When everyone had a glass, he raised his up towards the rafters and said, 'A toast.'

'*Salute*,' everyone said.

'May it be the best harvest ever,' Anna said.

'It's got every chance of being another medal winner,' David said. 'It's been a great growing season.'

It was the last day of October and Alex had driven up the day before at David's invitation to join in the celebrations.

'We're so thrilled to have you back in the country, we want you to come and celebrate with us,' he'd said a few days ago. 'Our last day of picking the pinot will be October 31. We're running a couple of weeks late this year. There wasn't as much sun as we'd have liked in September. But we've had a late run of it these past two weeks, thank God. The brix are getting up to a much more respectable level now.'

She'd been delighted to be asked again. The annual harvest blessing ritual was one she looked forward to, but being a consultant to the Rossinis – as opposed to an employee or member of the family – she cautioned herself every year that she might be overlooked on the guest list. She couldn't expect them to remember to invite her as of right.

'You're like family to us,' David always said.

But just the same she wanted to protect herself against disappointment.

She'd driven up in the M3 yesterday after lunch, getting Sharon to cover with her clients for the next couple of days. She'd felt guilty – it was only a month since she'd returned from New Zealand – but Sharon brushed her away.

'You deserve a break. Get back to those roots,' she'd joked.

Alex wasn't sure if she meant the vine roots or what. Her family roots were elsewhere – although, she figured, the Rossini's were just as much family to her as her own. David and Anna were much more concerned about her messy love life than her father had ever been.

'So have you found Mr Right?' was almost the first thing Anna had said as soon as they were alone, sitting at the big, worn wooden kitchen table over a glass of wine as dusk fell outside.

'You know me,' Alex had answered.

'Now what's that supposed to mean, *cara*,' Anna said. 'If I do know you, I'd say that you fell for the first tall, dark and handsome man you saw, and he turned out to be an absolute bastard.'

Alex almost choked over her pinot, only just managing not to splutter it all over the table.

'Well, you're absolutely right, Anna. That's exactly what I did. And he *was* a bastard.'

'And that was it?'

Alex debated with herself whether to spill the beans to Anna, and quickly decided she might as well confess the truth. If Zhi were to meet up with her in the next week or two, Anna would find out soon enough.

'Well, not quite.'

She told Anna about the scary trip to Queenstown – or as much of it as she needed to reveal to set the scene – and how Zhi had come to her rescue.

'So is he tall, dark and handsome too?' Anna asked.

'Not exactly, no. He's about the same height as me. Or maybe even a bit shorter.'

Anna burst out laughing.

'Then he's perfect for you, *cara mia*,' she said. 'If you can fall in love with someone…'

'I didn't say I'd fallen in love, Anna. I just like him…'

'Tssss, *cara*. Isn't that as it should be? How do you think love begins?'

Alex had never thought about that.

'I've always imagined it was like you always knew when someone was destined for you, like an electric charge.'

'Tssss. I don't think so. I think that's lust, not love. I think that's your hormones talking.'

'But…'

'No, *cara*. It's a big myth that Mr Right is going to arrive on a white charger and sweep you off your feet. The earth isn't going to move and the angels aren't going to sing. That's the stuff of fairy tales. The tricky thing about finding Mr Right is that, when you come across him, there's every chance you won't know. He'll sneak up on your psyche when you're not looking and slowly but surely you'll find you can't do without him.'

'Well, you'll be able to judge for yourself,' Alex had said then, feeling overwhelmed. He's coming back home to San Francisco in a week or two.

Anna had become very excited at this news and had rushed out of the kitchen to the lounge to tell David, who had abandoned the television and arrived moments later in the kitchen to congratulate her.

'Hey, hey, don't jump to conclusions,' she'd said, laughing despite her embarrassment. 'It's only the beginning.'

Just the same, she reflected as she sipped the ambrosial *Don Giovanni*, surrounded by the Rossini family and their friends, she did miss him and had kept a tally of the days until he was due to arrive back on home leave. Sixteen days and two hours precisely, she counted silently then castigated herself for it. She'd emailed him a few days ago, telling him she was taking a few days off to go to the harvest blessing and how she was looking forward to staying with the Rossinis again. He'd replied the next morning (or evening, according to the time record on his side of the world) full of good cheer about the seismic gear being fully operational at last and how excited they'd been a few days previously at a gas find off the New Plymouth coast. She wished he were here now to share the blessing and the following festivities with her.

Tucked away in his tiny cabin, bracing himself against the side of the desk to reduce the effects of the heavy seas, Zhi checked his emails. He was feeling unusually mellow, having partaken of more champagne than he should have in the officers' mess. Their gas find that morning had now been thoroughly celebrated, but at the expense of seeing if there was a message from Alex. He booted up the laptop and waited patiently while it went through the motions until he could open Outlook Express. Ping! There was mail. A message from his sister about Thanksgiving dinner and who would be there and would he be able to make it too; and beneath it a message from Alex. As he read through it, he experienced an unusual feeling of isolation. It had never bothered him before, being miles from the nearest port and cut off from his friends ashore. But Alex's message, short and simple as it was, made him realise how far he was away from the rest of the world. She was going to a harvest blessing and described what it would be like. Suddenly, he wanted to be with her, where he could smell the rain falling on the earth, feel the Californian sun beat down on his skin, see the mountain of grapes, and touch her soft fair skin again. The ship, his happy escape module for the past year, was now a prison, keeping him from being with her.

He shut off the laptop without even taking the time to reply and shot off down to see Franklin.

'When did you say the company told you we'd be back in port?' he asked as soon as Franklin opened the door to his cabin.

'And how are you, too?' Franklin said sarcastically. 'What happened to your manners? Three days, if all goes well. We've got two more days of tests and then they want to head back to port to check it all out.'

'D'you think I could take home leave, this time?' Zhi asked.

'Don't see there'd be a problem,' Franklin said. 'You haven't been back home in a while now. Why? You got a girl waiting back there for you?'

'Never you mind,' Zhi said defensively. 'I just want to get back home, that's all.'

Franklin continued to give him a hard time and Zhi put up with it. As long as Franklin gave him the leave he wanted, he didn't care what he said.

'Must be that California girl you met at the Vic Rose,' he said. 'Yes, Curtis told me,' he added, seeing Zhi's look of surprise. 'Don't worry, I'm not going to stand in your way. You go for it, Zhi. It's about time you got yourself a nice girl.'

Franklin had signed off Zhi's home leave and booked him the necessary flights home – New Plymouth to Auckland to Los Angeles to San Francisco. He could spend a couple of days with Zannie, have lunch with Sarah, and with a bit of luck avoid his mother and her prying questions about settling down. He didn't want to tell her about Alex yet. She'd want to meet her right away and that would put Alex off him for life. He'd swear Xanthia to secrecy and fob Mom off with tales of meeting a nice girl in New Zealand.

He could just hear her now: 'Noo Zeeee-land? Where ever's that? Don't tell me it's one of those islands in the South Pacific where they have natives running round in grass skirts? Santa Maria! Why can't you settle down with a respectable girl from somewhere round here?' She'd said something along those lines whenever he'd told her about a girl he'd met on his travels. Unless they were from a ten-mile radius of home, they'd never do for his mom. Although she'd been getting so desperate for him to settle down lately, she'd conceded she might consider a 'foreigner' for a daughter-in-law, if only he'd hurry up and get on with it.

On the first day of November, the day after the harvest blessing, Alex picked her mobile up off the charger and phoned her sister Kate. She'd awoken with a hangover and no amount of Berocca or black coffee or long runs could improve her mood. Finally, she'd realised with a shock she was grumpy because she was lonely and missing Zhi.

She'd tried to find Anna but was told she'd driven into St Helena with Manfred to help him prepare for his engagement party tomorrow night. David had agreed to open up the wine shop and the adjoining gallery where they started the wine tours with talks and a video, and had offered to supply the wine for the party. Manfred was organising the catering and entertainment. However, being a typical winemaker who could only think about one thing at a time, he'd forgotten to do anything until the last minute. This had all come out last night at the harvest blessing party, Alex recalled. Manfred, for once, had too much to drink and loosened up to the extent that he had gone over to his lodgings to fetch his guitar. She was astonished to hear him playing a string of Elvis Presley medleys – not what she would have expected from the serious German at all. He strummed and sang, with a passion and abandon completely out of character. And although she'd had quite a bit to drink herself by that stage, she'd observed that most of the others else seemed to be just as blown away as she was.

'Whatever's come over Manfred?' she asked David in between 'Rock Around the Clock' and 'Blue Suede Shoes'.

'He breaks out on rare occasions,' David said, laughing at her incredulity. 'I know, he gives the appearance of being a stolid sort of guy who takes himself far too seriously. But there's a lot more to him than the winemaker you see every day at work. He just needs a bit of a prod to lighten up.'

It was much later in the evening when Anna had asked him if he was playing at his own party that Manfred had confessed that, in fact, he hadn't organised anyone to entertain them on Saturday. Nor had he arranged the caterers.

'I'm going to do it myself,' he said grandly.

'Nonsense,' Anna said. 'You know perfectly well you won't have time to cook anything before then.'

Now with Anna and Manfred gone into town to arrange everything at the eleventh hour, the only person she could talk to about feeling lonely was Kate.

'So why don't you jump on a plane and go back to New Zealand and see him again?' Kate had said after finally calling her back. She'd been dropping Bas and Alexander off at the park for Bas's junior league game and was dashing across town to pick up Georgia from her sleepover. 'I can't talk now, hon. I'm just walking up the path to Georgia's friend's house and I'm late already. I'll call you back.' When she'd finally gotten around to do that, Georgia was singing loudly in the background with a Sophie Ellis Bextor song on the car CD player.

'Take me home, take me home,' was all Alex could hear.

'Sorry,' Kate shouted. 'But this is what it's like on Saturdays. You wanna join me?'

'No thanks,' Alex said.

At last, Kate managed to turn the disco-bop music down and she could hear her speak.

'I can't just get on a plane and go back like that,' she'd said.

'Why ever not?' Kate said. 'I would.'

'Murder on the Dance Floor' was now blaring behind her.

'Because… Because it wouldn't be right. Besides he's at sea right now. I'd never be able to find him until his ship returns to port.'

'Well, there you are then. You'll just have to wait for him to come home. It's not that long now, is it?'

'Fifteen days,' she said – and eight hours, she added silently.

Kate had gone on to relate a complicated story about Max and his wife Trish, and how one of Max's conservative architect friends from work had turned out to be the devil in disguise at one of the select dinner parties "Patrice" liked to stage. Alex was finding it hard to get a grip of all the characters, let alone who was chasing whom and in what closet they were discovered.

'Kate, please. You're telling me all this as if you thought I gave a damn.'

'You would have if you'd been there. The look on Trish's face was priceless. She looked like she'd eaten a lemon.'

'She always looks like she's eaten a lemon,' Alex retorted. 'Especially when I'm around.'

'Well, you should tell her about Zhi. She's dying for you to settle down like the rest of us.'

'Is she, now? Well you can tell her from me I haven't the faintest intention of settling down – not with Zhi and not for a long time.'

'Famous last words,' Kate said before the Sophie Ellis impersonator in the back seat drowned her out again.

At a loose end still, Alex checked her emails.

Nothing from Zhi, which worried her. She feared the distance might be putting him off.

A rude one from Magda, teasing her about finding a man 'who's, let's face it, a short ass,' Magda wrote. 'I wonder if that means other parts of him are not so short.'

Alex ignored that and flicked down her inbox until she saw Gen's name and an attachment beside it.

'Recipes for Grapeseed Oil,' the email was headed. Intrigued, Alex opened it up and read on.

'Ollie and I will never recover from the shock of overhearing you passing on grapeseed oil recipes to Mrs Lowe from along Clover Road.

We think it deserves a special PR award for ingenuity. We want to know what other recipes you have tucked up your sleeve to tame hostile opponents.'

Alex chuckled to herself and continued reading.

'Seriously though, Alex, you were pretty special to us in the all too brief time that you were here and we want you to know that you're welcome back any time. We won't go as far as to create another PR crisis for you to come and solve, but we really do want you to come back and visit us again.

'Your weeks with us have become inextricably linked with my family's heritage. You were here for such a short time and now you're gone, it almost feels as though you were part of a strange dream. If it weren't for the physical presence of Carrie's diary I don't think I'd be able to believe that it really happened. It's had a dramatic effect on me and especially on my Mum. She's been delving right back into the family history, aided by some of the clues the diary has given her, and has come up with a lot of new information about Carrie and Burgess. I can't get over how kind and gentle he was at home and yet when he was out robbing people he was a cold-blooded killer. He must have been a real Jekyll and Hide.

'Mum has decided to bite the bullet and "come out". She's taken the diary to someone she knows from the local Historical Society and they think she should give it to the museum in Isel. They reckon the museum might do a special display about Burgess. Apparently they've got something already, but it's fairly low key. This friend of Mum's thinks the diary might be the catalyst for a big recreation of the murders, a bit like they do in Australia with their famous bushranger Ned Kelly. After all, both Burgess and Ned Kelly learned their bushranging from the same teacher, so why shouldn't we create a bit of a legend around him too? Anyway, we will have to see how far they are prepared to go. For now, Mum is just relieved that she's not going to be ostracised for having Burgess in a hidden branch of her family tree. Her historical friend thinks it's wonderful. She says Mum shouldn't worry about what people will think, that it's such a long time ago now that any stigma or shame will be long gone. If anything, she says, people will romanticise Carrie's story. Mum could end up a sort of folk hero!'

The evening of the engagement party, Alex treated herself to a long soak in the tub with Anna's *Rush* bath foam, then dressed carefully in the same little black dress she'd worn in Queenstown that awful night with Rick. She'd been going to throw it away, but the further away that weekend was the less inclined she was to waste it. After all, it had cost her over a week's salary once. When packing for Rossinis, she decided to take it for Manfred's party. Nobody there would know about what happened in Queenstown, or what she was doing in the Prada dress. She hadn't brought the Blahniks, though. They seemed a bit over the top for St Helena.

She looked at her watch. She still had plenty of time before she was due to join the family in the lounge for a drink before they headed off to town for the party. She filled in the time doing her hair, applying make-up – something she always meant to do more often but hardly ever got around to – even painting her nails. Then, picking up her jacket and bag, she made her way down the long corridor to the main part of the house.

'*Cara, cara*, come and join us,' Anna cried when she walked into the lounge. The whole family was there, formally dressed for the occasion, but they all appeared to be grinning at her as if they knew something she didn't. She looked down at herself to check she hadn't forgotten something. When she looked up again, David and Anna moved apart and from behind them stepped Zhi, looking positively dashing in a beautifully cut dinner suit and peacock blue bowtie. She could feel herself gaping. The Rossinis were all cheering and laughing, and Zhi was smiling broadly.

'Hello, Alex,' he said. 'You look absolutely gorgeous tonight. You must have known I was coming.' His eyes were sparkling, teasing.

'How… how did you get here?' she stammered. 'You're supposed to be at sea off the coast of New Zealand.'

'Easy,' he said, moving forward and taking her hand. 'I caught a couple of planes and here I am.'

'But how did you know where to find me?'

'Oh, that was incredibly difficult,' he said, laughing. 'I looked up the phonebook yesterday and rang David. He told me about the party tonight and invited me out.'

'You all knew!' Alex said, tuning to the Rossinis.

'Anna, I'm surprised at you for not telling me. I don't believe you could have kept a secret like that.'

Anna came over and put an arm round each of them.

'You're right, it was hard to keep quiet. But it was worth it just to see the look on your face then.'

'It was a picture,' David added coming forward and giving her a hug.

'I think we should propose a toast to them both,' Pietro said, coming forward with a tray of glasses.

'Careful, Papa,' David said, quickly taking the tray from him and handing it around.

'As long as you promise not to sing, *ma che matto che sei*,' Madelena said to Pietro.

'*Salute*,' the Rossinis all said as one, raising their glasses. '*Salute*, Alex and Zhi.'

'May you find happiness,' David said, holding up his glass again and smiling.

'Thank you,' Alex said. 'Thank you for helping to bring us back together. Now I'd like to propose a toast. To the Rossinis.' She raised her glass, and Zhi did the same.

'The Rossinis,' he said, clinking his champagne flute softly against Alex's and briefly looking into her eyes before turning back to the family facing him expectantly. 'Thank you for keeping my secret. I can't tell you how overjoyed I am to be here.'

He turned back to Alex again and gently pulled her towards him. She didn't try to resist.

'I've been looking forward to this moment for a long time,' he said as he leaned over and kissed her, wrapping his free hand around her waist.

Alex felt safe in his arms, as if she belonged there.

There was a brief silence as they kissed, then the family started to clap and cheer.

'Bravo, *cara*, bravo,' Anna cried, coming forward to embrace Alex. Then she whispered in Alex's ear so only she could hear, 'I think Mr Right just walked in.'

'Come on, everyone, drink up,' David cried. 'We've got Manfred's party to go to.'

'We've been waiting a long time for this celebration,' Anna said, nudging Alex gently. 'It's about time.'

Dancing in the Wilderness
Felicity Price
ISBN 1-877270-15-6

A passionate and compelling saga of two women – Etta Jackson, a young, impressionable immigrant miner's wife and her granddaughter, Stephanie Hunter, sophisticated PR pro who has left behind her Gucci London lifestyle having been headhunted by a multi-national logging company to take on the environmental activists fighting to protect precious lowland native forests. Separated by three generations but linked by an emerging pioneering spirit, they each travel on their own journey towards finding themselves and coming to terms with the raw honesty of New Zealand's West Coast.

'Felicity Price's first novel offers something rare in New Zealand fiction – pace and tension. You can't bear to put it down… Price is gifted enough to write her story with a precision, eye for detail and balance that make it feel authentic… Price is a gifted storyteller who has gone to serious lengths to research her plot.'
– *New Zealand Herald*

Also available from Hazard Press
www.hazardonline.com

The Inca Tapestry
David Rawson
ISBN 1-877270-23-7

A stunning fiction debut: a large, award-winning suspense-laden thriller set in South America. Moving between the time of the Conquistadors and the present, the detail is staggering and will motivate travellers to visit the region for years to come.

Backpacking on the bleak but hauntingly beautiful Bolivian Altiplano, Daliah, a young Israeli with some time to spare between completing her studies and commencing her career, is presented with an ancient and previously hidden tapestry.

But others seek the tapestry for their own dark ends and will stop at nothing to possess it. For the tapestry, and the route of a perilous journey woven within it by an Incan concubine fleeing the conquering Pizarro, holds not only the answer to the origins of humanity itself but the power to control our world.

Also available from Hazard Press
www.hazardonline.com

Enemy Within
Richard Webster
ISBN 1-877270-14-8

The year is 1860 and celebrated entertainer, illu-sionist, mind reader and world traveller, Monsieur Cardot, is in the bustling town of Auckland to perform his wondrous feats. Invited to dine with the Wainwrights, a family whose fortunes are on the rise, Monsieur Cardot consents to daughter Sarah Wainwright's request that he tell the future of each family member by reading their palms.

And so begins the saga of a family that will be torn asunder through greed and ambition, of love unrequited and of love lost, of two brothers born into a life of privilege and possibilities whose radically different natures will pit them against each other for life – with devastating consequences for all.

Parrot Parfait
Sue Emms
ISBN 1-877270-27-X

Hello, *he'd say, and tilt his little head.* Hello. Who's a clever boy? *And some unsuspecting fool would forget what a brute he was and hold up a finger to stroke his vivid glowing feathers.*
One finger was all he needed to get a talon hold. A flurry of feathers, a triumphant squawk and that was it. Clever Pete, clever Pete, *he'd cry while tears ran down the unsuspecting fool's face and their mouth opened in an agonised shout.*

Love, hate and guilt, the glue that holds families together: or splits them apart. Paula Mason left home taking nothing but bad memories, her dreams, determination, and Pete. And a promise to her brother, Mark, that she would make it up to him.

She enjoys her life, her successful business, her lover, her friends, and her childhood is far behind. Until three disasters spin her around, turn her life upside down and she finds herself going home to face her family. The love, hate, and guilt, that's been holding them together, and apart, for so long.

Also available from Hazard Press
www.hazardonline.com

The Irish Yankee
Edmund Bohan
ISBN 1-877270-16-4

The Irish Yankee, Edmund Bohan's fourth Inspector
O'Rorke novel, opens in the Civil War-ravaged Tennessee
of 1863 – where a young Irish-American Union secret
agent – known only as Sean Brennan – is sent on an
assignment for General Ulysses S. Grant. Distracted by
his growing passion for the beautiful Louisa Beaumont,
and embroiled in a fatal web of deceit and treachery, he
fails.

In Christchurch, New Zealand, twenty-two years later in
July 1885, news of the death of ex-President Grant revives
uncomfortable memories for the police detective Patrick
O'Rorke. And when members of a visiting group of
American feminist and temperance lecturers recognise in
him the 'Irish Yankee' Brennan, whom they believed had
died at Gettysburg, they set out to gain belated vengeance.
But as O'Rorke, haunted anew by the bitter memories of
betrayed love and youthful failure, plans to lure his old
enemies into a trap of his own, he again puts at risk both
his career and his life, and brings tragedy upon those
around him. As crowds gather in central Christchurch for
a major political rally, the assassins stalk O'Rorke through
the city and out to his isolated property in Beckenham –
before the shattering secrets of the past are finally revealed.

'[Bohan] respects his readers' intelligence with the
enjoyable subtlety of his writing, and by allowing us to
see the hero's failings. Highly recommended.'
– New Zealand Herald

The Fourth Eye
Clinton Smith
ISBN 1-877161-57-8

Deep in the Indian Ocean an Oscar class Russian sub tests a revolutionary propulsion system. Above it a converted supertanker hides an appalling cargo. On the sub are the last people able to prevent world populations being turned into cattle. But it all hinges on one man's mind.

A faulty lift traps photographer Colin Blake on an unlisted floor of a high-security area. Within minutes, a SWAT team grabs him and he faces an inquisition.

Blake is sucked into a nightmare of intrigue and corruption. Though relentlessly pursued, he manages to connect with an underground trio – Kate, a Kiwi weapons expert, the crude but warm-hearted Sergeant Higgins and the mystical Mr Ko.

One man confronts the surveillance society. His only weapon – total recall.

As the action shifts across continents and oceans, Blake encounters everything from human experiments to slaughterhouses for unwanted populations. But he has one extra-ordinary weapon – his mind.

Written with meticulous military detail and inside knowledge, *The Fourth Eye* is an utterly convincing, non-stop descent into terror.

'Action-packed all the way and thrilling to the end.'
    – *Wanganui Chronicle*